Life as Planned

ALSO BY AMANDA PROWSE

Novels

Poppy Day

What Have I Done?

Clover's Child

A Little Love

Will You Remember Me?

Christmas for One

A Mother's Story

Perfect Daughter

The Second Chance Café

Three and a Half Heartbeats

Another Love

My Husband's Wife

I Won't be Home for Christmas

The Food of Love

The Idea of You

The Art of Hiding

Anna

Theo

PRAISE FOR AMANDA PROWSE

'Amanda Prowse reflects society in our times in her gripping novels'
—Katie Fforde

'A moving, romantic tale about finding your place in the world and the people who can help you get there'
—Libby Page, praise for *Swimming to Lundy*

'An utterly compelling and exquisitely crafted read. I loved it!'
—Heidi Swain, praise for *All Good Things*

'A candid, moving and inspirational book, I am blown away'
—Jonny Benjamin, bestselling author of *The Stranger on the Bridge*, praise for *The Boy Between*

'Amanda Prowse is the queen of family drama'
—*Daily Mail*

'A deeply emotional, unputdownable read'
—*Red*

'You'll fall in love with this'
—*Cosmopolitan*

'Captivating, heartbreaking and superbly written'
—*Closer*

'Uplifting and positive but you may still need a box of tissues'

—*Cosmopolitan*

'Warmly accessible but subtle . . . moving and inspiring'

—*Daily Mail*

How to Fall in Love Again: Kitty's Story

The Coordinates of Loss

The Girl in the Corner

The Things I Know

The Light in the Hallway

The Day She Came Back

An Ordinary Life

Waiting to Begin

To Love and Be Loved

Picking Up the Pieces

All Good Things

Very Very Lucky

Swimming to Lundy

This One Life

Ever After

Novellas

The Game

Something Quite Beautiful: seven short stories

A Christmas Wish

Ten Pound Ticket

Imogen's Baby

Miss Potterton's Birthday Tea

Mr Portobello's Morning Paper

I Wish . . .

A Whole Heap of Wishes

A Wish for Forgiveness

Children's books

The Smile that Went a Mile (with Paul Ward Smith)

Today I'm in Charge (with Paul Ward Smith)

Non-fiction

The Boy Between (with Josiah Hartley)

Women Like Us

Life as Planned

Amanda Prowse

LAKE UNION PUBLISHING

This is a work of fiction. Names, characters, organizations, places, events, and incidents are either products of the author's imagination or are used fictitiously. Any resemblance to actual persons, living or dead, or actual events is purely coincidental.

Published by Lake Union Publishing, Seattle
www.apub.com

EU Product Safety contact:
Amazon Media EU S. à r.l.
38, avenue John F. Kennedy, L-1855 Luxembourg
amazonpublishing-gpsr@amazon.com

ISBN-13: 9781662515224
eISBN: 9781662515217

Cover design by Jo Myler
Cover image: © Buch and Bee © mentalmind © RONIN001 © Vector Elements / Shutterstock

Printed in the United States of America

This book is for you, Sara Hartley-Prowse.
My beloved daughter-in-law. Life is indeed short and so live every minute of it! You are a ray of sunshine no matter the weather – never change, darling.
We adore you X

Ashleigh and Remy Brett

1972

Aged 10

Ashleigh

Five more minutes . . .

Ashleigh Brett prayed, and screwed her eyes shut at the sound of the bedroom door opening. Lying immobile in her single bed pushed against the wall, she wriggled further under her eiderdown and savoured the last few seconds of warmth, of stillness, knowing that once light had pierced the dark, and people moved about and words were spoken, the day would truly begin, and she would be forced to stir.

Wheels would then be set in motion, driving a machine that would carry her into her future. A machine, the sights and sounds of which she had been dreading since the first mention of the exam, almost a year ago now.

An exam.

Not just a test or a mere quiz, but an exam, a word with so much weight attached to it she could barely say it out loud without wanting to crumple with the effort of holding it on her tongue. This was a new and fearful experience and what scared her the most was how powerful it seemed, taking over each waking thought and wiping all the joy from her usually happy life. Lurking like a dark thing, the monster under the bed, a baddie behind the curtain, ready to pounce the moment she was alone.

A whole year of letting the fear build, of feeling the swirl of nausea in her tummy at the thought. A year of doing her best to bury the worry, and able with relief not to dwell on it *too* much because a year was a long, long way away. Then six months was far in the future, and then a month felt like an age, and then a week, which meant it was creeping closer . . . and now, suddenly, it was today.

Today!

In that moment, it seemed to have arrived in a blink.

'Rise and shine, little doves!'

There it was, the slightly irritating sound of her mother's voice, hollering into the small room she shared with her sister.

The room with the Cindy shelf their dad had built. A sturdy white, bold, bracketed affair, on which they displayed their favourite dolls. All the Cindys looked down at her now, as they stood in front of their caravan, with their bike, grill, dog, and backpacks, everything a Cindy doll might require for a decent weekend in the great outdoors. These just a few of a wide array of accessories from gramophones to ironing boards, even a tiny crib. They really did cover all bases when it came to Cindy's life choices.

They had been avid collectors, she and Remy. Relatives had for years delightedly presented them with new Cindys or Cindy related items on their birthday and at Christmas. Truth was, however, they didn't play with them anymore, and Ashleigh for one would rather have books on the shelf or her collection of Wade Whimsies, but her dad had built it and it felt like a big deal to ask if they could pack away these treasured things. Her mum had cried when they'd placed their Fisher-Price activity centre and record player into a box destined for the loft; goodness only knew how she'd react to a request for a removal of the dolls.

Ashleigh stared at them, the smiling lookalikes. All seemingly excited to go about their day of adventure. She wished she could be a Cindy, just for a day. More specifically, just for *today.*

Some might think it an odd wish, to sit on a shelf with someone who had the exact same face and physical features as you, but this was not strange to Ashleigh, who stole a glimpse at Remy, her identical twin, on the other side of the room. Identical in looks, build, size, shape, everything, but very different people this morning, as Remy was smiling while Ashleigh had to concentrate on not crying.

'One egg split in two, one person really, same genes . . .' her mum liked to remind them. Ashleigh didn't have the heart to say that just the thought of it made her feel a bit sick. Who wanted to be *half* an egg? Who wanted to feel like a person *split* in two?

Not her, that was for sure.

With her head still resting in the satisfying dent in the pillow, she opened one eye fully as her mum, Ruthie Brett, drew back the orange-and-brown swirl-patterned curtains to let the yellow glow of the streetlight fill their room. The window, always an indicator of the weather, carried small icy patches in the corners which, close up, looked like snowflakes. She sank down further on to the mattress, feeling the caress of the striped brushed-cotton sheet on her downy legs.

Remy, she noticed, was already sitting up, happily. This irritated her too, the fact that her sister seemed to be taking it all in her stride, as she did everything. She wondered, not for the first time, if that egg had been split equally, fairly, because it seemed to her entirely possible that her sister got more of the happy genes, the ones that made you care a bit less. It wasn't Remy's fault, but still Ashleigh had to smother the flames of jealousy that leapt inside her, wishing she could be more like her sister, who didn't seem to sweat things in quite the same way.

'Seven eights?' her mum yelled.

'Fifty-six!' Remy responded.

'Okay, this one is for you, Ashleigh, sleepyhead, what's the capital of Iceland?'

'Reykjavik,' she mumbled. *Duh! Everyone knew that.*

'My clever babies!' Her mum, in her lilac housecoat and quilted slippers, danced in the small channel between their beds, her excitement crackling from her like electricity. 'My clever, clever babies!'

She did this, spoke about them as if she had won a prize, as pride and delight dripped from every syllable. It was nice, sometimes, but not today.

'I don't think it's going to be that kind of exam, Mummy.' Remy caught her sister's eye and subtly pulled a face. Ashleigh smiled back. Aged ten, they were already proficient in humouring their mother and understanding the need for it.

'Well, it's still good to get your brains warmed up!'

The woman was both relentless and undaunted.

'What's heavier, a kilo of feathers or a kilo of tar?'

'They're the same.' Ashleigh sat up and rubbed her eyes, wishing she could turn back the clock to last night and sleep all over again, meaning this day would never come. Or better still, turn back the clock to when she had started school, when she now knew it would be wiser not to be so smart, instead to sit at the back and hang out with the gigglers, the slowcoaches, and the dumdums, who seemed to have much more fun than she did. It wasn't fair, how much she cared, how hard she worked and how she now had to sit the stupid exam.

'Ah, I can't fool you!' Her mum lowered her voice and pointed out of the window. 'This is an important day, and I want to talk to you about Mrs Jenkins who lives in that house on the corner, you know the one, don't you?'

They both nodded.

'She's got three spare bedrooms, *three*! And you, my little doves, will pass this exam and get a place at St. Jude's Academy, a full academic scholarship, where you will get the very best education, and that will get you the best job, which will pay you the best money, and you can buy the best house, with four spare bedrooms if you choose, *four*!'

'I don't think I'd like four spare bedrooms,' Remy piped up.

'Why not?' Her mum stared at her sister as if she just didn't get it.

'It just seems like more to clean, all that hoovering and dusting, more rooms to worry about.'

This time Ashleigh caught her mum's eye, and *they* exchanged a slow, conspiratorial look. Remy was right: she *didn't* get it. Ashleigh knew that if you could afford four spare bedrooms then the chances were you could also afford a cleaner or housekeeper to do all that stuff for you.

She wondered if Mrs Jenkins had a cleaner and tried to imagine a life like that. The big question was, what would you do in your house while your cleaner was in it? Her mum was always busy, constantly polishing, cleaning or scrubbing something with her Marigolds pulled up to her elbows and her hips shifting from side to side beneath the bow of her pinny. And if she wasn't doing that she was peeling, chopping, stewing, simmering, or mixing, preparing food for the family.

Ashleigh wasn't sure she wanted a life like her mum's when she grew up, and she had heard Nancy, who worked in the library, say that her boyfriend had cooked their tea! *Her boyfriend had cooked their tea!* It was so shocking she had mentioned it to Remy, who had been just as surprised. It had stuck in her mind; she was quite unable to imagine her dad doing anything in the kitchen, let alone cooking tea! It was an idea so far removed from their little life here in Church Lane it made her laugh, like suggesting her mum go out in the car every day to do her dad's job and come home expecting *her* tea to be on the table!

This wasn't what mums did.

But maybe to have a cleaner would be the answer, someone to do all those chores, while she had time to read! Yes, that was what she'd do if she had a cleaner in the house. She'd sit on the sofa and read book after book. It sounded lovely, a life like that, sitting around while someone else did all the work. A life that would probably not be hers if she didn't pass the exam. And just like that her stomach folded with nerves and she felt like she might be sick.

Remy

Remy was excited for the day ahead – a change in routine and missing lessons was always a novelty on a school day. Plus, she had a trip in the minibus to look forward to and a chance to look around St. Jude's. Oh, and the exam, which she had no doubt they would ace! But it was definitely the minibus trip that felt like the most exciting thing.

'Right, up and at 'em, little doves! See you downstairs in five!'

Her mum clapped as she left the room. Remy stared at Ashleigh, who looked less than keen to rise and shine.

'Did you have any sweet dreams?' Remy asked, as she arranged her soft toys on the pillow. They had an order and a rank that she liked to follow: Little Pigeon in the arms of Blue Cat, Mousey on the foot of Josephine the duck. And Mr Ted and Maureen the hedgehog behind her soft Holly Hobbie 'Heather' doll. It all made sense to her. She kissed the tip of her finger and touched each one, like someone of the cloth issuing blessings.

'No. I didn't dream anything.' Ashleigh was yet to leave her bed, and Remy sensed her reticence. 'I kept waking up.'

Remy had slept soundly, as she always did, knowing her sister was right there and her parents were in the room next door along the hallway. It was even nicer when she heard their voices chattering or the sound of music floating up the stairs from the radio, or their laughter coming from the kitchen, or the click of her dad's wedding ring on the banister rail as he gripped it to walk up or down the stairs. She might be ten, but still, at the sound of this background noise she felt the calming of her pulse, and the settling of her bones, happy to know her mum was within reach. Not that she'd be sharing this with Ashleigh, who would only think her a baby, or worse, a scaredy baby.

Ashleigh was braver than her, more adventurous; she liked to go out and about on her bike alone, or to wander up to the Old Sarum hillfort for a trek and a mooch, whereas Remy preferred to be in the kitchen, watching her mum whip up a Victoria sponge, or helping her peel spuds for tea. She liked to feel useful and liked it even more when her mum put her hand on her face and said, 'Such a good girl.'

There was nowhere Remy would rather be than inside, where everything she needed and everything she could possibly want was right there under the roof of their little house, the one without a spare bedroom. Her parents slept in the double, while she and Ashleigh shared their room, with the smallest room currently full of boxes, her mum's sewing machine and Christmas decorations, ready for one of them to move into *when they were ready* . . . this the vague timeline her mum had attached to the event. Remy couldn't imagine falling asleep without her sister, who she had slept next to since they shared the snug space inside their mum's tum, close by. Together before they even knew how to think, or how to be.

One egg, split in two . . .

She certainly wasn't yet ready to move her bed into the littlest room and, in truth, couldn't imagine a time when she might be.

'Are you worried about the exam?' She tried to guess at the reason for her sister's lack of enthusiasm to get the day started.

'No!' Ashleigh fired, and Remy knew her well enough to understand that this might actually mean *yes*.

'Because it'll be okay. You'll have me there, and even if you don't finish, Miss Delaney said that you can get enough points from the first three parts to pass, so we don't need to rush.'

'I don't care what Miss Delaney said! I told you, I don't care about the stupid exam! Or the stupid scholarship!'

Remy stared as her sister finally jumped out of bed, grabbed her towel, and headed for the bathroom to have her bath, choosing to say nothing rather than say the wrong thing.

Ashleigh got this way sometimes, a little snappy, a little mean.

She had learned it was best to ignore her until the storm passed.

'You all need to be good today. I don't want any naughtiness while I'm gone!' Remy spoke sternly to her stuffies lined up on her pillow. Instantly she felt bad for raising her voice a little, and sat down, running her fingers over their soft faces. 'What can we do to help Ashleigh? She seems a bit upset, don't you think?' As usual, they didn't reply.

Ashleigh

Ashleigh pulled her school jumper over her head and took a seat at the square kitchen table, disliking the uncomfortable feeling of her thick, curly locks trapped inside the neck of her polyester sweater. It made her itch. Her mum stood behind her and gently eased her mop from its woolly confines. The touch of her fingertips to the back of Ashleigh's neck made her shiver and jump, yet more irritation on this day that was already proving tricky.

'I hate my hair!'

'No, you don't.' Her mum did this, dismissed her views as if she could easily transform them with no more than a gentle steer. 'Your hair is beautiful, everybody says so. Besides that's the same as saying you hate Remy's hair, and you don't want to upset your sister, do you?'

Ashleigh shook her head. No, she didn't want to upset her sister. But she also didn't want to look exactly like her, finding nothing funny in the question, *'Now, which one are you?'* that she was asked countless times a day, by their neighbours, her mum's friends, parents at the school, teachers, even her dad, once or twice, although he did so quietly, as if wary of her mum hearing.

She also didn't want to discuss it anymore, knowing that this morning it would take more energy than she had spare to explain that it was not how her hair looked that bothered her, but rather the way it felt, like there was too much of it, and she wanted it to be neater, flatter, less in the way.

Remy, she noticed, was already tucking into toast and jam and glugging from a tumbler full of milk. Ashleigh wished it were dinner time, wished it were possible to blink and the day be done, and they'd be back here eating their tea, instead of breakfast. No doubt they would be quizzed about the exam and what exactly they'd written, and asked numerous questions about what St. Jude's had been like, but it'd be preferable, all of it, as it meant it would be over.

'Brain food!' her mum trilled. 'You have to eat. And talking of eating, I've got you a treat of a tea, all your favourites: toad in the hole, mash, onion gravy, and' – she paused, letting the tension build – 'a special pudding.'

'Yes!' Remy, who sported a large milk moustache, did a fist pump, and her mum's face lit up.

The truth was, Ashleigh barely had an appetite, but knew better than to let on, as this would only encourage her mother to give a half-baked monologue on the importance of breakfast on a day like this. Everything, it seemed, was geared towards keeping her brain in tip-top condition so she could identify shapes and match them on a page, find missing words hidden in code, fill in the blanks of numeric sequences, and circle answers to a passage of writing to show she comprehended it.

Easy enough.

She had done tons of practice tests. All four pupils who were to sit the entrance exam had spent hours doing just this. And she had passed every single one, sometimes finishing with so much time to spare she'd been allowed to take out her book and read, getting lost in the world Noel Streatfeild had created, while the other three continued to scribble furiously.

This felt different. There were three scholarships available and kids from all over the county were vying for them.

But it was more than the exam itself, much more, and she wasn't sure how she could explain it. It was a feeling of pressure, of something heavy on her shoulders and rocks in her stomach, a physical thing that was as new as it was scary. Supposing she didn't pass, supposing she fainted, supposing she couldn't remember a thing, or needed the loo, or her pencil broke, or she actually threw up.

'Ashleigh!' Her mother clapped, and again she jumped. 'Where were you? I've been asking you for the last minute if you want milk or orange squash?'

'I don't mind,' she whispered, trying to find a voice that was steady, trying to control the desire to vomit, as Remy chomped merrily on her toast, and even hummed. Ashleigh didn't want to be the one who wavered, the one who let the side down. The weakest.

'You have to mind!' Her mum laughed loudly, a noise that was an irritation, an upset. 'Milk or orange? Which one would you like best, which would you *prefer*?'

'Orange.'

'And while we are on the subject of fruit, can you name me three different varieties of apple?' her mother asked as she topped up the vibrant cordial with tap water.

'No.' Ashleigh blinked and reached for the glass, knowing the woman wouldn't be satisfied until she had sunk the lot. 'I can't.'

'Oh dear!' Her mum pulled a face that would have been more appropriate for the very worst kind of news. 'What about you, Remy? Three varieties of apple?'

'Nope.' Her sister kept eye contact, letting her know that she was there, and that she understood. Remy offered a small smile telling Ashleigh that it would all be okay. 'No clue.'

'Well, that's not very good, is it?' Her mum tutted.

'Maybe we should have spent more time on apple varieties and not worried about fractions and long multiplication,' Remy whispered sweetly as she bit her toast.

And for the first time that day, Ashleigh felt a smile forming on her lips. It was her sister's gift: she was funny.

'What are you two smiling at?' their mum asked, hands on hips.

'Nothing.'

'Nothing.'

They replied in unison. It was that way with twins. In sync, in tune and always having each other's back.

Remy

Remy was worried about her sister, knowing her well enough to recognise when she was struggling. This was the trouble with Ashleigh, she cared too much about . . . about everything!

Her dad walked into the kitchen, whistling, as was his way. He looked smart in his white shirt and company tie, which was red with a small gold logo on it. Her dad sold concrete. People always made the same jokes when they found this out: '*How does he carry his samples around?*' Or, '*Now there's a job you can really get stuck in to . . .*' He had explained to her in great, great detail that he sold concrete to companies who built things and it was probably the most important part of any project, getting the concrete right. Without it, the whole shebang could tumble down, literally.

Her dad took concrete very seriously. And as he liked to remind them, his smile gone, eyes blinking, 'There's a million people unemployed in this country. One million. I can't even picture that many of anything, fellas who can't put food on the table or shoes on their kids' feet. There'll always be a need for concrete, and for that I am thankful.' His tone and manner hinted that he was not only thankful but fearful too, the slow rise and fall of his Adam's apple suggesting that he was only one wrong move or one pay cheque away from being a fella like that.

She didn't like to think of kids with no shoes.

'How are we all doing?' He always said this, as if he were addressing a crowd. She suspected it was because there were moments when he couldn't tell them apart and was happier with this catch-all, often addressing them directly as 'sweetie' or 'love'.

'Mum's getting us a special pudding.' This, the thing that stuck in her thoughts from their earlier conversation. Remy had a very sweet tooth and was unashamedly motivated by the prospect of sugar.

'Not Arctic Roll, is it? What are we, made of money?'

'Don't be an old grump, Dennis, this is a big day for our little doves, and they deserve a treat!'

'Well, I'm going to work all day, so can I have some?' He winked at her, her lovely dad; she knew he'd never take their ice cream, spoil their treat.

'It's a home-made pud, actually, but I'm not going to say more than that!' Her mum beamed and gave a little wiggle. Excited, it seemed, at no more than the promise of her family around the table, all sampling her special pud.

'How are we all feeling about the exam?' Her dad got straight to it as he slathered marmalade over his toast.

'Well, Mum's excited.' Ashleigh spoke quietly, eyes fixed on Remy. It made them both laugh; there she was, beneath the frosty exterior, her smart sister.

'You'll do great.' Whether he hadn't heard, wasn't paying attention or simply chose to ignore Ashleigh, it was impossible to tell. 'I'll tell you something' – he paused, using his marmalade knife as a pointer as he aimed it at them in turn, verbally ladling on the expectation she knew would do nothing to help ease Ashleigh's nerves – 'when I drive past St. Jude's, do you know what I see?'

She shook her head, knowing he didn't really want her to guess the answer. Ashleigh rolled her eyes and took a deep breath.

'I see fancy cars, and fancy people. Drove past the other week and one bloke was in one of them new Ford Granadas. Cor, I'd give my left nut for one of them.'

'Dennis!' her mum shouted. Her dad was not allowed to say 'nut' in front of them. Unless it was of the pea, wal, or hazel variety.

'And the thought that my daughters will be right there among it.' He shook his head, his voice quavering with emotion. 'It's something I could never have dreamed of. I can't imagine what my old mum would say if she were still alive. She'd not believe it.'

Her mum came up behind him and squeezed his shoulder. It occurred to her then how she, certainly, might be taking the exam in her stride, but for her parents, and Ashleigh too, it was kind of a big deal.

'If we don't pass, don't get the scholarships . . .' She spoke as thoughts formed.

'It doesn't matter!'

'Doesn't matter a jot!'

Her parents replied simultaneously before she had finished the question. They shook their heads, held up their palms and spoke with gusto and false grins, as if they might be able to convince her this was the case. She, however, caught the way they shared a brief but meaningful, wide-eyed glance, as if it *did* matter. As if it mattered a lot.

The colour, she noticed, had drained from Ashleigh's face. Her sister placed her buttered toast on her plate, seemingly unable to take another bite.

'Five eights?' her mum yelled, obviously trying to change the atmosphere as she headed towards the sink.

'Forty-four!' Remy shouted.

'Forty-four?' Her dad pulled a face.

'Goodness me, Remy! Do we need to go over our eight times table in the car?' her mum asked nervously.

Remy smiled at Ashleigh, hoping to make her laugh, knowing her sister was well aware that she could recite all of the times tables perfectly in her sleep.

'I don't know, Ruthie, do we?'

This did the trick, and Ashleigh laughed loudly; the glass of orange squash shook in her hand, spilling over the wipe-clean tablecloth, and Remy's tummy felt warmed.

It was all going to be okay.

Ashleigh

'Here we are then, girls! We need to get a wiggle on as your dad needs the car back pronto. He's heading up to Bristol and won't thank me if he's late. But I wanted to drive you in – no bus for my little smarty-pants, not today.'

Ashleigh gave a brief nod of understanding, although why all the fuss she wasn't sure. She liked getting the bus, liked sitting with Tony, their friend, swapping their news, not that they had much news, and more often than not spoke about what they'd had for their tea. She looked out of the window on her side of the car, the right. She always sat on the right. Remy did likewise on the left.

'Now' – her mum adjusted the rear-view mirror, and spoke into it – 'don't forget, you are to have an early lunch – your form teacher is aware – then Miss Delaney will meet you by the minibus at the front of the school and she will wait *in* the minibus while you take the exam.'

That word, again . . .

It did little to help her nerves, hearing the plan, the schedule. Her mum pulled out the choke, turned the key, and the car juddered as the engine sputtered into life. Ashleigh wondered how badly she would be injured if she jumped out of the moving car. This wasn't a suicide mission, nothing like that! What she was after was the kind of injury that could mean a few hours in the casualty department, long enough to miss the trip to St. Jude's, and maybe a cast on her arm, to show authenticity and commitment to the cause. Yes, a broken arm would do it. Her writing arm! That would be perfect, but would it hurt? She wasn't very good with pain, and how awful if she sustained something horribly damaging or permanent. It felt risky, too risky. Maybe a faint might be better when they arrived? A graceful fall on to the playground floor, or, or . . . vomiting! That would be easy! She again felt nausea rise in her throat. A quick but meaningful vomit, all over her skirt and T-bar shoes, thus guaranteeing a trip home to get changed, suggesting enough of a bug that might mean isolation from all of her classmates and peers. This felt like the only option.

'Then she'll drive you all back,' her mum continued, 'and I will collect you from school as normal, only it won't be as normal, as I'll be driving you home, and it will all be done and you, my clever babies, will have taken the first step on the wonderful path that means so many great things!'

Four spare bedrooms! her sister mouthed at her, and rolled her eyes, before returning her gaze to the window.

Ashleigh felt her legs tense.

'I've checked your bags, and you've got pencil cases, an apple, and a little note each, not to be read until you are in the minibus. A kind of good luck and go-get-'em note!'

It felt like there was little point in reading it, now her mother had revealed the contents.

'You are both very quiet in the back there, little doves!'

'Why do you call us doves?' she had asked once.

Her mum had explained with her hand at her throat and tears in her eyes.

'On the day you were born, I remember sitting on the side of the bed in the ward, I was tired, so tired, but I couldn't sleep. I wanted to stare at those two perfect little babies who slept holding hands, always within reach of each other. I thought my heart might explode! I'd never felt love like it, not before, not since. You were both so beautiful – miracles! Two babies from one egg, rare and special. I was overwhelmed and just to think of it now makes me cry.' She had wiped her eyes as if to prove the point. *'And then, I heard a sound on the windowsill and when I looked there were two white doves, pretty things with keen eyes and beautiful feathers, and they were looking right at me, looking right at you two! And so I called you my own little doves, and that was that.'*

Ashleigh thought of it now and wished she were a little dove, an actual bird, who could, just for today, simply fly away.

Remy

Remy discovered Tony Newman sitting cross-legged on the floor of the cloakroom. It didn't seem to bother him that people had to navigate around him as they tried to stash their bags and coats for the day, clambering over him to pop things on to their pegs. His head was propped on his hand, elbow on his bony knee, and he stared at the floor.

'What's the matter, Tony?'

She dropped to the floor and sat in front of him. He was her and Ashleigh's best friend, and the kindest boy she knew.

'Nothing.' His reply was unconvincing, but his voice sounded a lot like there was *something* wrong and so she took his hand and held it briefly inside hers.

'Where's Ashleigh?' He looked over her shoulder.

'She's gone for a wee.'

He gave a single nod.

'You can tell me what's wrong,' she whispered, 'I'm your best friend.'

This made him smile and he met her gaze. 'I didn't like you not being on the bus. I got a bit . . .' He ran out of words, but his fingers twitched, his face crumpled, and she understood. He often got a bit . . .

'That's okay, Tony, I'm here now. Ashleigh too.'

'I guess I'm feeling a bit sad because I won't have anyone to hang out with at lunchtime, because you and Ashleigh are going to do your test.'

Tony wasn't like the other boys in their class. He wasn't rambunctious or sporty or loud or irritating. He was the opposite of all that, he was lovely. He read as much as she did, wore a jumper knitted by his mum instead of one of the boring, itchy school ones, and his older brother, Gregory, cut his hair. He smelled of mothballs and lavender and always offered to share everything he had with her and Ashleigh; his sweets, his lunch, his good advice.

He didn't have a dad. Well, he used to have a dad, but he had died by getting squished by a car when Tony was in his mum's tummy and his dad had stepped off the kerb without looking. He was also funny, the funniest, and could do the best impressions of everyone they knew, including Miss Delaney, the second-year teacher, who took them for gym and seemed, most of the time, to be in a bit of a tizz.

She noticed the shiny tears that sat at the bottom of his eyes gathering on his lashes but not falling down his cheeks, and it made her feel a little sad too. He was different to a lot of the other boys in this regard also, as he didn't mind crying.

'It's only one lunchtime, Tony. It will all be back to normal tomorrow.'

He nodded, but his bottom lip still looked a little wobbly.

'But if you both get into St. Jude's and I have to go to Milton Road on my own . . .' He let this hang, and it was the first time she reconsidered leaving her friend. She didn't like the thought at all.

'We won't worry about it until we have to.' Remy gave the advice her mother offered with regularity.

'I remember when you both got chickenpox and were off for a week,' Tony whispered. 'I made out to have it too because I didn't want to be here without you. My mum knew I was faking, but she let me stay at home anyway, as long as I did the work Mrs Harman sent.'

'I remember that.' It had made her like Tony's mum even more. 'While we're gone, you can go to the library and help Nancy with the returns, or you could see if Mr Vaughan might let you litter pick?'

'I'll go to the library.' He voiced the plan but sounded less than enamoured at the prospect.

'Nancy will look after you.' This she knew to be true. Nancy was a student who was at college and wanted to be a teacher. She was a grown-up, obviously, but had badges on her jumper that suggested she wasn't a full grown-up, and everyone called her Nancy, and not Miss . . . whatever Nancy's last name was.

Remy was excited about her trip, and was looking forward to the exam, but still she envied Tony the day ahead, knowing she would give anything to spend the lunchtime in the library with him and Nancy. It was the best place to be on any day.

Ashleigh

Ashleigh shut the door and sat in the stall of the bathroom. Her heart beat very quickly and she felt a little sick. It happened like this sometimes when the world felt very big, and she felt very small and entirely uncertain of her place in it. What she was certain of was that she did not feel able to take the trip to St. Jude's.

I can't . . .

I can't do it . . .

I can't take the exam . . .

I just can't . . .

Her top lip was wet, and she ran her finger over it to see if her nose was running, but it was sweat. All sounds were a little echoey in her ears. Her legs felt as if they were made of both jelly and lead.

I can't do it . . .

'Ashleigh?' The sound of Remy's voice made her instantly feel a little better, the familiarity of it, the concern in it and the proximity of her twin. 'Are you okay?' her sister asked softly, quietly, as she knocked on the door. Ashleigh let her in, and Remy locked the door behind her, her expression one of concern.

'No,' she began, 'I'm not . . . not okay.' Her tears came then. Springing from her eyes like leaks.

'Don't cry!' Remy held her hand. 'What shall I do, shall I go and get a teacher?'

She shook her head. 'No! No, please don't. They'll only tell Mum, or they'll try and explain why I *need* to go and take the exam, and I don't want to do it, Rem, I just don't!'

'But . . .' Her sister swallowed, and looked all around them, as if trying to figure out what to say, what to do!

'I . . . I can't . . . I just . . . just can't!'

'Course you can, it's only an exam!'

'It's not though, is it? It's an exam that says where we'll go to big school, it's the scholarship, and I know how badly Mum and Dad want us to get into St. Jude's. Milton Road is a rubbish school. Everyone knows it!'

Her chest heaved, and her breath came in short bursts.

'You don't have to do it, you don't have to do anything!' Remy tried to placate her, placing her hand on her arm. 'You're shaking!'

'I think I might be sick.'

'You sure you don't want me to get someone to call Mum?' Remy exhaled, her tone now edged with panic that echoed her sister's.

'No! Please don't! Please! I've *got* to do it, haven't I? And the last thing I want is Mum coming here to give me one of her talks about how great everything is going to be and asking me to name the capital cities of Europe. I need to try and figure it out.'

'It will be okay, Ash.'

Ashleigh wasn't sure she believed her. 'I've worked really hard – I *want* to go to St. Jude's. I do! I want to go there more than anything! I just . . .' Tears sheeted her face, leaving two snotty streaks that snaked their way towards her mouth. 'I just can't go and do it. I can't!'

'Oh, Ash!' Remy's face was contorted, as if it were hard for her to understand or to know how to fix it. Ashleigh understood; her sister seemed fairly ambivalent about the whole thing, supremely confident in her smarts and certain she would ace the exam. She aced every exam. They both did.

It was no coincidence that out of the fifty-six pupils in their school year, only four of them had been put forward to take the entrance exam.

'The thought of not doing it makes me feel better.' Ashleigh slumped down then on to the toilet, as if her bones, made soft with fear, could no longer support her.

Squatting down, Remy wrapped her mirror image in a loose hug. 'It'll be okay. Don't cry.'

'It won't though, will it?' Ashleigh looked up at her twin, tears flowing over cheeks mottled with distress. 'It changes everything!'

'I don't know if it does.' Her sister's contorted expression suggested she was wrestling with this. 'We're only ten, we don't know how things are going to turn out.'

'Mummy said she blinked when she was ten, and the next minute she was twenty! And so does that mean you blink and then you're forty and then sixty?'

Remy laughed. 'Then eighty!' She giggled because even in this dire moment it was too funny, and Ashleigh understood this too; it was impossible to imagine being an old, old lady of forty, let alone eighty.

'What are you going to do? You can't stay in the loo all day.'

'I'm going to hide.' It was as if the plan formed as the words left her mouth. 'I'm . . . I'm going to hide in the mower shed.'

'But . . .' Again Remy looked at a loss as to what to say to make it all better.

'Please, Remy, don't tell them, don't tell anyone.'

'I don't want you to get into trouble.'

'I don't *care* if I get into trouble,' she lied, 'and I'd rather get into trouble than have to do the exam.'

'Shall I stay with you? Would you like me to hide with you? I will!'

'No!' Ashleigh shook her head, unsure of many things, and touched by her sister's willingness to go along with her crazy plan, but adamant she didn't want Remy to miss out on a place at St. Jude's too. 'Please go and do the exam and pass it, like we know you can, and then go to that great school and get a house with four spare bedrooms and mix with fancy people who buy concrete and don't sell concrete.'

'I wouldn't mind selling concrete.' Her sister spoke softly, earnestly.

'I'd mind you selling concrete.'

'I can't imagine not going to school with you.' Remy's voice cracked.

'It will be okay, little dove.' Ashleigh wrapped her in a brief, tight hug. 'It'll be okay. Let's go to morning lessons and then, when the early bell goes and we're let out, I'll go and hide in the mower shed and come out when the minibus has gone, when it's too late for me to get to St. Jude's.'

'You've still got time to change your mind and come along. You might feel better in a bit, and decide you can do it after all, and that would be great!' It was the closest her sister had come to trying to sway her decision.

'Yes, I might.' Ashleigh smiled, knowing she would not change her mind, not at all, because unlike other tests, this felt different. The thought of failing, of letting everyone down . . . it was preferrable not to try, easier. She was also aware, however, of the need to give Remy this little hook on which to hang her hope, something that would help them both get through the morning. 'You go into class. I'm just going to wash my face and I'll be straight in.'

'Okay, Ash.' Remy took her time, stood slowly, and unlocked the cubicle door, as if unsure if leaving her sister alone was the right thing to do. 'I love you, little dove,' she whispered.

Ashleigh found a smile she hoped was convincing. 'I love you too.'

Remy

Remy wasn't very good at lying. Her dad said her face gave it away every time, and she knew this to be true, feeling the red flush of dishonesty mark her whenever she voiced an untruth.

'Who took my last Malteser?' he had asked as he proffered the empty box. *'Was it you, Remy?'*

She had shaken her head, but he knew.

'Which one of you little rascals has run over the wet kitchen floor? There are footprints leading to the fridge. Was it you, Remy?'

She had pointed at her sister, but her mum wasn't fooled.

This was no different.

As she spoke, she felt the spread of crimson on her chest and neck, picturing it like ink dropping into water, marking her out as dishonest.

'Where the devil *is* she?' Miss Delaney almost shouted, her face screwed up, eyes combing the playground, as she looked at her watch and scanned the horizon again.

'I don't . . . don't know!' A hot, clammy sensation engulfed her.

Tony always said she'd be a hopeless poker player or adulterer. Aged ten, she'd had to look up both poker and adultery in the dictionary. It had been fascinating. Tony, as ever, knew a little bit about everything. The result, no doubt, of having an older brother like Gregory, who spoke and acted freely in front of his younger sibling. Tony had even smoked, and seen three pictures of boobs torn out of a magazine, which he said he didn't get, unsure what all the fuss was about, as his older brother and his mates went into raptures about the milk balloons, as he called them, sitting rather limply on the chest of a woman in an undone negligée.

'Well, she can't have just disappeared! Did she not have lunch with you?' Miss Delaney sighed and huffed at the same time, indicating she was doubly mad.

Remy shrugged.

It made her feel bad. She knew *exactly* where her sister was, but wasn't about to rat her out. That wasn't the way with sisters. And certainly not the way with twins. Identical twins.

'Well.' Miss Delaney stared at her with a look of pure frustration. 'I'm now going to have to go and inform Mr Gerald, who will have to spend *his* lunch hour looking for her, and the minibus is not going to wait. It's unfair if her going AWOL makes you, William and Rukmal late, it's all stressful enough as it is.'

'I'm sorry.' She felt it wise to apologise, even if it wasn't really her fault.

Miss Delaney shook her head, and she felt the disappointment shower down on her like the dandruff that clustered on the shoulders of her teacher's black jumper. It was always this way, the collective praise, anger, or judgement directed at either one or both of them, as if everyone was aware that they were one person, split in two, and therefore it felt justified.

'Get on the bus. I'll be back in a jiffy.' Miss Delaney sighed again, as she shepherded the three of them on to the minibus where the engine was already running. 'What a silly girl!' was her parting shot, before leaving the three of them to sit amid the aged interior that smelled of diesel, sweat, and cheesy plimsolls. It was gross.

Remy wished she could open the windows.

Choosing a seat in the middle, she put her bag on the seat next to her to stop one of the others taking it. Inside nestled her ink pen, pencils, ruler, eraser, an apple which she was under strict instructions to eat on the way there, and a note from their mum that read:

> *My clever little dove! You can do this, just keep your eye on the prize; this amazing school! And if you don't pass,*

don't worry – either way, you are wonderful and your whole future awaits! We are proud and we love you! X

She knew the same note and a similar apple would right now be nestling in her sister's bag, which was probably doubling as a seat as she hid in the mower shed on the edge of the playing field.

Miss Delaney came back, her face red, eyes small, mouth thin.

'Thank you, driver, let's go!' she said as she sat down hard at the front of the bus. This was really happening: they were leaving without Ashleigh! And in that moment, Remy felt seven different types of sickness and nervousness! What would happen now?

Remy stared at the low red-brick building as the minibus rumbled out of the gates on to the main road and headed towards town, where St. Jude's was located, and she felt her heart flex for her sister. It had been horrible to see her so distressed, so scared.

She looked back at the rather nondescript squat design of their school, the mobile classrooms tacked on to the side to cope with the ever-expanding population. The vast metal dumpsters at the back of the dining hall which gave off the foul odour of Spam fritters and grey mashed potato.

She'd studied the glossy brochure they'd been given about St. Jude's Academy. It was pretty, no doubt, with snaking plants that hung over the doors, neat hedging, science labs, lecture theatres, tennis courts, a swimming pool, and its very own music studio! A school that was a world away from this little place that was crammed in among the 1930s housing estate where parking was a nightmare. St. Jude's had a wide gravel car park. Even the litter bins were pretty!

'Right.' Miss Delaney turned to face them all. 'I am so sorry for the last-minute disruption.' Remy felt this was directed at her, and her face coloured accordingly. 'I want you all to keep calm.' Her fast-paced speech and slight pant suggested she'd be better off taking her own advice. 'You have worked so hard for this, and you are more than capable! Enjoy it!' She gave a wide, false smile. 'It's a chance to see this fabulous school up close and its lovely facilities. We're all rooting for you. I know you can do it. And remember, if you don't pass, if you're not offered one of the scholarships, it will still be a valuable experience and you will all thrive, no matter what happens, so, no pressure!' The teacher swallowed and wiped her hands on her skirt. 'Relax, and do your best. Does anyone have any questions?'

William put his hand up.

'You don't have to put your hand up, William. There are only three of you in the minibus.' Miss Delaney spoke sharply.

'Erm, do you think Remy will get into trouble for missing the exam?' he half-whispered, as if he might be able to ask the question without her hearing. Remy turned to face him, giving him a hard stare that made him blink behind his gold-rimmed glasses and shrink back in his seat. And it was in that moment that an idea formed. Of course, he had assumed it was her who had not turned up! She was the more easy-going of the two, less conscientious than her sister. William thought she was Ashleigh, and Miss Delaney had not corrected him. Did that mean Miss Delaney thought she was Ashleigh too? Ashleigh, who wanted to go to St. Jude's more than anything . . . and she loved her sister more than anybody. And just like that, it felt obvious, easy even!

'Let's not worry about that right now, let's just concentrate on staying calm and maybe running through some of the practice questions in our head.' Miss Delaney shook hers, and twisted her lower jaw before turning around. 'Silly girl.'

There it was again. Remy heard her loud and clear and envisaged lobbing her apple at the back of the teacher's head before thinking better of it. It would be hard enough for her parents to deal with the fallout of the day without her being expelled for any apple-related injury Miss Delaney might sustain. Miss Delaney, who couldn't tell the difference between her and Ashleigh.

The silly woman . . .

Ashleigh

Ashleigh waited a good half an hour after the minibus had left, ensuring there was no way she could make the exam, before coming out of her hiding place. She felt lighter, happier, yet worried too about being in trouble. It seemed obvious to head to her happy place, and she went straight to the library, where Nancy was delighted to see her.

'Hello, Miss Brett. You've caused quite a stir, little one, Mr Gerald has been running around trying to find you, Miss Delaney said you weren't on the bus, but I'm glad you're here. Are you okay?'

'Yes.'

'I just need to call your mother.'

Ashleigh buried her head inside her reading book while Nancy whispered down the phone. It was a strange feeling, knowing she was talking to her mum about her.

'Now.' Nancy, having ended the call, bent down so they could speak quietly, calmly, without any of the hysteria she had feared. 'I've told your mum that you're safe.'

'Thank you.' Her voice was meek, her muscles uncoiled with something very close to relief.

'Where were you? What happened?'

'I hid in the mower shed because I didn't want to do the exam.'

It felt good, the honesty, the openness, letting the truth out of its cage. Holding it in was never an option. It would eat away at her.

'I see.' Nancy smiled and nodded with her eyes closed, as if she understood.

It felt nice, it always did, being here in this room with its peculiar smell of dust and the exhaled wonder and gasps of delight lingering in the air from everyone who had ever read a book inside the magnolia-painted walls.

'Would you like to help me put some books back on to the shelves?'

Ashleigh nodded. It was exactly what she felt like doing. Nancy handed her a small pile of books. She knew the drill. This was not her first rodeo.

'I just need to call Mr Gerald. As I said, he's been very worried.'

She listened to Nancy's phone call to the headmaster as she trawled the shelves, searching for the correct alphabetical spot, her stomach churning at the thought that she'd worried Mr Gerald, who was nice.

'Yes, yes, she's here, just strolled in. I've let Mrs Brett know. Nope, she's fine, not upset, no, just . . . quiet. Yep, uh-huh. She's going to help me in here for a bit, which I think is a good idea, let her settle and let the fuss die down. But she's safe, in one piece, and was apparently in the mower shed, hiding. Why? Oh, because she didn't want to do the exam.'

If Nancy was telling Mr Gerald, then it would only be a matter of time before the whole school knew. Her mum would definitely tell her dad, and on it went. In truth, she hadn't given much thought beyond hiding, hadn't properly considered the consequences at all.

Still, she knew with certainty that it was worth it. Whatever happened, it was worth it. Her stomach was no longer moving like a food mixer, she didn't feel faint (genuinely faint!), and gone was the feeling that she could burst into tears at any given second.

It was over; thankfully, and finally, it was over.

Her time in the library slipped by quickly, and just before the bell for home time, her sister appeared in the doorway. Remy rushed over and held both of her hands in her own.

'There you are, Remy!' Remy spoke with urgency, and Ashleigh wondered what on earth was going on.

'What?'

'I said, "There you are." Honestly, *Remy*, Mum and Dad are going to be so mad with you!'

'Ashleigh, please, be kind! Whatever reason Remy had for not wanting or feeling able to take the exam is neither here nor there, not now it's all over. We don't need to make today any harder for her.'

Ashleigh stared at Nancy, who had got the wrong end of the stick, confused them. 'But I'm not—'

'Not sorry?' Remy stared at her, eyes blazing. 'Well, you should be!'

'Okay, Ashleigh, that's enough!' Nancy shouted, and Ashleigh felt her insides shrink, not only at the rare occurrence of Nancy raising her voice, but also because it was starting to dawn on her what Remy had done.

Ashleigh stared at her, mouth slightly open, her chest heaving.

Remy gripped her hand. 'Come on. Mum will be here any minute.'

Nancy took her seat behind her desk and smiled at her. 'Try and remember, Remy, that these things only feel important at the time. But trust me, in a few weeks, a few months, a few years, you will barely think about it.'

Ashleigh nodded, hardly trusting herself to speak, as Remy led her from the room. They walked hand in hand. She felt like the condemned as they made their way to the pick-up spot in the car park where their mother, Ruthie, liked to collect them, knowing she'd be where she said she would be, arriving like clockwork, reliable. Unlike her, who couldn't even make it on to a minibus to take a stupid exam.

Remy let out a long, loud breath, suggesting she had been holding it in.

'Why?' Ashleigh managed, feeling perilously close to tears. 'Why are you doing this?'

'Because I don't care!' Her sister laughed. 'I don't care about going to St. Jude's, and you do, and I don't want you to be upset over something so daft. It doesn't matter to me, none of it, and I know it matters to you.'

'Did you put my name on the paper?' She tried to get the facts straight in her mind, to catch up.

'Of course.'

'I don't know what to say!' She shook her head, her confusion genuine.

'Don't say anything! It's done! I did it for you. I love you, Ash.'

'I . . . I love you, but . . .' This was a whole other level of subterfuge she had not banked on.

'No buts. It's all over!' Remy smiled at her.

'Did you pass, would you say? Do you think you got the scholarship?'

'Of course, it was easy-peasy pips, all of it.' Her sister spoke with conviction.

'Supposing . . . supposing someone asks me questions about it!' It was starting to feel horribly complicated and deceitful.

'They won't! There's only me, William and Rukmal who took it, and they're none the wiser. No one knows. No one questioned it. It doesn't matter!'

'*I* know, and it matters to me.' Ashleigh hated how worry over the exam was now replaced by worry over her sister's actions. What if they got caught? Were they criminals now?

'We need to forget about it and, as far as the whole wide world is concerned, you took the exam and I didn't, and that's the end of it. And now we just wait and see.'

'I still don't really understand why, Remy . . .'

'It's done, Ash! No one will ever know, and that's all that matters!' She sounded certain, and Ashleigh envied her confidence.

'You might get into trouble with Mum and Dad for not going to sit the exam even though you did! I think we might go to prison!' Her heart raced.

Remy pulled a face. 'We are not going to prison! You don't go to prison for things like that, you go to prison for robbing banks and setting fire to things!'

'I'm scared.'

'Don't be. I did it for you, and I know that if it was something important to me, you would have done the same.'

'I would.' The words easy to say, yet she was unsure if they were just that – words.

'We're not to mention it, not ever again. Just make out it hasn't happened, let everyone believe what they know to be true, that you took the exam, Ash. That's the end of it. Promise me!'

'I promise.' Her mouth felt dry. It was overwhelming that her sister had done this remarkable, daring, and crazy thing just for her. 'Thank you, little dove.' Ashleigh reached for her sister then and held her close.

That's how they stood, cheek to cheek, with their hands around each other's backs, curly hair falling over the other's arms and shoes toe to toe. The symmetry was stunning, these two little girls indistinguishable, almost; two halves of one egg, one person . . .

Remy

'Get in.'

Remy watched as her mum held open the car door, avoiding eye contact, but looking around as if she were a getaway driver making sure the coast was clear. She slipped on to the back seat. Ashleigh sat next to her, on the right.

Ashleigh always sat on the right.

Her mum, usually in a hurry to get supper on the table, sat still for a second. Slowly, she buckled up, missing the connection with the end of the seat belt; it took her two attempts before it locked in, and with her trembling hands she gripped the steering wheel.

'I don't honestly know what to say.'

Her tone wasn't what Remy might have expected. There was no shouting, no overt anger, no questions fired or judgement offered, nothing loud. It was worse somehow; far better the yelling that she would know how to react to. This was more reminiscent of when their grandpa had died and her mum had sat on the edge of the bed and said gently, *I have some really rotten news* . . . It felt the same.

Remy stared out of the window, avoiding the frequent blink of her mum's eyes in the rear-view mirror that she feared might be a forerunner to tears, and quite unable to look at Ashleigh. It was a dreadful thought that she might be about to make their mummy cry! She hadn't wanted that, definitely not that.

'I mean, I just . . .' Her mum shook her head, as if confirming that she really didn't know what to say. 'Me and your dad, we're at a loss . . . It makes no sense.'

And this was how it went. Her mum barely keeping the lid on her sadness, her confusion, as she pulled the choke, started the engine, and drove slowly out of the school gates. Remy stayed silent, while the atmosphere inside the car screamed loudly of all that they tried to contain.

'Honestly, Remy, what were you thinking?'

She felt her sister's hand creep across the seat and reach for her fingers. And there they sat, each staring out of the opposite window of the car as it moved towards home, holding hands. Both aware of what she had done and yet both sworn not to mention it, not ever. There was something very satisfying about having come up with a plan and executed it, knowing she had done so for her sister, yet any joy was tinged with sadness at the way her mum was now reacting.

'I even made a lemon meringue pie to celebrate.'

'I won't have any.' Remy spoke clearly. She thought it best to show she wasn't expecting any special dinner, not when she had, in her mum's view, let them all down so badly. At the thought of the promised treat – toad in the hole, mash and onion gravy – her stomach growled. It had been a busy old day, what with the exam and all, and she was hungry.

'That's right, you won't!'

Her mother spoke sharply now, as she shook her head; this no doubt just the first punishment to come Remy's way. She hadn't expected this anger, this uproar, it was, after all, only one exam.

She felt the tremble of her sister's palm and slowly turned to face her, wanting to help allay her fears, to smile and reassure her, but to her surprise, Ashleigh was not shaking with fright or nerves, she was instead laughing, quietly laughing until the tears rolled down her face.

Remy tried not to, knowing it might tip her mother over the edge, but it was impossible, and she too started to giggle.

'Well, I don't know what about this is remotely funny! I really don't. Mr Gerald was in a flap, thought you'd been abducted! We were minutes away from calling the police! Can you imagine how worried I was? He did four laps of the paddock with a stick, prodding every bush, looking behind trees. He had the caretaker search every cupboard and storeroom. They even took a torch into the crawl space under the terrapin!'

Their mother fired from thin lips, her voice a firecracker in the quiet, and it became clear that suddenly she knew *exactly* what to say.

Ashleigh laughed harder, wheezing now with one hand on her chest. This only made Remy giggle more, snorting in an almost uncontrolled fashion that was always the way when one of them laughed, and it was contagious.

'You can laugh now, but my God! All that money, the scholarship, beyond our wildest bloody dreams!' Her voice cracked. 'And when one of you is holidaying in Sardinia and the other in Southend, it won't be funny. When one of you is driving around in a Ford Granada and the other is taking the flippin' bus, it won't be funny! When one of you is running your own business and the other is emptying the bins, trust me, you won't be laughing, Remy Brett!'

Her mother had made it abundantly clear that she was the one who would be holidaying in Southend, having travelled there by bus, on a precious day off from bin-emptying. This dire prediction of her life felt so removed from her ten-year-old self travelling in the back of her dad's Austin that it was hard to picture.

Again Ruthie gripped the steering wheel so hard that the leather squeaked under her palms.

'I really don't see what is funny about it, about any of it!'

'What's funny,' Ashleigh spoke up, clearly and confidently, 'is that Remy doesn't even like lemon meringue pie.'

'I thought it was you who didn't like lemon meringue pie, Ashleigh? I've made you a mini apple Charlotte!'

'Nope, other way around.' Her sister smiled at her. 'Don't worry, Mum. It's easy to get us mixed up, everyone does it. It's hard to tell us apart sometimes.'

Remy sat back in the seat. Her sister was right: it *was* hard to tell them apart.

Ashleigh and Remy Brett

1975

Aged 13

Ashleigh

'Right, listen up!' Mr De Vere clapped and waited for hush in the junior common room. 'I know we are all excited, but there are a few things I need to remind you of.' Ashleigh rolled her eyes to make Jacinta and Harry laugh. The three had been tasked with loitering in the quadrangle and helping direct any lost or bewildered guests in the right direction. 'I want you to have fun, of course – speech day is something we should all enjoy – but also, be aware that you are representing St. Jude's Academy. I want top buttons done up, ties straight, blazers on and hair brushed.' Ashleigh patted her locks, which she kept in a tight plait, with any loose curls tamed by a brush and tucked in flat to her head. 'We have a reputation to uphold. This school has been here for nearly two hundred years, and we don't want today to be the day our reputation goes down the swanny because of some lapse in judgement from you lot!'

A ripple of laughter swept around the room. He was great, Mr De Vere; fun, handsome, quite trendy when out of school, in his flared corduroys and leather jacket. She had seen him in the Post Office in the holidays, buying stamps. Unlike some of the more stuffy masters, he spoke to them as if they were equals. Everyone had a tiny crush on him. He had long sideburns and reminded her a bit of David Soul.

'Now, you all have your roles, your tasks, your responsibilities, and I am trusting you to execute them wonderfully! Be polite at all times, and remember you cannot leave with your parents until the end of the school day and have to be signed out in the usual manner by your house master or mistress! No scarpering after lunch like we did in my day!'

There it was again, that laughter, like he was a mate. He was always keen to remind them that he was St. Jude's alumni and loved it so much he'd come back here to teach.

'Have a great time. This is your day – a chance to show everyone around our beautiful campus – so enjoy it!'

Ashleigh was glad to be outside, to stretch her legs, as an unidentifiable cramp squeezed low in her gut. It was brief, nothing to worry about.

'Are your parents coming?' Jacinta asked, as they made their way from the junior common room to the main quad to take up their posts.

'Yes, worse luck, and my sister.'

'Why worse luck? I wish mine were coming, but my dad's in Hong Kong and my mum's probably at home with a migraine or a severe case of can't be bothered.'

Ashleigh laughed; she was funny, Jacinta. Not that they were close, not really, but their interactions were always pleasant enough.

'I didn't mean worse luck.' She regretted her openness in the face of Jacinta's response. 'I'm glad they're coming, kind of.' She swallowed. 'It's just that my mum always makes such a big deal out of everything, and my sister's never been here before, so . . .' This was a small lie. Remy had of course been here once before, but only briefly, long enough to set wheels in motion that had affected her whole life – both of their lives.

'Consider yourself lucky,' Harry huffed. 'My parents will travel in separate cars, and scowl at each other across the marquee over lunch, only smiling or being civil when I'm there. They're halfway through a divorce and arguing about the house and money. My sister pointed out the other day that they're not fighting over us! Says it all, really.'

She and Jacinta shared a wide-eyed look. This was quite shocking. She didn't know anyone who was divorced and couldn't begin to imagine how a family like that functioned. She'd heard her mum say that divorce was a terrible thing, and that it was awful to be from a broken family. It *sounded* awful, a family *broken*, heartbreaking even. She was glad her parents still liked each other.

'My dad's got a new girlfriend, and my mum hates her, so' – he sighed – 'be happy your parents are coming here together. It'll be nice!'

'I guess so.' She smiled, still processing Harry's words, and knowing she could never explain just how she felt about her sister coming to see the prize that should have been hers. Not that they had ever mentioned it, not ever. It was a dark and deceitful episode that seemed to have put a splinter in all of their communication. Ashleigh avoided talking about school, sometimes avoided talking to Remy altogether. Preferring not to give her the details of all she was missing out on, this life that should have been hers. The trouble was, all Ashleigh could *think* to talk about *was* school and as it was a topic that was off limits [illegible] It sat like a poisonous thing between them, not to be discussed or prodded, for fear of awakening the whole sorry subject.

Not that it would have been easy to talk about. It was hard enough for her to get it straight in her own mind; how she felt about her place here, her life at this amazing institution and all the opportunities it afforded. But certainly guilty, torn, delighted would do for starters. That, and having to carry a secret had never sat well with her. Her life here at St. Jude's was undoubtedly wonderful, but it came at a cost, the duplicity and subterfuge around her winning the place a high price for her to pay, especially as it was something she had not chosen. It was conflicting, trying to understand this, but also knowing that, despite their awkwardness, Remy had only ever acted out of love.

It was partly why she chose not to pursue deep friendships here and could never have entertained bringing anyone from school back to her house. Not that she was ashamed of their less-than-grand abode with its lack of spare bedrooms, not that, but rather she feared getting close to someone and blurting out the truth, or worse, her sister blurting out the truth, being exposed as a liar. She had only recently realised that at the end of every school day the way she exhaled deeply and let her muscles uncoil was not the simple reaction to another day done, but rather relief that she had got away with it. Again. It was a good day if no one tapped her on the shoulder and marched her across town to the comprehensive school without its own swimming pool, array of science laboratories, lecture theatres and grounds pretty enough to rival any well-kept park.

'Jacinta!' A diminutive woman in a neat navy wool two-piece suit waved from the other side of the quad.

'Mum!' Jacinta's face lit up, and she turned to Ashleigh. 'Well, whaddya know? I guess my mother *is* coming after all!' The two met on the path and enjoyed a brief hug.

'Are these your friends? Hello!' The woman raised a gloved hand and Ashleigh took the opportunity to admire her pillbox hat, the pearls at her neck, her clip-top leather handbag and matching clickety-clackety kitten heels that made the most pleasing sound on the path. She was smart and fancy. Ashleigh felt the watery rise of inadequacy in her stomach. It was always this way when she met people like Jacinta's mum; she was aware that she was a little less than. A fraud.

'Yes!' Jacinta's face coloured a little. It was certainly an assumption, but she understood. Far better than admitting that, like her, most people in her year were no more than acquaintances, casual buddies with whom she could sit for lunch, chat to at the beginning and end of class. People to smile or nod at when you passed them in the corridors or on the sports pitch. But proper friends with the kind of connection that Remy and Tony Newman shared, the kind you giggled with until you collapsed, reminisced with about shared experiences, swapped in-jokes and the platonic love that wrapped them in an impenetrable bubble? No, nothing like that. Not even close.

'This is Ashleigh.' Jacinta beamed.

'How do you do, Ashleigh?'

How do you do . . .

'Good, thank you.' She kept her vowels well rounded, emulating the way Jacinta spoke.

'And this is Harry.' Jacinta gestured towards the boy.

'Hello, Harry.'

'Hello, Mrs Wentworth.'

Mrs Wentworth . . . yes, of course! Ashleigh knew she should have addressed the woman in this way and made a mental note for the future.

'Well, this is all very charming!' Mrs Wentworth laughed without making a noise. 'What are you planning on doing when you leave, Ashleigh?'

'Oh, probably just go home. My mum will have cooked tea.'

This time her laugh was audible, but only just. The woman's nose gave a slight wrinkle of distaste. 'I meant when you leave St. Jude's.' *Of course you did* . . . 'We've told Jacinta it can only be Oxbridge and that she should read the law like her father and grandfather. Her brother is currently at Brasenose.' The woman spoke with reverence, and as if Ashleigh should be aware of what this meant.

'That's good,' she managed.

'I'm hoping for medicine, Christ's, Cambridge,' Harry piped up confidently, part of the club. 'It's where my father went.'

'Wonderful!' Mrs Wentworth almost glowed with approval.

And there it was . . .

Just a tingle at first, but quickly this spread into something almost paralysing. A feeling. The same feeling she had felt at the prospect of sitting the entrance exam. A heaviness in her limbs, a sickness in her gut and a pressure that sat across her shoulders and pushed her down and down . . . *law or medicine* . . . *Oxbridge* . . . too much, all much too much for her to cope with. She was without doubt brighter than Jacinta and Harry; her grades alone proved this. But the idea that she was as *capable* as them, as *worthy* as them, not at all. They carried a confidence that eluded her, a self-belief that meant they would set their goals, aim high and succeed. But for Ashleigh? She was not from the same stock. A scholarship girl. Her dad sold concrete, her mum made shepherd's pie and fussed over the arrangement of the faux flowers on her dining table. A girl who had never sat the entrance exam because of that tingle, that feeling – like she was in freefall.

Remy

Remy closed her bedroom door and took a beat on the top stair, steeling herself for the day ahead as she peered across the narrow hallway into the room she used to share with her sister. A space she now avoided.

'Come on, little doves, flutter up to bed!'

She could still hear her mum saying that when they were small: *'Up you fly!'*

It hurt to think of it, even now, nearly three years later; the casual nature of her sister's request, spoken over supper, as she sat in her green wool blazer and long skirt.

'Okay, so I was thinking' – Ashleigh's voice was clear and confident, addressing their parents who hung on her every word – 'I'd quite like my own bedroom. Can I move into the little room?'

Remy had felt winded, stunned, and then came the unexpected bloom of tears. Hot, snaking glass rods of distress that trickled down her cheeks. Her mum and dad didn't notice, staring at Ashleigh as she spoke. For Remy, it seemed like the beginning of the end to have separate rooms, not to wake and see her sister's face looking back at her. There was already a thin sheet of separation that had never existed between them before, but with different friends, different schools, different expectations and what felt like a different standard in their education, this request felt a lot like punishment for a crime she didn't know she had committed.

Only that wasn't true: she *did* know, and so did Ashleigh.

It seemed that her actions on exam day were at the heart of their separation, and it killed her.

'If that's what you would like, love,' her mother replied, keenly. 'I suppose I can move my sewing machine up into the loft and your dad can find a place for all the boxes.'

'Great!' Ashleigh had forked baked spud and beans into her mouth, but avoided eye contact with her, because she would have known – Remy was convinced that her sister would have *known* what this meant, and how it *felt.*

'I suppose it makes sense in the long run, all that homework and proper studying, special textbooks. Clever girl.'

Remy had stared at her mother. What did she think, that her textbooks were less informative, riddled with errors, books for dumdums? Frustration had bubbled in her veins, and she'd stared at Ashleigh, and in her gaze she fired the words, *We both know the truth and I know that's why you can't look at me and don't want to see me when you wake up in the morning. We both know it* . . . It was doubly galling because she rarely thought about the bloody exam, but it was obviously a big deal for her sister, who had changed so much since starting at St. Jude's. Her voice was different, her mood a little sullen, her expression serious, and she never shared anything about her school life, not a thing, as if Remy wasn't worthy of being party to such things. Excluded. She wasn't sure she'd even *like* the girl if she met her for the first time now. Not that she'd share this with anyone, ever. Not even Tony.

'In fact,' her dad had piped up, 'why doesn't *Remy* move into the little room, give you the space you need?'

'Yes, that's a brilliant idea!' She had jumped up. 'Why don't I? Or better still, why don't I just put my bed in the shed and Ashleigh can have both rooms? One to sleep in and one for all her very important, special, clever textbooks!'

'There she is!' Her dad pulled her from these thoughts now, calling upstairs, 'Come on, love, car's running!' He rubbed his palms together as if it were cold.

'Coming.' She reluctantly trod the stairs, stepping out of the house and watching as her dad shut the front door behind them and pushed it, twice, just to double-check it was properly closed. Her mum was already buckled up in the front seat.

'I don't see why I have to go. Can't believe I'm taking a day off school for this!' Sitting in her dad's Austin, Remy's mood wasn't helped by the fact that she had a stomach ache, a gripping pain, no less. She pulled at the mustard-and-red kilt that had been bought for her cousin's wedding almost a year ago and now sat some inches above her knees. The whole affair would, she knew, be a lot easier to bear if she'd been allowed to wear her corduroys and a nice blouse. The kilt was itchy, unfashionable and a little tight around the waistband. The fact it was paired with a thin red turtleneck did little to help. Her tights were American tan, and she hated them too, nearly as much as her brown clumpy school shoes which she felt finished off the whole ensemble with just the right level of shitness. She felt like a wally, already uncomfortable enough going into this strange environment where she knew she'd feel out of place. The only saving grace was that Tony would not see her in this get-up and would therefore be robbed of the ammunition to tease her with in the coming weeks.

She smiled to think of him, hoping he'd be okay, a full school day without her. He'd survive, but only just.

'So, ready for the gossip?' he'd asked her yesterday as they made their way to class, heads together, tittle-tattling.

'Always!' How she loved him.

'You remember Nancy from the library at primary school?'

'Of course I do!'

'Well, she's pregnant!' he gasped.

'Pregnant? I didn't know she was married.' She wondered if she'd got hitched to her boyfriend who had cooked her tea.

'That's the thing, she's *not*!' Tony had enunciated, stressing the horror of it. 'I heard my mum telling her sister on the phone.'

'Oh my God!'

'Exactly!'

'Are you two *actually* joined at the hip?' Mr Morgan, their biology teacher, had yelled at them as they dawdled arm in arm along the corridor.

'I think, Mr Morgan, that as a biology teacher, you'd know that would make us conjoined twins, and we are most definitely not that,' Tony had replied without a whiff of irony, earning himself a detention for insubordination. It would be worth it, she knew, as this was the kind of story they'd laugh about for months.

'For the love of God, Remy! Please not this again!' her mum snapped, rubbing her forehead as she turned to shout at her through the gap in the front seats. 'You have to because it's important! We are going to support your sister! It's her first speech day! You're only invited when you leave the prep and go into the big part of the school. It's an honour!'

An honour my arse. Remy bit the inside of her mouth and swallowed the sentence. Words she knew would only be incendiary to her mother who for days had been rather worked up about the whole event. That morning she'd had her curlers removed and her hair combed out before having it sprayed into a fixed helmet that a hurricane couldn't budge. Her dad, too, sat tall in the driver's seat, his sports jacket with gold buttons hanging on the coat hook above the rear passenger window behind his seat. His company tie was around his neck, his white shirt pressed and starched. His grey slacks steamed. His black shoes shiny. Proud, so proud.

'Ashleigh won't care if I'm there or not,' she half mumbled.

Her mum's finger appeared then. Jutting towards her. She knew things were bad when her mother's finger appeared.

'That's it, smartarse! I do not want to hear a peep out of you for the rest of the day. No moaning. No whispers, no mumbles, and no embarrassing your sister!' The finger recoiled, and she was glad of it. 'This is what I was talking about when I told you there'd be consequences.'

Ah, perfect. This was just what she needed, her mother kicking off about the bloody exam. Again she bit her cheek and stared out of the window as they trundled past Old Sarum.

'People are rewarded for putting in effort, Remy. I don't think that's something you've quite grasped yet. You had the chance. You both did. We've never treated you girls any differently. Never. We love you just the same.' Her mother drew breath.

Wait for it . . . there's a but coming any second now . . . She half wished Tony was in the car to witness the perfection of the moment, knowing he would get it and find it as funny as her. Not as funny as her grotty kilt, however.

'But . . .' There it was, right on cue! 'But not taking the exam put you on a different path, my little love, one that you now no doubt regret, but there's not a whole lot we can do about it. We did try and explain to you.'

'We did,' her dad chipped in, eyeing her in the rear-view mirror.

'It was a chance, an opportunity, and there's no saying you'd have passed or got the scholarship, of course not – the other two kids from your school failed to get in – but Ashleigh . . .'

She was sure her mum was still talking, but rather than listen, yet again, to the many ways Remy had royally, to the best of her mother's knowledge, cocked up her future and flushed all chance of success down the pan, she stared out of the window that was starting to fog up, and in her head she played the latest Bay City Rollers song that the radio loved.

Bye Bye Baby . . .

Her dad pulled into the car park and drove with caution between a khaki-coloured Wolseley and a shiny claret-toned Jaguar.

'I tell you one thing, Ruthie,' he chuckled, 'I definitely cannot afford to bash anything in this car park, for the paintwork repairs on these beauties alone, they'd take the house!'

She saw her mother's shoulders tense, as if this new worry, making it off the premises without losing their home, was one to now occupy her mind. It sent a shiver of regret along her bones; she needed to be nicer to her mum today.

Before they left their car, which looked tiny and a bit battered, her dad tried the driver's door handle to make sure it was locked, twice. With his eyes popping, he took in the array of expensive vehicles that filled the place.

He whistled and shook his head as he put his arms into his blazer and straightened his tie, the one with the little gold logo on it. And she hated it. Hated how impressed he was with the overt displays of wealth, the way her mum grabbed his hand and held it fast, trying to look confident, doing her best to fade into the background. Although that was never going to be easy. Her dress and matching overcoat with their bold floral pattern of pink and orange were beacons, bright, bright things among the clipped hedges, the ivy-covered flint walls, the raked gravel and pretty litter bins. In another mood, on another day, she'd have given thanks that with her mother dressed like that, no one was going to give her kilt and clumpy shoes a second glance.

But not today.

A thought struck her then, an unpleasant one: was part of her reticence to attend because she had known it would be like this? Her mum and dad bending over backwards to fit in, while sticking out like sore thumbs – and how would Ashleigh react to the lot of them being on her turf, in her world, if only for a day?

'Isn't this beautiful?' She spoke with false joy, arms wide and strength to her tone, doing her best to make the day the best it could be, for them all. This was what she did, fixed things, for Ashleigh; for her parents too.

Ruthie Brett beamed at her, clearly relieved, happy she was on board, yet with an underlying sadness to her tone as she spoke. 'It really is, my love. Quite something.'

Remy trotted beside them towards the main school building and the quadrangle beyond, filling in the blanks of her mother's sentence, *and it could have been yours too . . .*

'Good morning!' A random master with his gown flapping behind him in the breeze walked past and greeted them.

'Hello.'

'Hello!'

Her parents held on tightly to each other and responded in tandem.

As the three walked forward, she looked through the stone arch towards the quadrangle in all its Gothic glory, and there in the middle of it was Ashleigh, standing with a boy and a girl in the St. Jude's dark-green uniform with the gold braided edging. The school crest was visible on their blazer pockets. They were laughing and talking to a woman who looked very Jackie O, reed thin and head to toe in navy. It was curious and fascinating to observe this snapshot of her sister in a setting that was unfamiliar, with people Remy had never seen before.

Ashleigh: her identical twin, two halves of one egg, yet never had she felt more separate, further away than she did in that moment. This was the time when the penny dropped. Not when they had trawled around the school outfitters' buying the long list of uniform that was compulsory for her sister's first term at St. Jude's. Not when Ashleigh announced a boy in her class was having a birthday party and she was invited, and his parents were taking the whole class to see the movie *Jaws* in London, where they were to travel by luxury coach, followed by a slap-up meal in a swanky restaurant – the *whole* class! And not when Ashleigh started to add the words, 'Okay, so . . .' at the beginning of her sentences with a slight drawl. Not when the summer break arrived and Ashleigh told her about the trips her classmates would take to Provence and Tuscany, while the Bretts set off on a camping trip to North Wales with the Swingball safely secured on the roof of their dad's car. Not when her sister called on the phone and sounded more like Princess Anne than her sister. Not even on that day when Ashleigh had announced that she would like to move into the small room, the box room, the room that had lain in wait for one of them to make the break.

No, it was *now*, as her sister stood in the quadrangle with strangers who were not strange to her: this was the moment when Remy realised they had indeed taken different paths, were on different tracks and were heading to very different destinations.

One to Sardinia, one to Southend . . . One in a Granada, one on a bus . . . One running her own business, the other emptying bins . . .

She would have laughed had she not been forced to swallow her tears, as the realisation struck her in the chest like an ice pick and hurt just about as much. The hardest thing to fathom was that she had done this – she had put her sister in this uniform, set her on this path! Remy might think her sister was an arsehole a lot of the time, but how she *missed* her.

'Look at her, Dennis!' Her mum put her free hand at her throat and spoke with thinly disguised emotion as they stared at her twin, framed by the view.

'I know, Ruthie, I know . . .' He patted her arm, and she watched the two grow inches in height and stature.

Ashleigh

Ashleigh smiled and nodded, as polite chit-chat was swapped between Harry, Jacinta, and Jacinta's mother. She spied her family through the arch and watched as they stopped and stared. Her mum was dressed so brightly she felt the flicker of embarrassment, followed by a sharp jab of guilt at having momentarily wished her mother were more like the other mothers, demure and calm, before remembering that Jacinta had doubted her own mother would come at all, and Harry's mum was more interested in money and property than her kids. *Her* mum, she knew, would put her and Remy first in every situation, and always had. She lifted her hand in a small wave. It felt a lot like giving them permission to proceed. They walked slowly forward, as if wary of interrupting, and her heart ached for them, wanting them not to feel so self-conscious and to enjoy the day they had been talking about ever since the gold-rimmed, stiff-card, crested invitation had arrived and been propped on the sideboard in pride of place.

Remy, she noticed, was unusually ill at ease, her hands clasped awkwardly in front of her. No doubt because she was wearing the awful kilt they'd both been kitted out in for Cousin Sian's wedding. It had been bad enough to be both wearing it when they could take solace from the other's discomfort, revelling in a kind of mutual despair that had been almost comical, but to wear it alone! It was like turning up to a fancy-dress party to find yourself the only one in costume.

'Goodness!' Mrs Wentworth gasped as she turned and spied Ruthie and Dennis Brett walking towards them. Ashleigh didn't have time to fully interpret the one word, but instinct told her it was unkind, mean, and for that reason alone she felt nothing but hatred for the woman in blue. No wonder Mr Wentworth liked to jet off to Hong Kong.

'Hello, darlin'!' Ruthie trotted the last few feet and wrapped her in the kind of hug that was more appropriate for long-awaited reunions and gave no indication that she had seen her daughter only hours before at the breakfast table.

'Hi, Mum! Dad! Rem!'

'Well, this really is something. Bit different from my old school, I can tell you.' Her dad put his head back and surveyed the architecture of the quad, taking in the walled recesses which held statues of Greek and Roman gods, all in a state of undress.

'I'm Jacinta's mother, Tuppence Wentworth.'

Tuppence? She exchanged a brief but meaningful glance with Remy, knowing without a doubt that like her she wanted to burst out laughing and holler, *Tuppence? What kind of a name is that?* It was the way with twins, the understanding, the closeness, and she was glad of the reminder. It warmed her. Everything always felt a little bit better when Remy was close by. The earlier feeling of being in freefall faded and, in its place, a small rise of confidence.

'Oh, yes, how rude of me, sorry!' Her dad stuck out his hand and shook Tuppence Wentworth's with enthusiasm. 'I'm Dennis, and this is my wife, Ruthie.'

'Hello!' Her mum waved rather than shake hands, and Ashleigh felt her heart flex with love for her mother.

'I so enjoy speech day. Our eldest son was here. He's now at Brasenose, studying law.'

'How clever. You must be very proud.' Ruthie spoke with genuine awe, and Ashleigh wondered how often Tuppence said the words *Brasenose* and *law* on an average day. 'This is our other daughter, Remy.'

'Hi.' Remy took a small step forward and kept her eyes on the floor.

'Twins!' Jacinta called out, as if she might be the only one to notice.

'Yep.' Remy gave her a double thumbs-up.

'And where are you at school, dear?' Mrs Wentworth asked.

'I'm at Milton Road Comprehensive.' This time Remy looked up and held the woman's eyeline.

'Oh!' Again Tuppence offered one word that was so much more than the sum of its parts.

'Remy's the clever one,' Ashleigh stated.

'I see.' Ashleigh knew Mrs Wentworth did not see, not at all. How could she?

'We were just talking about what these youngsters might do when they leave St. Jude's. We've told Jacinta it's law and Oxbridge or don't come home!' There it was again, that silent laugh. 'What would you like to do, dear?' She addressed her sister directly. Ashleigh wondered if the woman had a secret hankering to be a careers advisor, she seemed so desperately interested in everyone's future plans.

Remy answered without missing a beat. 'What I'd *like* to do is sit on a beach and read, but what I'll probably do is work on the bins and go on holiday to Southend, if I can find the bus stop.'

Harry laughed loudly. Mrs Wentworth opened her mouth like a fish looking for krill, and her parents coughed and tutted to hide their embarrassment.

'I guess one good thing' – Ashleigh pointed out the obvious – 'is that if you're working on the bins, you can throw that kilt away easily.'

'Very good point!' Remy smiled at her, and it felt like a moment of healing, of connection, unified against the rather unpleasant Mrs Wentworth.

'I don't know what I want to do when I leave school' – Ashleigh spoke now with certainty – 'but I know it won't be law or medicine. Maybe English or history, and then, who knows!' She shrugged, almost excited by the prospect.

'Would anyone like a Mint Imperial?' Ashleigh watched as her mum ferreted in her handbag for the small white paper bag that bulged with the little sweeties, anything to change the subject, as if aware that neither her husband nor she wanted to hear their daughter's plans *not* to become a doctor or a lawyer.

'Ooh, smashing!' Her dad placed his fingers in the bag and came out with not one but two sweets. Harry too took advantage of the offer. Jacinta and her mother both politely declined, Mrs Wentworth with a look of mild disgust on her thin lips.

'So, what would you like to see first?' Ashleigh smiled at her parents, wondering where to direct them.

'Tell you the truth, I'd quite like to go back to the car park and look at some of them motors!'

Harry's face lit up. 'An American boy in the year above us, his father has a Jensen Interceptor, 7.2 litre engine, V8, convertible.'

'Cor, I'd love to see that!'

'Not sure if it's there, but we can go and look around.'

She watched as her lovely dad wandered off with Harry, the boy whose own father was locked in a messy divorce.

'What about you, Mum?'

'I really don't mind.' Ruthie clutched her bag to her chest.

'Tell you what.' Remy took her mother's arm, and Ashleigh was glad her sister was there to look after her. 'Why don't we have a mooch and see where we end up?'

Ashleigh smiled, watching as they ambled towards the art block, her sister pulling at the hem of that hideous kilt and her mother glowing like a neon bouquet against the brickwork.

It was typical of Remy, happy to wander without a plan, content to see where she might end up . . . and in that regard, Ashleigh could only envy her.

Ashleigh and Remy Brett

1982

Aged 20

Remy

It was a typical Saturday night.

With her tape recorder providing the background music, and her poster of John Taylor taped to the ceiling above her bed, Remy was quite lost to the new Duran Duran album, *Rio*. 'Oh, turn this one up!' she instructed her best friend, who did as she asked as '*Hungry Like the Wolf*' filled the room.

'My eyeliner's wonky.' Remy coughed into the mirror propped on the chest of drawers before spitting on her finger to remove the outer eye flick that was not quite as straight or as bold as she wanted. She was aiming for part Siouxsie, part Debbie Harry, but right now looked more like Robert Smith of The Cure.

'Do you want me to do it?' Tony paused, hairspray can in hand, his eyeliner perfection, and his backcombed fringe now gloriously upright with just the right amount of tousle to his roots.

'Bloody hell! I've got hairspray in my throat!' She coughed again.

'We must suffer for beauty. You know this!' He tutted and shook the can, which rattled.

'Can you do the back of mine?' Angling her head, she could see there were one or two areas where her crimped layers had fallen flat. Her hair was wild and huge, the perfect volume and texture to fulfil every girl's, and some boys', dream of having big, bold hair. Tony picked up his comb and went to work on her locks.

They were precious, these Saturday nights. Something she looked forward to all week while working at the garden centre, where she sat on a stool at the checkout desk and ran plants and bags of compost through the till, waiting for whoever was buying to baulk jokingly at the price before handing over their pound notes and trundling off to the car park with a trolley full of greenery. There were some lovely regulars, elderly people who would peruse the shrubs, sniff the flowers, and treat themselves to a cup of tea and a toasted tea cake (which she got for free with her afternoon cuppa) in the café ran by Leering Len, who she knew not to be alone with, not ever.

Her job was quite unlike Tony's; he was an apprentice with a photographic company in Bath. A natural, he had already learned the mechanics of taking pictures and was, apparently, outshining the senior team with his artistry and brilliant eye. The garden centre had been a stopgap. A job to fill the days after leaving school at eighteen, while she thought about what she *really* wanted to do. What she wanted to do was earn money and buy make-up. Well, two years of living the dream, and it was, she had decided, time to get serious. She just wasn't entirely sure how. Her parents were, she could tell, a little puzzled by her laid-back attitude. What she couldn't make them understand was how reluctant she had been to rush into something and get stuck; far better, she felt, to take her time and make the best choices. Her mum had told her she had her whole life ahead of her to do something meaningful, but the question was, what? With this in mind, she had begun to quietly explore the idea of getting a degree.

Tony was already talking about making the jump to a bigger firm, or a smaller firm, or going freelance! His dream was to work with models instead of podgy kids as he snapped school photos, or needy brides who often had a very unrealistic list of demands, wanting to look like Fawcett or Fonda when they were not similarly blessed.

Ashleigh too seemed to have a set path and had gone straight from St. Jude's to Exeter University, where she was now two years into her three-year history degree.

'What's she going to do with that? Work in a bloody museum? I mean, you hear it every day, don't you? "What the world needs is more historians!"' Her dad had, despite her sister's protestations to the contrary, been hoping she might go into medicine or law. A fancy-pants career for his fancy-pants girl. But it seemed it was not to be.

Remy had begun to feel as if she were being left behind, knowing the garden centre was not where her future lay, no matter how good the free toasted tea cakes. This thought had started to poke her awake in the hours before her alarm. And this was why she had a secret stash of prospectuses under her mattress. It felt prudent to keep them hidden, not wanting her parents to get wind of her idea and run with it at a million miles an hour as they always did, enthusing and beaming wildly as they steered the topic until she became no more than a passenger in what turned into their plan. Ironically, she felt drawn towards law, not that she'd share this with her mum and dad, knowing they'd have her wig, gown and gavel ordered and business cards printed if she so much as mentioned it as a possibility. There was also a small part of her that wanted to show her parents how smart she was, to make up for the disappointment they had felt at her not chasing the prize of St. Jude's.

She decided not to say anything until she was sure of what she wanted to do, but a law degree certainly sounded interesting, and she had the grades. Had got the grades easily. Not that it was always on her mind. Tonight it was all about having fun with her best friend, unsure how she would break it to him that she was thinking of leaving Wiltshire and heading off to college, possibly even somewhere as far afield as Bristol. Just the thought of it was enough to make her truly appreciate every minute of their Saturday nights together.

'What are we thinking? Pub then Concordes? Then a drive?' Tony suggested.

'Yes! Fab!'

Driving was their thing. The car a place to be that was away from home, going out, feeling free! Tony was teetotal, and with access to his mum's Austin Allegro, it had become part of their routine. Plus, and she hated to admit it, travelling in the car to and from places with him or simply driving randomly was nearly always the best part of the night. With a mixtape blaring, they would chat and laugh at nothing in the lovely warm bubble of their own making. It was always a high point. Ensconced in that little motor she felt full of infinite possibilities as they giggled and gossiped and sang – oh how they sang!

There was a knock on her bedroom door, and her mum walked in.

'Goodness me. I can't see the carpet, it's covered with clothes!'

She did this: pointed out the obvious.

'Yep.'

'And the noise!' Her mum shielded her eyes with her hand as if this might quieten the music.

She caught Tony's eye in the mirror and they both stifled laughter. Not only because Ruthie Brett was nothing if not predictable, but because they were giddy on life and almost everything was funny. The floor was indeed covered in various items that they had tried on, rejected, and flung. She'd clear it up tomorrow or the day after that. It was hard to keep a tiny room tidy. She looked now at the floor, where the soft layer of shirts, jackets, and waistcoats made a lovely spongey layer underfoot that was not only nice to walk on but also hid the burn mark where her forgotten and briefly unattended hair crimpers had left a deep, dark gash, two sticky tarry lines on the cream pile, which had melted. Ruthie, she knew, would not be happy when they were discovered.

'Could you turn it down a bit? Can't hear myself think!' Her mum rubbed her temples as if the volume of Le Bon's voice was in some way damaging.

'Sorry, Mrs Brett.' Tony turned it down.

Keener . . .

'Goodness me, it's like fog in here!' Her mum flapped her hand in front of her face. 'Shall we open a window?'

Remy quite liked the fog, a heady mixture of White Musk, the scent they both wore, and Elnett Firm Hold, a can of which lasted them a weekend at most.

Tony stood and opened the smallest window.

Total keener . . .

'We're just getting ready, Mum.' It was her turn to point out the obvious, which was actually code for *leave us alone.*

'I can see that, love.' This, code for *don't be so bloody rude.* 'Just wanted to know if you would like something to eat? I've got a shepherd's pie in the oven, or I can make you both a sandwich? I've got fish paste or sandwich spread.'

Remy felt a little mean for wishing her mum would disappear when she'd only come to offer them food.

'I'm okay, thanks, Mum.'

'I'm okay too, thank you, Mrs Brett.' Tony smiled.

'And your dad says do you need a lift anywhere?'

Her dad was always on standby to run them around whenever they needed it. It was evident that he rather liked being their taxi, any excuse to hop into his blue Ford Escort; he could scarcely disguise his disappointment when Tony had passed his driving test.

'I've got my mum's car. But thank you.' Tony was so polite. Remy pulled a face at him.

'Did you know your sister called earlier?'

'No.' She held her eyeliner still, waiting to hear whatever tidbit of news Ashleigh had shared.

'She's going to a ball with that boy she likes! A ball!'

'Like Cinderella?' Remy couldn't help herself. It was typical of Ashleigh, who, the last time she had come home on one of her brief visits, had displayed a whole new level of airs and graces. She had been this way since she'd met Archie Fitch, or rather since she'd become an item with Archie Fitch, who, her dad had rather delightfully pointed out, had not been born with a silver spoon in his mouth but a whole canteen of cutlery. He certainly didn't sound like Remy's cup of tea, the yuppy. It had irritated her beyond belief, hearing Ashleigh drone on and on to her and Tony about Archie bloody Fitch!

A ball! What was that other than a fancy name for a big old gathering, and one where tickets cost considerably more than if they'd just called it a party?

'Don't be like that!' Her mother tutted. 'Be pleased for her. It's the circles she mixes in now.' Remy shared a look of amusement with Tony, who was the circle *she* mixed in. 'She's got a black taffeta off-the-shoulder frock with a big bow at the back. I bet she'll look beautiful.'

'She will.' At least on this Remy could agree.

'And did you see the picture of Princess Diana and the new baby?' This Ruthie addressed to Tony, knowing he was as much of an admirer as she was.

'I did. I loved that green on her,' he enthused.

'Oh, me too, and I said to Den, someone's done her hair. It was gorgeous. She looked tired, mind.' Her mother spoke as if it were her concern to have.

'I said the same.' Tony sighed, as if he were Ruthie's companion, not hers! 'But I guess she has an excuse, having just given birth to the little prince!'

'Ah, yes, William! Lovely name. What a smashing, happy little family they all are. Her and Charles, a real-life fairy tale!'

'Really is.'

Remy bit her lip rather than express her bemusement at just how these two people she adored could be so interested in the lives of complete strangers.

'Righto. Well, I'll leave you to it.' Her mum retreated, smile fixed, and closed the door behind her.

'Which lipstick?' Tony ran his hand through their shared make-up bag, selecting their favoured Rimmel lippy in Heather Shimmer, which they liked to top off with a clear lip gloss, the applicator stick of which was a rather curious shade of red/pink, and the once transparent contents of the tube were now decidedly murky.

'Yes.' She nodded her approval. 'If ever there was a night for Heather Shimmer, it's this one.'

As they made their way downstairs, excitement fizzed in her veins, as it always did at the prospect of a night out.

'Don't get separated,' her mother instructed over her shoulder as she scrubbed baked-on mash from the shepherd's pie tin, her orange Marigolds going like the clappers.

'We won't,' Tony replied.

'And don't be too late, Remy. You know I don't like you being out when we're asleep in case you need anything.'

'You go to bed at nine o'clock!' She pointed out the obvious. 'If we have to be back by then we might as well not go out at all!'

'You know what I mean.' Ruthie gripped the Brillo pad and scrubbed harder.

'If you need picking up, anywhere, anytime . . .' Her dad abandoned his newspaper, laying it flat on to the kitchen table, offering his services, as he always did. It was clear that despite his promotion to manager, now able to sit at a desk all day in the head office of the concrete company in Trowbridge, he missed the days of repping with his car as his chariot, the open road ahead and as many Little Chef breakfasts as he could wangle on expenses.

'Thank you, Mr Brett, but I've got Mum's car.'

She caught Tony's gaze and rolled her eyes: how many times was he going to have to say it!

'Well, the offer's there, son. The Escort likes a run out, and I always have the keys within reach.' As if to prove his point, her dad patted the pocket of his slacks, and they all heard the jangle of the keys.

'He thinks more of that bloody car than he does of me!' Ruthie huffed.

'And I've told you countless times,' her dad replied without missing a beat, 'that if ever you want an oil change and a quick run around the block, I'm happy to oblige!'

'Idiot!' her mum spat, but her face still split with a smile that made her look almost girlish.

'See you tomorrow. Love you.' Remy walked over and kissed her mum's cheek.

'Love you too, and don't accept drugs from strangers!'

'What?' Remy let out a peal of laughter. 'I don't . . .' She didn't know how to respond. 'I don't *do* drugs, Mum. I never have, they don't appeal to me in the slightest, but if I *did* want to do drugs, I cannot think of a single close friend or family member that might be able to supply them, which kind of suggests I'd have to get them from a stranger.'

'You know what I mean.' Her mum paused from her scrubbing.

'I really don't,' she confessed.

'It was on my mind, that's all. They were talking about it in the hairdressers'. Mrs Butterworth was saying that her son lives in London, and everyone there is taking drugs.'

'Everyone in London?' she asked for Tony's benefit, knowing it would make him laugh.

'Yes, pretty much.'

Even her dad shook his head and returned to his paper.

'I'm just thinking about the millions of people who live in London, including the Royal family, Margaret Thatcher, Denis Thatcher, the Bishop of Westminster, Felicity Kendal.' She could go on.

'Well, obviously none of them!' Ruthie tutted.

'But everyone *apart* from them?' Remy knew she was winding her mother up, but it was too ridiculously rewarding not to.

'Probably.' Her mother shrugged. 'And drive carefully, Tony.'

'I always do.'

'You read about those kids, don't you, who are larking about in the car, and the next thing you know their mothers are laying plastic-wrapped bouquets by the side of a tree that came at them from nowhere on a bend.'

'Erm . . .' Tony stared at her mum, clearly as lost for words as she was.

'Bye, Mum!' Remy grabbed her friend by the sleeve, and they left the house, both committed to look out for trees on bends that came out of nowhere.

'I love Felicity Kendal,' Tony sighed as he got behind the wheel.

'Everyone loves Felicity Kendal,' she pointed out as she adjusted the front seat of his mum's Allegro.

'True.' He turned the key and the little engine shuddered to life.

'A ball?' Remy scoffed; it had been on her mind, and she changed the subject with ease. 'What does it even mean? A ball!'

'Let it go!' Tony shouted, as he navigated the lanes that took them into town, where they'd park near the pub.

'Nothing to let go. I'm not bothered, I'm not!'

What did bother her, and the thing she found hardest to voice, was the further weakening of the bond between her and Ashleigh. The blurring of the sharp edges of the shape of them. Sharp edges that meant as kids they slid together forming a perfect one. Now, they could get close, but never as close as they were. They were altered, had grown into their own people in a way that she could not, as a child, have envisaged. And it wasn't only a physical thing, although it was always a little jarring, a surprise to see her blonde, straight-haired sister who from the back was nothing like her. It hurt in a way that was as hard to reconcile as it was to explain. Inevitable, of course, the ageing, the separation, the evolution, and yet that had been her thing, their thing, being special, one seed split in two.

They were now very different people. Very different people whose communication was sporadic and even a little awkward, as it was when you had very little in common with someone's day-to-day.

One who went to Southend, the other Sardinia . . . It wasn't that she wanted Ashleigh's life, not at all, but equally, she didn't want to be written off either. Maybe that law degree would redress the balance. A bubble of excitement rose in her gut at the possibility.

'You sound a *bit* bothered.' Tony kept his eyes on the road.

'I'm not! It just irritates me. Only Ashleigh would go to a *ball*. It always has to be that bit more than anyone else does, a bit grander than you've experienced or seen, a bit more expensive than most of us can afford, and she's a bloody student. I don't know how she does it!'

'A student with a full grant and a very wealthy boyfriend, according to what she was saying when she came home last. His parents were at their house in Italy, and he'd gone sailing. *Sailing!*'

'I remember.' She snorted and pulled a face. 'But hardly a boyfriend – she'd only been seeing him a few weeks. What was his name?' She clicked her fingers.

'You *know* his name, Remy! Be nice! She is your sister, your twin.' He shook his head, reminding her so much of her mother it made her chuckle. 'I miss my brother. I'd give anything to have him close by.'

She knew this to be true; his brother Gregory had emigrated to Australia a couple of years ago and was living and working in Sydney. It sounded brilliant, sunny, warm and, with a beach on his doorstep, what was not to love? But so very far away. The furthest she had ever been was France on a day trip; they'd gone by hovercraft from Dover to Boulogne. It had rained all day, but she'd got to eat a baguette and said 'please' and 'thank you' at passport control in French. Job done. But who knew where she might travel in the coming years, or what her future might hold? A qualified lawyer with a job in a sunny place . . . that'd do.

'Archibald. *Who* is called Archibald?' She changed the topic, not wanting the absence of his brother to be a downer on their evening. 'Why can't she have a nice normal boyfriend with a name like Jamie!'

'At least she has a boyfriend.' He pulled a face.

'And as I've told you before, darling, we're waiting for the right ones. We are discerning, not desperate.' This, her justification for their drought in the man department. She'd had a couple of harmless flings at school, nothing serious, and more often than not went out with boys because they'd asked rather than because she really liked them. University was, she reckoned, going to offer rich pickings when it came to boys. Her virginity sat around her neck like an eye-catching weighty necklace. She was aware of it, irked by the presence of it at times, and yet in no real hurry to whip it off. It was, she had to admit, hard to meet fabulous and eligible men at the garden centre. Well, that wasn't strictly true, as she found herself propositioned with offers of afternoon tea or garden walks daily; what she meant was fabulous and eligible men under the age of eighty.

'I think the trouble is, any potential suitors might think we're a couple,' Tony offered without irony.

Turning her head to study her friend, she took in his perfect make-up, his well-tended do, his practised pout, and didn't mention his affection for Princess Diana or the discreet tattoo on his collarbone that was a homage to his greatest love, Barbra Streisand, her face in profile. 'Tony, I adore you, but I literally do not think *anyone* who has met us has *ever* thought we were a couple!'

'None taken.' He sucked his teeth.

The trumpet toot introduction to 'Geno' filled the car and she felt her gut swell with excitement at no more than the sound.

'Love this! *Classic!*' She beat her feet on the rubber mat in anticipation.

'Turn it up!' Tony yelled. 'Turn it up!'

She obliged and turned the knob to full volume, until the speakers rattled and threatened to blow.

This is how they travelled, singing and drumming on the steering wheel and dashboard, high on life! High on 'Geno'!

Ashleigh

Ashleigh felt a little light-headed, but there was no way she was going to eat, not with the waistband of her black taffeta frock sitting so snugly. She loved this dress, and as it hung on her wardrobe door, had run her fingers over the shiny fabric every night before climbing into bed. Excitement kept her awake as she waited desperately to step into the skirt, lift the bodice and zip it right up, counting down the days, knowing Archie was going to practically swoon when he saw her. Changing her body shape was easy: a couple of days of eating little and she felt the sharp bite of her hip bones and her cheekbones seemed to pop.

Archibald Oxton Fitch . . . That was the name of the boy she loved. For despite knowing him for mere weeks, love him she did. She loved saying his name, loved telling people all about him, loved the way he looked, the way he spoke and, more than anything, she loved having sex with him. It was a strong and powerful glue that she couldn't have imagined existed.

Archie wasn't her first lover, nor her second, third or fourth. The sixth form at St. Jude's and the first couple of years at Exeter had been a time of discovery. She would always remember those boys fondly, the Davids, the Johns, the Peters and Michaels of the world, who had been fun, and with whom she'd shared experimental flings of the sweetest nature. But if these boys were grey, then Archie was golden! The last few months had taught her that what she had felt for her previous conquests was inconsequential, in no way comparable to the mighty arrow of complete and utter adoration that had skewered her the moment she'd clapped eyes on Archibald Oxton Fitch.

He was blond and smiley with very neat teeth and a gravel to his voice that was almost as intoxicating as the whisky sours they liked to concoct in his tiny student kitchen after a night out.

All the boys that had gone before were now nothing more than smoke in her thoughts, and she could quite confidently say, had anyone asked, that she would be entirely happy if he were her last lover. The last ever. It was a drug. The scent of him, the touch of him, the memory of their fabulous and numerous trysts enough for her to want him all over again. She was impatient to learn every inch of him, hungry for his touch. Beyond excited, as they knitted themselves together, building a connection, a union, the prospect of which brought her more joy than anything she had or ever could have imagined. It was impossible to see him, spend time with him, be close to him without sex being their destination, their ending. *Impossible* . . .

The question that kept her awake, when she wasn't staring at her ball gown or having sex with Archie, was whether he loved her too. She hadn't said it out loud, and he hadn't mentioned the word at all. But if he did, *when* he did, she knew it would be the icing on the rather moreish cake.

They had met through Guy, who had casually mentioned over a pint in the Students' Union that his old school friend from Clifton College had made the transfer from Durham and was joining next term. She had barely given it a second thought, but would forever, with hindsight, be thankful to him. Guy was the boy who had started as no more than someone in her tutor group, a funny, handsome klutz who had seen her name on the registration sheet, written as Brett Ashleigh, and had understandably assumed she was a boy called Brett, and had called her Brett ever since.

Guy was everything she might have looked for in a boyfriend, apart from one crucial ingredient: the magic X factor that made her want to rip his clothes off. She had never and could never feel that way about him. He was like a brother, definitely just a mate, someone she could hang out with, spend time with, rely on, and he was fun! A bit like Tony was for Remy, not that she and Guy were *that* close.

After only a few weeks of joining St. Jude's – while she was still trying to build a solid friendship group, testing the water with girls like Jacinta, who she thought she might like to hang out with, and chatting to boys who seemed nice, boys like Harry – Remy and Tony had become joined at the hip, as if her twin couldn't bear to be alone, and just like that Tony filled the spot Ashleigh used to occupy. It had hurt her, to be so excluded, replaced. To come home and find the two of them giggling about things of which she had no knowledge made her feel isolated, lonelier than she would have thought possible in her own home. It made her regret leaving their shared bedroom, remembering with a stab of nostalgia the warm, safe feeling of waking with her twin within reach, snoring.

They were still like it now, a little clique of two. Tony would say one word to Remy, just one word, like *conjoined*! And they would fall about laughing. It had irked her for years. Ashleigh had never managed to work out if it was a dig at her, something to do with being twins, but she was damned if she was going to ask. It was one of the reasons she didn't always go back to Salisbury in the holidays, finding the gruesome twosome with their in-jokes and shared make-up bag a little too hard to fathom. And the way they dressed! Ashleigh did her best to adopt the Sloane Ranger look, with Peter Pan collars peeking from under her jersey collar, padded velvet headbands, pearls at her neck and in her ears and a Barbour thrown on with smart jeans, while Remy's clothes were slouchy. She looked like she was auditioning for Dexys Midnight Runners. And not that she would ever say it out loud, but her sister's fashion sense embarrassed her a little, showed the world they were not really Sloane Ranger stock, another thing that marked Ashleigh as an imposter.

She tried not to let it bother her, the closeness between her sister and Tony. He was her friend too, after all. Besides, she now had Guy. Guy who was *her* study buddy, her drinking partner, her wingman and protector, her great friend.

She had gone to meet him at the red-brick four-storey house on Pennsylvania Road where eight boys lived the student dream.

If that dream was a sink full of dirty dishes and an old grill pan full of soft bacon fat the scent of which lingered. A place where mismatched pint glasses, stolen from various establishments in the city, cluttered up the countertops. Empty tequila and champagne bottles were lined up like trophies on top of the kitchen cupboards, and there was a dartboard on the wall of the living room. And for some reason, which she was yet to fathom, a life-size cut-out of Clint Eastwood in the bathroom which, she had been reliably informed, was taken during his *Dirty Harry* era.

It was while she sat on the sunken sofa, surrounded by the detritus of a night well spent, careful not to step in the sticky remnants of Chinese food upended on the carpet, to nudge the overflowing ashtrays on to the already stained upholstery, or kick over the abandoned bottle of Bolly on the floor, that in walked the boy who would change absolutely everything. At no more than the sight of him, her heart jumped in a cartoon-like fashion, booming in her chest, as her legs trembled, and a warm feeling of self-consciousness crept over her. There was something about him, the X factor for sure.

'I'm Archie.'

'Ashleigh.' She'd smiled, demurely, yet holding eye contact. His grin had been broad, knowing, suggesting he too had felt the visceral leap of attraction.

'I was at Clifton with Gigi.'

'Gigi?' She was confused.

'Guy Gallow, GG, which quickly became Gigi!' he explained.

'Makes sense.'

'So are you two . . . ?'

'No, we're not!' Her tone emphatic. 'I mean, we're friends, but not . . .' She let this trail, conscious of her posture, holding her stomach in, shoulders back, head tilted to one side, looking up at him through her lashes à la Diana. They all did it.

'Archie?' a female voice called from the hallway and then a leggy brunette walked into the lounge. Ashleigh folded her hands into her lap, doing her best to look a little more demure. She had seen the girl on campus a couple of times and smiled as she stopped fluttering her lashes.

'Ah, yes!' He clapped. 'This is Tamara.' He blinked and she felt her cartoon booming heart sink down to the bottom of her navy loafers.

'Hi, Tamara.' Ashleigh waved.

The girl lifted her chin in a greeting of sorts and slipped her arms around Archie's waist, which was both galling and thrilling. Galling because it was a clear message, letting her know that he was taken, and thrilling because such a display was only ever necessary if you felt under threat. Tamara was clearly smart as well as gorgeous because her assumption was correct. At times like this Ashleigh liked to remind herself of the St. Jude's school motto – *qui se applicat spoliis fruetur* – which roughly translated to *he who applies himself shall enjoy the spoils.* It was adopted long before the admission of girls, but she had always figured it applied to her too.

It had taken three weeks for her to win the spoils and for Archie to declare his hand. Three weeks during which the anticipation of progression had crackled between them like electricity. After a great night out, standing close to her in the kitchen of his grotty digs, with eyes half closed, a little unsteady on his pins, he tried, in his drunken state, to explain.

'Just want to say, that Tamarara and I . . . we are not, not any longer, not.'

'Not?'

'Well, we were, but now we can't be, because I think you're gorgeous.'

'Thank you,' she'd whispered sincerely. 'So, you and Tamarara.' She smiled. 'Are you saying you're not a thing or . . .'

He had silenced her with a kiss, and as she had placed her hand on the small of his back, underneath his cotton shirt, touching her fingertips to his skin, it was like . . . it was like igniting a spark, as flames leapt to life in her stomach. Flames that she knew would never expire because it was all-consuming in the way that fire was. She wanted to never stop touching him, never, even if it meant she got burnt.

Now, as she stood in front of the full-length mirror stuck to the inside of the Formica wardrobe door, she was warmed by thoughts she could never share with a soul, not wanting to be boastful, but knowing as she studied her reflection, her dyed blonde locks blow-dried into a bouffant flick, her shoulders and décolletage shimmering under a generous dusting of Body Shop bronzing beads, her make-up subtle and her faux-diamanté choker catching the light, that she looked beautiful. Beautiful, unique and whole, no longer a half, but a *new* person altogether. A girl who could meet someone and know that they would remember her face, *hers*, and not wonder which twin she might be, which half of the egg.

It had been a slow transition, the erosion of their closeness, the severing of the bonds that kept them tied together as one, completed around the age of fourteen, when she had properly discovered boys, and Remy had become fashionable. Her twin and Tony had fortified their impenetrable gang of two with shields made of music, clothes and make-up. She loved her sister, of course she did, but she understood it was different now, and had been different for a while. Did Ashleigh miss her, miss what they had once shared? Yes, especially at times like this, when she wanted Remy's opinion, her approval.

How do I look, Rem? Will I do?

'Archie's here!' Fran, her flatmate, called from the hallway.

''Kay!' she replied, reaching for her dress, but then turning sideways, studying her slender frame in the mirror as she stood in her knickers and stockings, deciding the dress could wait. They had at least half an hour before they had to leave and go meet the gang for pre-ball cocktails. Ashleigh slipped on to her bed. 'Send him in!'

She smiled and lay seductively on her side, hair over one shoulder, hand on hip, head tilted just so. They could do a lot in half an hour.

◆ ◆ ◆

Dozy now and satisfied, calmer, Ashleigh lay back on her pillow. She liked watching Archie get dressed, the care he took in his practised movements, slipping his arms into his shirt, pulling on his trousers. It felt just as intimate as the sex they had just shared. No longer paying heed to the clock, caring less if they made it for drinks, she sat still, hair tousled, her skin still singing with the memory of his touch. Despite it being mere minutes since their union, in her gut rose a deep ache of want that was present whenever he was close by. In that minute, if Archie had suggested they forfeit the ball altogether and spend the night in bed with crisps and wine, she'd have agreed in a heartbeat, no matter she'd miss the opportunity to wear her frock.

'I have a little surprise for you.' He spoke into her mirror, as he popped his cufflinks back into the double cuffs of his dinner shirt, fastened the bow tie that she'd hastily undone and thrown into the air, and smoothed his now tousled hair with his palms.

'Ooh, I like surprises!'

That wasn't strictly true; she found the thought of them to be agony, wary of being unprepared for any event or happening that might require preparation and planning. The idea of being whisked off on an unexpected sunshine break with hairy legs and a lack of personal grooming was enough to bring her out in hives, but any surprise from Archie was going to be wonderful. Plus, a little surprise was going to be just that, a bottle of something cold he'd popped into her fridge, flowers he'd asked Fran to arrange? Her smile broadened at the possibilities.

'My parents are coming to the pre-ball drinks.'

'Your parents?'

She sat back against the pillow and took a moment to let her pulse settle. This was huge, nothing little about it. It was a big deal, and it was too much! She wasn't ready to meet his parents, not yet! They'd only been dating for a short while, and while she knew it was love, she found herself completely thrown by the thought of having to make a good impression on his mum and dad.

In her mind she would meet them eventually after asking lots of pertinent questions and building a picture that would help her chameleon her way into their favour – if they liked Greek architecture she'd gen up, if they favoured cinnamon over lemon she'd bake cookies awash with the bloody stuff! This felt a lot like going in blind and she was instantly petrified. It was another way in which she missed Remy, knowing that in her early years, when she had been one half of the little doves, she'd rarely had to face anything alone and nothing was ever going to be that awful because her twin was within reach.

And the one thing she hadn't been able to face, Remy had taken care of.

This thought, as ever, a pill coated with shame and guilt that was still very hard to swallow. The prospect of Archie finding out that she'd effectively stolen her sister's scholarship left her a little clammy, with that tingling in her limbs and a feeling like she was in freefall.

Her body shivered at the thought of having to make small talk with the Fitches. It was always there in the background, the unpalatable thought that she felt less than, when compared to someone who had grown up as Archie and Guy had. Not for her a country house in Gloucestershire, a London pad for when they were in town, summers spent idling on the Amalfi coast, a low red sports car waiting on the gravel driveway when she passed her driving test, a love of sailing, a chunky gold signet ring bearing the family crest gifted to her on her eighteenth birthday; no trust fund, no attending a truly prestigious public school like Clifton because it was where her father and grandfather had gone, and therefore no membership of the Old Cliftonian Society that held meet-ups worldwide for its alumni. None of that. Attending St. Jude's held some weight locally, but it wasn't one of *the* public schools that people knew of.

It shouldn't have made a difference, of course it shouldn't, but it did.

And it wasn't entirely about money, but more about the things money allowed you to do, the access it gave you to other worlds! The things you learned on your travels, the freedom and confidence that came with such a life that meant you were comfortable asking questions, stating an opinion, exploring, and expanding your horizon beyond the corner of the street where Mrs Jenkins lived in a house with three spare bedrooms. *Three!* It was far from pleasant, living with the fear of meeting new people and having nothing of value to say.

She wasn't *ashamed* of how and where she had grown up, not even a bit, but she was acutely aware that it might matter to others, specifically Archibald Oxton Fitch's parents.

'Gosh, that's . . .' She swallowed, not wanting to dim the light of excitement in his eyes.

'You're going to love them. Elaine is a hoot! And Dickie will rib you, he does all my friends, he's known for it, but he's great fun. There's no harm in him.'

'And is that how you're going to introduce me, as one of your friends?' She hated how much she craved his words of reassurance that would in turn fuel her confidence to go and meet Elaine and Dickie.

Archie twisted his cummerbund until it was sitting neatly over the waistband of his trousers, before taking a seat on the edge of her single bed. He reached for her hand and the two locked eyes. She held her breath, unsure if he was about to offer the reassurance she craved or if he'd had a change of heart and was about to break up with her. It was torturous, waiting. He shook his head.

'No, I'm going to introduce you as Ashleigh Brett, my girlfriend.'

She tightened her grip on his hand, as relief and a rush of breath made answering impossible; a nod would have to suffice.

'Truth is' – he licked his lips, took his time – 'I love you, Ash. I do, I love you. You are under my skin and inside my bones, part of me.'

It was as these words flew from his mouth and spiralled out of the sash window, with wings of hope and promise beating fast, carrying them into the night sky where they would land among the stars, that the emotion she had been trying to contain burst from her. Tears ran down her face and her mouth twisted.

'I love you too, Archie, I really, really do!' This, the first time she had said it out loud and a moment she knew she wouldn't forget, not ever.

'Don't cry, Ashleigh Brett. Please don't cry.' He leaned forward and rested his forehead on hers, and there they sat for a while, revelling in the closeness of this new and thrilling world into which they had stepped.

It was wonderful, magic, the fairy tale! And as he held her close, running his fingers over the knobbles of her spine as she fell into him, she felt her nerves melt away. Anything and everything was possible because Archibald Oxton Fitch loved her. He *loved* her! She was under his skin and inside his bones and that was, she knew, a place she could happily stay forever.

Remy

Remy linked arms with Tony as he walked around all the doors, locking and checking his mum's car.

'Where first, Anchor?' They fell into step. She quite liked the Anchor and really liked the look of a boy who worked behind the bar there sometimes, not that she'd be sharing this with Tony, knowing his capacity for meddling.

'Why not. And remember, if anyone asks, we're not a couple!'

'And as I said, my love, I really don't think that's why we are both single.' She nudged him with her elbow. 'Would you like to meet someone?'

It was a topic they didn't usually dwell on, knowing it was hard enough for her to find a love interest living in a small city, and it was a darned sight harder for Tony, who had only been open about his sexuality in the last couple of years.

'It's taken me a while to figure it all out,' he'd explained.

'It's nobody's business but yours.' She'd held him tightly before they'd jumped up to dance.

'Would I like to meet someone? Hmm.' He stroked his chin in an exaggerated fashion. 'No, I want to remain single for my entire life, die a virgin and end up living in a leaky cottage full of cats.' He tutted.

'You know what I mean!' She pulled his arm towards her. 'I guess I'm asking if you're ready to meet someone, because it's different isn't it, at our age?'

'God, what are we, fifty? We are young with our whole lives ahead of us!' He threw his head back and called out to the starry sky above. They got this way when they were dressed up and heading out, excited at all the possibilities of what the night might hold. She felt a bubble of pure happiness rise in her stomach.

'Yes, but as Ruthie is fond of telling us, we shall blink and be forty, then sixty . . .'

'Well, aren't you a little bowl of sunshine this evening!' He pursed his lips.

'I don't want to put us on a downer, but it *is* different though, isn't it? It's much more than snogging at discos. We're at that point in our lives when it can get very serious, very quickly.'

Not entirely averse to the idea, she was curious about her next chapter, about sex, love and all that came with it. Maybe university was the portal to take her to that world. Again she pulled Tony's arm into her, knowing these moments were even more precious because they might be on a timer.

'Well, someone's been reading *Cosmo*! And, actually, right now, I'd settle for snogging at discos.'

'I can see I'm not going to be getting any sense out of you tonight.' She gave up.

'I kind of feel that serious conversations are for Monday through Friday, but in the words of Elton, Saturday night's the night for dancing!'

'I don't think they're the words.'

'Let's make out they are!' He laughed, and they sped up, giggling, keen to get to the pub.

'Oi!'

The shout was loud, determined, spoken with an intent that suggested it was a forerunner to more words. If she had to guess, it had been hollered with particular consideration given to the volume, as the single word ricocheted around them and landed uncomfortably in their ears.

Remy wondered who was shouting and who they might be shouting at.

Tony too stopped walking and they both looked back over their shoulders, quickly understanding that it was one of a group of lads who was yelling; clearly they travelled as a pack. Fear sloshed in her stomach, as she counted *one, two, three, four, five* of them. Their very presence intimidating, as they stood resplendent in their oxblood Doc Martens laced high on their shins, tight jeans rolled and cuffed at the top of the boots, white T-shirts tucked into their waistbands with braces under green puffy bomber jackets. Their heads were shaved, and they gave off a collective energy that sent a white-hot rod of fear through her very core. She had never been in a situation like this, never experienced this horrible sense of foreboding. Yes, there had been one or two calls of 'Poofter!' shouted by cowards from moving vehicles, but they'd ignored it. Tony said it was par for the course where he was a rarity and was always adamant he wasn't going to let some dickhead homophobes spoil a night out. The second thing that became clear was that they were shouting at her and Tony.

'We're just going to the pub!' she replied in a sing-song voice that she hoped might let them know they were friendly, in case it was a matter of mistaken identity, smiling broadly to indicate they were not persons of interest, no one to be bothered with. Just two friends going to the Anchor for a pint, although she wished they weren't. She wished in that moment with a growing sense of fear that she had taken her mum's advice and that they were on the sofa, in her house, with a nice cup of tea.

'Who's your friend?' One of them, possibly the one who had yelled out, with eyes that were chips of flint, gestured with his cigarette towards Tony. She felt him tremble next to her.

'My friend?' She played for time, wondering where to run, looking behind the gang of five to see if there was anyone else around. There wasn't. The shops to the right of them were closed and there was no one else in the car park. Trapped.

'Yeah, your friend, what's her name?'

Tony spoke then, holding up his free hand, the other still linking him to Remy.

'Look, we don't want any trouble.'

The men shared nasal bursts of laughter, and the spokesman dropped his cigarette on to the floor and trod it under the sole of his DM.

'Is that right, Shirley? And who says it's you who gets to decide whether you're in trouble or not?' They took a step closer.

Remy felt her mouth run dry and her legs turned to jelly.

'You wearing red lipstick?' a different man asked, and the other four snickered. She could see the hatred in their faces. Hatred for her and Tony, strangers. It was as petrifying as it was unfathomable.

'Run, run, now, Remy!' Tony's voice was a quiet warble of fear spoken from the side of his mouth.

'No!' She was resolute, believing they would not hurt a girl and that she was therefore his best form of defence.

'What *are* you anyway?' the mouthpiece asked, and his mates laughed again; one hawked and spat.

She knew Tony was aware of the loaded question, but he didn't falter and answered in a steady voice. It was an act of bravery that she knew was the mark of the man.

'I'm a photographer.'

'Oooh! I'm a photographer!' The one who had asked about the lipstick mimicked Tony's voice, exaggerating the feminine lilt, walking with his hand on his hip and making out to toss long hair over his shoulder.

What happened next was quite unexpected. Tony shrugged free of her arm and took a step towards them.

'Ah, it all makes sense now.' Tony stood with his back straight, chin jutting, his voice bearing only the slight betrayal of fear as his words, sounding a little sticky to her knowing ear, came from a nervous mouth. 'The lipstick you were interested in, and which, by the way, I think would really suit you, is not red, it's actually Heather Shimmer. And may I say you've got that walk off pat. I can see I've found a kindred spirit. Fancy a quick one?' He jerked his head towards the alleyway between Dolcis and Rumbelows.

There was a second, maybe two, of stillness, as if they were in a play and were all a little unsure of the stage direction given, or whose line it was. Of one thing she was sure: it was about to get very serious, very quickly. It was then Remy remembered the words of the Elton John hit. It was fighting that Saturday night was alright for, *fighting*, although at that moment in time she would have given anything in the whole wide world for it to have been dancing.

She froze.

Holding in her breath, her words, her terror, as in the next second the world began to turn in slow motion and all hell broke loose.

The five thugs seemed to surge, in a manner which, upon reflection, would suggest it was well choreographed. Their mouths she would remember, shrunk to angry arseholes, as their eyes blazed. It was almost instinctive, the way she lifted her arms to shield her face from the impact, as if they were still in the Austin Allegro about to hit the tree her mum had warned them about, the one that could come at you from nowhere on a sharp bend.

They charged at them, a melee, a gaggle, a tangle of angry limbs all working in unison with the intention of causing damage, of committing violence. Two hands pushed her backwards, thumping her with such force in the chest she toppled, whacking her elbow and shoulder on to the pavement as the wind rushed from her lungs, landing hard. It was shocking, a surprise, leaving her quite dazed by the unexpectedness of such an act. The pain was instant and intense, not that there was any time to consider it, as almost immediately, and still while she struggled to take a breath, a boot came heading towards her and she felt the heavy blow against her ear, which set everything ringing and sent her vision a little fuzzy. But it was the other four who had set upon Tony that drew her concern. Panicking as finally she drew breath, she managed to shriek, as best she was able, as loud as she could, 'Leave him alone!'

It was then that she realised her mouth was bleeding as the syrupy, iron-flavoured loss sprayed over her shirt and the bib of her dungarees.

It was hard for her to stand, to move. Thankfully the pig who had hurt her had backed off. The bad news was he immediately went to join his buddies, mere feet away, as they kicked and stomped on Tony.

Stomped.

Their boots now working like pistons, a machine whose mechanical sounds were the grunts and exhalations of fetid, hate-filled breath, as they expelled energy through their uneducated noses.

Levering herself up into a half-sitting position, she looked around, trying to find someone, anyone who might be able to help. Her friend wasn't moving, wasn't fighting, and she screamed out, 'Tony! *Tony!*' before stopping to catch her breath. 'Stop it! Get off him! Leave him alone! Please leave him alone!'

Remy felt as if she were caught in a riptide, fighting for breath. As fear and pain rendered her immobile, it was all she could do to scream until it felt as if her lungs might burst: 'Stop it! *Tony!* You'll kill him!' she sobbed. 'You're going to kill him!'

They came out of nowhere.

Suddenly.

Men.

Her chest was tight in anticipation: were they going to hurt Tony more, her too? If she had learned one thing in the last few minutes it was that she couldn't trust anyone. Scouring the floor, she tried to see if there was anything she could use as a weapon, something, anything with which she might be able to mount a feeble defence, but a defence nonetheless. There was nothing. She braced her limbs as best she could, somehow figuring that if she wasn't supple, compliant, injury might be harder, more difficult for them. Her breath came in stuttered gasps, her mouth so dry and still she cried, calling out, shouting when able, 'Leave him alone! Get off him, get *off* him!'

With one eye now closing, she could make out their shapes, young, like her and Tony, how many it would have been hard to say; six, maybe seven. They were in jeans and shirts, short hair, a group of lads on a night out, and here they were, joining the affray. It took a second for her to realise that they were indeed hauling punches, bent low, delivering blow after blow, but they were not hurting Tony, they were in fact lugging the thugs from her friend.

They were help.

They were helping . . .

They were helpers.

Her whole body sagged with relief.

One by one they picked off the aggressors, knocking three out cold and tossing the other two with bloody noses and split lips on top of them.

'You're alright, lad.' One of the men spoke to Tony, as he lifted his head and placed a jacket under it. Tony didn't move, but made a whimpering noise, a low, moaning response, but it was something. 'Help is on its way. One of our lot went to call an ambulance. Lie still, and breathe. We've got you.'

It was as if she went under then, sinking beneath a wave of relief, giving in to the riptide as the remaining strength left her body, and she slumped back down on to the pavement.

He was in good hands. He was being taken care of.

Tony, her very best friend.

Ashleigh

The taxi was overly warm. Ashleigh wound down the window, enjoying the cold blast of night air on her face. There was something about being so dressed up, so sparkly, that put her in mind of Christmas and all good things.

'I hope they like me.' She spoke her words out into the dark as the car zipped along.

'How can they not?' Archie lit a cigarette and blew the smoke in a steady stream.

'Do you really call them Elaine and Dickie?' She turned to face him.

'It's their names. What else am I going to call them?'

'Mmmn.' She didn't have an answer, not wanting to offer 'Mum' and 'Dad', aware of how pedestrian it sounded. Trying to imagine calling *her* mum and dad Ruthie and Dennis – they'd laugh and tell her not to be so daft, for sure.

'Anywhere here is great, thanks.' Archie tapped the back of the front seat.

The taxi stopped and he paid the cabbie.

Conscious of their lateness, the two now tripped along the cobbled street and made their way to the wine bar with a view out over the river. The steamed-up windows were edged with fairy lights, and as he opened the door, the roar of greeting was almost deafening. He was popular and loved, this boy of hers. She followed him, his hand behind his back, holding hers, leading her in from the cold. Doing her best to smother her nerves with thoughts of how she had looked in the full-length mirror, she concentrated on that, and the fact that he loved her!

'There he is! How good of you to show up!' A man's voice – Dickie, she presumed – boomed at the sight of them. He stood among Archie's friends, at ease, as if he'd known them all forever.

‘Dickie! You old fart!’ Archie laughed loudly at his father, who sported a soft jersey tied over his shoulders, the arms draped over his navy-and-white checked shirt. He looked like he’d just stepped off a yacht, his worn Sebagos doing nothing to temper this. The man came forward and enveloped the boy in a brief, crushing hug, before shoving a glass of bubbles into his hand.

Guy rushed over and stared at her. ‘Wowsers! You scrub up well, Brett!’

‘Thanks. You too.’

It was true, they wore evening dress well, these boys who were accustomed to bespoke suits, well-cut shirts, and good shoes.

‘Gigi!’ Archie slapped his mate on the arm, before pulling her towards his parents, who stood back to back, a few feet between them. Dickie stared at them; his mother, however, was engaged in conversation. Ashleigh took the opportunity to study her.

Elaine Fitch was thin, so thin, with a grace and elegance that came with such a build, hair swept up in a loose chignon to show off her delicate neck; willowy arms languid inside the sleeves of her ivory silk blouse, the hem of which was tucked into a velvet tight-fitting skirt that stopped on her knee. Black tights showed off her endless legs and on her feet were the most darling pair of soft black pumps with the telltale double C Chanel logo on the front.

When Ashleigh saw *her* mother after any time away, Ruthie almost bubbled over with excitement. Irritatingly running her hand over Ashleigh’s face, touching her hair, holding her close, staring into her face, and kissing her as she spoke. It was therefore with interest that she stared at Elaine, who with a glass of champagne in her hand, smiled once in her son’s general direction, and let her eyes sweep over Ashleigh’s frock, but didn’t break from the chat she was having with Bruno, a boy who was on Archie’s course and who had gone to Stowe.

Archie leaned in and whispered to his father.

'Oh, fuck right off!' Dickie shouted from under his bushy moustache. 'She is not your girlfriend. She is way too pretty for you, you mangey reprobate!'

It was then she tuned in, and realised Archie's dad had sworn in jest and that they were talking about her. And no one was shocked, and no one gasped, as if your dad saying the F word loudly in public to your friends was the most ordinary thing in the world. She couldn't imagine how her parents would react if they heard this.

'Let me look at her!' His dad put on gold-rimmed spectacles that had been secreted inside the front pocket of his shirt. She noticed then he wore the same signet ring as Archie. 'My God!' Dickie smiled approvingly, revealing teeth that would only benefit from a trip to a dentist. 'She is exquisite! If I were you, I'd get her bed, fed, and wed quick as you can!'

Ashleigh laughed then, because everyone was laughing, and it felt rude not to. It was conflicting, to be so considered and commented upon, as if she were a broodmare or a new hound. It was insulting, yet it sounded a lot like approval, and for that she was ridiculously thankful. Besides, Archie had already told her that his father had no harm in him, and she believed him.

'For God's sake, Pa!' Archie shook his head despairingly and winked at her, confirming it was all in jest. A pantomime, no more.

In that moment she was glad Remy was not with her, knowing she wouldn't have laughed, and guessing that by the time her sister would have finished speaking out, Dickie wouldn't be laughing either, and that might just ruin everything.

Ashleigh watched Elaine Fitch, as she finally, having listened intently to Bruno drone on about his parents' ski chalet in Les Deux Alpes, gently dismissed him by placing her hand on his forearm and gracefully stepping to one side.

Dickie was still holding court with Archie and the rest of the boys, who were all hanging on to his every word. As their volume increased, more bottles of champagne were duly deposited into silver buckets full of iced water. She wondered if they were ever going to get to the ball. Not that she wasn't having a good time, she was, but the more people who saw her frock, the better. The more people who saw her and Archie together, a couple to be envied, the better, because to be envied meant she was worthy of envy; it meant she wasn't a fraud, but was one of the girls who was winning, winning in her own right.

'You must be Ashleigh.' Archie's mother let her gaze sweep her head to toe. Only yesterday, this kind of scrutiny would have had the power to erode her confidence, like taking an axe to the vines of self-assurance that wrapped her and kept her upright. But this was not yesterday, this was today, when a boy like Archibald Oxton Fitch had told her that he loved her! More than that, he had woven words into poetry, the power of which made her feel almost invincible! She was under his skin and inside his bones.

'I am. It's lovely to meet you, Mrs Fitch.' She smiled.

'Lovely to see you too.' Ashleigh made a mental note, *Lovely to see you*, to use in the future. 'You like it here in Exeter?'

'I do! I really do. I'm from just outside Salisbury, so another beautiful cathedral city.'

'And what is it you're studying?' Elaine sipped her bubbles.

'History.'

'Mmmn. I like history.' It felt a lot like approval and Ashleigh felt her chest bloom with joy. A very different reaction from her parents, who had looked at each other, mouths open: *History! What's the point in that?* 'What period?'

'At the moment, I'm looking at the economics of war, mainly the Second World War.'

'Oh dear! That sounds a little dreary, I rather like the Tudors. All that lovely architecture, infidelity, and the most marvellous frocks!'

Ashleigh laughed loudly, not because she felt it the right thing to do, but because the woman was funny.

'You're right. It is a little dreary, but I only have a year left, then out into the big wide world.'

'And what then? What's the grand plan?' Elaine's ice-blue eyes gave little away, and Ashleigh felt she was still making her mind up as to whether she was a suitable date for her only son.

'No plan, exactly.' She clicked her tongue against the roof of her mouth, deciding that honesty was the best policy. 'Much to the annoyance of my parents, I have a very clear idea that I want to work for myself. Not sure in what capacity yet, and I don't know what area of business.' She drew breath, almost as if she anticipated questions. 'But Guy and I have talked about working together. We get on well and have the same outlook on life. We agree we want to work hard when we're younger and then sit on a beach when we're older.'

That was the dream. She could picture Archie sitting right by her side on the sand.

'Interesting. Of course, Guy and Archie were at Clifton together. I know his mother.' The woman narrowed her eyes as if deep in thought. Ashleigh wasn't sure if it was interesting good, or interesting bad. And as was the case in moments like this, she babbled, a little.

'I do know that, succeed or fail, I want it to be on my own shoulders. My dad has worked for the same company since he left school and could only ever progress when someone else set the framework. It was always on their timescale, their terms, and often those promotional leaps weren't leaps at all, more like small sideways hops, with a pat on the back for good measure. I admire my dad.' She spoke freely with a lump in her throat at the thought of him in his company tie, eating his cereal each morning. 'But I guess I want more.'

'Well, good for you!' Archie's mother seemed genuinely impressed. 'You can't underestimate the importance of independence and self-reliance, and strength, especially when there's a crisis. It's the difference between surviving or sinking. I learned that.'

Ashleigh pulled a wide-eyed expression of agreement at the loaded statement, remembering that, according to Guy, Archie's mother had never worked in a traditional sense, but spent her days, and Dickie's money, decorating and redecorating any one of their three homes. It didn't sound like independence or self-reliance to her.

'And what is it your parents do?'

My mum fusses, cleans the kitchen, worries over us, and loves us with a ferocity that could shame a tigress.

'My father's in concrete.' She spoke with pride, picturing her lovely dad, hoping Elaine didn't want to delve too deeply into his exact role.

Elaine laughed loudly, open-mouthed, revealing small, uneven teeth.

'Well, that sounds jolly uncomfortable. Do we need to head over there with a chisel or two?'

'Ha!' Ashleigh, entirely aware of how she had set the woman up, laughed again; this time it was affected, but she knew it would help build a bridge.

'So what do you think, Ma?' Archie placed his arm around her shoulders and addressed his mother, a cigarette dangling from his bottom lip. 'Isn't she great!'

'I think she's charming.' Elaine spoke softly, as if Ashleigh were not present.

'Isn't she just.' He clumsily plonked a wet kiss on Ashleigh's cheek in a manner that told her he had consumed more than a glass or two.

'Why don't you bring her out to Mulverton? Daddy and I are there for a few days before we go back to London.'

Ashleigh liked the way the woman said *London*, giving it emphasis, as if it really was the only place to be. She was also more than a little chuffed with the invitation. Mulverton was the Fitches' Gloucestershire country house, a pretty red-brick Queen Anne mansion, according to Guy, with perfect symmetry and an unparalleled art collection that was open to the public once a year.

He had been very keen to give her all the details, telling her how Archie's wealth had been a great source of interest, even at a school like Clifton, where the termly boarding fees were the equivalent of an average year's salary. She would be lying to say she hadn't found it fascinating, alluring even, but knew at this point that even without money, she would still love him, love everything about him.

'That'd be great! What do you think, Ash? Can you cope with a few days of board games, real fires, wet country walks in wellingtons, and stodgy food cooked by Miss Mallory, who you'll love?' Archie lowered his hand and placed it just above her bottom, applying pressure with his fingers that she knew was an indication of his want for her. She kept a straight face as she looked at his mother.

'I think that sounds fabulous. I'd love to!' She did her best to contain her delight, knowing that to whoosh around the room like a firework, fizzing with anticipation, would not meet Elaine's approval. But an invitation to Mulverton! It felt a lot like acceptance. Not only was she keen to have a look at the grand house, she also knew it was the perfect way to all get to know each other. It would help seal the deal with Archie.

'Splendid.' Archie's mother gave a tight-lipped nod of approval.

'Ouch! Oh my God!' Ashleigh yelped.

It was sudden, scary, and painful. Ashleigh jerked, as her arm shot out. And there she rested, doubled over briefly, and leaning to one side with a sharp pain that tore through her left shoulder and arm, so acute it caused her to catch her breath.

'What's the matter?' Archie held her hand with a look of concern.

'Should we get you a seat?' Elaine looked over her head, as if searching for a chair.

'No, no, I'm fine!' She straightened and took a second to breathe slowly. It was the most curious thing. Almost as quickly as it had occurred, the pain went. She rubbed her shoulder and flexed her wrist. She was desperately not wanting to make a fuss and a little overawed at the severity of the discomfort that had, thankfully, been brief.

'What on earth happened?' Archie stood in front of her, and seemed to study her face, looking for clues.

'I don't honestly know.' She forced a smile. 'It just came out of nowhere, a sharp pain, like an electric shock in my shoulder and arm, but it seems fine now.' She rolled the shoulder that carried the faintest lingering twinge of discomfort, but nothing compared to the searing pain that she feared returning. Her breathing was a little laboured.

'Have you been doing any vigorous exercise today?' Elaine asked with a tone of concern.

Archie grinned at her, and she felt her blush spread over her face, neck, and chest.

'No, no, not really no.' She looked at the floor.

'How very odd.' His mother again looked her up and down.

Ashleigh could only agree: it was.

Remy

The blue light on the top of the van spun around, flooding the market square with its eerie glow. Remy took great comfort from its presence, which felt a lot like coming to rest on the dock beneath the safety of the lighthouse. Finally out of the water, thankful to be on solid ground. Safe.

Their attackers were duly cuffed and thrown into the back of the meat wagon, spitting, snarling, and swearing at those who arrested them as they went. She couldn't look directly at them, but rather concentrated on the cloud of their venom that hovered above them, venom with the power to infect them all.

Sitting up now, and in spite of her trembling limbs, she breathed a little easier, knowing they were gone and couldn't hurt her anymore. Straining her neck, she tried to glimpse what the medics were doing with Tony as they crowded around him on the cobbled floor. She could see they'd cut his jacket and shirt and were bent low, busy, attentive, and she was grateful for their urgency.

Don't die, Tony . . . Please don't die . . . I love you so much . . . She silently pleaded with the universe to help her friend, to spare him. She wished Ashleigh were there, wished her twin were holding her hand, right by her side, remembering when they'd crouched on the floor of the cubicle at their primary school, Ashleigh crying, holding each other tightly, knowing that to be in such close proximity made everything feel a bit better.

'Please . . . please . . .' She spoke quietly into the ether, part praying now, part wishing, part asking for help from whoever and whatever might be listening.

'Let's get him into the ambulance.'

She watched as two paramedics carefully lifted him on to a stretcher and carried him to the vehicle, where two open doors awaited.

'Here you go.' She looked up at the sound of a voice, a nice voice, kind, as a tall boy of about her age slipped his jacket around her shoulders. She was grateful for the warmth it offered.

'I don't want to get blood on it.' Her voice carried the slur of one whose lip was split, bleeding and swollen.

'Don't worry about that. Where are you hurt?' He knelt on the pavement by her side.

'I don't know.' It was as this fact registered that her tears sprang and offered something close to relief.

'Don't cry. You're going to be okay. I promise you. What's your name?'

'Remy,' she managed.

'Rennie?' He cocked his ear.

She shook her head. 'Remy.' She tried again.

'I'm going to call you Ren for short.'

She didn't mind. Ren was close enough.

'I'm Midge.'

Reaching for the sides of his jacket, she pulled it closed at her neck, trying to stem the chilly tremble that shook her whole body.

'You're in shock. But don't worry, these guys will get to you in a mo.'

'Are you a doctor?' She assumed he was a medic.

'No,' he laughed. 'I'm a Royal Marine. We all are.'

'Marines?' She twisted her head to look at the group, who were folding down their sleeves and wiping their hands on the thighs of their jeans.

'Yep, we're on a training exercise not far from here and we were just off out for a bite to eat.'

'Midge?'

'Yes?' He leaned in closer, a big man who radiated tenderness.

'Is Tony, my friend, is he alive?' She hardly dared ask, as the prospect of losing him sat like a stick wedged into her throat and about as painful.

'He is. He's alive.' His reticent tone suggested that this might not remain the truth as the night wore on.

Her tears were ribbons of distress that washed her face and now offered scant respite at the fact that her friend was not out of danger. She couldn't imagine a life without Tony in it.

'They, they hurt him!' – she hiccupped – 'for no reason! We were just walking along,' she sobbed. 'Just walking along!'

'Don't cry. I never know what to do or say when a girl cries.'

She sniffed up her tears as best she could.

'Are you with the young lady, sir?' A policeman knelt beside her.

'No, no, we've just met.' He smiled at her, a nice smile, a nice face.

'You're one of the men who came to the rescue?'

'Yep.' Midge nodded.

'Do you mind if I give you some advice?' The officer lowered his voice.

'Please do.' Midge leaned in.

'Get out of here, all of you. Get out of here before my over-officious colleagues start taking names and addresses.'

'Right.' He took a sharp breath through his teeth. 'Will you be okay, Ren?'

She nodded, and with the one arm that didn't hurt, went to remove his jacket.

'Keep it.' He smiled.

'I can't keep it.'

'Yeah, you can. Give it to me the next time you see me.'

He held her eyeline, and just the thought of seeing him again was a thin beam of light shining in this, the darkest of moments. She didn't want him to leave, wary of being alone here; what if the bad men escaped from the police van and found their way back to her?

'I mean, it won't be for a while. We're off to the Falklands.' He kept his eyes trained on her. 'But when I get back, I'll look you up. Is your number in the phone book?' He spoke with confidence, as if the policeman wasn't present.

'Yes.' She gave a small nod and winced as the movement hurt her cheek, her eye, her lip, her jaw. 'Brett. We're on Church Lane, Broadhaven.'

'Got it.' He stared at her face, as if taking her in for the last time, this stranger who had saved her, saved Tony. 'I hope your friend's okay.'

'Me too,' she managed. *Please let him be okay!* Mentally she offered up the prayer.

He smiled broadly, knowingly, and her heart, despite being encased in sorrow, gave a little squeeze.

'See you in a bit,' he said softly, and then he was gone.

'See you in a bit,' she whispered.

'Now, what have we got here?' A medic appeared and dropped down on to the pavement, shining a light towards her face. 'What's your name, lovey?'

'Remy.'

'And how old are you?'

'Twenty. We're twenty.'

'Right, Remy, have you been drinking?'

'No.'

'Have you taken any substances that it would be useful for me to know about?'

She thought of her mother and their drugs conversation earlier, *before* . . . her gut bunched at the thought of the conversation they were going to have. And who would tell Tony's mum?

'No.'

'Where are you hurt?'

'Everywhere.' This the truth, as her body and mind caught up and she replayed the horror of what had happened. 'Can I go and see my friend? I need to be with him.'

'We're taking you to the hospital now.' As he spoke a second ambulance appeared and with the help of the medic and the policeman she stood on shaky legs, and they guided her towards it.

The ambulance made its way through town as she lay on the gurney, strapped in, staring at the ceiling. A strange and unique mode of transport that she had often thought about, wondering what it might be like to be ensconced in the back of one. They had given her something for the pain, which curiously didn't stop it, but rather muted it, made it less acute, and she certainly cared less about it.

Her shivering was so intense her teeth chattered. The kindly paramedic tucked the blanket around her, but Remy knew it was not only an issue with temperature that caused her tremors. It was something harder to explain, something that had happened deep inside of her. Her core, shaken. Her belief in human nature, shaken. Her faith, shaken. Her optimism, shaken. It had taken mere minutes for her to understand that she now lived in a different world, a dangerous world, undermining all she had thought she could rely on. This in turn induced such fear that she shook some more.

She had lost track of time; they might have left home minutes ago or hours. How long were they on the ground? How long did they kick him for?

Tony . . .

And then more tears at the memory of the one word that had changed everything, *Oi!* The noise like a burst of gunfire in her brain, *Oi!* And still so loud.

'Can I see him?' she asked, as they ferried her into a small anteroom in the bustling casualty department.

'Not right now.'

One of the paramedics patted her good shoulder as he pushed the trolley beneath the row of strip lights, so bright they were an affront to her eyes. Having been wheeled into position, she was transferred to a narrow, raised bed, wary of getting blood or dirt on to the pristine white sheet that covered it. She felt embarrassed to be so grubby. The medics clearly didn't have the same concern, and positioned her, shoes and all, on to the bed, before laying a clean, soft, wool blanket over her. 'We'll leave you now, but you're in good hands. Someone will be here in a little bit to get you fixed up.'

'Thank you,' she murmured, feeling like she might fall off the bed and aware of a wooziness that made her feel nauseated. It would only be in hindsight that she would regret not thanking them more profusely for the job they did, the help they had given and all they had done to care for Tony.

Tony . . .

A nurse came in, older, busy, distracted.

'Can I see my friend, the one I came in with? I really need to see him!'

'I'm afraid not,' the woman said, as she fixed the blood pressure cuff around her arm and popped the glass thermometer into her mouth. 'Just hold that under your tongue. He's in the very best hands and you would only get in the way. I'll get someone to come and talk to you as soon as they can.'

She nodded, the woman's response giving no indication that her friend was going to make it. Remy thought she might be sick. Seconds ticked by and the nurse took her readings, removing the glass thermometer.

'Thank you.' There it was again, that mealy-mouthed two-word catch-all that didn't convey half of what she wanted so desperately to say.

Please, Tony . . . Please don't leave me . . . Please be okay . . .

'Try and rest, and if you need anything, just pull this.'

The nurse looped a red cord that looked like the bathroom light at home over Remy's shoulder and into her hand before she left and closed the door behind her. It was the first time she had been alone since the assault and she stared at the door, her heart racing, wary of who might walk in.

How can I be sure the police have kept them locked up? Or are they out? Could they find me here?

She ran her thumb over the red cord and took comfort from knowing it was there, that all she had to do was pull. Closing her eyes as the drugs riddled through her system, she felt herself on the verge of dozing and let her body sink deeper into the trolley bed on which she was perched.

Oi! There it was again, that gunshot.

She came to with a start at the sound of the door opening. Her heart raced as, momentarily stunned, she took a second to remember where she was and why.

'Oh, my baby! My baby girl!' Her mother spoke as she rushed towards her, making no attempt to hide her distress, her dad following behind, his face ashen. Ruthie Brett stopped short of the trolley and placed her hand over her nose and mouth. 'Oh my God!'

It occurred to Remy then that she hadn't seen a mirror. Aware that she was injured, she felt a leap of fear in her chest as, judging from her mother's expression and demeanour, she figured it must be bad. It was some small consolation that her mum was a little prone to exaggeration, if not hysterics. With this in mind, she managed to remain calm. It was, however, the sight of her dad, whose knees seemed to buckle when he saw her, reaching for the edge of a sink, leaning on it hard as he pushed his thumb and forefinger into his closed eyes and breathed deeply, that worried her.

'Mum!' She spoke softly, her voice now scratchy, coming from a throat riven with exhaustion.

Ruthie took her tenderly into her arms. 'My little dove, my darling. I love you Remy, I love you so much. I'm sorry! I'm so, so sorry!'

Remy wasn't sure what she was apologising for but welcomed being held. It was everything.

'How did you know I was here?' she managed to ask when her mum released her hold and took her hand.

'The police came to the house. I was in my nightie, just cleaning my teeth, when they knocked on the door.' She broke away to shake her head and cry some more. 'It's every parent's worst nightmare, and there they were,' she howled. 'I thought we'd lost you. I thought there'd been a crash or—'

Oi! There it was again, and her body jolted.

'Not a crash, no,' Remy whispered. 'How's Tony? They won't let me see him.'

'He's holding on, my love. He's holding on.'

Holding on . . . it sounded fragile, and she again offered a silent prayer into the ether.

'He's my best friend, Mum.' Her tears came again.

'I know, my love, I know.'

Her mother tentatively stroked the hair from her face. Some of it caught, trapped, she would discover, stuck fast to her skin with globs of dried blood.

'Ouch!'

'I'm sorry! I'm sorry!' Ruthie shook her head once again.

Remy looked over at her dad, who had gathered himself, a little.

'Hi, Dad.'

He stood on the other side of the bed and let his tears drip down his face.

'I'll kill them! I swear to God, I will fucking kill them!' His voice was high and unnatural, each word dragged over vocal cords plucked tight with anger and distress. It was the first time she had ever heard her dad use the F word, the first time she had ever seen him cry like this. It felt appropriate, all of it.

'We'll have no talk of killing.' Ruthie pulled a tissue from her sleeve and wiped her eyes. 'There's been enough violence tonight to last us all a lifetime.'

'What have they done to you?' her dad asked softly, and she knew him well enough to know he didn't actually want the details. All in good time.

'We've left a message for your sister with her flatmate.'

'Right.' She was glad Ashleigh wasn't home to get the message, hoping she was at her ball having a fabulous time.

'God, I hope she's okay!' Ruthie spoke to her husband, her face contorted. Remy, who ordinarily would have laughed at her overprotective mother, did nothing of the sort, understanding that if something like this could happen to her . . .

The door opened, and in stepped a doctor, his white coat open to reveal a brown cotton shirt and beige Farah slacks and a black rubber stethoscope hanging around his neck. A fancy-pants career for sure. And even though she didn't admit it, not yet, somewhere at the back of her bruised and bashed head she understood that what had happened tonight had changed her, changed everything. She wouldn't be going off to university, wouldn't be taking up the law, but would stay close to home, where she'd coil in bed, take warm baths and sit with her mum and dad on the sofa. She would seek out peace and safety. A quiet life, away from those boots and that noise, *Oi!*, and that fear. That awful, awful fear.

That was all she wanted, that and for Tony to pull through.

Tony . . . please . . .

'Right, Remy.' He studied the clipboard with her chart attached, before smiling at her briefly. 'You've been in the wars.'

She nodded, reassured by his presence, this man who was unemotional, calm and who would help make her better, fix her up enough so that she could go home.

'Can I go and see my friend? I really need to see him!'

'Um, I don't see why not. Let me go and grab a wheelchair. We need to get you down to X-ray anyway, but you can stop by on the way. But literally just to say hello.'

'Thank you!' At last someone had listened to her. She cried now, but these were tears of gratitude and tasted different.

It was awkward, painful, and cumbersome transferring into the chair, which her mother pushed. Her dad, by her side, kept reaching out to touch her good shoulder, letting her know he was close. It meant a lot, knowing he was right there. Her dad would never let any harm come to her.

'Just a minute, no more.' The doctor spoke sternly and knocked on a door before walking ahead. He turned to face them as she and her parents waited anxiously. 'In you go.'

Remy knew she would never forget the sight that greeted her. The person on the bed had a grotesquely swollen head and face. No discernible features, no pretty eyes, no small nose, no pouty lips that always knew what to say to make her laugh, lips that favoured Heather Shimmer. Instead, he was a bloated, bruised ball that looked more balloon than human. There was a white stretchy tube in his mouth, a drip in his arm and a machine that beeped, attached to his chest via wires.

'What happened?' Tony's mum, Mrs Newman, who had been sitting by his side, her head resting on the small gap on the mattress, fired the question at her. Her eyes bloodshot with distress, her skin grey and loose on her cheekbones, as if felled by the sight of her boy. And Remy understood. This woman who had lost her husband, Tony's dad, when she was pregnant, this woman who already knew pain. There was something in the rhythm of her question, the emphasis on the word *what*, the almost imperceptible curl of her top lip as she voiced it, that coated the question with accusation.

Remy's response was the only one that felt fitting, as she felt the ligature of culpability tighten around her throat: 'I'm so sorry.'

Had it been her idea to go into town?

Were they laughing too loudly, drawing attention?

Why did she not advise him not to wear so much make-up?

Had her response goaded their attackers?

Was it her fault?

Could she have done more to help her friend?

Why hadn't she stood and joined in the fight, tried to beat them, clawed them, anything?

Ashleigh had suggested she ditch the off-the-shoulder T-shirt and oversized dungarees. Maybe she was right?

In that moment she felt an instinctive need to see her sister, to be near her, to be wrapped in her arms, her other half, as if believing that in some way, that contact might help restore her broken self. Make her whole. *Two halves, one egg . . .*

For broken she was.

Ashleigh

With feet sore from dancing, her head a little dizzy from the gin, wine and champagne she'd consumed, Ashleigh waltzed through the front door of her flat and threw her keys on to the side table. She was in that pleasant stage where she'd gone from drunk to almost sober. With it enough to function competently, even passing to an unknowing ear as clear-headed, but with just enough booze in her system to coat the world in a pleasant haze of joy. A warm and comforting sleepy kind of high that was always the perfect end to a perfect night.

For perfect it was.

Having jumped out of the cab, Archie had kissed her long and hard on the doorstep before going to buy beer from the twenty-four-hour off-licence. She had been too cold to go with him. Plus, the last thing she wanted was beer, she was far keener to pull Archie's shirt from his body and get to bed, longing to feel him next to her, skin to skin. She figured she had approximately twenty odd minutes to shed her frock, shower, climb beneath the covers, and wait for him. Although she had to admit, it felt like a shame to have to take off her fabulous dress. It had been quite the draw.

An invitation to Mulverton!

She danced her feet on the spot with her eyes closed and her arms in the air. It might now be nearly three in the morning, but she wasn't sure how she was going to sleep, not with her adrenaline pumping, so excited about the next few days. The big question was what to pack. Her one decent pair of pyjamas, for sure; wellies, obviously; and a nice gift for Elaine – flowers? Chocolates? Both? Not that she'd explicitly said *Call me Elaine*, but that couldn't be far off.

'Ash?' Fran called from her room along the hall.

'Oh, sorry, love. Did I wake you up? I was trying to be quiet. Archie's gone to get beer. We've had the most amazing night! We started off at the wine bar, I met his parents, who were a hoot' – she stole the phrase – 'and then the ball. We all arrived late, missed dinner, but the band were brilliant! My feet are killing me – whoever thought dancing in heels was a good idea! And tomorrow we're off to stay with his parents for a few days! I say *we*, because we are, officially, a *we*!'

Fran appeared in the doorway of her room, hair mussed, glasses in lieu of her contact lenses, which quite changed her appearance, her pyjamas crumpled from sleep and an air of fogginess that was to be forgiven at this hour. Her flatmate, it seemed, shared none of Ashleigh's enthusiasm for her news, which was mildly disappointing.

'Your mum called earlier.'

'Oh right. Well, thank you, darling, I'll give her a shout tomorrow.' She knew her mother would want all the details.

'No,' Fran shook her head and walked into the hallway. 'She was quite insistent. She said that you needed to call her the moment you got in from your party.'

'Why?' She couldn't think of any good reason for such an instruction and her heart lurched at all the possibilities. Was her dad okay?

'She didn't say. She just made me promise to tell you to call when you got in. So here I am.' Fran raised her arms and let them fall by her sides.

'Well, I can't call now. She goes to bed before nine p.m., and it's three in the morning!'

'She said to say, *call her even if it's two or three in the morning.* Those were her actual words.' Fran shrugged and sighed; message delivered.

'How did she sound?'

'She sounded like she wanted you to call her!' Fran displayed understandable impatience at the fact that this conversation was happening at this time of the morning, and finished with a slight shake of her head.

'Okay, thanks, Fran. Sorry!'

The girl sloped back to her room and Ashleigh stared at the phone on the small table by the door, unsure if she wanted to hear whatever it was her mum had to tell her. If it *was* something bad, she'd almost prefer to leave it until tomorrow, unwilling to spoil the joyous fairy tale that had been her evening, yet understanding her mum well enough to know she wouldn't settle until she had relayed whatever it was she had to say. On the other hand, *knowing* Ruthie as she did, it could be something and nothing. Maybe a letter had arrived for her; did she want it opening? How was the ball? Did people say her dress looked nice? It was a relief to think this was more likely the case.

Her shower would just have to wait.

With her face screwed up in anticipation, she lifted the receiver and exhaled as she dialled her home telephone number. Holding the phone under her chin, she cringed, imagining the ring echoing all around their little house in Church Lane, disturbing the quiet, raising her parents from their bed. She pictured her mum sitting up in bed and running down the narrow stairs while she struggled to get her arms into her wool dressing gown, as her dad boomed, 'Who the bloody hell is that at this time of night!'

The phone rang.

And it rang.

She gripped it tightly and willed them to answer.

It was at that point that Ashleigh felt the pleasant haze of joy, the warm and comforting, sleepy kind of high spiral from her body. And in its place: a cold and sobering intensity that was as scary as it was unwelcome.

They didn't answer.

They weren't home.

It was a little after three in the morning.

Where were they? Of course, she had no way of knowing where they were, but one thing was for certain, it was nowhere good. How could it be? It was at this realisation that the strength left her legs. She put the phone back into its cradle and slid down the wall until she landed on the wooden floor. Her dress bunched up around her waist, her head buzzing, and a feeling of dread in her limbs that made the prospect of moving unpleasant.

'Where are you?' she whispered into the stillness, as her thoughts raced. Was one of them ill? Had one of them died? Had they been burgled? Were they being held against their will? With her hand on her stomach, she did her best to control her desire to vomit, and considered calling again, but didn't want them not to answer, knowing it might just send her over the edge. With an ache to be at home, curled warmly in her childhood bed with her sister in the room next door and her parents snoring through the wall, she wished she had called more often. Wished she had visited. Wished she and Remy were closer. Wished she'd told them all she loved them, wished she knew where the hell they were.

The phone rang.

'Thank God!' Jumping up, she felt a new surge of energy fuelled by relief – they were home, and she had woken them, and they had just taken a little while to get to the phone. Her mum would no doubt give her an earful, but she'd happily take it! Beaming and desperate to hear the voice of her mum or dad, she lifted the receiver.

'Hello?'

There was the unmistakeable sound of coins dropping, a payphone. A call from a payphone . . . Her heart raced.

'Ash.'

'Remy!' Ashleigh sang. Thank God. Remy was on the phone. 'I've just phoned the house! I would never have called this late, but Mum left a message with Fran, and I had a bit of a panic, and so . . .' It was that burbling-when-nervous thing again.

'I didn't know you'd called. We're not at home.'

We . . .

'Not at home?' She gave a short, sharp, nervous laugh. Unable to fathom where her family might be at this hour, together, the three of them, but without her. 'Where are you then?'

'I'm at the hospital.'

Oh God! Oh God! Oh God! Oh God!

'Rem!' She exhaled.

'Mum and Dad are here. They've just gone to the machine to get a cup of tea. The nurse has brought the phone to my bed.'

Nurse?

'Okay.' Her breathing calmed, a little. 'Okay.' If her mum and dad were off getting a cup of tea, then they were not ill and certainly not dead, and if Remy was on the phone, ditto that.

'Ashleigh . . .' Remy cried then. Her distress wasn't loud or jarring. Hers were not hysterical tears. Neither did they carry the suggestion of tiredness or frustration; they were instead the calm kind. Tears drawn from a deep, deep place where pure sorrow lies in wait, rearing its head on only the very worst of occasions. 'I have some really rotten news . . .'

'What's happened, little dove, what's happened?' Again Ashleigh sat on the floor, hands shaking, her back against the wall, waiting for her sister to explain, wishing she *would* explain, so that Ashleigh could take a breath.

'We went into town, Tony and I.' There was a pause while the sounds of Remy's stuttered breaths came down the line. 'We'd only just got out of the car, and, and we were attacked.'

'What do you mean, *attacked*?' Ashleigh shook her head. It didn't make sense! Who would attack her and Tony? *Why?*

'Some men.' Her sister's voice was a thin whisper, as if to recount it was too painful. 'Some . . . some men.'

'Remy, Remy, my little dove! Are you hurt?' Her own tears came then; just the thought of her sister, injured, damaged and she hadn't been there to help, to protect her!

'I've got a broken shoulder and wrist.' Ashleigh nodded; she had *felt* it. 'And my face.' Remy swallowed. 'My face is very bruised. I've got stitches on my forehead, my temple, and my bottom lip.'

No! No! No! No! No!

'My love! Oh, my love!'

'I'm okay.' Remy coughed; the beeps went. Ashleigh felt a flare of panic; thankfully, her sister deposited more coins. 'But Tony,' she sobbed, her voice barely audible, riven, Ashleigh could tell, with the pain of it, 'they've really hurt him, hurt him so badly.'

'Poor Tony!' It was unthinkable. Tears ran down Ashleigh's face, leaving inky black rivers of mascara. 'Is he going to be okay?'

'He's not going to die. The doctor just told me that.' Her sister spoke with the first glimpse of resolution to her tone, as if this were a fact she clung to. 'But you should see him, Ash. His face . . .'

'Rem!'

'So many broken bones, his ribs, eye socket, jaw. I can't even . . .'

'Oh my God! I can't believe it!' She felt helpless and useless, wishing she were by her sister's side, there at the hospital with her family in the world that was hers, not here, in this frock, wearing faux diamonds and drinking bloody champagne while her sister had been attacked – *attacked*!

'I thought they'd killed him.'

'I don't know what to say.'

'I'm scared, Ash,' Remy whispered.

'What are you scared of, my love?'

'Everything.' This one word shook down the line, and Ashleigh felt the power of her admission. It was devastating to hear her sparky sister so cowed. 'I need you, dove. I need you right now.'

Archie let himself in with the key she'd given him and held the can of Skol Special Strength in the air. More cans were stuffed into the pockets of his dinner jacket and a cigarette dangled from his mouth. One glance at her, however, and he too dropped to his knees, placing his can of lager on the floor. He put his hands on her legs, his expression one of concern.

'It's my sister,' she explained with her hand over the mouthpiece.

'She alright?' he mouthed.

Ashleigh shook her head. No, no, she was very far from alright.

'I'm coming home, little dove. I'll be home tomorrow. I'll be there as soon as I can. You just hang on. You just hang on, okay?'

'Okay. Okay.'

After her call, they sat on the hall floor for a while, Ashleigh letting the facts permeate, while Archie, still drunker than her, did his best to offer platitudes. She was, however, glad of his physical presence.

'I can't come to Mulverton. I hope your parents understand.'

'Of course they will.' He kissed her.

'My sister and her friend, our friend, Tony, they were attacked by a group of men.' The words sounded monstrous, even to her own ears.

'God, that's awful!' He sat back against the opposite wall, he too stunned by the terrible fact.

'It is. Really awful. I need to go home. I'm going home. I'll get the first train tomorrow.'

'Shall I come with you?'

It was a sweet offer from the boy she loved, the boy who loved her back, but these were not the circumstances under which she wanted him to meet her family or for them to meet him.

'Thank you, Archie, but I'll go on my own.'

She took a deep breath and sat up straight, knowing that in a crisis, independence and self-reliance were important. Sometimes, they made the difference between surviving or sinking.

And of one thing Ashleigh was absolutely sure: she was not about to let herself, or her sister, sink.

Ashleigh Brett and Remy Aller

1983

Aged 21

Remy

The sky took on the pinky hue of dusk, as Remy, who had lost all track of time, stared out of the window of the taxi. Sleep had been sporadic over the last couple of days. It happened like this, when your day was no longer punctuated by a work routine, or the eating of breakfast, lunch, and supper. No commute, no clocking in or clocking out, no being late or early, no framework within which to exist. It had been this way since the incident, which she didn't really know how to name, cloaked still with shock and something close to embarrassment that it had happened to her, happened at all. Weren't smart people supposed to avoid situations like that? And that nagging and persistent doubt that she could have done more, done less, done differently.

The police called it an assault, grievous bodily harm. It had certainly been grievous to her body, had harmed her for sure, and yet if people asked her what had happened she felt her mouth go dry and she'd mumble, 'We were . . . hurt, my . . . my friend and me. It was, it was bad . . .'

And they'd more than likely nod and change the subject. She understood. I mean, what was there to say that wasn't either flippant or invasive?

Sorry to hear that . . .

Glad you're on the mend.

Bad, what do you mean, bad?

How's your friend?

How *was* her friend? That was a good question. He was at his mum's and didn't leave the house. He was in bed most of the time, taking copious quantities of painkillers while his bones continued to knit. He attended physical therapy, saw a shrink, and was holed up with a small TV in his room on which he watched TV-am, *Sons and Daughters* and *Blockbusters* just to pass the time.

'You got away lightly.'

That was what Tony's mum, Mrs Newman, had said to her when she'd been there to eventually welcome him home from hospital, and she supposed she had. The woman had spoken with subtle undertones of anger, of blame, as if Remy should have taken *half* of the beating metered out to Tony so it wouldn't have been as bad on him, a dilution of his injuries. It was nothing she hadn't considered herself, no matter how misplaced.

Watching as the ambulance pulled up slowly to the kerb, one or two neighbours found jobs in the front garden just to catch a glimpse. They'd wheeled him out the back, down a ramp and helped him up the front step. He'd looked old and bent and small and grey and more like a husk of the boy who had banged the steering wheel and yelled, 'Turn it up!'

It was so sad to see, and to be so helpless; she felt like her heart had turned to dust and swirled its sadness in her veins.

Tony didn't want visitors, didn't want to chat, or be chatted to, didn't want her to sit in his room and watch him watching TV. He wanted to be left alone, and so she did, she left him alone. But my God, how she missed him. Feeling the absence of him like a dark thing hovering. Ashleigh had come home, and suggested they grab a pizza and go and surprise him. It angered her, her sister's lack of awareness, too busy racing ahead with her life plans, and without a shred of comprehension that a surprise of any kind was the last thing Tony needed. Her twin was horribly out of touch.

Oi! This was the word that infiltrated her dreams and pulled her from sleep, the word that ricocheted around her head when she walked along a pavement or entered a lift or crossed a park or was in a public space that was strangely quiet. Her heart would race, her breath coming in short pants, and she would sweat and shake, so much so she preferred not to go outside alone if she didn't absolutely have to.

She had thought, in the wake of her attack, that she might stay close to home. A quiet life, away from those boots and that noise *Oi!* and that fear. That awful, awful fear. But that wasn't quite how it had worked out.

And as the cab now trundled out towards Broadhaven, she yawned. Her shoulder ached. It was the norm, and she therefore rarely mentioned it. This, along with limited movement in her wrist, which the doctor told her would improve with time, and the criss-cross of angry red weals on her face, raised and unpleasant both to see and touch, daily reminders of just how lightly she had got away with it.

One scar, across her forehead above her left eye, was about an inch in length, with small, vertical lines where long stitches had pulled the skin together. Stitches applied to her skin by an impatient and possibly tired hand in the early hours. The second scar, longer but finer and running from her cheekbone up to her temple. One of Jamie's friends, Higgins, had nicknamed her Scarface. They'd been in the pub, all laughing, all sloshed, and he'd said it, pointing to her empty glass, 'What you 'aving, Scarface?' as he stood to buy a round.

The atmosphere had changed in an instant, like turning off the light.

Jamie had laughed only once, a short snort, before launching himself across the pub table and smacking Higgins in the face. He'd had to leave, spitting blood, and wiping tears from his eyes as a tooth plopped into his palm.

She had stared at Jamie, his expression searching, whether wanting her thanks or approval it was hard to tell; unable to explain to him that the very last thing she needed or wanted was to be around more violence, more blood, more injury.

Jamie . . .

Just the thought of him was exhausting. And now she sat in the back of the taxi, mentally fatigued, too tired to think straight. There was some small solace in knowing she was heading home.

What the hell do I do now? she asked the pink sky that met the wide sweep of countryside, unable to appreciate the beauty of her surroundings, too worn out even for that.

'I won't be that long! I'll be home soon. We can talk when I get back.'

That was what Jamie had said, but she knew the moment he closed the front door and left her, despite her pleading with him to stay, that she would not be there to talk to when he got back, not this time. Plus, it was most probably a lie. *Another* lie. He would not be home soon. She'd simply run out of energy to have the same conversation, in any number of variants, about what she needed, what she expected and what he was prepared to give or not give, which was more to the point.

I've messed up . . . I've really messed up . . . how is this my life?

These thoughts and others did nothing to aid her state of mind, which could best be described as fragile.

She paid the cab and grabbed her heavy bag from the back seat. It was hard to do with Sophie balanced in her right arm.

Her baby girl stirred, lifting her small hands to her face, and pursing her tiny lips.

'Shhhh, go back to sleep, little one, go back to sleep.'

Remy trod the path to the front door of her parents' house in Church Lane and placed the heavy bag on the floor. It was stuffed with clothes for Sophie, nappies and blankets, a pair of jeans for her, and some other bits and bobs, but essentially it was what she had managed to grab in the forty-five minutes between deciding to leave and arriving here.

Raising her knuckles, she hesitated, wishing she'd practised what she might say to her parents, what she might be asking, but deep down confident that there wasn't really a need for any rehearsal, knowing she could always return. It was more the sense of failure that dogged her, the awful dragging feeling that she was *that* girl. The one who had met a boy, fallen for a boy, got pregnant by a boy, married the boy in a crappy ceremony that took no more than half an hour on a grey, wet Thursday morning. Discovered the boy was not who she had thought he was and was now here, babe in arms, coming home. It was as desperate as it was clichéd.

It was shortly after the assault that she'd met Jamie Aller. He had been working on the new wing at the hospital where she kept her appointments and medics told her she was healing nicely.

The cocky, chirpy scaffolder with all the chat had bombarded her. 'Here she is, hello gorgeous!' or 'You not talking to me then?'

he'd holler, as she smiled and made her way in and out of the automatic door of the outpatients' department.

'I don't know you,' she replied, once.

'Well, we need to put that right, don't you think, beautiful?'

She hadn't felt beautiful, the opposite in fact, but it had been nice. He'd pushed, and she had been drawn to the man. A new person who was interested in her, even in this state. A man who was brawny enough to keep her safe from the one thing she feared more than any other, physical attack. She was lonely, afraid, damaged, and so instead of staying coiled and remaining quiet, she had jumped into his arms and into this life, and it had felt like a tornado, whipping her up and spinning her around until she didn't know which way was up.

Jamie was good-looking and funny, *so* funny, in a very unsophisticated kind of way. He was no Tony, but still she laughed as he mispronounced words, got the wrong end of the stick and was self-effacing. All of it the very best medicine, making her laugh long and hard until her sides hurt, her nose ran, and she needed to pee. He was a distraction from the trauma, the twisty turn her life had taken, the absence of her best friend, the guilt, the lack of closeness with Ashleigh, who was in London living her best life, and the fact Remy couldn't bear to look in a mirror. Hooking up with Jamie meant she was not stagnating, not dwelling on the bad, bad thing that had happened. She gifted him her virginity, they became a couple, they shopped for pasta and sauces in jars and giggled at the doctors as they discussed due dates and birth plans. It meant her life was moving forward, it meant she was not broken. The laughter and the man who had instigated it the very best of diversions, or so she had thought.

Her parents were noticeably thin in their praise of the man. She saw the way they thickly covered Archie with compliments, beaming at him as he walked in the door on the one occasion he'd come home with Ashleigh. Listening to his every word like he was a guru spewing details of his new job in finance, and how he and Ashleigh were having trouble sourcing decent marble for the guest bathroom in the renovation of their *London* home. Poor things. When she spoke of Jamie, or he came with her to eat bacon sandwiches, chewing with his mouth open at her mum's kitchen table, they offered no more than small-mouthed nods of approval. Even her mother, who usually had so much to say. There was, she noted, a quiet lack of enquiry whenever she mentioned him, as if they really didn't even like him, but were aware that she had been through something, and that any branch of happiness was one worth grabbing.

It made her want to stay away from home, and so she did, spending more and more time in his tiny, messy flat. Ashleigh never called her there, and that was fine. Jamie would only have listened to their conversation and mocked her in the background.

Things had changed when she'd discovered she was pregnant with Sophie, who was now four months old. It had been a shock – was still a shock! The last thing she had done before moving out of her little room and moving (officially) into Jamie's two-room flat above a bookmakers' in town was kneel by the side of her childhood bed, scoop the prospectuses for universities from under the mattress and pop them in the bin.

She had felt numb almost, carried along by the current of life, simply grateful to have her head above water, to be safe. It was enough.

It was a horrible, horrible experience, living with him, being married to him. An expectant first-time mum, she was lonely, skint, and silently struggling with the after-effects of the assault, yet on more nights than she cared to count had been forced to sit up, waiting for him to walk through the front door, stinking of a night well spent. A satisfied swagger to his walk and a mouthful of lies that he thought she was dumb enough to swallow. It had been the most terrible time, and she was still reeling from it, still walking with hesitation, untrusting of the very ground beneath her feet.

'Where have you been?' she'd asked that very morning as he'd put his key in the door at a little after 5 a.m., having left the flat the day before to go for a quick drink with the lads.

'Oh, here we go!' He'd exhaled through his nose, thrown his keys on to the table and grabbed the milk from the fridge, drinking it straight from the carton.

'I can't live like this, Jamie, I just can't.'

'What did you think, Rem? What did you think life was going to be like with me? I ain't no Archie, there's no family estate, no fucking bus fund, no title, none of it. You just got me, and I ain't never lied to you, I'm a scaffolder who likes a pint and a laugh. That's it!'

'Do you mean trust fund?' She had lost the thread a little.

'Yeah, what did I say?'

'I don't . . .' She shook her head; it didn't matter. 'The point is I never wanted you to be anything other than who you are. It was enough, or I thought it was, but you *do* lie to me, you lie all the time, and that's the thing I can't stand. *Knowing* you lie and watching you spend so much time trying to convince me that you don't is literally driving me crazy.' She'd knitted her fingers into her hair.

He'd stared out of the window, eyes wide, hands on hips, clearly irritated.

'I can't be crazy, Jamie, I've got Sophie to look after. I need to put her first, put us first. I don't like this life, this life with you.'

He had stared at her from a distance. 'I'm going to have a shit and a shower and then a sleep.'

'Please can we just talk?' she'd asked. 'We need to talk, Jamie! Or nothing changes! Please!'

Remy had watched him walk into the bathroom and lock the door. Sophie, the angel, had mewled in her crib and Remy had known it was time to go. She waited until he emerged from the bedroom post his very long nap, all spruced up, ready for another night on the town, and he bent down to kiss her. His liberally applied aftershave filled her nose.

'I won't be that long! I'll be home soon. We can talk when I get back.'

She rapped now on the door of her parents' house, and held her baby girl close, kissing her perfect scalp and inhaling the addictive scent of her. She was home, where she'd curl up in bed, take warm baths and sit with her mum and dad on the sofa. She would seek out peace and safety. A quiet life.

Ruthie opened the door wide, and sighed, taking note of the big bag on the path. Her mother's expression spoke volumes, and Remy got the message loud and clear. *I told you so . . .*

Ashleigh

'Here she is!' Ashleigh stood on the front path and could hear her mum almost squealing. 'Ashleigh's here!'

'I heard!' Remy's voice, her beloved twin, the reason she had ventured home this weekend and was missing Purdy and Raff's brunch because Ruthie had phoned her in tears.

'You should see her, Ash . . . we just don't understand it at all, any of it, she's lost her spark . . .'

And so she had changed her weekend plans, made her apologies, packed a small bag, and bought a train ticket, because that was what you did when your other half was hurting.

The door was flung wide, and her dad stood there with his arms open. 'Come in, love!'

He held her tightly and she looked over his shoulder as her mum pulled off her apron and shoved it in the broom cupboard. It was an odd thing to witness, her mum behaving as she did when a guest arrived, someone she might want to impress. Ashleigh would have found it hard to express her sadness at it.

'You look so lovely!'

'How was your journey?'

'Shame Archie had that work thing . . .'

'How's the house going?'

It was a bombardment no less, and she didn't know what to respond to first.

'Hey.' Remy came out of the kitchen with a tea towel in her hand. It was a shock to see her complexion; almost grey, with dark, dark circles under her eyes. She looked exhausted.

'Hey.' She smiled at her sister and wished she hadn't taken so much care over her appearance – her straightened blonde hair, her ditsy-print Laura Ashley frock with the dropped waist and mutton-leg sleeves, her black patent pumps – knowing there would be the inevitable comparison drawn between the two of them, when only ten years ago it had almost been impossible to tell them apart.

'You do, you look lovely.' Remy spoke sincerely, and ran her hand over her own short, tight curls.

'You chopped it off.'

'Observant as ever.' Her sister pulled a face and returned to the kitchen.

Ashleigh exchanged a brief look with her parents, who stood like scared mice, hands clasped by their chests, stock still, unusually quiet, waiting for what, she wasn't sure, but they now looked at her like she just might be the cavalry.

'Cup of tea?' Remy called.

'Yep. I'll give you a hand.'

Her parents shuffled into the lounge, in an obvious display of leaving the two to talk. The atmosphere was tense, as Ashleigh folded her arms across her chest, feeling a wave of pity for her parents, who had to live in the ripples of this negative, soul-sapping energy that emanated from her twin.

'You've lost weight, Rem.' The observation made as her sister reached up to the top shelf of the cupboard by the kettle to get the big mugs, her 501s gaping at the waist, revealing her ribs and back, without an ounce of spare flesh on them.

'Haven't really got much of an appetite.'

'Half your luck, I'm eating like a horse!' She laughed, trying to lighten the mood.

'That's me. So very very lucky.' Remy clicked her tongue on the roof of her mouth.

This wasn't like her sister at all – the snarkiness, the hurt, the lack of interest in her appearance. Ashleigh felt a little afraid for her, more than a little. They hadn't spoken much since Remy had taken up with Jamie, and when they did their chats had been perfunctory, brief. The formal and awkward nature of their conversations meant she preferred not to call. It was that simple, although the sight of her sister right now made her feel guilty and awash with intentions to do it differently from here on in.

'Where's Sophie? I'm dying to see her!' Her enthusiasm was genuine, the thought of holding her niece! It thrilled her.

'Sleeping.' Remy pointed at a baby monitor from which came the faintest sound of snuffly breath that was at once cute and hypnotic.

It had been a huge shock to find out her sister was pregnant, an even bigger one to hear that she had – one lunchtime, her manner almost furtive, the news spilled from her narrowed mouth, eyes downcast – married the absolute dipstick that was Jamie Aller. Ashleigh recalled the first time she'd met him, right here in this kitchen. He was good-looking, if short men with big muscles, deep tans, floppy hair, and white teeth that were constantly masticating gum, was your thing. It certainly wasn't her thing, and she would, up until that point, have sworn that it wasn't Remy's either.

'Two of you!' He'd pointed at them with his index fingers, his expression one of perplexity.

'Yup!' Her grin had been deliberately brief and insincere; she wanted him to know she thought he was a dipstick, could never entertain ending up with someone who wasn't her intellectual equal.

'How does that happen then?'

'Well, essentially there are monozygotic and dizygotic twins. One known as *identical*, the other as *fraternal*; we are of the monozygotic variety. One egg, one sperm that split in two . . .' Ashleigh had looked at Archie, showing off, which she knew was mean, but who the hell was this meathead her sister had hooked up with? It was infuriating and frustrating to see her stoop to this level, and it was nothing to do with money or class or status, nothing like that, but rather the fact that he was clearly a dunce. A handsome dunce, but a dunce nonetheless. And Remy was smart! *So* smart! But, like anyone else, would only properly thrive, only grow, with the right mental sparring partner. She couldn't stand the thought of it, Remy settling for *this*, as if he had trapped her when she was low . . . She wanted more for her sister, so much more.

'I suppose Mum called you.' Remy lobbed teabags into the old brown earthenware teapot that had been hanging around the kitchen for donkey's years.

'She did, yes. She's worried about you.'

'I'm worried about me.' Remy gave a wry smile.

'What happened?' Ashleigh took a seat at the kitchen table, thankful her mum was aware enough to give them this time alone.

'Not sure how far to go back.' Her sister abandoned the tea making and took the seat opposite her. Ashleigh noticed her grey, baggy T-shirt with a food stain on the front.

'As far as you need to. You've kind of dropped off the radar, I hardly ever hear from you.' She swallowed the emotion that threatened.

'And I hardly hear from you.'

Touché.

To speak of their distance out loud was like peeling off a plaster, and she didn't necessarily want either of them to have to face what lurked beneath. It felt a little shameful, the lack of contact, the ebbing of the closeness that had always been their foundation, until it wasn't.

'It's felt easier to just' – Remy looked skyward as if searching for the words, and she understood, knowing it was indeed *easier to just* – 'deal with it all on my own.' Remy rubbed her face in the way she did when she was tired.

'Deal with what? Tell me.' Ashleigh reached across the tabletop and took her sister's hands into her own. The same hands. *One egg . . . split in two . . .*

'Since the thing with Tony, I haven't been myself.' Remy spoke softly.

'That's understandable, it was terrible.' Just to remember that night, the phone call, the fear leaping in her throat at all the awful possibilities.

'It was.' Her sister freed her hands and ran her fingers through her short hair. 'Jamie was like, I don't know how to phrase it, a staging post, a place to rest. It was like I was made of sand and a big, powerful wave had come along and flattened me and he scooped me up and saved me for a bit, or at least I thought he had.'

Ashleigh bit her lip, not wanting to add her less than favourable commentary, staying silent to enable Remy to talk and to talk openly.

'I was able to forget about what happened when I was with him, because we were either sloshed or laughing. He made me feel safe, physically safe. I knew if I was walking around with him then no one was going to hurt me.'

'Oh, little dove.' The admission of her sister's state of fear was enough for her to feel the sting of tears at the back of her nose and throat.

'I didn't really mind where we lived, what we did or didn't have, none of it. And then getting pregnant, well,' – Remy took a deep breath – 'it felt like a sign. I didn't exactly have a plan. It was as if the universe was telling me this was how to lead my life; I was going to be a wife and mother and I was certain I could make a go of it.'

'But?'

'But Jamie was bored, I could tell. Not his fault, not really, he's just not, not ready. And he's not, erm . . .'

'Not for you?' She finished the sentence.

'Apparently not.' Remy let this trail. 'He went out most nights with his mates, like he always had, and I'm certain he was sleeping around. Which, funnily enough, meant I didn't want to sleep with him at all. It was the opposite of making me feel secure.'

'God.' Ashleigh could barely hide her disgust. *How dare he?*

'Actually, that wasn't the worst thing. It was the lies; telling me he'd be home in an hour and then coming back after six hours. Saying he would eat, so I'd cook, then announcing he'd already eaten. Staring at me as if I was mad when I suggested he had been with other women, when I could see it, could sense it.' She swallowed. 'And then, a couple of days ago, I just, I had enough. I felt like I was losing my mind. He was making me crazy! And being holed up in the flat with Sophie and no one to talk to. Arguing round and round in circles, never getting anywhere. Worrying about Tony, not seeing you, Jamie being a shit, it all just . . .' – she paused – 'I'm so tired.'

'Oh, Rem!'

'So here I am, and I'm not sure what comes next, but I'll figure it out.' She sat up straight.

'Of course you will! You are the smartest, the most beautiful, you will figure it out, and I know that it must feel like you've veered off course right now—'

'Just a bit.'

'But it won't always feel that way. I promise.' She hoped this wasn't a lie. 'We need to keep in closer contact. I don't ever want you to feel like you're holed up with no one to talk to, not ever. I'm always there for you. Or I want to be.' This she added, aware of how little they had seen of each other.

'Thanks.' Remy held her eyeline. 'It's tricky, though, isn't it, when you're in London and doing so much and are busy. I don't feel like I want to disturb you, and I don't feel like, like you get it a lot of the time.'

It was an accusation that stung, partly because there was truth in it. Ashleigh *was* always so busy and *didn't* really get it, but this was not the time to defend her position. Remy was raw, vulnerable and any discourse could wait.

'I want to get it. I do. You need to tell me, and you are never disturbing me. You're my twin sister.'

On cue, the sound of sweet murmuring came from the baby monitor.

'I'll go grab her.' Remy left the table, and Ashleigh poured the hot water into the teapot, letting the bags steep.

Her sister returned not minutes later, and she was smiling. Her face momentarily one she recognised. With her baby girl in her arms, gone was the hardened frown of unhappiness, the clenched jaw of dissatisfaction, even the heavy eyelids of fatigue. All of it gone, for a few seconds.

'There she is!' Reaching out, Ashleigh scooped Sophie into her arms. To feel the trusting weight of her was something quite beautiful. 'Hello, cutie! Hello, littlest dove!'

'Don't drop her,' Remy instructed as she grabbed a baby bottle from the cumbersome sterilising unit that took up a large chunk of her parents' countertop.

'I won't drop her! God, give me some credit!' She stared at the face of her baby niece and felt the tug of love. She and Archie had spoken about kids, of course they had, and both agreed that it would happen, or not, when the time was right; they were far too busy being busy and having fun to consider it yet, and while she might not have said it outright, she would be just as happy if it was 'not', unsure if she'd be any good at it. Another paper cut of self-doubt that came as a result of living and feeling like a fraud.

'How long are you staying?'

'Bloody hell, Rem, I've only just got here!'

'I was just thinking about the sleeping arrangements, that's all. Archie not coming?'

'No, he's got a work thing. Hector, his boss, is a nightmare, working him into the ground. He's actually a friend of Dickie's, and so Archie can hardly complain, poor love.'

'Yes, poor love.'

Ashleigh didn't like her sister's tone but reminded herself again that Remy was having a hard time right now; the sole reason for her return home.

'And what about you, Ash? You've heard the delights of my life right now, what about you? How's things in the big smoke?'

'Well, you remember Guy Gallow, my uni mate?'

'Yes.'

'We're thinking of going into business together.'

'I thought you liked your job, getting to nose in all those pricey houses around town?'

'I do, but I'd like it a whole lot more if we had our very own estate agency. We've looked at the numbers and we think we can do it. A small loan from the bank, guaranteed by Guy's mother, cheap premises to start with, no other staff, no wages, but luckily Archie has said he'll look after everything at home, financially, until I'm on my feet.' She felt the swell of pride in her stomach, a rare thing for a girl who had always felt like an imposter, but school was over, this was the real world, and she was sure she could make her mark.

'It sounds fancy.' Remy smiled at her.

'It would be fancy.'

'Come to your nana!' Ruthie marched into the kitchen and reached for Sophie.

'I've only just got her!' Ashleigh pulled the baby towards her.

'We never had this problem. There was always two of you to hold, to feed, to sit with. Everyone got their fair share.'

'I can't imagine having two, Mum. Looking after one is hard enough.' Remy beamed again at her little girl.

'It gets easier, love.' Her mum smiled and ran her fingers over her granddaughter's head. 'She's not got your curly hair.'

'Lucky thing!' Ashleigh laughed, having never made a secret of her preference for more manageable locks. 'You don't regret cutting yours?' She was curious, the first time she'd ever seen her sister with hair this short.

'Not really. It's easier with her.'

She was confused. 'I don't get it. Why does having a baby mean it's easier to have short hair? I don't follow!'

'No, you wouldn't.' Remy rolled her eyes and Ruthie laughed, leaving her feeling left out. 'But there are days when I don't even get to piss without holding her on my lap, I don't have time to shower, and so it felt easier to have short dirty hair than long dirty hair.'

'That's . . .' She was gobsmacked.

'What, Ash? What is it?' Remy stared at her.

'Gross!'

'Yes, love, that's definitely been the grossest thing about giving birth and becoming a mother, having to cut my hair short!'

Ashleigh watched as she and Ruthie laughed again, as if in on the joke that again left her feeling like an outsider. It was a moment of realisation that no matter how much she loved her sister, her parents, and coming home, Archie Oxton Fitch was her life now, her future, her other half. She looked at the clock on the wall and decided to give him a call in a bit, knowing just the sound of his voice, the man she trusted never to lie to her, never to make her crazy, would make everything feel just a little bit better.

Ashleigh Brett and Remy Hughes

1995

Aged 33

Remy

Remy raced as best she could up the wide stone staircase of this vast country pile, doing her darndest not to trip or spill the bowl of ice. Her Buffalo platform trainers made the job a little trickier, but who cared when it gave her a lovely extra couple of inches of height? Her baggy jeans sat pleasingly over the top; she liked this look. The lady who seemed to be running the kitchen had been very kind, helpful, when she'd explained that Sophie, her twelve-year-old daughter, had a bit of a temperature.

'Oh lordy!' the woman had remarked, abandoning a tray of choux buns she was delicately tending to, as if as aware that illness, this weekend, was an absolute no-no.

'I'm sure it's nothing!' She'd done her best to smile as if her words were true, fingers crossed behind her back.

Walking into the large bedroom with a sweeping view of the immaculate, striped rear lawn at Mulverton, she deposited her ice on a magazine on the chest of drawers. Sophie was still curled up on the pull-out bed that had been set at the foot of the imposing four-poster.

'How are you feeling, darling?' Remy bent low and placed her hand on her daughter's clammy forehead. It was warm, very warm.

'Bit sick.'

'Oh, Soph. Keep sipping water. I've got some ice. I'll soak a flannel in it and put that on your head; it'll cool you down. Where's Dad?' She looked towards the vast bed, just to check he wasn't lost under the heavy silk counterpane.

'In the bathroom. Harper's being sick.'

'What? No!' Pushing her long hair behind her ears, she rushed to the bathroom, where Midge stood by the sink of the rather grand en suite and wiped at the front of his shirt with the damp corner of a towel. Harper splashed in a bath filled almost to the brim with bubbles.

'You got enough bubbles there, Harps?'

Their little one smiled. Aged three, she was at that adorable time in her life when everything made her giggle and nearly everything was of interest. Remy watched as she heaped bubbles on to the back of her hand and blew them against the tiled wall.

'She looks alright.' This she noted with relief, hoping it was the over-indulgence of Jammy Dodgers in the car on the way here that had made her sick and not a bug. *Please, please, not a bug! Not this weekend.*

'Well, she does now, but a few minutes ago, it was like a scene from *The Exorcist*. Projectile doesn't come close, it was . . .' He shook his head.

'Poor love.'

'I'll survive. Just washing splashes off my shirt. Wish I'd packed more than three.'

'I meant Harper!' She tutted at the big oaf of a man she adored.

'She was sticky' – he pulled a face – 'so I thought it best to give her a bath and get her into her PJs.'

'It's only four o'clock,' she pointed out.

'I know! But if she's ill, I thought, snuggle her up in here with Soph. I'm happy to sit with them, get them some soup, I don't know!'

'Hmmm, you wouldn't be using the girls' sickness as an excuse to hide and avoid the celebrations now, would you?'

'As if!' He winked at her in the mirror. 'You know there's nothing I'd rather do than spend time with The Right Honourable Archie of Mulverton and his mates. When are they arriving? Wouldn't want to miss it!'

'Midge, my love,' she began, running her hand over his back, about to issue another reminder of why this was important to her, to Ashleigh, and how it would soon be over.

'Mumma!' Harper suddenly wailed, and as Remy grabbed her, her little girl proceeded to vomit the watery remains of her stomach into the bubbles.

'It's alright, my love, I've got you.' Having whipped her out of the warm water, Remy swaddled her daughter in a huge white bath sheet and, with her safely on her lap, rocked her, using the loo as a makeshift seat.

'What do you think it is?' She wanted Midge to give her the answers. It was what he did. Her rock, her guide, her great, great love.

How they had got together, seven years ago now, was still the stuff of all good rom-coms. Remy had not been looking for a relationship. The opposite, in fact, as scars on her face and body were matched by the scars on her heart, carved by her short-lived, disastrous marriage to Jamie. Riven with shame at what she now saw as a lack of sound judgement, it had eroded her confidence, making her doubt her choices to the point when even choosing between coffee and tea had felt like a ridiculous pressure. In the face of her assault, her life had become small, her bedroom tiny, her horizon within reach, all of it wrapped in subdued loneliness. She had, however, resigned herself to it; there were, she knew, far worse lives for her and her daughter than being in a warm, safe environment, where they were both so loved. The memory of Jamie's damp flat where she felt anything but welcome was there for perfect recall.

Then Midge appeared, took her hand and led her into a wide, open space, a whole other universe where she learned not to berate herself over what had happened with Jamie, understanding that she was reeling from the after-effects of the attack, searching for something, anything that might act as a safety rope. The marine never stopped trying to fill her with confidence, to make her feel loved, and she knew that if she could spend her days with him by her side, she would want for nothing else. It was a peaceful, happy and fulfilling life, based around her little family. Being with him kept her fear at bay, and living a happy life meant she no longer hankered for degrees or to prove herself in any way. It was enough. She had enough.

And it had all started on that day seven years ago, when having finished her shift at a local builders' merchants, where she inputted data and chased payments in the chaotic office, she had collected Sophie from school, thinking it was any other day. Still living at her parents' house, she could hear her mum and dad chatting to someone in the sitting room.

'That'll be Remy, now!' She heard her mum and, curious, had poked her head inside the door.

There he was, the nice-faced helper who had given her his jacket. It was only the sight of him that made her remember the jacket. She had no idea what had happened to it but hadn't seen it since she'd arrived at the hospital. It was shocking, surprising and yet wonderful to see him, remembering how his face, his words, his kindness had provided something good to focus on amid the bewildering chaos of that rotten night. She'd told Tony all about him and he'd teased her lack of nous in getting his number. It had then fallen to her to remind him that she had been a wee bit preoccupied, to put it mildly.

When, eighteen months after the attack, he had finally crawled from his dark hibernation, her beloved Tony had listened intently about the tall man who had appeared from nowhere with his mates, and quite simply saved his life.

'Like Batman?' he'd queried.

'Yes, exactly like Batman. But without the tights.'

Midge had, true to his word, disappeared to the Falkland Islands, and she had all but forgotten about him. In truth, of all the vivid memories of that horrific night, meeting Midge and him giving her his jacket had not ranked highly. She did, however, remember his parting words: *See you in a bit*, as if confident that he would.

It had been a nice thing to say.

In the intervening years, reeling from her best friend upping sticks and shipping off to Sydney, where his brother lived, concentrating on getting through every day, she had felt the icy grip of solitude. Ashleigh was understandably preoccupied with her business, which was taking off, and Tony moving so far away was a wrench. She felt the loss of him keenly, still did. Not that she blamed him, not a bit. The attack had changed her best friend, as it had her. He lost his sparkle for a while, his confidence too, his ability to hold eye contact, his sense of humour, not that you'd know it to see him now, flying high! He was a photographer, well known for his stunning portraits, and was deeply and madly in love with his maths teacher beau, Raul. She was so very proud of him and loved him still. Would love him always.

See you in a bit, yes, that was what Midge had said, and there he was as she'd hung her coat on the hook in the hallway, turning the day into something extraordinary, a beginning no less.

He had stood from the sofa, mug in hand, his sharp intake of breath the only clue that he might be a little nervous too. 'Hello.'

'If you've come for your coat . . .' She smiled.

It was good to see him, really good. He stared at her as if taking her in and it was one of those moments when the world stopped spinning and the planets aligned and she felt the warm spread of possibility trickle through her veins at no more than the proximity of him. Something that felt a lot like desire leapt in the base of her gut and all she could do was laugh, because it was bonkers! Utter madness! This man who had come to her aid when she had needed it most, Batman, no less, was now in her parents' sitting room and was drinking tea.

'I remembered what you said, Brett. Church Lane, Broadhaven.'

'Apparently so.' She did her best to contain the crackling fire of joy that threatened to burst from her, sparked at no more than the sound of his voice.

'He's a Royal Marine!' her dad chimed.

'I know, Dad.' She'd nodded.

'Muuum! Can I have some crisps?'

He'd looked towards the sound of Sophie in the kitchen, and she half expected him to pop the mug on the table and leg it. But he didn't, he hadn't.

'Yep!' she called in response.

'I did say I'd look you up.' He spoke confidently, as if they weren't being observed by her parents.

'That was a long old tour. Did you get lost?'

He laughed then. 'In a manner of speaking, yes.' His double blink told her that he too had a story. And she knew right there and then that it was a story she wanted to hear.

'Muuum!' Sophie called now from the bedroom. With her hands full, Remy watched through the open bathroom door as Midge ran into the room, grabbed the decoupaged waste paper bin from the floor and held it under Sophie's mouth as she too was very sick.

Shit . . . Her worst fears were realised: this was no Jammy Dodger-fuelled incident.

'What are we going to do?' Midge read her mind.

'Tie the sheets together, escape out the window and do a runner?'

'We can't run away from your sister's wedding.' He sighed.

'No, but we can't let our kids give every guest a sickness bug either. Ashleigh would never forgive me.' Her sister was, to put it mildly, a little strung-out over the whole affair, and Remy knew that a nasty bout of vomiting into the canapés or over the train of her Amanda Wakeley frock was not going to make matters any easier.

'I'm more afraid of Elaine,' her husband confessed.

'Oh God, me too!' She pulled a face.

'I feel a bit better.' Sophie wiped her mouth and sipped her water. Remy carried Harper to the bed, while Midge disposed of the bin's contents down the loo.

'That's good, darling.' This was a relief.

'Can I still be bridesmaid?' Sophie asked, her voice a little weak.

'Erm' – she shared a brief, knowing look with her husband – 'not sure, little dove. I mean you can't if you are going to throw up as you walk down the aisle or if there's a risk you might give it to someone else.'

'But I really want to wear my dress!' Sophie beat her fists on the duvet. 'The material! It's so beautiful!'

'I know, my love.' Remy understood. It was indeed a beautiful, beautiful dress of the palest pink, with acres of tulle under the skirt, a simple fitted silk bodice and sweet matching ballet shoes to grace her tootsies. 'I know.'

Having cleaned the tub, Remy decided to take advantage of the gloriously opulent bathroom and ran herself a deep bath. It was all very different to their flat-fronted 1970s rented bungalow, which had the advantage of being cheap and near the garage and repair shop that Midge was trying to get off the ground. She lay back in the water and let the fatigue of the day leach from her muscles.

Midge knocked on the door.

She replied with an elaborate knock on the side of the bath and watched as her husband crept in.

'What was *that*?' He looked at her quizzically.

'It was a code knock, me saying, yes, it's only me! Come in!'

'It's only a code knock if you've already established the code with the person who might be receiving it, otherwise it's just a series of random bangs.'

'You spoil all my fun. How're the kids doing?' She leaned up and peered into the bedroom through the door he held wide, staring at Sophie and Harper, both sound asleep in the middle of the vast four-poster bed. 'Bless them.'

'Yes. Neither has been sick again, and I figure just let them sleep.'

'Definitely. Did you see the huge marquee in the field? All decked with festoon lighting. It's going to look spectacular tomorrow. I really hope the girls are okay. I want them to experience it all!'

'This is all taking me back, making me think about our wedding.' Midge sank down on to the floor and ran his hand over her face, letting the tip of his finger trace her scars, as he often did.

'My beautiful girl.' She pulled him to her and let him hold her tightly in his arms. His shirt, once again, now soggy.

'Really? What part of this is similar?' She laughed. 'There was only you and me there, your mates as witnesses, and the vicar bloke.' It had been perfect, and simple, just the two of them exchanging vows inside St. George's, the garrison church at Bulford. Her second wedding, sure, but different in every way; she was in it for the long haul, they both were, no doubts. Her parents had been mildly and briefly offended not to be invited, Ashleigh had only sounded relieved that she wasn't required to venture outside of the M25, and with minimal fuss and no distractions, Remy had spoken her vows with a clarity and hope that had been sadly missing when she had wed Jamie.

'I guess, I just remember what I felt like the night before.'

'How did you feel, Midge?' She leaned up and kissed the side of his neck.

'Lucky, so lucky that you were going to be mine. I couldn't believe it, still can't sometimes.' It was his turn to kiss her. 'I'd been thinking about you since that night we met.'

'Yeah, thinking about me so much it took you years to drop by!' She sank back in the water, and he leaned against the tub.

'I've told you, I was unstable, posted all over the place, didn't know if I was coming or going, and I wanted to wait until I could look you in the eye and say, I'm here and I'm not going anywhere.'

'I'm very glad you did.' She closed her eyes. Moments like this, without the TV on, a kid needing something or a chore to do, were rare.

'I was scared too, scared you might not turn up! Scared I might not be able to make you happy.'

'Are you kidding me?' She touched his dark hair where it lay on his collar. 'I turned up early! Keen as mustard, and for the record you do, you make me very happy. You gave me back my confidence, my faith in humanity, you're everything. Our little family.'

'I remember when we got home after the service and we picked Sophie up from school and we said, we have some news and it felt like a big deal.' She laughed quietly at the memory, knowing what he was going to say, one of their favourite stories, she was always happy to hear it. 'And you said, "Guess what, Soph? We got married today," and she said, "What's for tea?"'

'What's for tea?' they chorused.

It had been lovely, seamless, the way little Sophie had just accepted this man into her life, calling him Dad, calling Jamie Daddy, and without seeming to apply the complexity to it that Remy had been fearful of navigating. It was both a blessing and a curse that Jamie wasn't ever present. Truth was, she preferred the lack of contact, but worried that he wasn't a constant in Sophie's life. He had, since she was a toddler, popped up on the odd occasion to take her out for a burger and to spoil her with a gift. Sophie, in fairness, didn't seem to expect or hanker after anything more. And Midge certainly provided constancy.

'I didn't need a big wedding. I wanted a marriage, I love you, Midge Hughes.'

'And I you.' He reached for her hand and knitted it inside his.

'We *are* lucky, aren't we?' She smiled, feeling a little smug and hoping that Ashleigh would enjoy her day tomorrow. Hoping too that it would be everything her mum and dad hoped for. Her sister had, after all, kept them all waiting for a long, long time.

'We really are, Ren. And I know things have been tight for the last couple of years, but the garage is picking up and I'm getting more regular customers, and so if you want to go to college, I know you used to want to study, or if you want to go and see To—'

'I don't want to do either of those things,' she interrupted. 'Midge.' She drew breath, hadn't planned on this being the moment, but it felt right.

'What?'

'I don't know how to tell you this.' Her mouth felt a little dry with nerves.

'You're running away with one of Archie Huffington Smythe's chinless school mates?'

'No!' She sat up in the water to face him, knowing this was important.

'Oh God, that's your serious face. Just say it.'

And so she did, she took a beat, and just said it!

'I'm pregnant.'

She stared at his face, waiting for the tell, the little clue that would let her know how he felt without him saying a word.

'Wow!'

'Yes, wow.'

'How pregnant?' He leaned over the bath and put his face into the water, kissing the flat of her stomach before surfacing with a wet face and hair.

'Just a little bit,' she whispered, knowing she wouldn't forget that this was when she told him, this day, in this room. With water dripping from his nose and chin, he looked her in the eye, and smiled, as if to say, *I'm here and I'm not going anywhere.*

'My clever girl.' His eyes misted with tears. 'My clever, clever girl!'

Ashleigh

Ashleigh was doing her best to keep calm. But if one more person asked her one more stupid question she thought she might scream!

Do you know where one might find some florist twine?

Do you know where Archie is?

Wine waiters to pour or leave opened bottles on the table tomorrow?

What time exactly are you planning on cutting the cake?

Do you know where Archie is?

Does the DJ know the gate code for the rear paddock?

It was exhausting.

And no, she did not know where Archie was.

In fact, she hadn't known where Archie was pretty much since they'd arrived at Mulverton last Tuesday, when he was either playing golf, in the pub, out with the dogs or catching up with old friends, while she ran around at the beck and call of every idiot with a question! She'd spent an inordinate amount of time with Elaine, which was never easy, feeling very much like her fiancé had abandoned her.

Having seen Dickie and Elaine Fitch up close over the years, she had watched the gilt she had mentally coated them with fall away, noticing small things at first that didn't sit well with her. The way they slipped into French or Italian to exclude anyone who hadn't stuck with languages post school or hadn't picked up the lingo while summering in Europe. But nothing irked her as much as the fact that she now knew what his parents felt for each other bordered on detestation. Their jovial veneer fractured every time they drank gin, which happened most days at around 5 p.m.

It was to her a frightful way to live and a salient lesson to look behind the facade, picturing her mum and dad wittering away as her mum dusted the ornaments and her dad organised the bins like it was an exact science. She was sure he gave more thought and planning to the refuse situation in their house than entire government departments who couldn't seem to organise the overflowing bins or solve the associated rat problem on the busy streets of the capital. Yet her parents were happy. It was all she wanted for her and Archie, that closeness.

It wasn't as if she could offload any chores to Remy, who was up to her neck with two kids and a job. She'd watched her mother's face fall, when with the best will in the world, Ruthie had suggested that to save on expenses, she was happy to make hundreds of sausage rolls for the buffet. Ashleigh had to explain that even the word *buffet* would send Elaine into shock. There would be canapés, a wedding breakfast and then cake, that was it! Her mum had stared at her as if offended.

'But people love my sausage rolls.'

'I'm sure they do, Mum, but no!'

This thought about food reminded her to make a phone call. The linen napkins that had been delivered were bright pink and not the rose pink she had ordered. One more frustrating thing to be dealt with. But it did need dealing with. Bright pink would throw her whole aesthetic and she couldn't have that.

'You all right, Brett?' Guy called from one of the leather sofas in the library, where he sat with an open book in one hand and a tumbler of something amber in the other. The sight of him caused a weird reaction that raised both envy and dislike. How she would love nothing more than to sit, read, and enjoy a drink like it was any other weekend, and how irritating was it that he and everyone else, it seemed, was so relaxed while she ran around like the proverbial headless clucker!

It wasn't fair.

'I'm not sure.' She walked in and closed the library door behind her. 'There's so much that needs doing! And explaining what needs to happen to other people only makes the chore take twice as long. It's easier to do it myself, all if it!' she vented. It felt good to get it off her chest.

'You're getting married tomorrow.' He snickered like a schoolboy.

'So it would seem.' Sinking down at the other end of the sofa, she stretched out her legs until her bare feet, and recently pedicured toes, were touching his jeans. They'd been good mates for a very long time, and he had always been an anchor in the storm.

'If you don't mind me saying, you don't seem to be shitting glitter and rainbows, which I think is what's expected of all brides-to-be.'

'Hmm.' She took a deep breath and reached for his drink, took a sip and, discovering it was whisky, handed it straight back. She hated whisky. 'First, let me tell you it's all a conspiracy; the joy, the fun, the shared sweet moments, the pampering, the memory making. All I've done since I agreed to this bloody wedding is chores! Choosing things, writing lists, trying on frocks, fretting over seating plans, arguing over guest lists, making endless phone calls, organising transport, sampling food, being at the beck and call of my soon to be mother-in-law, and having to gee up Archie in all of the above just to get him to participate. It's been bloody hard work, and it's not over yet! I knew it would be like this. I told Archie I was happy being his fiancée, we work perfectly well as we are! But apparently his parents had started to raise eyebrows about our *long* engagement and the fact we weren't strictly legit. I'm sure it's got more to do with tax and inheritance than romance,' she joked, because she adored Archie, and her friend knew it.

Guy threw his head back and laughed loudly. 'That's the spirit!'

'Am I awful?' she whined.

'No, just a realist, and a perfectionist, and a control freak, but that's why I love you.'

'You do love me, don't you?' she laughed, and dug her toes into his jeans, her lovely mate.

And then Guy stopped laughing and looked straight at her, and there was a flicker, a moment when she felt the weight of the question, and after what seemed like an age he responded. His voice barely audible, his eyes wide.

'Since the moment I met you.'

It was ghastly, unbearable, excruciating, and unexpected. She felt the cold sweat of unease coat her skin. Guy was her best friend. Archie's best friend too. She had only ever, ever seen him as a friend. As if scolded, she folded her feet beneath her legs and smiled broadly, doing what she did best, as she changed the subject.

'I think the Sutton property will go through this week, fingers crossed.'

She watched him double blink and take a large glug of his drink.

'I do too, and then we can pay the rent, get the windows cleaned, put petrol in the cars, eat!'

They both laughed.

She had done it, steered them on to safe ground. Here they rested, talking about their business. Their hard-won, much-loved business that now paid them a paltry salary as they ploughed every penny into it, watching it grow with a reputation for excellence. Gallow and Fitch estate agents, into which they had both invested so much time, energy, and money that to have it derailed by a single moment when one of them had sipped too much whisky and had given in to a misguided, wistful slip of the tongue . . . well, that would be too terrible to contemplate. And that before she considered what it might feel like to have to tell Archie, to have to confront Guy, to have to admit to herself what had just occurred. Guy was her go-to, her buddy; the thought of upending their friendship and not having him on the end of the phone was unfathomable.

'I'd better crack on. No rest for the wicked!' She jumped up, relieved and ridiculously wishing she'd left the library door open, knowing it would have made their whole exchange feel less clandestine.

'It'll all be over in a blink, Brett. Before you know it, you'll be heading back down the M4 with a hangover.' He laughed and went back to his novel.

She paused, hand on the door, and turning to him, asked, 'We're okay, aren't we, Gigi?'

'Of course we are. We'll always be okay.'

It was what she needed to hear as she closed the door and made her way up the stairs to find Remy, still undecided if she should share the awkward conversation with her sister or not.

Not, she decided, as she reached the guest room in which Remy, Midge and the kids were staying, believing the old adage, least said soonest mended. It seemed obvious that if no one knew what had happened then she could simply make out it hadn't. Plus, telling Remy was as good as telling Midge, and who might he then tell? She knocked quietly in case little Harper was napping.

The door opened, but no more than an inch, as Remy, hair wet, pressed her face to the gap.

'What are you doing? Can I come in?' Ashleigh pushed the door with her foot.

'No! No, you can't! Say what you need to say and then go away, far, far away!'

'Why are you being so weird?' She tried the door again; this was the last thing she needed right now, her sister playing the idiot. Remy didn't let it budge.

'I'm not being weird, I'm being prudent.'

'Remy, it's not funny! I just want to talk to you! I've got so much to do and I'm feeling a bit overwhelmed.' Hating the emotion in her voice, she was aware of how on the edge she sounded.

'Fine!' her sister huffed, 'I'll meet you on that patio that runs along the back of the house. We can talk there, outside.'

'The terrace?'

'I don't bloody know! Yes! The terrace! Whatever you want to call it. Who needs a house this big! It's ridiculous!'

'I know, right, Rem! All that hoovering and dusting, just more rooms to worry about.'

'Exactly!' Remy sighed as if, finally, someone got it. 'I'll see you down there in five.'

Ashleigh flinched as her sister unceremoniously closed the door.

Walking quickly past the library, she kept her eyes trained forward, not wanting to see Guy, not right now. It was a relief to find the terrace empty as she took a seat on one of the steamer chairs positioned with a view over the lawn. Truth was she was still a little stunned by their odd exchange. How *long* had she known Guy? He had *seen* her in her underwear! They had shared a *bed* when there was no choice! She'd helped him court and ditch any number of great girls who had caught his eye, and she'd talked to him *endlessly* about how much she loved Archie! Never, ever had she thought . . .

'What's up, dove?' Remy pulled the lounger next to her another few feet away and sat on the end of it.

'What's up with you? Your behaviour is stranger than usual! It seems to be the day for it.'

'Nothing's up with me! I've just seen Mum, Dad and Archie's parents all standing around in the garden room. Mum was offering everyone a Mint Imperial.'

Laughter burst from her. Remy, as ever, providing just what she needed.

'Was she really?'

'No, but I like to think she might.' Her sister waggled her eyebrows. 'That little paper bag with all those fluffy mints stuck in a lump in the bottom.'

They both laughed, and it was good, and she felt some of the tension leave her shoulders.

'Rem, I'm exhausted, could quite easily sleep all weekend and forgo the whole walking up the aisle thing. I love the man, you know I do, but all this fuss!'

'Well, you might have to forgo the whole thing if everyone starts yacking up. The kids are sick.' Remy pulled a face that suggested even saying the words was torturous. 'That's why I'm being weird, that's why I'm sitting over here, keeping my distance, and why Midge, Harper and Soph are confined to barracks. I don't want everyone to get sick!'

'What do you mean, *sick*?'

'I mean, vomiting in the bin sick. Throwing up in the bath sick! A bug maybe, I don't know, but they're clammy, clingy, and poorly.'

The awful possibilities filled her mind. 'Shit!'

'Not yet, but . . .'

'Poor Soph. She was so excited about wearing her dress!'

'I know, and she still might be able to. We've got a whole twenty-four hours for her to perk up and feel better. It's like that with these things that fly around school; one minute they're at death's door, the next they're driving you mad with their energy and demands for Pop Tarts.'

'Oh God! I don't want everyone getting ill. That would be the icing on the bloody cake!' The reality of what that might mean struck her then: poorly guests, empty seats, the beef carpaccio going to waste. 'We can't let anyone else get it!'

'Well, gee, thanks, Ash, for making me and my kids feel so welcome. You think I *want* to spend the night in a strange room with the kids throwing up? It's a nightmare!'

Ashleigh winced. The idea of spending time in any room with kids throwing up was abhorrent. Remy was a natural at parenting, and Ashleigh loved her nieces, she really did, but having seen Remy struggle up close, she wasn't entirely sure motherhood was for her. In fact, given the idea of so much disruption to the lovely life she and Archie shared, at thirty-three she was almost certain it wasn't for her. She and Archie had always been relaxed, leaving the idea of parenthood up to fate, almost. It had taken all of her courage to tell him that if they didn't get to hear the pitter-patter of tiny feet, she was more than okay with that. He had kissed her on the mouth and told her she would feel differently if it happened. Maybe he was right.

'Well, gee, thank *you* so much for coming and for all *your* support!' she sniped.

'Jesus, Ash!'

'Jesus, yourself!' she fired back. Her sister just didn't get it! So much planning had gone into this wedding – for it all to fall at the last hurdle would be the final bloody straw. It was enough that Guy had said what he had. Now this!

'Tony would probably bang our heads together if he was here.'

'Oh, Rem! I wish he was.' And just like that they were back to being friends; it was how it was with sisters, with twins. The flare of discord and the instant forgiveness.

'He said he was going to send a filthy telegram just so it had to be read out at your reception by one of Archie's Old Cliftonian pals. I told him not to, although it would have been funny.' Remy made out to unfurl a piece of paper and put on an affected voice. '*Darling Ashleigh, we were so glad to hear that you finally got the all-clear from the STD clinic and that the new in-laws never found out about the time you tied up their son and spanked—*'

'Ashleigh?'

'Oh!' She was aware that she'd shouted, as if the volume might erase any lingering echoes of her sister's inappropriate joke. 'Elaine! Everything okay?'

'Yes, thank you.' The woman, holding her generous gin and tonic aloft, her thin lips set, eyed her twin with suspicion. 'Just wondered if you knew where Archie was?'

'No! I really don't!' She smiled and spoke as sweetly as she was able. 'But if I had to guess, maybe playing golf, or in the pub, out with the dogs or catching up with old friends?'

'Are you quite all right, Ashleigh?' her mother-in-law-to-be asked without a hint of jest.

'I think maybe I'm a little tired and there's probably a bit of pre-wedding jitters setting in.'

'Right.' Elaine nodded and downed her gin. 'Well, I'll say to you what my mother said to me the night before my wedding.' Ashleigh waited with bated breath for the advice. 'Buckle up!'

She watched the woman turn on her heel and make her way back into the house.

'I'm scared of Elaine,' Remy whispered.

This too made her laugh out loud.

'We're all scared of Elaine,' she admitted. 'No one more so than Dickie!'

'I'd come over there and give you a big old hug if there wasn't the slightest chance that I might infect you.' Remy smiled at her.

'I'd like that,' she confessed. 'The hug, not the infection.'

'Can I ask you a question?'

'Course you can.' She sat back against the sun lounger and took a deep breath.

'Why now, after you've been together for *how* long?'

'Thirteen years, nearly fourteen.'

'That's what I'm saying, why after all this time? I thought you were happy with the vast engagement ring and the idea of marriage. You even named the business Fitch!'

Ashleigh looked at the huge diamond that she barely noticed anymore. 'It made sense. I knew I'd be a Fitch one day. The truthful answer is, I'm happy as we are, not that getting married won't be wonderful, it will! But I've been, I don't know, bit scared, I suppose.'

'Scared of what, Mrs Fitch?'

'It's hard for me to put into words, Mrs Hughes.' She gave a nervous laugh.

'Try.'

Ashleigh swallowed and kept her voice low. 'I want to be Mrs Archie Oxton Fitch. I want that more than anything.' She thought of the night of the ball when they'd been no more than kids, when he'd first told her that he loved her, and how she had dreamed of becoming his wife. 'I guess, I never thought it would require so much effort, or be so involved. I kind of wish it could just be Archie and me, somewhere quiet. Does that make sense?'

'Oh, it does, my love. It really does. It worked for us.'

'I get it now, Rem.' She smiled at her sister, with a mixture of admiration and envy. 'I love him. I can't wait to be his wife, to be *someone*.'

'You are someone, Ash! You've always been someone! Please don't ever put your happiness in the pocket of someone else! I mean, I love Midge, I adore him, but even I don't do that.'

'It's easier for you though, isn't it,' she ventured.

'What does that mean?' Remy stared at her.

'I mean, you don't have to live how I do.'

'How do you live? What are you talking about? And you haven't answered the question. What do you mean, that you're scared?'

Ashleigh took her time in responding, doing her best to get the wording just right. Glancing around to make sure they were alone.

'Scared because I spend a lot of my time waiting for discovery! Waiting for someone, Archie, Mum, Dad to find out that I didn't take the entrance exam, that it wasn't my scholarship, that it was yours, that I'm a fake!'

'Don't be so crazy! Surely you can't *still* think about that, not after all this time! You're not a fake, Ash, you're remarkable. You have your own business, you and Archie have that great big whacking expensive bloody house that you're renovating, you have a lovely, lovely life – you have it all!'

'Do you ever think we *should* tell people, come clean and not have to worry about it coming out?' It was, for Ashleigh, a conflicting thought, equal parts wonderful and terrifying. She dreaded the thought of it, yet guessed it would mean she no longer woke in the early hours in a cold sweat, having dreamed of discovery and banishment from her lovely, lovely life.

'No!' Remy almost shouted. 'I don't! That would be bonkers, like taking a massive sledgehammer and smashing up our lives! Can you imagine what it would do to Mum and Dad? It was a long, long time ago, it's dead, buried, and telling people would only *make* it a big deal! I've lied too, don't forget. Midge would find it hard that I've never told him, and he has enough on his plate right now.'

'What's he got on his plate?' Her sister's words worried her.

'Just life, Ash! Life without the safety net of in-laws with a cazillion quid in the bank and a big old country house you can escape to if the going gets tough!'

Her sister's words were as hurtful as they were dismissive. It had taken a lot for her to raise the topic, and yet Remy wouldn't even entertain the conversation. But it was her truth. She didn't want Archie marrying a fraud and was torn as to what to do about it, not wanting him to leave her because she was a liar, not ever, but also wanting there not to be any secrets between them. It was a paralysing and complex dilemma.

'There they are!'

Ruthie and Dennis made the interruption and came and sat next to them.

'Are you getting excited, love?' Ruthie beamed.

'A bit, Mum, yes.' She kept her nerves to herself, aware of how much her parents were loving the whole affair, especially staying here at Mulverton, which even had more spare bedrooms than Mrs Jenkins'.

'You should see the size of our room!' Her dad whistled. 'It's bigger than our lounge! Can't wait to go to bed and run around it! Plus, your mum's put a box of Maltesers in my suitcase. Reckon I'm all set.' He chuckled. 'I was going to save them, but it's my birthday coming up and so I'm bound to get more. Not that I like a fuss.'

She and Remy smiled at each other. It was nice, the way her parents did these lovely, small things for each other.

'Where's that wifey of mine?' She heard Archie's voice calling and recognised that his vowels were lubricated with alcohol.

'I'd better go and find him!' She didn't want her parents to see him sloshed, knowing he had a tendency to be a little open, enough to make even Remy's fake telegram seem tame. 'Back in a mo!'

'Ah, love's young dream!' Her mum clapped with delight.

Ashleigh made her way through the garden room, heading towards the kitchen, and there he was, her love, her fiancé. And just the sight of him . . . She ran and he rushed towards her, and they met somewhere in the middle. His grip on her was fierce, as he lifted her up and held her against him.

'Can we run away, just me and you? Let's go to Vegas and come back married!' he whispered into her hair.

'I wish we could' – she kissed him hard on the mouth – 'but your mother has ordered the flowers. And the string quartet is booked.'

'You've been my wife since the day I met you. I love you, Ashleigh, and I always will, for ever and ever and ever. And even that won't be long enough. I just love you! You're under my skin and inside my bones!'

He spun her around and she closed her eyes, happy! For the first time that day, *truly* happy, in his arms, his words lodged in her heart. Maybe Remy was right. Why would she take a massive sledgehammer and smash up their lives? Nothing else mattered, not taking an exam when she was a little girl, not her mother offering all and sundry a Mint Imperial, not even the wrong-coloured napkins.

Nothing.

Ashleigh Fitch and Remy Hughes

2002

Aged 40

Remy

'I can't be late!'

Remy hollered up the stairs as she hopped with one rolled-down Ugg boot on her left foot, before steadying herself on the console table in the hallway where her car keys and the unopened mail nestled.

Midge trudged down from the landing, and yawned with that smile on his face that irked and amused her in equal measure.

'What?' she asked, as she shoved her mass of curly hair up into a top knot and fastened it with the favoured hairband of the month, khaki, faux velvet, with just the right amount of give, not too tight when it lived on her wrist post eight at night, when she released her mane, peeled off her socks, shrugged off her bra and undid the top button on her baggy combat trousers.

'Nothing!' He raised both hands in submission. He walked past her into their narrow kitchen cum dining room, and she smiled. His T-shirt strained across his wide back, the residue of his summer tan still visible on his neck below his hairline. She felt the usual flare of attraction in the base of her gut for this man of hers. Thankful that after fourteen years married, he still had this effect on her.

'No, come on.' She scooted into the kitchen and poured her second or third cup of coffee. It was easy to lose count when she'd been up since five, and it was now seven thirty, the start of the day for some, but for her, practically mid-morning. It seemed to be the only way to get the laundry done, kitchen floor mopped, dishwasher unstacked and all the other jobs that, uncompleted, would be other worries to add to her already busy day. 'What was that look for, Royal?' She sipped the dark brew that was nectar in her veins, her get-go juice that fuelled her days.

'What look?' he asked through a mouthful of Frosties, some of which fell back into the bowl.

'Urgh, you eat like a toddler. Has anyone ever told you that?'

'You tell me that every time you watch me eat cereal and hotdogs.'

'Oh yes.' She pulled a face of disgust. 'I'd forgotten the hotdog thing, the licking of the sauce, the shoving of it in two bites into your mouth as if you're scared someone might take it away from you.'

'I can't help it, I LOVE hotdogs!' he yelled, spraying the countertop with Frostie fragments.

'I know you're doing it on purpose so I'm not going to rise to the bait.'

'Me mee me mememe mme mee me . . .' He did a vague impersonation of her rhythm in a high-pitched tone. This was standard, the ribbing, the humour, the way mates did in a pub over a pint, or the girls might over a long lunch when the vino had been flowing. She knew they were lucky. Good friends. It was the secret to their happy marriage. She still looked forward to seeing him when she arrived home, still shaved her legs, and popped on her silky knickers for a weekly romp with a bit of Norah Jones playing in the background. Despite the daily threat of fatigue, it was always a delightful moment of contact that bound them closer.

'You're not funny.'

'I think I'm a little bit funny.' He shovelled more cereal into his mouth. 'And if you really want to know, the *look* was because you shout it out every morning: *I can't be late!* As if by shouting it you're going to make it happen.'

'I think they call it manifesting.'

'Is that right?' he asked quizzically.

'Yep, apparently you put what you need or desire out into the universe and it comes to you.'

'Why has no one told me about this before? You mean there's me grafting my biscuits off since I left school and all I had to do was shout out what I wanted and it would be delivered, by some kind of cosmic postman?'

'Yes, that's exactly how it works.'

'Why are you wearing one boot?' He stared at her left foot in its pink-and-green striped sock.

'I can't find the other one.'

'Have you tried manifesting it?'

'No, and don't say, *where did you last have it?* because that drives me crazy, if I knew where I last had it, I'd go to that place, pick it up and put it on, wouldn't I?'

'I guess you would. Sassy-pants.'

She needed to get a wiggle on, could not be late for her shift. Remy worked in the call centre of a large insurance company, a customer service representative in their initial claims department. She hated it. Hated everything about it, but it was a job, it was a wage, and it was reliable. It also made up half of their household income and kept their heads above water, while allowing her to make small savings that would ensure after-school clubs, birthday presents, Christmas gifts, the odd takeaway, and a once-yearly purchase of fancy Uggs or similar, were all within reach. This job was no more than one of the necessary cogs that kept the wheels of their lovely life turning. Unlike Ashleigh or some of the corporate ladder climbers she worked with, her reward, her joy was to be found behind her front door. It had been this way since she'd had Sophie and had only been reinforced since she married Midge. It was enough, more than enough, *more* in fact than she'd ever hoped for!

She had never had a strong desire for material things, nor the ambition that seemed to drive her sister. The attack in her formative years and having a child when she was young had put things into perspective. She was happy to plod and leave the ball-breaking to people with more energy and inclination. People like Ashleigh. She liked forgetting about her job the moment she got into the car at the end of a long day.

Having gulped the last of her coffee, she shoved the small china mug in the sink, the one their six-year-old son, Bertie, had painted at a pottery café. On it, scrawled in a spider-like script, the words MUMMY IS A CU. His clumsy hand and poor spatial awareness meant he had run out of space. She hadn't known whether to laugh or cry as she'd unwrapped it last Mother's Day. Midge had known *exactly* what to do, and had to leave the room, lest he damage their young son's artistic confidence. She had heard him snorting his laughter in the lounge.

'Wowsers!' she'd yelled. 'That is . . . that is marvellous! I shall use it every day for my morning cup of coffee.' And she did.

Bertie had beamed.

'I was going to put Mummy is a curly head, because of your hair, but I ran out of space.'

Phew!

'Well, I love it, thank you, Bertie-bee.'

The hands on the kitchen clock seemed to be whizzing.

'Right.' She drew breath.

'Oh God, here we go.' Midge braced himself. 'I can't believe I've been out of the marines for ten years and I'm still getting orders barked at me daily by the domestic chief of staff!'

Remy ignored him, more concerned with making sure she didn't miss any of the detail, knowing her thoughts wouldn't settle until all of the information had been downloaded.

'Packed lunches are on the side.' She glanced towards the countertop, and there on the floor lay her missing Ugg, with a Barbie stuck in it, head first, her legs sticking up comically in the air. They both laughed. Having flung Barbie from her sheepskin nest, she shoved the boot on her foot without missing a beat. 'Harper's got cheerleading squad after school, so don't forget her kit when you pick her up; there are snacks in her bag, so she can have something before supper. Bertie is going to Max's for tea and pick-up is at six thirty. If you're running late, Mum said she'll go and get him. I've made a chicken casserole which you need to shove into the bottom oven, just before you leave to collect Harper, and I'll do the spuds when I get in. Postman, not cosmic, just regular, is bringing me the Next catalogue. Check in case he leaves the box outside; he's a bit of a moron. I think that's everything.' She drummed her fingers on the tabletop as her husband stared at her, his spoon midway between bowl and mouth, the milk-doused cereal now looking decidedly sodden. 'Oh! Shoot! Yes, I know what it was, I said you'd help Dad fit the outside tap near the new patio, but if you can't manage that today, tomorrow will do, or the weekend. Right, that really is everything.' She swooped forward and plonked a kiss on his cheek. 'Keys, bag, water, lip balm, banana.' She ran through the mental checklist before making her way into the hallway, and yelling up the stairs, 'Kids, I'm off! Dad's picking up, and he knows all about your stuff and snacks, and Nanny will get you from Max's, Bert, or maybe Daddy, but someone will! Have a great day and make good choices!'

'Bye!' Harper yelled from her room.

'Mummy?' Bertie called, in a measured way that paid no heed to her rising anxiety and the fact she was already cutting it fine.

'Yes, my love?' she replied, her tone curt.

'I can't find my, my . . .'

'No no no!' Midge appeared in the hallway. 'Let me guess.' He put his hands on his hips, as they both stared at their six-year-old, who stood in his pants with hair still mussed from sleep.

'Football kit?'

'Nope.' Bertie shook his head vigorously.

'Homework?'

'Nope.' He sighed.

'School shoes?' She willed him to get to the point. 'What have you lost, buddy?' She did her best to speed things along.

'I've lost Morty.'

'Can I leave this with you?' She wrinkled her nose at her husband.

'Yep, hamster location services are a big part of what I do now, when I'm not a taxi driver for the kids, acting as your parents' handyman, or getting involved in pom-pom club.'

'It's cheerleading squad!' Harper corrected, her voice coming down the stairs.

'I knew that,' he replied.

'I guess those are the perks of being self-employed – all that flexibility.'

'I still actually have to work though, Remy. I'm a mechanic, in case you'd forgotten, and all them cars aren't going to fix themselves.'

'I know, but you've got Lincoln to help you. He can hold the fort, can't he?'

'He'll bloody have to, won't he?'

'It's only for today, then I'm back to my usual shift from tomorrow onwards.'

'Remind me why you're doing earlies and a double shift, again?'

She held his eyeline; he knew full well. 'Because I work for a dickhead, and I don't want to lose my job.'

'Got it.' He nodded.

'Oh, and Sophie's coming home with us after her end-of-term show on Friday. She was thinking of going to Newquay with some of her friends, but instead she's got some shifts at the petrol station next week!' She clapped, delighted at the prospect, and happy Sophie had her head screwed on enough to know that earning money was more useful than a drunken weekend at the seaside. Plus, when Sophie was home, Remy slept differently, knowing her daughter was safe.

Oi! It was her worst nightmare, the thought of something bad happening to Sophie in the way it had her, knowing how it could alter the course of a life.

'Great.' Midge huffed. 'Well, that's my weekend viewing scuppered. I had it all planned. Six Nations on the Saturday and Sunday, with F1 qualifying early hours Saturday, although I don't know why I bother watching, Schumacher's pretty much got it sewn up with Ferrari – and now I'll have to wrestle a space on the sofa while you and Soph huddle under a bloody blanket and cry into tissues while Leonardo Di whatever his name is, floats away from a sodding door! It's not like you don't know it's going to happen, and yet still the tears!'

'You have no heart!' she yelled.

'And you have no taste when it comes to movies!' His counter-argument was predictable and weak. But my God she loved him, that was the simple truth of it. Theirs had not been the bumpy start for many who fell in love with someone who was already a parent. Quite the opposite: he saw the addition of Sophie as an absolute bonus and stuck to his belief that as long as he didn't try to be her dad – the girl already had one of those – they would be fine, and it had worked. More than worked; he adored the girl, and she him.

'Oh, and I meant to say, Jamie asked if he could come to her showcase.'

'Fantastic!' He gave a forced grin and a limp thumbs-up.

It was a delicate balancing act, allowing Jamie, who was still a sporadic figure in Sophie's life, enough access to preserve the father/daughter relationship, while doing her best to preserve her own marriage, as Midge, quite understandably, thought Jamie was a knob.

Midge leaned in the kitchen doorway and gave her an approving look, the way someone did when they liked what they saw. It made her feel good, sexy, and confident, a lovely boost, no matter that she sported messy hair and crumpled Uggs.

'Lamborghini!' he suddenly yelled.

'What the—?'

'A villa in Ibiza!' This time, louder, and she worried that Mr and Mrs Smith next door might bang on the wall. Again. 'A fridge that doesn't make that humming noise, and a hot tub in the back garden with a beer fridge by the side of it!' he screeched.

'What on earth are you doing?' She stared at the man, who was clearly having some kind of an episode.

'I'm manifesting.' He chuckled. The idiot. 'Go get 'em, tiger!' he called.

'I bloody love you.' She smiled, grabbing her bag, as she opened the front door.

'Come on, Dad! I can't go to school if I don't know where Morty is!' Bertie called down the stairs.

'Good luck.' She blew him a kiss. 'See you in a bit.'

'See you in a bit, Ren.' He smiled, as she made her escape.

Ashleigh

Ashleigh stood with her face turned up towards the shower, letting the hard jets pummel her skin and wash away the sweat of exercise. She liked this time in the morning. These few unallocated minutes when she had already achieved so much, a six-mile run, her suit for the day selected, blouse pressed, muesli consumed, and now a hot, restorative shower.

Running her fingers over the slippery wall of the wet room, there wasn't a day she regretted the upheaval, mess and huge expense of the building work that had created this incredible home. It still thrilled her, to arrive home after a long day and park on the gravel driveway, looking up at the Crittall windows and the soft honey-coloured lighting coming from within, knowing this was her house! She loved nothing more than giving her address:

'Oh, we're on Clarendon.'

'Clarendon? Oh, how lovely! Which one?'

It was a road with a certain reputation, as all the palatial houses were distinct and everyone in the locale knew which house was which.

'Erm, gosh, how best to describe, the one with the Crittall windows, the Crittall windows in grey beige, the one with the sandstone extension and the wrought-iron gates?'

She couldn't help herself. It made her feel good, gave her a feeling of self-satisfaction that she had lived without for the longest time. The success of her business, knowing just how to decorate their house, looking just right and spying the envy of those on the outside of her circle was enough to dilute the feelings of inadequacy that had dogged her for much of her life. There were still days, moments when the cold creep of imposter syndrome wrapped its tendrils around her and threatened to pull her down, but in the main, she had it under control.

Her shower pulsed and beeped, letting her know it was time to get out and dry off. One of her non-negotiables, a little bit of deserved luxury, a clean and fluffy white bath sheet, fresh every day. Marguerite knew to keep a ready supply.

She descended the sweeping stone staircase that allowed her kitten-heeled Choos to echo as she clip-clopped in a kind of dance down towards the entrance hall, taking a second to admire the vast glass chandelier that hung low over the black-and-cream tiled floor. This, a main feature of her home, based on the grand foyers of all the fabulous hotels they stayed in. Fran, her old flatmate, and one of her dearest friends since university, always joked that for a couple with their dream home, they sure did like spending time away from it! It was a reminder to call Fran; she hadn't seen her for months, or spoken to her, actually. It was wild how time flew.

She found Archie sitting at the kitchen island, a broadsheet covering his face. His oaky cologne filled the room and the signet ring on his little finger caught the light where the morning sun hit it.

'I left you a muesli pot on the side.'

'Yep.' He shook the newspaper. 'Thanks, but I had a croissant.'

Ashleigh felt the grip of irritation in her gut. 'Well, don't moan at me when you can't fasten your cummerbund next month if you're going to eat croissants!'

Her husband lowered his newspaper, revealing his handsome tanned face against the collar of his pale-pink Oxford.

'Jesus Christ! I'm allowed a bloody croissant if I feel like it.'

This was not how she liked to start the day.

'Of course you are, you're allowed to do and eat whatever you want. You're a grown-up. All I'm saying is that you can't have it both ways, getting angry when your clothes don't fit or your shirts gape and then choosing to eat shit.'

'How lucky I am to have you to keep me on the straight and narrow.' He took a sip of coffee.

She didn't have time to rise to his provocation, not today. Not any day. It was as tiresome as it was futile, this little rut of bickering then making amends that had been their routine for a while now. Making up was always spectacular. They'd go out for an expensive dinner, eat fantastic food, get drunk, dance barefoot in their palatial home when they returned, drink some more, smoke as if they were back at university sharing a cigarette out of her bedroom window, and not forty-year-olds with a grown-up life and responsibilities. They'd then have sex, good sex, on the sofa or by the pool, wherever they happened to be when the music stopped.

It kept the sniping at bay, for a while.

'Where's Evie?' She was yet to see her daughter, who liked to hide away, illegally watching cartoons before school.

'In the den.'

'Has she had her breakfast?' she asked as she pulled the green juice from the fridge and poured a small glass.

'Well, I hardly dare respond.' Her husband widened his eyes.

'You gave her a croissant!' She was sure he did this purely to irritate her.

'And jam!' he mouthed, and pretended to fall backwards off the leather barstool, clutching his hand over his heart.

'You can be such an arsehole.'

'So I've been told.' He clicked his tongue on the roof of his mouth and re-covered his face with the broadsheet.

A quick glance at the oversized clock above the shiny black Aga told her that Marguerite would be there any minute. Ashleigh didn't know what she'd do without her, the woman who bought and prepared their food, gave the house a quick once-over, reminded Evie to do her homework, and took care of them all. Marguerite was the fuel that ran the machine of their London home. Ashleigh had made it clear after Evie was born that she needed help if her life was to work.

'Help?' Archie had asked when she'd announced her plans to return to work as soon as she was able.

'Help! Yes! For when I go back to the office, which I want to do as soon as possible.' She had worked too hard to watch the business slip through her fingers now. Plus, Guy was counting on her.

'But, who's going to look after the baby?' She'd been a little taken aback by her husband's question, assuming he'd understood her need to get back into the swing of things, knowing *exactly* who he had married, and it wasn't a pinny-wearing homemaker.

'I don't know, Archie. You? Why don't you have a word with Hector and see if you can work from home or take her into the office with you?'

He had stared at her, the slow rise of his Adam's apple suggesting he wasn't entirely on board with the idea.

'Maybe help is a good idea,' he'd conceded.

It made her smile, even now, to think of Marguerite's rather unorthodox interview.

'So you'd be looking after Evie, as I'm going back to work in a few weeks.'

The woman had nodded. 'Yes.'

'Do you like babies?' Ashleigh had prompted, feeling her enthusiasm slipping away at the woman's rather no-nonsense attitude. She had hoped for someone like her mother or Remy, someone with that lovely, soft, maternal edge.

'I'm not sure, but I figure I don't have to like them to do a good job.'

Ashleigh had laughed out loud, uncertain if the woman was joking. It became a moot point almost immediately. Marguerite's face when she saw Evie for the first time was something she wouldn't forget, the wide smile, the sweet burbles of affection she lavished on her. She had hired her immediately and Marguerite had fallen in love with Evie, who loved her in return.

'I have a dinner tonight,' Archie informed her.

'Fine. To be honest, I've got such a day, I'll probably be fast asleep by the time you fall through the door.' She drained her glass and winced, unable to find a liking for this brand, but she'd persevere, a little obsessed with the whole idea of juicing and cleansing her gut.

'It's not a boozy one, strictly business with a complete bore. A partner in the Berlin office.'

'Won't he want beer? Isn't that what Germans drink?'

'I have no idea what Germans drink.' His hand appeared from behind *The Times* and reached for the mug of coffee. 'And actually, Ashleigh, I can't remember the last time you didn't have *such* a day, or, come to think of it, a night when you weren't fast asleep by the time I got home.'

It was true.

But today promised to be a stressful one, an early meeting in her Chiswick office with the rather fed-up owner of a 2.3 million-pound Edwardian villa on Hartington Road, who was fuming about a lack of progress on his house sale. The fact she had valued it at £1.5 million and the listed price was at his insistence was frustrating. It happened sometimes, when pure greed and not sound demonstrable property and land variables dictated the asking price. Ashleigh knew theirs was the third agent to take the property on, and while it looked good on her books, she knew it was a case of lowering the price or she'd be having these conversations with the fuming vendor on a regular basis. The thought alone was depressing. Having so far only dealt with his nervous wife, she wondered if it was worth the hassle. Maybe she'd tell Guy to pull the plug, tell him it was a case of 'new price' or 'adios' – yes, she'd get Guy to do it, depending on how their chat went this morning.

'You're right, Archie, there is always a meeting, and I'm always in a mad rush. I guess it's not my fault my business is so in demand that I'm permanently rushed off my feet!' She put her empty glass in the sink.

'Hmm, I don't think it's being in demand that's the problem.' He lowered his newspaper. 'In fact, I'm pretty sure if I came in and spent a day looking at your processes, your admin procedures, your—'

'I'll stop you right there.' Her husband might be a very fine management consultant, specialising in streamlining and re-financing inefficient businesses, but she would never, could never, let him get his hands on her mini empire. It was the one thing that was hers and hers alone. Her success, her validation. 'Guy and I have built this from the ground up.'

'I know. I was there when it was first suggested and have been there every day since!'

'Yes, but my point is, it runs how we like it, and it works, for us.'

'And *my* point is, people pay a hefty daily rate for my expertise, and I would do it for you, in exchange for no more than sexual favours and roast lamb on Sunday.'

'Think I'd rather pay your hefty daily rate,' she half-joked, and he again shook his newspaper before hiding behind it.

'Maybe I should go to Gigi directly? Isn't he the senior partner?' he goaded, and ducked as if she might lob something at him. He was not wrong. Sadly, with only her phone and a glass fruit bowl within reach, she had nothing to hand that wouldn't cause serious damage either to his head or the item.

'In name, yes, and only because we were advised to do it that way by our accountant because Guy's mother put up surety for the first loan. Which we paid back a while ago now,' she reminded him.

'I'm joking, of course. We all know you're the brains of the outfit.'

'Correct!'

She spoke with her hands on her hips and was not about to confess to her husband that she and Guy were a little worried about their pipeline. Sales were slowing, instructions taking longer to come on board, commission percentages were being whittled by penny-conscious vendors, and with the uncertainty of the world economy, people were, it seemed, a little reticent about rushing into huge mortgages or upsizing when neither jobs nor financial stability was guaranteed. They'd figure it out. They always did.

'Better dash. See you later.'

She grabbed the gold knot earrings from the mother-of-pearl trinket dish next to the oversized orchid on the counter and put them into her ears, tucking her neat, straight, blonde hair behind her ears. Hair that she kept in check via her permanent hair-straightening treatment that set her back a small fortune every six months to fix any curly regrowth. It was, in her book, worth every penny to rid herself of those darned ringlet curls that had been the bane of her younger life.

Popping her sleek head into the den, she found six-year-old Evie lying recumbent on a vast leather beanbag, still in her soft pink pyjamas. The girl was indeed transfixed by a loud, flashing animation of high-kicking ninjas, whose saccharine-sweet, squeaky voices were akin to nails on a chalkboard. For Ashleigh, at least.

'Mummy's leaving, darling.'

''Kay.' She didn't look up from the screen.

'Marguerite will be here any second and Daddy's in the kitchen.'

'Yep.' Evie inserted her index finger into her nose. Ashleigh looked away.

It was another ritual that felt a little pointless, her explaining to her daughter every morning when she was leaving, where everyone was, as the child seemed to pay her no attention. A throwback no doubt to her own childhood, when it had always felt important to Ashleigh to know these things. Although, in fairness, in her parents' small home she had always known where everyone was as she could either see or hear them, but still.

'I shall try and be home before supper, and we can have a chat then. How does that sound?'

'Good.' Evie laughed then, not at her, but at one of the high-kicking ninjas who had fallen on his bottom with an accompanying wail of distress that made her ears ring.

She left her to it, unsure what to say next, what to do next, aware of the invisible barrier that made her hold back and which had always been there. It was her secret shame. And it wasn't that she didn't love the child, she did, would *die* for her! But that didn't mean she was comfortable with her or knew how to be one of those mums who grabbed their kids and wrapped them in love.

'Morning!' Marguerite hung her coat on the stand in the vestibule, removed her book from the pocket, and slipped out of her Ugg boots, which she paired and placed by the front door. *Revolting, sloppy things*, Ashleigh thought, and knew she wouldn't be seen dead in them.

'Morning, Marguerite. What are you reading?'

'*The Lovely Bones*, by Alice Sebold.' Their housekeeper held up the pale-blue cover.

'Ooh, what's it about? I don't have time to read, so I have to live my reading life vicariously through you!' There was the undeniable throb of sadness in her breast at this truth.

'It's about a girl who has been raped and murdered and she watches her friends and family from heaven and sees what happens next. It's beautiful.'

'Oh!' It wasn't quite what she had expected. 'It sounds . . . anyway, only Evie for supper. Archie is out for dinner, and I'll probably just grab some crackers or whatever's in the fridge.'

It was partly how she kept trim, not sitting down for big meals. It also meant less time wasted when she could be catching up on work admin.

'Okay.' Marguerite smiled. 'Have a lovely day.'

'Yep, she's in the den, watching that awful cartoon. She's had a croissant.'

'I'll turn it off.' The woman spoke matter-of-factly and without the guilt that would have made the task almost impossible for Ashleigh. 'She needs to read to me before we go to school.'

'Right.' Ashleigh nodded and swallowed the uncomfortable lump at the base of her throat.

It had been easy for her to conceive, she'd had a dream pregnancy and the birth was straightforward. Her heart lurched for all those she read about or knew personally who struggled with all three. What she could never confess was that the conception, pregnancy, and birth had actually been the easy bits. It was all the stuff that came after she struggled with, caring for and spending time with a child she had nothing in common with. It was a mystery to her, how at ease Remy was with all three of her kids. Ashleigh knew she didn't fare well in comparison to her sister, the brilliant homemaker. The one doctor she had confided in had told her that it would happen in time; the bonding, the love, the emotional investment.

Well, her little girl was now six years old, and she was still waiting.

What she *hadn't* told the doctor was that as for so many aspects of her life, she just didn't feel like she deserved to be a mum to a fabulous kid like Evie, and there it was, that tingling in her limbs and a feeling of being so overwhelmed, she thought she might topple.

Remy

Remy made the mistake of answering the call from her mother as she pulled into the business park.

'Remy, are you there, love?'

'Yes, sorry, was just parking the car.' She locked her Vauxhall Corsa and shoved the keys in her handbag, staring at the building, knowing she had eight minutes to get inside and log on, her Nokia now resting under her chin.

'It's me, it's Mum.'

'Yep, I've told you before, Mum, your name comes up, so before I even answer I know it's you!'

'Yes, that's right. Anyway . . .' Her mum began to talk so slowly that Remy felt her blood speed up in her veins. She needed to get to her chair and get that computer fired up. '. . . So, do you remember I told you last week about the newspaper going astray? Well, it turns out that the lad who delivers it has been dropping it at Mrs McFarland's. I asked her if he had, but she shook her head and trundled indoors, but I said to your dad, Mrs McFarland only usually has *The People's Friend* and her hands had looked suspiciously full as I chatted to her—'

She cut her mother short. 'Mum, I don't want to be rude, but I have to go inside and start my shift. Is everything okay? I told Midge about the outside tap.' She tried to pre-empt the reason for the call with the sole purpose of hurrying things along. 'He'll either get to it today or tomorrow or the weekend and he'll let you know later about picking Bertie up.'

'Oh, smashing! Just a sec.' She heard her mum shout out, 'Dennis! *Dennis!* It's Remy on the phone. Midge is going to do the tap today or tomorrow or the weekend . . .' There was a silent pause. 'Hang on, I'll ask her.' Remy felt her jaw tense. 'Your dad says does he have the washers or should he pick some up? He's happy to go to B&Q. He's got a discount card. He quite likes going and having a gander at the concrete.'

Remy did her best to stay calm. 'Erm, not sure. Get Dad to call Midge and ask him.'

'Righto.' Again her mother pulled away from the phone and shouted out: 'She says call Midge and ask him about the washers!'

'Mum!' she yelled, aware that she was in a car park and that people were coming and going. 'I need to go in.'

'Of course, Remy, I don't want to keep you. Reason for the call is that you know it's your dad's birthday on Sunday.'

'I do.'

'Well, he's asked if we can all go for lunch on Saturday at The Plough. You know he doesn't like a fuss.'

Doesn't like a fuss apart from a grand outing to the pub en masse for lunch and then a fancy cake and singing with a few pressies thrown in for good measure . . .

'Lovely. Yes, of course, I'll book it. It's great timing, because Sophie's home. I was going to get him a voucher for the garden centre and some chocolate, of course.'

His fondness for Maltesers was legendary.

'Wonderful, and I'll let you know for how many once I've spoken to your sister.'

Remy rolled her eyes. Of course everything would hinge on what Ashleigh said and did. She loved her sister, but it bothered her, how she stayed away and yet was presented with the crown every time she graced them with her presence. She and Midge worked their butts off to keep her parents happy, always on call, always in demand. It was conflicting, she wouldn't have it any other way, but she wanted some recognition just once in a while.

'Doubt she'll come down for a lunch at The Plough, birthday or not.'

'Don't be like that, it doesn't suit you. I've told you before you've got no reason to be jealous of her.'

'Mum!' The accusation stung as much today as it ever had and spoke volumes about how her parents measured success. 'I am not jealous of her, not even a little bit!'

'If you say so, love.' This was her mother's irritating way of dismissing her truth. Remy felt the flame of frustration lick her skin. It was a worn topic that she had neither the time nor inclination to revisit. Remy wasn't jealous of anyone, it wasn't in her nature; besides, she had everything she had ever wanted and more, a lovely, lovely life, happy to be with her husband and kids in their little bubble. 'I'll let you know what she says.'

'Smashing!' she offered with false enthusiasm, wondering how to break it to Midge that not only did he have the joy of spending time with Jamie at Sophie's end-of-term fashion show this Friday, but now he'd also be required to be civil to her sister and her husband, who he'd recently nicknamed 'Posh and Specs'. Not that her brother-in-law wore glasses, but rather on account of the fact that he wore such garish shirts, mustard-coloured cords and braces, making him look like a '*right old spectacle*'. It was mean, she knew, but still made her laugh.

'Have a lovely day, little dove!' Her mum, it seemed, was happy for her enthusiasm, false or not.

Rushing in, Remy bent awkwardly low and presented the pass around her neck to the turnstile entry, which beeped its approval, then waved to the security guard on reception, who always smiled, and raced across the foyer and up the stairs, scooting across the industrial royal-blue carpet and landing on her chair, earphones on, mouthpiece in position and computer logged on, all in the nick of time.

'By the skin of your teeth, Remy Hughes.'

She dug deep and found a smile. Graham, her supervisor, had worked with her for the last five years, and had vaulted the hallowed line from colleague to boss with more self-satisfaction than if he'd climbed Everest, smashed a record, won gold at the Olympics or cured world famine. Clearly, he was a man delighted by the perks of his junior managerial role; his very own allocated parking space, access to the early-bird insurance offers for family and friends, an annual invite to the manager's Christmas dinner buffet that was held in a roped-off corner of the vast dining hall, and crucially, the right to stroll, hands behind his back, as he was wont to do, around the desks, paying particular attention to . . . everything!

His manner bothered her, bothered them all, not that there was much she could do about it. Midge had suggested she talk to HR, and she'd laughed at the thought.

'And say what? *You know Graham, who seems not to have a home to go to? The one who arrives early and leaves late, who makes sure I am at work on time and adhere to my breaks and that my call times are efficient? The one who's always there with the right answer to any query, based on his extensive and detailed knowledge of our policies? Yes, him, well, is there anything we can do about his revolting cardigans and his tone that borders on nasal?*'

'You raise a good point,' her husband had conceded. 'Do you want me to punch him?'

She had sprayed her laughter over him. 'You can't do that in the workplace anymore. It's a little frowned upon. There are rules.'

'*What?*' he'd scoffed. 'Next you'll be telling me I can't send the kids up the chimney and that women can have the same pay as men! Where will it end?'

'Yep.' She gave Graham a weak double thumbs-up and placed her banana on the table, next to her water bottle.

'Remember, no unsealed drink units on desks.' He pointed towards her water.

'It is sealed, Graham. As you can see, it's a bottle with the lid firmly attached.'

'No harm in reminding you.' He fastened his hands behind his back, and she wondered if Midge's offer was still on the table.

Tyler caught her eye and raised his eyebrows and lifted his chin in greeting without missing a beat of his call. Tyler, who wore a shirt and tie even though there was no formal requirement to do so. Tyler, who kept pens in his top pocket for just in case and jumped to life when a call came in. Tyler, whose stats were impressive, the highest customer satisfaction score, the most calls taken and the winner of every bonus and incentive going. To her certain knowledge he had enjoyed a golfing weekend, a giant Easter egg, and a couples massage at the local sports centre. He was what Tony would have described as *a right keener* back in the day. This thought alone was enough to make her smile and dilute the irritation of Graham's lingering presence. It was some small comfort that even though her lovely friend was on the other side of the world, he could still lift her mood. It was nice to think back to those days, when she and Tony had danced and laughed and sung until their throats were hoarse. Before that night.

Oi! Still she heard this call at the most random of times, and still it was a gunshot and about as terrifying. That night when she had known the true meaning of fear, the very worst of times, and the very best too, because she had met Midge.

She wished Tyler would stop shouting. Yet to take a call, his energy made her somehow weary.

'Now let's see what we can do about *that*, Mrs Williams!' He grinned.

He was *so* loud, almost as if this job were a performance and he was desperate to guarantee that even those in the cheap seats at the back could hear every word. She liked to study him over the privacy board that offered none. It sat between the two rows of facing desks like the Berlin Wall, only it was thinner, smaller, and upholstered with cheap, grey, hairy fabric.

The call centre operated two shifts, meaning customers could get help or at least vent into a willing ear from eight in the morning until ten at night. She wasn't sure who occupied her seat when she was off but had arrived one morning eight weeks ago to find a large, wonky penis scrawled on the privacy board. The cleaner had tried to remove it with a soft cloth and detergent but had only succeeding in smudging the balls a little. Despite no doubt tackling the tackle with the very best of intentions, the smudging had somehow made it worse. As if the neat, narrow lines of the phallus might have been ignored, but this distorted, faded, obvious and crude art demanded attention whenever she approached the desk.

'I would like to apologise, Remy Hughes, for you having to look at that.' Graham had visibly coloured.

'Oh, no worries.' She had smiled, deciding not to share that Midge had a fondness for similar artwork on any icy surface, a snow-covered window, anything steamed up, or if the kids left a pen within three feet of an envelope. 'It can't be that hard to find out who drew it, can it? I mean, who was sitting at the desk, or who was sitting next to them? Don't we have CCTV?'

'I'm afraid it's not that straightforward.' Graham had pushed his glasses up on to his nose. 'They were agency staff, temps, and I don't think they're coming back again. They drew a similar image on the bathroom wall and wrote something unsavoury about Melanie in marketing.'

'What did they say about Melanie in marketing?' She was curious. The girl was lovely and wore a short top that showed off the diamanté dangler in her naval, she laughed at whatever anyone said to her, whether with nerves or in genuine bemusement, it was hard to tell, but she was lovely nonetheless.

'It wasn't very nice.' Graham blushed.

'What was it?' Her curiosity knew no bounds.

Graham had sighed and looked to his left and right, as if checking the coast was clear.

'It said something like, Melanie the minx and her most marvellous melons.'

Remy guessed it was not *something like* but was in fact entirely accurate in his recollection. The banal, sexist, juvenile wording was obviously disappointing, and yet she was quietly impressed by the half-decent alliteration. It was conflicting.

'Nothing amusing or clever about reducing a woman to the sum parts of her body.'

Remy had stared at the team leader for her section and given him a warm smile.

'You're absolutely right, Graham.' It was a nice moment when his irritating flaws were diluted by his clear sense of indignance.

Her headset beeped to indicate a call was coming in and her computer screen automatically brightened. She glanced at the timer in the corner of her screen. It popped up automatically when a call was answered and ticked second by second in a grassy-green digital display. The colour chosen presumably to remind her of nature, of life outside this vast square building where the grass grew while she toiled. After three minutes, the green changed to a rather muddy orange and after seven minutes it became bright red, reminding her of failure, of blood, of emergency and the fact that Graham would see a red mist if she couldn't keep her call times down.

Speedy!

Helpful!

Interested!

Timely!

This was one of Graham's motivational initiatives that had been plastered all over the kitchenette areas and in the lifts. She had roared her laughter, yet chose not to disclose the unfortunate mnemonic, delighting in seeing it every time she made a scalding cup of tea or waited for her floor. It seemed someone else had chosen not to remain so tight-lipped, as the posters were removed as quickly as they had appeared.

It still made her chuckle to think of it.

'Good morning. Thank you for calling Castle Care, you are through to Remy. How can I help you today?'

And just like that she was out of the blocks.

Ashleigh

'Come on, parking fairy!' Ashleigh banged the leather-covered steering wheel of her shiny Land Rover. 'Just one measly space! Just one! Please!'

She hated that often the most stressful part of her day was finding somewhere to park her fat-bummed car. Having driven up and down the streets at a snail's pace, hoping, praying, and doing her best to manifest a spot, she spied a man wearing a red-and-blue striped beanie hat sitting in the driver's seat of a shiny Mercedes. Whether with the intention of moving or having just arrived, it was impossible to tell. Either way, her heart lifted with joy at the prospect of getting this lucky.

'Ooh, are you going?' she mouthed, pointing at his car and then the road ahead. He stared at her through the window and ignored her. 'Are you going?' She shouted this time, as if he might be able to hear over the hum of traffic, the beep of horns, the roar of engines and through the two sturdy panes of glass that separated them. 'For the love of Jesus, ARE YOU LEAVING?' she roared, and knocked on her window with her knuckles. The man wound down his window and shook his head, before looking down at his phone. 'Beanie-wearing dickhead!' she yelled.

This was what London had reduced her to, hating and abusing a stranger who was doing no more than going about his business, and yet was on the receiving end of her sharp tongue as her adrenaline surged, her muscles bunched and her irritation flared, all because she could not park her massive car. She hated how ugly she had sounded, acted. It was, she knew, a result of how stressed she was about the business. It wasn't that they were against the wall, nothing like that, but still it was a worry, this drought. Gallow and Fitch was her thing, how she measured her success, and she could not imagine a life without it.

With her phone resting under her chin, she punched a call to Guy, as she did at sporadic points throughout her day; he was a big part of her routine. In a traffic jam, bored at lunch, waiting for clients to show up to a viewing, she called Guy. Wanting to share something funny or irritating, she called Guy. Theirs was an easy and comfortable friendship. It was much to her relief that any fleeting embarrassment over his admission of love had been just that, fleeting, and they had thankfully put it behind them the minute they returned to London.

She started speaking the moment he answered.

'Can't park the bloody car!'

'Good morning to you too.'

'We've got Mr Whatshisname coming in about the Hartington house,' she reminded.

'I'm well aware. Clara has the coffee machine primed and we even have croissants.'

'Don't you start with sodding croissants.' She shook her head and stopped her car, eyeing a space that she knew was at least two feet too short, but that didn't stop her staring at it, wishing that the cars either side had only shifted up and down a bit.

'Am I to assume that you didn't get out of bed on the sunny side of the street this morning?'

'I just need to park the car! There's not a single space!' she boomed.

'Well, thank goodness you called me, as I can make that happen from here in the office. Just a second while I grab my magic wand.'

'Why is it always when I'm in a hurry!' she whined.

'There's never a parking space. Difference is, when you're not in a hurry you care a little bit less.'

'You might be right.' This was what her friend did, offered the voice of reason, calmed her with his logic. It was mollifying and maddening in equal measure. She didn't know how his wife, Ada, put up with it. Ada, who had snared the former self-proclaimed lifelong bachelor and was about to give birth to their first child. Ada who didn't work outside the home, liked pretty things, and cooked from scratch for the husband she adored. It was strange for Ashleigh that Guy's wife was not one of her friends, not one of their gang or someone who had been introduced, a friend of a friend of a friend. She was instead an unknown who Guy had fallen for hard and fast. Ashleigh would have to admit to feeling the tiniest bit of trepidation when he'd announced he was getting married, not wanting their relationship to change.

'Doesn't she get bored, Gigi?' she'd asked Guy when he'd announced that his wife-to-be would more than likely be staying at home to look after the house, the kid they planned for, and the Dachshund called Ben they doted on. The Dachshund called Ben with his own wardrobe that included a tiny Sherlock Holmes coat, deerstalker, and pipe. Nuff said.

'No, or tired.' He'd let this hang, and she'd felt the weight of exhaustion on her bones, having spent the day rushing from appointment to appointment in heels more appropriate for sitting; her head throbbed, and she needed a shower.

'Huh!' She'd given a wry laugh, wishing for a brief moment that she could be more Ada.

'And while we're on the subject . . .'

What subject? She had been a little confused by his segue.

'Ada would prefer it if you didn't call me Gigi. She doesn't like the name, not for me, because, because . . .' He sounded nervous and very much like he was reciting practised lines.

'Because what?' she prompted, wondering what else Ada didn't like.

'She says it's exclusionary, of a time and place when she wasn't there.'

'But she wasn't there!' Ashleigh had pointed out the obvious, wondering what Archie would make of *this*.

'Exactly.'

'But it's your school nickname, long before uni, before me.'

'Ash.' The way he said her name sounded very much like the old Guy, like Gigi, who was sweet and funny and not so stressed he tied himself in knots trying to please his rather demanding wife. 'Please.'

Her heart lurched for him. He sounded under pressure and the last thing she wanted was to add to that.

'What about if I just don't call you it in front of Ada? Would that work?'

'Yes,' he sighed. 'That would work.'

And they had shared a rare, lingering look, as if both mentally acknowledging that it wasn't the only thing they wouldn't mention to Ada.

The car behind beeped and she moved forward with a small wave of acknowledgement in the rear-view mirror.

'Anyway, just thought I'd let you know, I'll be there as soon as I can. Keep Mr Doodah happy.'

'Oh, don't worry. I have many more magic tricks to show him. This wand does lots of things.' Guy snorted.

'Could you magic me to the Seychelles just for a day, or maybe two, or three, I just want to sit in the sun, and for someone to bring me lovely things to eat and drink.'

'Looking at our current account, I'd say a day in Margate might be more budget appropriate.'

'Spoilsport.' She tutted. 'Should I be worried, Guy?' She closed her eyes briefly, hating to mention the concern that she knew would dog him too.

'No more than usual.' He made a tsking sound. 'But go back to the Seychelles, a much nicer place for your thoughts to rest.'

The memory of her perfect honeymoon was enough for her to feel warmth on her skin.

It had been bliss – perfection! The country wedding of her dreams at her in-laws' house, everything she had wanted and more. Little Sophie, who at one point in the proceedings seemed like she might miss the whole ceremony due to a sickness bug, had been the happiest of bridesmaids! Her parents had of course loved every second of her special day.

This, followed by two whole weeks of sleeping when the mood took them, eating such delicious fresh food that she still yearned for it, and lots of lovely sex . . . Sex that had meant she returned with more than tan lines and sand between her toes, as Evie had, without invitation, taken up residence in her womb.

It wasn't something she had planned, far from it, and it wasn't only the timing that had thrown her a little. They had barely finished the house renovations, and she had wanted to enjoy the post-wedding glow, to revel in the perfection of that wonderful day! *A baby* . . . she had laughed in public and cried in private at the news. Archie had been beside himself with joy, which proved to be the driver in her own acceptance. Of course, she wasn't getting any younger, and hearing the thrilled reaction of her mum and dad and Elaine and Dickie, she'd got rather wrapped up in the whole circus, but a *baby* . . . a whole event in itself that required a huge mental adjustment. Truth was, she was still trying to catch up.

Thinking about their glorious trip made her wish she hadn't snapped at Archie earlier. It was, after all, only a croissant. She had been trying to help, wanting him to live a long and healthy life so they could grow old together and do all the things they had been planning since university; to go to Nepal, charter a mega yacht, buy a seaside home, take a classic car to drive along the Côte d'Azur, where they would walk among the lavender fields of Provence and stop for lunch in Cannes. All of it, right there on their wish list for that time when things slowed down.

He might know how to push her buttons, but he was still that boy she had met at university who had danced at the ball with his tie around his head. A handsome boy who had been mad for her, smothering her with love and wrapping her in promises that anyone would have found hard to resist.

You are under my skin and inside my bones . . .

She decided to call and leave him a message by way of apology, knowing it would do the trick . . .

'Just park and get your arse in here. No one likes to hear you feeling sorry for yourself, Brett.'

Guy's words made her smile; the small and meaningful connection that spoke of their history. He was, after all, the reason she had met Archie, shaping her future, all of their futures.

'He's loaded!' Guy had whispered to her out of the corner of his mouth when he had caught her eyeing up the handsome blond with the big laugh and big personality. 'Archibald Oxton Fitch, absolutely loaded!'

'I don't care about things like that,' she'd fired back, but on reflection, she knew she had cared, a little bit. That kind of wealth was a ticket to the life she had always dreamed of. A life she had glimpsed at St. Jude's, where, unlike her, most of the kids didn't have to worry about the next instalment of their scholarship being paid on time, as their parents could simply write a cheque for the large sums that bought membership. Her membership was won, although not by her, a stolen prize. She shivered now at the thought.

The car behind beeped again, this time a long-drawn-out toot, intended, she was sure, to intimidate, hurry her along and make her blood boil. It achieved all three and she put her foot down, making her way out of the road and heading for Sainsbury's, where she could park and leg it all the way back to the office. It was inconvenient, a hassle, and she would no doubt arrive late for her meeting looking like a sweaty mess, but at this point there was little she could do about it. The most frustrating thing was that her next mid-morning appointment would mean haring it back to the car and heading off to the viewing the minute Mr Hartington Road had left.

'Shit!' She hit the steering wheel for the second time that morning as she turned out on to the main road and hit the nose-to-tail traffic. A call came through and she grabbed the phone from the front seat and again tucked it under her chin.

'Hello, love. It's me, it's Mum.'

'Yep, I've told you before, Mum, your name comes up, so before I even answer I know it's you!'

'Yes, that's right, anyway . . .' Her mum began to talk so slowly that Ashleigh felt her blood speed up in her veins. She needed to get to the office, familiarise herself with the property on Hartington and get her ducks in a row before she faced Mr Greedy. Fat chance of that now she was crawling along, going nowhere fast. 'I've just got off the phone with your sister, and she's going to book it up.'

'Book *what* up, Mum?' She jumped in, finding her mother's rambling lack of specifics more than a little irritating.

'Oh!' Ruthie laughed. 'The Plough for your dad's birthday. You know he doesn't want any fuss, but he'd like us all to go out for lunch.'

Ashleigh smiled, remembering the time there had been a mix-up on the buying of the birthday cake and they'd found themselves without his favoured chocolate gateaux, and at the eleventh hour had been forced to sing 'Happy Birthday' while her mum held up a mini roll on a saucer with a single candle in it. He'd been stroppy, to say the least, fed up even, for one who cared so little about fuss.

'Right.' She looked skyward, trying to remember the excuse she'd given last time to avoid schlepping all the way back to Salisbury to spend a few hours in the pub and then having to schlep all the way back to London. She loved her family, loved them dearly, but trips home felt like such a faff when there was always so much to do around the house, and the prospect of mustering Evie and coercing Archie to come along, and the fact that her job took up so much of her time and thoughts . . . Besides, it was only six weeks until her and her sister's birthday when attendance was mandatory, couldn't she just give him his birthday present then? She and Remy only spoke occasionally; it was just how it was. There had been no great fallout, no animosity, nothing so marked. It was more a quiet separation as they pursued different lives in different parts of the country, a natural easing of the ties that bound. Even for twins.

She made a mental note to call her dad on his special day, get a gift, send it over. 'What day is his birthday?'

'It's on Sunday.'

'Course it is! Ah, that's a shame, Mum. I'm afraid we can't make Sunday. Evie has a match, and then a classmate's birthday party that I've already replied to, and Archie has got a work thing. I'm gutted because we are free on *Saturday*, nothing in the diary, but Sunday is tricky.' She pulled a face, knowing she was going to hell.

'Oh well, that's wonderful. I was just about to say that his birthday is on Sunday, but we're going on Saturday, so I'll let your sister know. That's so great, little dove. I know your dad will be over the moon!'

Her mouth moved, but she couldn't think of a way out of it, having already stitched herself up like a kipper.

'Brilliant.' She closed her eyes briefly. Already trying to think of how to sell it to Archie, who had never been that enamoured with Midge, who was, he felt, a little rough around the edges.

'It'll be lovely for the kids to spend some time together.'

'Yep.' She took a deep breath, trying and failing to feel enthusiasm for the whole event that meant a four-hour round trip *if* the roads were kind. And the thought of Evie spending time with Bertie, who might be the same age, but was – how to phrase it politely? – dancing to his own tune, and Harper, who just seemed moody . . .

'Hang on a mo.' Ashleigh heard her mother pull away from the phone, briefly. 'She's coming! I told you she would.' Her joyful tone was enough to swamp her with guilt. 'You on your way to work?'

'Yes, well, trying to. I can't find anywhere to park.'

Her mum laughed loudly. 'You funny little thing. Can't find anywhere to park in that big city! Why don't you pop the car in one of the side roads near your office?'

Now why didn't I think of that? Her mum's lack of understanding of what life in the crowded capital could be like was both endearing and frustrating.

'That's a good idea.' She sat back in the seat and took another deep breath.

'Speak soon, darling.'

'Yep, speak soon.'

It always had a strange effect on her, hearing her mother's voice, a reminder of that slower, simpler life that meant time for cups of tea, popping in and out, and even meeting for pub lunches in town. A life that hadn't felt like hers for the longest time, not since she'd taken up her place at St. Jude's, when she'd had to adapt to fit in. The trouble was, and what she hadn't banked on, was that changing shape to fit into her new life at school had meant she no longer quite fitted in at home.

Already late, she abandoned the car in Sainsbury's car park and ran as fast as her Choos would allow her, all the way to the office, arriving with a red face, hair that was less than pristine, the desire for a shower, aching feet, and horribly squished toes.

Guy, she could see, was leaning forward at his desk, talking earnestly to the man in the chair in front of him. The man who owned the big house on Hartington Road. The man who had quibbled over the asking price. The man who drove a shiny Mercedes. The man who wore a striped red-and-blue beanie hat.

Shit! Her mouth felt sticky with nerves, and she cursed her quick-tempered and terrible reaction to the man earlier.

'Here she is.' Guy stood to introduce her.

The man turned to face her, his deadpan expression filling her with relief – he didn't recognise her! *Phew!*

'I am so sorry for my lateness, the traffic is foul! Absolutely foul! I'm Ashleigh, Ashleigh Fitch, Guy's business partner.'

The man stood and reached for her outstretched hand, shaking it gently.

'I'm the beanie-wearing dickhead.' He stared at her. '*Mr* beanie-wearing dickhead.'

Guy shot her a look that spoke of his confusion. Her blood ran cold.

Not for the first time that day, Ashleigh felt a little lost for words and a little stitched up like a kipper . . . although this time, she had no one to blame but herself, as it had been her who was holding the needle.

Remy

Remy pulled the car on to the narrow drive behind Midge's van and ratcheted up the hand brake. It seemed that every light in their new-build house was on, and she smiled, imagining what her dad would say: 'Looks like Blackpool bloody Illuminations! What are you, made of money?' This would no doubt be followed by his detailed observations on the concrete that made up their driveway and the general construction of their home. It was his obsession.

He had been on first-name terms with the team who had laid the foundations and screeded the driveway, watching the house rise in a matter of weeks, keen to tell anyone who would listen that this was his daughter's plot, waiting for them on the pavement like a proud father, to smile, nod and thank them for a job well done. He'd been a little devastated when they finally moved in and the team moved on. It made her smile even now.

How she loved this moment in her day, knowing her family, bar Sophie of course, were all safe and sound inside, feeling smug at having completed her double shift with satisfied tiredness clinging to her limbs, keen to walk into the chaos and hear about everyone's day.

Her phone flashed with a message from her mother.

YOUR SISTER IS COMING TO DAD'S BIRTHDAY! ISN'T THAT WONDERFUL!

She sighed, again trying to fathom how she and Midge ran around after her parents day after day without thanks or acknowledgement, and yet news of her sister setting foot in the county and her mum went into raptures. Almost as if the novelty of Ashleigh and the fact she was preoccupied with her London life made any visit doubly precious. Maybe it was; maybe Remy needed to be a bit kinder, a bit more understanding.

GREAT! she replied.

No sooner had she put her key in the door than the cacophony assaulted her ears. Either Harper had McFly over for tea or was playing their music loudly in her bedroom. Remy didn't mind, knowing if the lads were here they could easily make room at the table, grab the spare chair from the landing; some would have to stand, of course, or eat in the lounge on their laps, but they seemed like nice enough lads who wouldn't mind.

Midge was in the kitchen.

'Please, kids, put your school stuff away and tidy the mess up in the lounge. We don't want Mum to come back and think we've been burgled.'

'Too late!' she called in response.

'Mummy!' Bertie ran from the kitchen and threw his arms around her waist. She inhaled the scent of her boy, who was a little stinky – he often smelled like a dirty straw after haring around all day, in a way that her daughter never did.

'You need a shower, baby boy.'

'I had one yesterday!' he responded without a whiff of irony.

'Yep, that's how it works: you have to have one every day. Did you have a nice time at Max's?'

'It was okay. They've got a cinema room.' He sounded impressed, and she had to admit, it sounded fancy. 'But his mum made garlic bread and she put *cheese* on it!'

'Oh no! That's awful! What is *wrong* with her?' She liked to match the drama. 'What did you do?'

'I said I didn't like cheese, and she said scrape it off, but it was stringy, and I didn't want it on my fingers, so I left it.'

'I'm sure Max's mummy won't mind.'

'We had Haribo for pudding, so that was good.' His eyes sparkled with delight, and she suspected a healthy smack of sugar coursing through his veins.

'Lucky you. I hope you said thank you for having you.'

'I did.'

'Good.' He was a lovely kid, polite and chatty. Her heart swelled to be this close to him.

'You'll never guess where we found Morty this morning?'

'In Max's cinema room?'

'No!' He laughed.

'In the bath?' She kissed his forehead and ruffled his hair.

'Nope!'

'In the fridge?'

'No!'

'Erm.' She sat on the bottom stair and pulled off her Uggs and socks, wiggling her bare feet on the cool laminate flooring, which felt quite blissful. 'In your school bag?'

'Mum! Come on, guess!' His skinny legs danced on the floor with impatience.

'I *am* guessing!'

Midge appeared behind their son, a tea towel slung over his shoulder, as he drew a circle with his finger; she was grateful for the clue.

'In the washing machine?' She gasped, that could have ended very differently.

'He was inside my football, the one with the hole in it. He'd eaten the hole bigger and was having a nap inside it!'

'D'you know, I don't blame him. That sounds so snuggly. I think I'd quite like to have a nap inside a football.'

'I'm going to go and check on him!' She watched his little feet clamber over her and head up the stairs.

'Washing machine?' Midge pulled a face.

'I thought you were drawing the round door.' She stood and leaned against him, gratefully receiving the kisses he dotted on her lips.

'Remind me not to pair up with you for charades next time we play.'

'Ha!' Slipping her arms around his waist, she let the day catch up with and wash over her. She yawned.

'How was work?' He spoke into her hair.

'Same old. Graham was on form, as per. Tyler was very shouty, and in my head, I can still hear the beep, and I'm saying, "*Thank you for calling Castle Care. You are through to Remy. How can I help you today?*"'

'I've got something you can help me with.' He squeezed her tight.

'Oh yeah, what's that?' She looked up at him.

'The spuds, you did say.'

'On it.'

Reluctantly she let go and, with fatigue firing arrows of ache into her heels and spine, she headed to the kitchen. It appeared she had stumbled into the aftermath of a very rowdy party or police raid. Harper's school bag had been upended on the floor; its pink-and-pastel contents made it look like a Care Bear had thrown up. The sink was still full of breakfast things, topped with drinking glasses and sticky plates. The cutlery drawer was open. The dishwasher flashed to indicate it had finished its cycle. The butter, lidless on the countertop with a knife still sticking out from it, looked like it had been murdered, the weapon of choice abandoned. The peanut butter jar was a mess, with great gobs of the stuff snaking down the glass and on to the breadboard. The floor carried the faint dusting of biscuit crumbs, and empty crisp packets (salt and vinegar flavoured) had been deposited near the bin, next to the bin, but not in the bin.

'Flippin' 'eck!' She rubbed her face and reached into the freezer for oven chips, suddenly losing the energy and inclination for any form of spud that required more effort.

'I was just having a tidy.'

'Well, I would have hated to have seen it before you tidied!'

'They're like animals, Ren. They come in and tear through the kitchen in seconds, looking for the chocolate stash, which they failed to find, and this is the result. I find it overwhelming. It feels easier to just stand back and wait till they've retreated before I do a thing. It's like coming back to camp and discovering bears have found your picnic. Far better to let them finish than confront them – safer. I honestly don't think they're children; I think they're part locust, part wolf. I'm actually scared of them when they're hungry, and I've served with the Royal Marines! I've faced hostile territories! I got a flipping medal for bravery!'

'I know, my love, I know.' She closed her eyes and smiled in his direction, bless him. 'I'm here now.'

Truth was, despite her tiredness, she couldn't care less about her home being pristine, understanding it was just that, a *home*.

He slumped down into a chair at the table, as if it were all a bit too much. 'And just a heads up, Harper asked me if she can get some tampons. I said that was your department.'

'Thanks. What does she need tampons for? She hasn't started her periods yet. Or maybe that was her way of telling you that she has.' Her heart lurched for her daughter. 'I'd better go and have a word. Stir the casserole and turn the chips in a few minutes.'

'I think I can manage that. Oh, didn't manage to get your mum and dad's tap done, but I told them I'll get over there tomorrow.'

'You're a love.' She blew him a kiss and climbed the stairs, before knocking twice on Harper's door, as she had been instructed.

'Come in!' Her daughter called over the music.

Remy found her in bed, knees up, leaning against the headboard, entombed by her fleece blanket.

'Hello, darling. Can we turn it down a bit?'

Harper's shoulders fell and she rolled her eyes, as if the request was as irritating as it was predictable. Her daughter leaned over and lowered the volume.

'Ooh, that's better. Couldn't hear myself think!' She sat on the end of her little girl's bed.

'You always say that.'

'Do I?' It was official: she was turning into her mother. God help them all!

Her daughter nodded and flattened her legs.

'How was cheerleading squad? What did you learn?'

'Not much.'

'I see.' Harper was at the odd in-between age; neither child nor teen. Her joy seemed to fluctuate, displaying wild excitement for the most mundane of chores to suddenly sighing as if she carried the weight of the world on her narrow shoulders. Today, it appeared, her daughter erred towards the latter. Remy understood. Being ten was an age that had stuck in her mind for a million reasons, and Harper was right: it was a lot.

This was your chance! Your one bloody chance! And you've blown it! It makes no sense, like being offered a raffle ticket where the prize is the best thing you can possibly imagine and not taking it!

This was one of the only times she had heard her dad lose his temper, raise his voice. She remembered how it had felt, wanting to crawl inside her skin and hide, wanting to run out of the front door and go far, far away. It had changed her, shaped her, that and the attack, both guiding her along a path that led to home. The place she wanted to stay, the place she felt safe. Somewhere to step inside and close the front door, somewhere warm, while doing her utmost to be the very best daughter she could be for her mum and dad. Trying every day to make amends for 'letting them down', for not taking her shot.

'What's up, pup?'

'Nothing.' Her daughter stared at her blanket, toying with a loose thread.

'Well, I know you *say* nothing, but it feels like something. You don't seem happy right now, and you're certainly not chatty and you asked Dad to get you tampons.' At this, Harper let her gaze flick upwards towards her mother's face. 'You've got your panty liners at the back of your knicker drawer for when you need them. Tampons have to wait a bit. You can talk to me about anything, anytime. And I know you *know* what to expect, but is there something you want to tell me? Have you started your periods, Harps? Or feel like you might be? Or are you just feeling a bit . . .' She pulled a face.

'I haven't got my period.' Harper slunk down and flipped over on to her side, head on the pillow, her face away from her.

Remy couldn't help the relief that swept over her. A reprieve, a while longer for her little girl to be a little girl, without the encumbrance of bleeding, the hormone surges, the slow creep of womanhood that would bring her so much but rob her of so much too. The emotional roller coaster and all that went with vaulting this line from little girl to little girl who menstruated. The fine seam of blood that ran from grandmother to mother and daughter, a slow trickle that left their bodies and changed their lives and made possible some of the greatest things and some of the less favourable. Babies, maturity, discomfort, and more nights coiled around a hot water bottle with Mount Vesuvius on her chin than she cared to remember. Aware of how adulthood and motherhood had been delivered to her within the space of a year; the assault, marriage to Jamie, giving birth, divorce . . . A neat parcel of awakening that had taken her years to properly unwrap. Not for her the gentle realisation through experience of all that existed in the grown-up world. No, hers had been a baptism of fire! One minute she was dancing in the car to 'Geno', wondering about kissing boys, and the next she was in the delivery suite, pushing a baby from her body while the bloke she'd met only months before smoked, paced and planned a night out with his mates. It had been ghastly, and to think of it now saddened her as much as it ever had. The one good thing was that it made her yearn for no more than the quiet, violence-free, love-filled life that she now enjoyed.

'I'm kinda glad you haven't got your period, little one.' She toyed with the fine ends of her daughter's hair.

Maybe Harper would be lucky, lucky like her Auntie Ashleigh, who barely noticed the change in her cycle; the loss and upheaval, in her case, minimal. They had started their periods on the same day, aged thirteen, speech day at St. Jude's. They had laughed at the fact, as they sat in their pyjamas on the sofa, hot chocolate in their mugs, hot water bottles on their tums. Their dad strangely conspicuous by his absence; 'Women's business,' she'd heard her mum whisper before ushering him up the stairs. A unifying and lovely thing after a day that had confirmed how remote she felt from her sister and her life. Funny she should think of it now.

'So did you . . .' She trod carefully, aware of the fragility of Harper's mood. 'Did you want the tampons for some other reason?' She was struggling to think what that reason might be – an art project? *Unlikely.*

'No-wah!' Harper banged her little fists on to the mattress.

'Okay. Okay, love. I'm just trying to figure out what's going on, because I'm your mum and I love you and that's my job. So, I'm going to stay right here until you let me in on the inside story with the tampons and tell me what the McFly is going on!'

She saw her child's shoulders shudder with laughter, and it felt good, to know she could still break through the ice of a low mood with no more than a joke, a cookie, or a cuddle.

'Please look at me. I like seeing your little face.'

Harper twisted around until she was facing her mother. Her mid-brown curls spread out on the pillow. Remy smiled at how beautiful this human was, this little person that she and Midge had made in haste, knowing it was right, certain it was what they wanted; to start their family. A sister for Sophie.

'Casey and Ella didn't let me sit with them. They were on the bench, and when I went over to get changed near them, they moved.'

Grrrr . . . Remy felt the growl of angry mummy tiger in her gut and knew she had to tread carefully, suppressing any possible rage she might feel towards a couple of young children, *because* they were young children. Not wanting to pour fuel on to a fire that might be no more than a flicker of flame, all doused, smothered and extinguished with love and a friendship bracelet by tomorrow. It happened this way sometimes when girls hung out. Not for the first time she felt a rush of love for Tony, the very best friend they could have asked for. He was all of the fun and none of the meanness. It was a reminder to call him soon. It had been a while.

'That can't have felt very nice.'

'It didn't.' Harper's bottom lip wobbled.

'Are you sure they did that, or were they distracted, mucking about . . .'

'No, they did that, Mum. They were whispering too.'

'Urgh, whispering's the worst! It makes you crazy, thinking of all the things they might be whispering about.'

'It did.'

Remy reached out and ran her palm over her daughter's head.

'I'm sorry you had to go through that today, but tomorrow is another one and it will all feel different in the morning.'

'I know, Mum.' Harper's agreement didn't stop her eyes blooming with tears that were hard to see.

'Also, I'm struggling to see where the tampons fit in?' This she said with no pun intended.

'I knew Casey could hear me, and so I said it to Dad when we got into the car because I thought if she thought I had my period then she'd think I was cool and interesting.'

'Oh, I see.'

It tore at her heartstrings, words spoken from a young mouth, by a child who'd had only the tiniest glimpse of the world and was trying to figure out the puzzle of life, searching for the missing pieces. She thought it prudent not to mention that she was forty, and still trying to figure it out, searching for the missing pieces. Like how to communicate better with her sister to be a bigger part of her life, how to be more tolerant of her mum, who had the ability to irritate the shit out of her, how to get closer to Evie, who she rarely saw, and how to win the lottery so she could spend every day with Midge.

'Firstly, you *are* cool and interesting, and secondly, telling fibs about periods is not how to win friends. I have never, in my whole life, met anyone who wanted to be *more* friendly with someone because they had a period. I'm pretty sure I haven't anyway.'

Harper smiled and wiped at her eyes.

'I just wanted them to let me sit with them.'

'I know, darling.' She bent low and kissed her forehead, remembering how lovely it had been to always have her sister close by – company, a friend, her other half, before life had put them on different paths . . . before *she* had inadvertently put them on different paths.

A thought occurred then: had Ashleigh struggled to make friends at her new school? She wondered what it must have been like for her sister to traipse off to St. Jude's while she and Tony got to chat on the bus as they travelled to Milton Road. It made her catch her breath. She hadn't really considered it before, but what had it been like for Ashleigh, togged out in her new uniform, making her way to a building she had never entered, to take up a place she had been given, having had no part in the decision, the plan? Was this why they had grown apart so soon after? Her throat felt tight with all it was trying to contain.

'I'm sure tomorrow will be better, Harps, but if you want me to speak to anyone about it, or get involved . . .'

'I don't!' Her response was almost panicked.

'Okay, I won't.'

'Promise?'

'Cross my heart.' Remy made the sign on her chest. 'Now, why don't you wash your face and come downstairs?'

Harper nodded and sniffed.

'My little dove.' She liked to call her daughter by the nickname that was her and her sister's too, a name threaded with their history, every strand woven with love.

'Love you, Mum.'

'And I love you, more than I can possibly ever tell you.'

'Dinner's ready!' Midge hollered from the hallway. 'Last one at the table is a loser!'

The sound of Bertie's feet racing down the stairs was all it took for Harper to throw off her blanket and run from the room.

Remy knew there was no point in rushing and so took her time, arriving in the kitchen to see the three of them sitting around the kitchen table, all beaming in her direction.

'Loser!' Midge pointed at her.

'Yep.' She winked, took a seat, and popped a hot chip into her mouth. 'But I'm a loser who knows where the secret chocolate is hidden.'

Ashleigh

Ashleigh waited for the gates to open before pulling into the driveway and sitting for a second or two, always a little stunned by the majesty of her beautiful home. It gave her a thrill every time she returned and took in the many windows, the beautiful craftsmanship and the fact that this was a house in a postcode beyond her wildest dreams – until it wasn't, and Archie's parents had gifted them the very hefty deposit that made it all possible.

Her parents' reaction when they first saw it replayed in her mind.

'It's a bloody palace, Ashleigh!' Ruthie had gasped.

'Like a film star's house!' Her dad had stood in the hall and stared upwards. 'Can't imagine how much concrete a place like this took!'

It had felt a lot like validation, and she liked it.

She smiled now, thinking of how her mum, who she suspected wasn't as green as she was cabbage-looking, had skilfully got her to commit to her dad's birthday lunch. Archie's mother, Elaine Fitch, had none of Ruthie's deftness, and Ashleigh was aware that had she declined an invitation to lunch, or drinks, or the opening of a gallery owned by the son of a friend, or last-minute tickets to a tiny theatre to see a one-man show, her mother-in-law would have gone full ice queen until they hurriedly reorganised their diaries and made amendments to keep her happy.

There was a lot of that.

She was thankful that she and Archie required no such drama. Not that they were perfect, and she was determined to find more time to spend with her love, and with Evie, creating the family moments that had shaped her childhood. The question was how, and was she brave enough? Every time she failed to make a connection, was rebuffed or ignored by Evie, it felt as if another strand of rope connecting her to her little girl frayed, leaving her more afraid of estrangement than if she hadn't tried. Looking up now at the bedroom windows, it was difficult for her to admit that she half hoped Evie was already in bed, wary of another unsatisfying interaction that highlighted just how bad she was at motherhood.

'I'm sorry, little one.' Words laden with sorrow she whispered towards the landing light, wondering how she could break down the barrier, how to get better at it and who she could ask for advice. Remy was the obvious choice, but it was almost impossible to broach such a mighty subject without inviting judgement or admitting to her shame. Especially when Remy seemed to effortlessly get it so right. She and Midge radiated bliss and contentment and were so at ease with their kids, displaying a closeness that she envied because it used to be hers, before she stepped away from all that was familiar and headed off to St. Jude's. A familiarity that, up until the age of eleven, had cocooned and kept her safe, before she had been driven to her new life, in her new uniform, while Remy and Tony waited at the bus stop arm in arm. Feeling herself cut loose and letting self-doubt settle into every pore had dogged her ever since, even when it came to communicating with her own child.

It was hard to talk about it to her husband, who tended to offer broad verbal brushstrokes designed to placate or calm her rather than actually offer a solution.

'Do you think I'm a good mum?' she'd asked once, as he walked up and down the kitchen with tiny baby Evie against his chest, winding her and cooing into her ear as she cried. He had offered a brief and unnatural smile before replying, 'Better than *my* mother!'

It had done little to reassure her.

The Fitches were a different breed, which meant Archie had grown up without the closeness that had been so wonderful. Elaine and Dickie were remote, cool when sober, and seemed barely interested in what she and Archie got up to. The type of people who believed that giving compliments did not help shape a person's character, and that showing too much emotion meant weakness. The kind of people who didn't care about common ground, quite the opposite, only favouring a preoccupation or hobby if no one else had done it or it was out of the reach of mere mortals, usually because it was prohibitively expensive. The moment Guy, at the dinner table some years ago, had chimed in with 'Oh, Machu Picchu? Yes, I went in my gap year, isn't it incredible?' taking the gloss from Elaine's story, she'd changed the subject to the time they tackled a gale in the Bay of Biscay before eating sea urchins on the yacht, the spiky delicacy plucked straight from the sea.

Ruthie had been spot on in her summary of the woman she'd met only a handful of times. 'Elaine? Oh, she's lovely! In very good shape, very smart, very pleased with herself. Mint Imperial, anyone?'

Ashleigh knew she would never forget how her in-laws-to-be had laughed when she'd pronounced the Cambridge college where Archie's cousin had studied as 'Mag-da-layne' and not 'Maudlin' – it made her feel like a dumdum and she'd almost fled the room, puce with embarrassment. It didn't take much. A reminder of all the things she didn't know, of the tiny world she had come from. They had made her feel small, in a way her parents never did. Her lovely mum and dad, who, after all these years, were still aglow with the fact that she'd won a place at St. Jude's. Archie's parents, after enquiring where she'd gone to school, had given tight smiles, and mumbled, 'Charming!' as if it were anything but.

In fairness to her in-laws, they had thawed a little since she'd gifted them a granddaughter who apparently looked exactly like Archie at the same age. This hadn't stopped them hinting that a sibling for Evie *'might be nice . . .'* A second child was, however, not on the cards, and she had made this clear to Archie. How on earth would her business thrive? How would they function if there were not one but two kids to consider? This, of course, was a smokescreen for the fact that she just didn't feel like a very good mother, and to be reminded of it by two children would surely only double the feeling of inadequacy. Her own private sadness that she masked with busyness and a jam-packed schedule. What else could she do?

She let herself in to the house and was surprised to hear The Strokes playing on the stereo, meaning either Archie was at home, or Evie had put on her dad's CD in lieu of watching cartoons.

'I didn't think you'd still be here!' She smiled at her husband, who was mixing a whopping gin and tonic into a highball glass on the countertop.

'Came back for a shower. The German wanted to freshen up, so we're meeting at Nobu.'

'Nice.' She yawned.

'You're very welcome to join us? Be doing me a favour!' He grinned.

She felt bad, particularly after their rather rocky encounter this morning, and didn't want to let him down, but the thought of smiling and making polite conversation with a stranger was no match for the lure of her silk pyjamas, a movie in bed, the slathering of Dior face cream on her dry skin, and a one-way ticket to the land of nod.

'Do you mind if I don't, darling?' She let her head hang to one side, indicating just how knackered she was.

'Course not.' He smiled at her, this gorgeous man who got her like no one else, apart from Remy, but that was a given. 'Good day?'

'Not really, bit shitty actually. We lost the Harrington Road house and I've agreed that we'll go to my dad's birthday lunch at The Plough.'

'Want one?' He lifted the glass in her direction.

'No, thanks, love.'

Her husband took a large glug of the sparkling aperitif.

'So, talk to me, what happened with the listing? How did you lose it?'

'Erm, there was an issue with the . . . with the parking . . .' This was not strictly untrue.

'That sucks.'

'Yep.' It sucked and meant a dent in their forecast for the month in a market that seemed to have stagnated a little, neither of which was good. They needed more property, more viewings, more sales, more everything! To have messed up today hit hard.

'When's your dad's lunch?'

She was glad he hadn't pressed her for the details of the house cock-up, knowing it didn't show her in the best light. 'Saturday.'

'Oh, shoot!' Archie put his hands on his hips.

'Let me guess. A work thing, golf with the lads, tickets to the Grand Prix, washing your hair?'

'Don't be like that!' He looked a little hurt and instantly she felt guilty. 'The German partner's still here and I've been lumbered with organising entertainment. Until we get this merger done, they are keen to keep them sweet.'

'What are you thinking for entertainment, juggling for him or magic tricks?'

'You're in a funny mood.' He held her eyeline.

'I'm sorry' – she rubbed her forehead – 'it's been a *really* shitty day, actually. Guy's angry with me about the Hartington house but making out he's not, and that's made me angry with him.'

'Has Gigi got his knickers in a twist? Do I need to come to the office and bump your heads together?'

'Ha, no, but do you think he's changed since he married Ada?'

Archie held his drink midway towards his mouth and narrowed his eyes. 'Is it a trick question? Try and find me a man who is not changed the moment he puts a ring on it and waltzes up the aisle!'

'In a good way though, right? Changed in a good way?' Staring at him, she swallowed the small bite of fear that he might not be happy, might want out, because he'd sussed she was no more than a front. Her bottom lip trembled, and she turned away to get a grip.

'Of course, my sweet!' His sarcasm made her laugh; he had always been able to do this, shift her mood, butter her up, lighten her worries.

'Seriously though, Archie, I feel like Guy is a bit more judgey now, as if some of Ada's uptight quirks are rubbing off on him.'

'Ada? Uptight? I'd not noticed.' There it was again, that sarcasm.

'Something he said has bothered me a bit.'

'What was it?' He took a seat at the island and rolled up the sleeves of his crisp white shirt. She liked the contrast of his lingering summer tan against the pale cotton, remembering how chuffed she had been to introduce her yachtie boyfriend to her sister. Archie had been sweet and patient during that dark, dark time, when she had felt so helpless, living far away while Tony recuperated in hospital and Remy was waiting for her face to heal, her bones to repair and for her faith in human nature to be restored. Jamie, the bozo, had been a placeholder, but it was Midge who had done that, good old Midge.

Ashleigh studied her man, who was still, in her eyes, devastatingly good-looking.

'You know we've been toying with the idea of expanding, opening a rental department, poaching Letitia from JB Fox and Sons?'

'Yep.'

'Right, well, we haven't discussed it for a while. The market is a bit unpredictable, and today, out of the blue, he said that he and *Ada* think it's the wrong time to borrow more money.'

'He's probably right.'

'That's not the point.' She leaned against the countertop. 'It's the fact that he and *Ada* have discussed it.'

'We're discussing it, and she is his wife.'

'No.' She felt the rise of frustration; she needed to clarify. 'It was the way he said, *Ada and I think . . .* I mean, what does Ada know about anything? Apart from making jam and being overly in love with that bloody sausage dog!'

'Hey, leave Ben out of this. He's a great dog!'

'I would have to agree, Ben is a great dog, but you know what I'm saying. I'd never say, *Archie and I . . .* wouldn't need to throw your name in to add weight to anything.'

'None taken!' He took another drink.

She took a beat. 'Am I being mean?' It wouldn't be the first time that day. Her stomach bunched as she recalled the way Mr blue-and-red striped beanie had dismissed her.

'Little bit, maybe.'

'I just . . .' She found it hard to voice.

'It's understandable, Ash. You've been Gigi's go-to since we left uni, and now he's going to Ada instead, and that must be hard.'

'You think I'm jealous?' Her voice had gone up an octave; it was ugly, unattractive, and entirely possible. It was a horrible thought that she might be reeling from no longer being Guy's number one. Not that she had ever wanted him in that way, never. But it really wasn't that complicated when she analysed it; Guy had been the person who *saw* her, invited her to join the gang, caring less about who she was, or how she had got there. He had simply included her the moment he'd met her, and yes, loved her, he had loved *her!* He had picked her on merit, and it was the first time since starting St. Jude's that she didn't feel she had to fight for approval or friendship; he had simply offered it. To have it withdrawn even only slightly made her feel just like that young girl with the fear of exposure jumping in her gut every time someone called her name.

'Maybe, or a little oversensitive.' He sipped his gin.

'I don't want to be.' She pushed out her bottom lip, feeling vulnerable and slightly ashamed, wanting Archie to see her as strong and capable, all the things he and the Fitches most admired.

You can't underestimate the importance of independence and self-reliance, strength, especially when there's a crisis. It's the difference between surviving or sinking. I learned that . . .

'I know, but it's human nature, a fragile thing.'

'Alright, sensei. When did you get so philosophical?'

'Hello, Mummy.'

She spun around at the sound of her daughter's voice. There she was, not asleep. Ashleigh was aware she needed to say . . . *something!*

'Hi, Evie, how are you?' Her tone was overly enthusiastic, false and jarring.

''M okay.' Her daughter shrugged and walked over to Archie before leaning on his leg. 'I'm tired, Dad.'

She noted the physical interaction between the two, he so comfortable with the child resting on him as Evie leaned, trusting him to catch her if she fell. It was an ease Ashleigh didn't feel, often a little awkward, self-conscious when Evie was close to her in this way, as if the child were, in so many ways, a stranger. She wished it were different, wished she could reach for Evie's hand and hold it tightly in the way she saw Archie do, wished she weren't so overly aware, so hesitant, nervous with a ridiculous and misplaced embarrassment that she didn't know how to overcome, and a horrible feeling in her gut that she was a fraud and didn't deserve any of this lovely life. Waiting, waiting for that instant and glorious maternal bond to kick in. She hoped it might happen soon, for all their sakes.

'You want me to carry you up to bed before I go out?' Archie put the empty glass in the sink.

Their daughter nodded and rubbed her eyes. 'Marguerite is cleaning my bathroom.'

'Oh, well, she can head off, now I'm home.' Ashleigh smiled brightly, falsely.

'I wish she could stay with me sometimes,' Evie added quite nonchalantly, as Archie lifted her on to his arm, words that Ashleigh found hard to hear because Marguerite was only there when she wasn't, and if Evie wanted Marguerite to be there more, then . . . was Evie saying she'd rather Ashleigh wasn't at home? Again, she smiled broadly lest she give away her thoughts, knowing she had to keep that oversensitive, green-eyed monster at bay. To keep smiling, to stop her mask from slipping and revealing to the whole wide world that she was an imposter.

'Sleep tight, Evie.' Her words were a little calmer now.

Her daughter stared at her over her dad's shoulder as he carried her from the kitchen. Ashleigh lifted her hand in a small wave, wanting so badly for the child to wave back.

She didn't, and the absence of it sent a shard of glass to pierce her heart.

'Yep.' Ashleigh spoke to no one as she opened the fridge door and reached for the hummus. 'A bit of a shitty day.'

Remy

Remy ran the washcloth over her face, and was, as ever, slightly icked out by the grime and sludge-coloured mascara smears that she transferred from her face.

'I know I need to be more patient, but Mum really annoyed me today.' She leaned out of the tiny en suite and spoke to Midge, who was already in bed, flicking through the channels of the TV on the wall, no doubt trying to find any of the sports that were his preoccupation.

'That's not news. She annoys you every day,' he pointed out without lifting his eyes from the screen.

'True. I guess I should have said she annoyed me more than usual today.'

'What did she do, promise you decent spuds and then at the last minute swerve on the deal and give you oven chips?'

She angled her head and stared at him. 'No, but if she had and did so at the end of a very trying day with only the smallest amount of energy left for the task in hand, then I'd have absolutely forgiven her, because I'd think she was doing her best and, in fact, I'd be grateful for her cooking me anything at all, smartarse.'

'Oooo-oooh! Someone's tetchy!' He gave her that grin, the one that spoke of love and attraction and she knew was just for her. It was his superpower and could disarm her with no more than a glance, a word, a kiss.

'Moving on.' She turned back to the mirror and tilted her face to the right to better see the healed wounds that marked her.

Oi!

This was the sound, the gunshot that still echoed in her thoughts and had the power to pull her under into a nightmare or to leave her shaking on a sunny day when she was safe. A powerful sound that had changed the course of her life, and Tony's.

She'd had no idea that the imprint of the coarse stitching on her face would be there for life. A constant reminder of that night, of what they had endured. The scars had faded over time, and were now finer, silvery, almost delicate, like the craze in glazing on something old or the fractures in ice when seen close up. Not beautiful, never that, but better.

She also studied the horizontal lines of ageing on her forehead and the vertical grooves that had started to appear at the side of her mouth; marionette lines they were called, and she thought this ridiculous. Marionettes were traditionally carved from wood, their faces unchanging as the years passed. What was happening to her was the opposite, a soft and slow decay, the loss of volume, the slackening of skin and the inevitable maturation that saw everything living metamorphose into the shrivelled, collapsing version of its younger, vibrant self.

'Do you think I look old?' She sucked in her cheeks and pulled back the skin under her chin.

'No, I bloody don't! You're beautiful.' He had always said this, and she knew that for him it was true. It was the greatest gift.

'You're biased!' She smiled as she hopped under the duvet.

'Maybe.' He ran the pad of his thumb over her cheek. 'But to me, you are the most gorgeous woman in the world.'

'Thank you.' She shimmied down on the mattress until her head was on his chest and she could feel the warmth of him on her cheek.

'I don't like it when Jamie pitches up at her events.'

The fact the man was coming to Sophie's end-of-term fashion show had obviously been on his mind. Her husband did this, let things stew during the day and then offloaded them just before sleep.

'I don't like it either.' Any interaction with Jamie was a reminder of that brief and oh so unhappy period of turbulence, but not all bad, given her beloved Sophie. 'But we'll do what we always do; smile, greet him warmly and show Soph that she never has to choose and that she never has to feel guilty or uneasy.'

'Yep, I just wish . . .'

'I know, baby.' She kissed his chest.

She wished it too, that Sophie was theirs in the truest sense, and that Jamie would volunteer for a lifelong Moon mission. Although how much call there was for scaffolders up there, she wasn't sure.

'So what did your mum do to upset you?' He put the remote control down and wrapped his arms around her.

'Upset's a bit strong. It was more a small irritation.'

'A small irritation that you've carried all day and felt the need to mention now, so tell me.'

The irony wasn't lost on her that this was precisely what he had done with Jamie.

'We were talking about Dad's birthday lunch, and she said she was going to invite Ashleigh, and I told her I doubted she'd come, and she said something like, "*There's no need to be jealous of her.*"'

'Ouch!'

'Yes, ouch! I'm not jealous of anyone, especially her! I feel like I could say it all day every day and it would make no difference. It started when she went to St. Jude's, and in their view, I was left behind. It was like they mentally put us on two different paths. As if she went off to the land of opportunity that meant university and landing Mr Moneybags and starting her own business, moving to the big city, wearing fancy wellies, and driving a big old car even though she's in the city. Like she switched up!'

'While you got saddled with this downmarket existence with the man of your dreams.'

'And thank God for that! I love you, love my life, all of it. There's nothing downmarket about it.' It was, as she gratefully acknowledged on a daily basis, enough.

'Do you ever wish you'd been the one to take the exam, and were now driving around London in a big old country car?'

'No.' She laughed, hiding the uncomfortable truth from her husband and feeling terrible that she did so. 'I like my little car!'

'It's not going to change, not ever, love. Your parents have that belief. It doesn't occur to them that you always had choices. You're so smart, you could have done anything you chose with your life, still could.'

She felt the heat of discomfort on her skin, knowing she was lying to him about the fact that she had won the scholarship. It sat between them, the only thing that did, but she knew that to tell him now, after all this time, might only cause a rift, and she couldn't stand the thought of that. It was obvious with hindsight that she should have told him when they met, the event not pressing in her thoughts in those early years, but time had passed, and the path had been set.

'What I *chose* was to keep Sophie. To make her my priority, to start a family; even though I knew eventually I'd be doing it without Jamie, I didn't mind. I always figured that it would be harder in some ways to do it alone, but easier in so many others.' She shifted in the bed so she could face him. That night, the one that gave her scars, had robbed her of so much, filling her with fear that out in the big, wide world, strangers, for no reason she could fathom, might want to hurt you. 'It's a weird one.' She coughed, and shook her head slightly to rid the image of those boots, *pistons*. 'How much value they placed on going to St. Jude's, as if it was the answer to everything!'

'It was for them, giving you both chances they never got. They saw it as your ticket, like it was the only way to harness your cleverness.' He let this hang.

'They made me feel for years like I let them down. Not that they said as much, but their faces, the little shrugs, and glances when we all had to traipse into town to get my sister's uniform, then the day she started, and I went off to Milton Road. It was always a thing. They revelled in the open days, the sports events, speech days, the music recitals, all of it, as if they'd won the place!'

'Well, you shouldn't feel like that. You do so much for them, like you're afraid to let them down.' She blinked, knowing there was more truth in his words than he realised. 'And in their defence, it's kind of like that, isn't it, we *do* feel pride for our kids' achievements.

I know you'll be looking at Sophie's creations at her show, thinking, That's my girl!'

'I will.' She took a deep breath. 'But even when we sat our final exams and I got better grades than Ashleigh, I swear they somehow believed that my exams had been easier and weren't the *exact* same A levels, set by the exact same exam board that Ash had sat! I could have gone to university had I not got pregnant, I could have done lots of things, but I didn't want to. For a million reasons I didn't want to. I was so scared, I needed to stay home, to be still, quiet.'

'I understand, my love. Please don't let it bother you.'

'What bothers me is the way my mum won't let it drop. As if they can't understand that I'm happy, satisfied with my lot.' She closed her eyes, readying for sleep. This wasn't strictly true. What bothered her most was being reminded of her part in the whole debacle and the deceit that had dogged her more and more in recent years. They were angry that she'd deliberately let them down, and she was unable to explain that she hadn't meant to, not at all. And worse still was the fact that if she came clean now, they'd be let down anyway, because she'd lied to them, made Ashleigh lie too! She wished it would all go away.

'Anyway, I don't think you need to worry. I doubt your sister will make it to your dad's birthday. She hasn't for the last two and missed Mother's Day last year.'

'Ah, well, you'd be wrong! She's coming, apparently.'

'Wow!' Midge tsked. 'I expect your mum will be thinking about redecorating or getting the carpets cleaned, buying a new sofa or putting up a banner across the street.'

'Probably.' She smiled, no matter how much his assessment irked her.

'Aren't you looking forward to seeing her? It's been a while.'

She thought how best to phrase it. 'I am, of course I am. But it's complicated.'

It was hard to accurately explain the relationship with her twin, the inseverable, deep connection that bound them. It meant she would fight for her, protect her, and often knew if something was wrong, how she might be feeling, if Ashleigh was going to call before she did. There was an inexplicable thread of comprehension that was beyond the material, and always had been. But that didn't mean she always liked her. 'I love it when she comes home, but I love it just as much when she leaves! And I hate how she says the word *London*, as if it's a special pronunciation for people who live there, like people who put a "th" into chorizo because they spent a wet weekend in Bar-th-elona, or people who say sked-yule instead of shed-yule because they watch too much American TV! Things like that. It annoys me.'

'I can tell, and if it's any consolation, I feel the same about Archie the chinless wonder sharing second-hand tales of all his pals who went to Sandhurst – it really gets my goat! "*Do you know Gerry Buntingford McAllister? He was with the Household Cav?*" as if I bloody would! He has no clue about life in the military, but because he's heard a couple of stories and one of his distant relatives fought at Waterloo, he thinks he knows it all. He wouldn't last a week.'

'You have to be patient. You have to be kind.'

'I will. I am.' He took a deep breath. 'Do we know for a fact that Master Archie of Fitchington is coming too?'

It was funny, the names he came up with for the man that were always spot on.

'Not sure.'

'I think the only person who will be praying more than me that he doesn't have to attend is Lord Farquaad himself.'

'Lord Farquaad?' Her laughter cackled from her. 'You have to stop it, or one day you might inadvertently call him one of these names and it would be terrible!'

'It would. You're right. Especially if it was one of my less favourable ones like The Right Honourable Chicken Pox, because he's about as welcome and makes my skin itch!'

'Honestly, Midge, no more!'

'Okay, it seems that we can strike a deal.' He twisted towards her.

'What kind of a deal?' She stifled a yawn.

Midge kissed her firmly on the mouth and she felt her body respond, yielding to the escape he promised, this man that she so loved.

'Mu-um!' Bertie called as he entered their room.

She sat up, as Midge leapt to his side of the bed and was almost instantly re-engrossed in the remote control.

'What is it, love? You should be asleep.'

'I was asleep, but Harper woke me up. She's crying. I can hear her through the wall.'

'Oh no! I'll go and sit with her. She probably had a bad dream.'

It wasn't unheard of: bad dreams, tummy aches, feeling sick, being too cold, too hot, the room being too dark, too light, needing a drink of water, or questions about the universe that meant her babies couldn't sleep – things like, did *everyone* die? And what would happen if *she* died? The sudden remembering that they needed to take in a hamper for the harvest festival, a robot made of tinfoil, a hat for a parade, a project about otters, a knight's costume, or a raffle prize. The reasons they had been pulled from slumber over the years were numerous and varied.

'She didn't have a bad dream, she's crying because Casey's been mean to her today.'

'Yes, she told me. Don't you worry about it, Bert. I'll deal with it.'

'Casey said she was smelly and called her Farter instead of Harper again.'

Again?

To hear that her baby girl had been so cruelly addressed and that she'd chosen not to share the detail was heartbreaking.

'Who said that to her?' Midge fired.

She saw the way her husband's jaw clenched and his muscles drew tight on his bones, as if someone had pulled a cord on his anger.

'I'll tell you about it in a sec.' She placed her hand briefly on his arm, knowing it would calm him, and flung back the duvet. 'You get Bertie back to bed and I'll go and talk to her.'

'You mustn't ever call people names, must you, Mum?'

Remy looked over her shoulder, giving Midge a hard stare, as she grabbed her dressing gown from the back of the door and went to console her baby girl.

'No, you never must.'

Ashleigh

Ashleigh parked the car in a side road and took her time walking to the office. The sun on her face was a comfortable blanket to warm her bones and ease the autumnal gloom. It was her favourite season: the smell of damp leaves, the aroma of real fires, hot chocolate on dark days, and who didn't look good in an oversized neutral-shade cashmere knit and a decent pair of jeans?

Archie had arrived home after she'd fallen asleep last night. This morning she didn't mention his croissant for breakfast or the fact that the white shirt he'd worn for dinner the previous evening was spattered with red wine that would be a pain for Marguerite to launder. It was her intention to eat with him tonight, Evie too, like one of those families you saw on TV that sat around the dining table and discussed their day. It felt like a good place to start, a way to connect with her daughter around the kitchen table, sharing food and tales of their day. She'd make an extra effort and, having left instructions, looked forward to the lasagne Marguerite would whip up for them.

Memories of her own childhood were peppered with images of the four of them laughing and eating around the dining table, her parents chit-chatting over their heads as she and Remy did all they could to make each other laugh. In fairness, it hadn't taken much, no more than the insertion of chip fangs or a pea up the nostril. Simpler times. It would be nice to see her sister when they went out for her dad's birthday. Nice, but she'd also be looking forward to jumping into her car and heading back to the big smoke. She loved her twin, of course she did, but it was complicated.

Clara was tip-tapping away when Ashleigh arrived at the office. The smell of coffee cut through the air.

'Morning, Clara!'

'Morning, Ashleigh.' The girl with her overly serious demeanour barely looked up. 'I'm just heading out, actually. I have an early viewing at Grove Park Gardens, and I want to make sure it's warm, put the lamps on.'

'Good call. No sign of Guy yet?' She looked behind her at his desk, which was obviously and unusually empty.

'Nope.' The girl shook her head. 'Shan't be long.' Clara spoke as she grabbed her handbag and left.

Ashleigh leaned back in her chair, feeling the same sense of satisfaction she always did when alone in the classy, pleasantly styled premises. The glossy magazines on the glass-topped coffee table were angled just so. The beautifully arranged white roses that spoke of understated class. The mink-toned cushions on the pale sofa with centre chops that made them look pricey and inviting. In short, they tried to replicate the kind of decor in the kind of homes they sold to the kind of people who could afford to live in houses like this.

It filled her with a sense of achievement like no other. The business had not come about through luck or because of a handout from Archie's parents. She was not in the chair because someone *knew* her and had given her a leg-up; it had not been gifted. It was instead hard won, grown from the smallest of dreams, a structured loan, and the hardest of grafts, and it was hers. Well, more specifically, it was theirs. One of the few things in her life she felt was hers on merit.

She put a call in to Guy.

'Buongiorno!' She did her best Italian accent.

'Hello, you. Are you in the office?'

'No. I've decided to not bother today, going to get my nails done instead.' She tutted. 'Of course I'm in. Clara's got a viewing on Grove Park Gardens.'

'Oh yes, good! Good.' He let out a long, slow breath. 'It's been quite the night.'

'You alright?' He sounded a little out of sorts, the man who was never ill, never absent, never anything other than on form. 'Did you hit the sauce last night?' It was the first place her mind went, that he might have overindulged, picturing him at uni, the boy with the voracious appetite for fun, never knowing when to pump the brakes.

'No, nothing like that.' He gave a brief laugh. 'And I'm more than alright, actually. Ada went into labour yesterday evening, a little earlier than we anticipated, but he's here! He arrived, a couple of hours ago.'

'Guy! Oh my God! *Guy!*' She felt the whoosh of joy at this marvellous, marvellous news. '*He* – a boy! Oh, mate, that's wonderful! I'm so happy for you.' She couldn't help, in that moment, but picture him as the idiot member of the crew he'd been in when they were younger. The one who drank the most, was sick first, would walk miles to find a kebab or a Maccy's when the booze glow ebbed, and the one who had her back, the one who always had her back.

'We're okay, aren't we, Gigi?'

'Of course we are. We'll always be okay.'

She felt the tightening in her throat, quite overwhelmed with a rush of love, heavily flavoured with nostalgia. It happened like this, these reminders that they were no longer carefree students with their whole lives ahead of them and barely a care in the world. It had been a lovely time. The loveliest. 'That's so cool. Mother and baby doing well? I think that's the standard question!'

'Yes, yes, really well. He's awesome, Ash, so tiny! But just . . . awesome!'

She heard the crack of emotion in his words and was pleased for him, pleased for them both. It was something she understood, even if it didn't reflect her own feelings around becoming a mother. She had seen and felt the elation in those all around her, none more so than in Archie, of course, and that had felt like enough, to know it was her effort, her body, her sacrifice that had made the whole thing possible.

'We've decided to call him Ben.'

'You've decided to call him *Ben*?' she asked with undisguised shock, her words coasting on laughter.

'Yes.'

'I can't tell if you're joking?' She hardly dared ask, the tone of his voice suggesting a distinct lack of humour.

'I'm not joking, no. Bit controversial, I know, but . . .'

'Bit controversial? Your dog is called Ben! Ben the dog! Ben the dog with his many, many outfits!' She pointed out the obvious, wondering if maybe in a state of post-birth delirium and with a heady cocktail of drugs whizzing around Ada's system, this had been decided in error.

'Yeah, and honestly, Brett, there's no name we like more, so Ben it is!' He laughed.

'That's absolutely mad!' She laughed too.

'It's not mad. It's practical, and we like it, so.'

'Well, obviously you like it, proof being that you already named your much pampered *dog* Ben and now you've called your *son* Ben. What will happen if you have another baby, a girl maybe, will she be Ben too? Benita? Benjamina? Or maybe you could just number them all: *Number five, your tea's ready! Number three, phone call for you!*'

'I'm, erm . . .' He didn't laugh in the way she had anticipated, and she felt her gut fold with having got it so wrong, as the clock ticked loudly. It was strange, to feel so awkward and ill at ease when chatting to Guy. *Guy!* 'I'm going to let you go, Ashleigh.' *Ashleigh*, she noted, not *Brett*. 'I know you must be busy.' His thinly veiled dismissal was jarring, and she knew that the old Guy, the pre-Ada Guy, *Gigi*, would have laughed loudly at the thought of having a whole brood of Bens. But *this* Guy . . . It was a marker of where they were at – matured, a little estranged, grown up?

All three. His reaction hit her like a thump in the gut.

'Give Ada my love and give Ben a kiss from me. That's Ben the baby, not . . .' Ashleigh let this hang. She heard his mouth open as if to say something else, but then he was gone. His absence echoed down the line, and she smothered the desire to cry. There was far too much to do today for that. She sat for a while, composing herself, staring out of the window at the comings and goings along Chiswick High Road, wondering if it was her.

Ben? She stifled her laughter and couldn't wait to hear what Archie thought of it all.

A quick squizz on the Peter Jones website, and a bouquet of baby vests was to be sent to their address, along with a bottle of champers and a box of cupcakes from the bakery they loved. No expense spared.

The door opened and in walked their accountant, Bernie. She wasn't expecting him, not that it wasn't nice to see him. He was smiley, round and calm, the perfect antidote to her call with Guy.

'Hey, Bernie. I've just got off the phone to Guy. You're not going to believe it, but the little one's arrived!'

'Oh, fantastic.' He dumped his leather bag by the chair and sat down hard. 'What variety did they get?'

'Little boy, called Ben.'

'*Ben?*' She watched his brow furrow as the fact landed. 'But isn't that . . .'

'It is,' she confirmed. 'I can't even . . .' They both laughed with their hands over their mouths, as if to do so in the business that was half Guy's was not the done thing.

'Well, that's um . . .' She watched the man try to find the right thing to say and mentally matched his confusion. 'It's going to be fun when one of them is naughty: *Ben, stop eating grass!*'

'*Ben, don't cock your leg on the wheelie bin!*'

'*Ben's bitten the postie!*'

'*Ben, stop sniffing Fifi's bottom!*'

'*Has Ben had his worming tablet?*'

They both chuckled again before Bernie calmed and coughed, as if trying to find a level of gravitas befitting his role as their accountant. He pointed towards the door.

'Shall I come back when Guy's here, or do you want to go through the paperwork now? What's best?'

'Erm . . .' She hated missing appointments or having meetings sprung on her when she had forgotten the intention or detail. It happened sometimes; everyone messed up. The image of a blue-and-red striped beanie floated into her thoughts and made her shudder. 'What paperwork?'

'The . . . the . . . the partnership stuff, for, for, Ada.'

His nerves were evident.

Ashleigh was glad she was sitting down, as she felt a little light-headed.

'Partnership stuff for Ada?' she asked with a fixed smile. Finding it hard to take a full breath.

Bernie's neck positively glowed with an instant rash of embarrassment. 'Oh God, Ashleigh, have I put my foot in it? It's just that I assumed you and Guy had discussed . . .' He stopped talking.

'Discussed what?'

'Making Ada a partner of Gallow and Fitch.'

'Yes, yes, he did mention it, of course,' she lied, not wanting to admit to Bernie that not only was she blindsided by the news, but that it was a slap in the face that Guy had done this sneaky thing behind her back. 'You can leave the paperwork, and we'll get it all sorted and back to you.'

'Cheers, Ashleigh.' He removed a sheaf of papers from his leather bag and placed them on her desk. She put her hands between her thighs, trying to halt the tremble to her fingers.

'Obviously, no rush! I can imagine he and Ada will have their hands full over the next couple of weeks with the Bens.'

'Obviously.' She found a laugh that she hoped might disguise her desire to vomit.

'What do you think I should send? Flowers, is that the best thing?'

'I think flowers would be lovely.' It was incredible to her that she was managing this conversation while the room spun, and the air felt like it was being squeezed from her lungs.

After Bernie had left, she sat for a while and let her pulse settle, staring at the paperwork that was so much more than the sum of its parts. She and Guy had been good friends since they were eighteen. He and Archie, even longer. The three had been through all the exploits that went with this phase in their lives, drunken misspent evenings, the many dating disasters, falling in love, marriage, watching their careers take shape as they turned into the men and women they were always destined to become. Guy was one of the three people in her phone she could say with certainty she could call at one in the morning, and he'd be there, offering help, no questions asked. Guy, Archie, and of course, her sister Remy; the three pillars that she knew would remain upright in her life, even if she crumbled.

In ordinary circumstances, she'd have called Guy immediately or raced to his house or tracked him down as her anger grew and her frustration gathered and words of discontent and hurt queued up on her tongue, which she would no doubt unleash in a garbled, emotional manner at the sight of him. It wouldn't be the first time.

'You absolute dipstick, you could have been killed! You just walked out in front of the fricking car! You're drunk, go home! Jump in a cab right now and go home! You're a liability and I'm not your mother!'

Or:

'You told Archie I liked him? I told you that in confidence, you knob! And now I can't even look at him or be near him because he knows I like him and he's so far out of my league it's just excruciating! He's seeing Tamara and now I can't face her either! Thanks a bunch. God, I hate you!'

This felt very different.

Not only was he at home revelling in the baby bubble, which she, no matter how hurt, was not about to burst, but she also recognised that this discovery was not something that required anger or a flare of discontent. It was more than that: deeper, more affecting. And this was where she felt the hurt; at a visceral level. The deceit, the planning, the exclusion, the discussion with Bernie while she was in the dark, all sharp knives that she felt sticking into her chest. Gripping the desk, she took deep breaths with a terrible feeling that she had almost known it was coming, in one way or another. Waiting for it all her life – the exclusion, the unmasking, the stripping away of something she had no right to. A fraud.

She called Archie.

You have reached the answerphone of Archie Fitch.

She ended the call. Maybe it was a good thing he was otherwise occupied, knowing she needed to think very carefully about what she wanted to say, what she wanted to do, and that probably meant reading the infernal document that seemed to glow on the desk in front of her.

With her phone in her hand, her actions almost instinctive, she made the call.

'Hey, little dove.'

'Hey, little dove! Long time no speak!' Remy replied, and just like that Ashleigh felt the sob leave her body as her tears ran down her face, no doubt smudging her Dior mascara, but that was by the by.

How could Guy do this to her? Why would Guy do this to her? What the hell was going on?

'Oh. Ash, don't cry! Don't cry! What's the matter? I hate to hear you upset. What's happened? Did someone take the last Curly Wurly?'

And just the sound of her sister and this reminder of a different time, when she had sobbed upon discovering her dad had eaten her Curly Wurly, was enough to make her smile through her tears that just kept a-comin'.

'Nothing's the matter!' She sniffed.

'Yes. Ignore me. You do actually sound on top of the world!'

Ashleigh laughed and took a deep breath. 'Have you got a minute?'

'For you' – her sister spoke slowly, sincerely – 'I have two.'

'I don't know what to do,' she managed to say, her voice no more than a strangulated whisper.

'About what, my love?'

Her sister's sweet and empathetic tone only made her tears fall harder. It seemed that once she started talking, she couldn't stop, and it all came pouring out.

'About everything! I want to spend more time with Evie! I do, but it's not easy! Archie and I hardly see each other, we're always working, and who has a bloody baby and names it after their dog? I mean, I like the name Ben, I do, but what the hell? This is *my* business, my thing! How can someone just dump paperwork on my desk and tell me that's how it is? Is that right or fair?'

'Okay.' She heard Remy take a deep breath. 'Let's take this one thing at a time.'

'Okay.' Ashleigh wiped her face and breathed deeply. She pictured crying in the cubicle of their loo in primary school and how her sister had been there, holding her tight. This was what Remy did, made everything feel a little bit better.

Remy

Remy shifted on the uncomfortable plastic chair as she stared at the closed office door in front of her, nervously looking from left to right, not wanting Bertie or Harper to spy her while she waited outside the head teacher's office. It had been unusual for Ashleigh to call, and even more strange that she had been crying, babbling. She was usually so in control. Yet nice, nice that her sister knew that when she needed her, Remy would be there on the end of the phone.

You need to look after each other, always. You are, after all, miracles, two babies from one egg, rare and special!

Not that she'd entirely got to the bottom of her sister's distress. Something to do with a dog called Ben, her accountant, and worrying that she didn't spend enough time with Evie. It sounded like a typical case of overload and Mum guilt, which she understood. For her a hot bath and an early night usually did the trick. She'd no doubt get the full story when they went for lunch at The Plough. Guilt tingled in her veins at the fact that she'd been a bit less than enthused about her sister coming down. It was difficult to explain. She would *always* love her, but it was hard, watching Ashleigh arrive like a well-groomed hurricane and upset the balance of everything. Her voice, opinions, manner, it was all a little forced, and if Ashleigh didn't relax, no one did. No one could. As if she filled the room with an energy that crackled and kept them all on their toes.

A message arrived on her phone from Jamie.

WHAT TIMES KICK OFF TNIGHT?

His lack of etiquette and inattention to grammar and spelling bothered her more than it should. She chose to ignore the fact that had this exact same message been sent by Midge or anyone else, she would scarcely have noticed, but any contact from him . . . It was as if she were predisposed to feel this intense level of irritation. The Jamie Aller effect. When they'd parted, she had spent a year, maybe more, riven with intense frustration that verged on dislike, sobbing herself to sleep with the grip of failure in her gut. Hindsight had taught her that Jamie wasn't a bad person, just a selfish and unreliable one. Someone who was not and never was meant for her. It was a salient lesson not to confuse lust with love that she wished she had learned earlier. Not that she would change a thing, because they had made Sophie. Her heart flexed at the thought of seeing her later. The fact she and Jamie shared a child meant they were bound forever, whether they liked it or not, and that was just the way it was.

SEVEN O'CLOCK

She replied without any pleasantry that she was sure he would neither notice nor care about.

'Remy! Hi! Sorry to have kept you waiting. Come in!' called the jovial woman, who had had a hand in educating all three of Remy's kids, as she blustered along the corridor.

'Not at all. I'm just glad you could squish me in, Jane.'

She followed the headteacher into her small office that smelled of dust and disinfectant.

'Sit! Sit! Sit!' Jane pointed to the chair in front of her desk.

Remy sat.

'Right, what's up?'

She exhaled, trying to recall all the words and phrases she had practised on the way here, suddenly aware that it all sounded a bit meh, a bit *is that it*? She wished she'd phoned instead. Far easier to cringe and end the call unseen.

'It's Harper. She's having a bit of a tough time.'

'No! I'm sorry to hear that. In what way?'

She swallowed. 'I don't want to sound like one of those parents who wade in and whinge and try to fight their kid's corner or make them seem oversensitive or like they can't cope or . . .'

'Remy, it's fine. Just take your time and tell me what the problem is. And when I say take your time, you have precisely six minutes before I have to go and help the nursery with forest school.'

'Right, sorry, yes.' She took a beat. 'Harper doesn't make friends easily, as I'm sure you know, and she tends to cling to the ones she's got, desperate to be liked, worried they might drop her.

She frets over it. Which means *I* fret over it, fearful of what would happen if they did all fall out.'

'Poor little lamb.'

'Oh, it's not like I obsess over it, more that—'

'I meant Harper.'

'Course you did!' She blushed. Remy liked the woman enormously. 'Yes, anyway, yesterday there was a bit of a, don't even know what to call it, but a couple of her friends were mean to her, and I just wondered if you could keep an eye. I'd have spoken to Miss Hutchinson directly. She's great' – Remy didn't want Jane to think she found the teacher unapproachable – 'but I didn't want Harper to see me coming in and out of the class or get wind of it, don't want her to know that I've interfered. She made me promise not to.' This didn't exactly sit well with her.

'It's not interfering, it's raising a concern, and that's your job.'

'That's kind of what I said to her.' She breathed out, happy to hear confirmation she was doing the right thing.

'Right. Who was mean to her and what did it entail?' Jane leaned back in her chair, her expression serious, her stance legitimising Remy's concerns, which in turn helped the words flow.

'It was Casey and Ella, who I know are sweet girls, but they called her names and wouldn't let her sit with them, stuff like that. She was upset.'

'Of course she was. I'm sorry to hear that.'

'I'd rather anything wasn't said directly. You know how these things can blow over, enemies to besties in no more than a heartbeat, but . . .'

'But what?'

'Harper didn't tell me about the name calling, she told Bertie, and I got the feeling it wasn't the first time.'

'I'll do a general mention in assembly about kindness and looking after each other, all the usual reminders, and let's see how it goes. But come in any time, email, call with any concerns. Try not to worry. You're right, these things tend to blow over, but it's my absolute mission to ensure every child here feels safe and protected while they're in my care. And if Harper is distressed then something's not working.'

'Thanks, Jane.'

'Right, that's it! Your time's up. I'm off to forest school!'

'And I'm off to work. And then off to Sophie's end-of-year fashion show!'

'Stop it! It feels like five minutes ago she was running around here in her tutu.'

'I'd forgotten the tutu stage!' Picturing her chubby-faced darling in her pink net skirt was enough for Remy to feel a surge of emotion. It happened this way sometimes.

'She wouldn't take it off!' Jane laughed. 'Oh! Oh, look, you're crying!'

Remy couldn't help it. Just the thought of how quickly the time had flown and tears misted her eyes. Sophie had had a similar attachment to her bridesmaid's dress and would wear it to the supermarket, school disco, wherever and whenever she felt like it, paired with chunky boots; she had always run her own race when it came to fashion.

'It goes so quickly,' she sniffed.

Her mother's words still stuck in her thoughts, how she had blinked and decades had been erased. Sophie was twenty; a blink, and her daughter would be forty! The forties, according to Ruthie, seemed to have lasted the longest, a fact Remy was thankful for now, as she had the whole wide world and, apart from restoring the closeness she had once shared with Ashleigh, didn't want a thing to change.

'That's why I love my job. I get to live in this wondrous stage, year in, year out.' The woman put her hand on Remy's arm. 'Give Sophie my love and don't worry about Harper. We're on it.'

The car park was full as she pulled into the business park.

As if on cue, her mum called. Remy felt the familiar flare of irritation. It was of course always nice to hear from her mother, but ye gods, her timing!

'Mum, listen, you'll have to be quick, just pulled up at work.'

Jumping out of the car, she shoved her bag on her shoulder, wincing as the electric current ran over the top of her arm and along between her shoulder blades. It happened this way sometimes, one awkward move, an unfamiliar twist, and a pain that felt like a wire inside her arm and shoulder, a twinge, a shock that took her breath away. A reminder of that night when her body had become damaged, and her heart and spirit were so badly bruised. It was no longer a surprise that two decades after the attack, she still felt the physical after-effects. How she hated that those men, boys really, still had the power to cause her discomfort.

'Oh, don't let me keep you, love. Just wanted to check you've booked The Plough and that you told them Ashleigh was coming.'

'Yes, I emailed, and no, I didn't specifically name Ashleigh' – *she's not as famous outside of our house as she is in it*; this she kept to herself – 'but yes, all taken care of.'

'Smashing. I was wondering' – Remy rushed to the front of the building and felt her pulse increase as her mother continued – 'do you think if we asked, they would give us that lovely table near the window, the one we had year before last at Easter, do you remember? It was nice, quite private, and if we get that one then no one is going to disturb Ashleigh.'

Remy pulled the phone from her ear and stared at it, trying and failing to think of a single reason that someone might want to disturb Ashleigh mid beef and Yorkshire pud, as if she were Madonna, who most likely *would* court attention in the pub on a rainy Saturday.

'I could ask.'

'You're a love. And you're picking us up, is that right? Only your dad was asking earlier about the plan for his birthday. You know he likes to know the details.'

'Well, I *can* pick you up, but it means Midge will have to take the van and put the two kids in the front and I'll have to take Soph with me in the car, which leaves two spaces for you and Dad. *Or*' – she lifted her tone to show her next suggestion was her preference, knowing Midge would find the whole arrangement a right faff when it really didn't need to be – 'you and Dad can drive or get Ashleigh to pick you up on the way through, and then *we* can all go in one car and go straight there. Plus, that would mean Midge doesn't have to park the van in that tiny car park, and of course, Ashleigh's car has plenty of space, but it's up to you.' She paused and waited for her mother's decision, hoping she had done enough to persuade her on the best logistics to make the day work.

'Smashing, so you *can* pick Dad and me up. That sounds great. What time? We want to get there a bit early, before your sister arrives.'

'To get the fanfaring trumpeters in place . . .' Remy whispered through gritted teeth.

'What was that?'

'Nothing, Mum.' She rubbed her forehead. 'Yep, I'll pick you up. About one?'

'One on the dot. We'll be ready! And we must make sure Bertie brushes his hair.'

'God, yes, we absolutely must!'

Her mother's silence meant she had heard and understood her sarcasm.

Remy stood with the phone in her hand, wondering how such a short interaction could leave her feeling so frazzled. And that was before her working day had even started.

'Anyway, got to rush. Mum, but see you tonight. It starts at seven.'

'I know. I put a note on the fridge.'

'Great.' She ran towards the front steps.

'Looking forward to it! I'm in a bit of a dither over what to wear to a fashion show!'

'Youcanwearanythingyoulike.' She took a sharp breath. 'GottagoMum, seeyoulater!'

'Always rushing . . .' She heard her mother's lament as she ended the call and pulled the pass on her neck until she could place it on the automated system and gain entry. The security guard smiled and waved.

Reaching her work station in the nick of time, she shoved her bag under the desk and placed the headset on her head, readying her computer and preparing for her first call.

Graham appeared from nowhere, as if magicked from the cheap carpet like a supervising genie.

'The skin of your teeth, Remy Hughes, the skin of your teeth!'

'No Tyler today?' She looked over the courtesy board and realised that the place had a rare and welcome serenity. There was no shouting, no performance, no fake and deafening laugh . . . She hoped he wasn't poorly, but my goodness, it felt like a treat!

The prospect of not leaving the place with her head confuzzled and the lingering memory of his roar filled with her joy. It was going to be a good day! Her headset beeped and she took the call with a certain jollity to her tone.

'Good morning. Thank you for calling Castle Care. You are through to Remy. How can I help you today?'

The timer on her screen glowed green and, yet again, in this groundhog day of a job, her shift had begun.

Ashleigh

Ashleigh had taken her time in the shower; wearing the fatigue of a poor night's sleep meant she was starting the day on the back foot.

Her mood and movements were both a little sluggish. Wrapped now in a thick, white towel, she stared at her line-free face in the mirror. It had certainly paid off, getting tweakments before the first sign of wrinkles, and at forty, she carried the waxy, smooth complexion she'd been blessed with since her twenties. A fact that usually made her feel good, but not today. Today, like last night, she was distracted, trying to mentally filter the hurt and understand how Guy could have taken such steps, could have engaged their accountant, and could be thinking of doing something that would change the whole fabric of their business, their friendship, and had done so behind her back.

As hurt as she was angry, she knew she'd have to wait before confronting him, as becoming a father top-trumped anything work related, even this. There was also some small element of relief, the fact that she couldn't call him immediately and therefore didn't have to face it head on. It gave her time to process it. How she was going to break it to Archie without him going crazy was also a concern. It had never been an issue, her and her husband sharing a best friend, but this had the power to fracture their trust, even damage their future. She dressed and joined him downstairs.

'Morning, darling.' Archie smiled from the island, where he sipped orange juice and was, as ever, engrossed in his broadsheet.

'Did you have a nice time last night with the German?' she asked, only half interested in the answer, as she grabbed a slice of pumpernickel and spread it with organic peanut butter. Her plans for a family dinner had again been foiled, as Archie had come in late, and Evie had filled up on cheese on toast.

'I did, but' – he stared at her breakfast, his expression one of mild disgust – 'that looks . . . unappealing.'

'It's good for energy.' She took a tentative bite, and found a smile, unwilling to confess that when she felt a little low like this, a little knocked off course, what she really craved for breakfast was a big bowl of Frosties, or a toasted tea cake, or toast with thick, thick butter and jam, or chocolate, just bloody chocolate, an eclair, a bar of Cadbury's, she wouldn't be fussy, and she'd wash the lot down with a cold Dr Pepper, the sugary kind.

'Think I'd rather have no energy.' He pulled a face.

'So, big news.' She wiped her mouth. 'Ada has had the baby.'

'What? No way! Oh, that's great! Way to go, Papa Gigi!' He folded the paper and threw it on to the countertop, giving her his full attention. 'What did they get? Give me the details!'

'Well, I don't have too many, but mother and baby are well, and it's a little boy and they've called him Ben.'

'Ben?' He looked about as confused as she felt. 'Did you mean to say Ben?'

'Yes, I did. I meant to say Ben. Honestly, Archie, I can't even—' She stared into the garden, looking for inspiration, or at least clarity. 'It's Ben, as in the name of their dog, the dog Ben and now the baby Ben.' She shrugged.

'Is it like a . . . a holding name until they figure out what they actually want to call him? Remember we called Evie *Peanut* for the first few days, while we chose a name?'

'I do.'

She smiled, *Peanut* . . . it had felt nice, surreal, unpressured. Visitors fussing over her as little Peanut slept in the bassinet, everyone pitching up at the Lindo Wing, bringing her fruit and flowers, as she lay in a post-birth, warm cocoon of low lighting. And Archie, Archie looking at her in a way he hadn't before, like she was a goddess, his beautiful goddess who had done this miraculous thing. It struck her then, the before and after – from the time they had met until the moment they left the hospital, when everything had changed, when *she* had changed. It had just happened, as if shutters had gone up and there were no instructions on how to lower them again. And she might mentally be hammering on them until her fists bled, but it seemed no one could hear.

Archie hadn't looked at her in that way for the longest time; she felt the bite of sorrow about her throat that made speaking and breathing a little tricky. How she would love him to look at her like that again. She coughed and swallowed the hard ball of sadness that she felt had no right to be there, not when she had so much. But there it was, the belief that it shouldn't really be hers, not any of it.

It's done, Ash! No one will ever know, and that's all that matters!

But I know . . . She ran her fingers over the sparkling granite work surface and smothered the thought.

'No, not a holding name,' she clarified. 'Guy sounded adamant, even got a bit shirty when I questioned it. Ben, that's his name. Baby Ben.'

'Was he drunk?'

'Baby Ben? No, I think he's still only on milk.' She laughed. 'I do love you, Archie, I do. I really love you.'

It came out of nowhere, out of context, her need to say it almost overwhelming and her need to know he loved her in return, and that no matter what, they were solid, even greater.

'Ash . . .' He stood from the bar stool and came to hold her, wrapping her in his arms where she let her head rest on his chest, eyes closed, blocking out the hurt at the fact that Guy had let her down, upset her, was possibly trying to edge her out. 'Are you okay?' he whispered, and she inhaled the scent of him, his lemony fragrance, and the peppery smell of his skin.

'I'm fine.' She eased away and dropped the remainder of her breakfast into the bin, before running herself a glass of cold water. Archie retook his stool and picked up his paper.

'We should do something, tonight, you, me and Evie, all three of us, what do you say?'

'Yes, great. What were you thinking?' She turned to face him.

'Supper, all three of us eating together.'

Her gut rolled with hunger at no more than the thought of it. This was what she wanted: family time. It sounded perfect.

'Brilliant! I was thinking similar. Let's do that.' It delighted her how in sync they were. She looked up as Marguerite came into the kitchen and headed straight for the coffee machine. 'Morning!'

'Morning, Ashleigh. How was the lasagne?'

'Oh, we didn't, erm . . .' She felt a little embarrassed, having asked her specifically to make it. 'It looked lovely, but Archie got in late, I wasn't really in the mood for food, and Evie was a little tired, so she had cheese on toast.' She smiled, trying to disguise the desolation she had felt as she climbed between the sheets, the house quiet, Archie absent and no one with whom she could discuss the turmoil of her day.

'Will you eat it tonight, or shall I freeze it?'

They were, she reminded herself, busy people with busy lives; there was no need to feel so embarrassed. 'We're going to have it tonight, all three of us, eating together. That's the plan. I'm looking forward to it!'

Marguerite looked nonplussed and opened the fridge to no doubt admire her handiwork, as she removed the milk for the coffee she liked to make the moment she arrived.

'What would you think, Marguerite, if a couple had a baby and gave the new baby the same name as their dog?'

The woman stopped to think about this before facing them both. 'I'd think they were either the dumbest people on the planet or the laziest. Or maybe the funniest if the dog and baby were both called Rover or Rex or K9.'

'Ben.' She gave the context. 'They've named their son Ben, and the dog is called Ben.'

'Idiots!' Marguerite shook her head. 'Absolute idiots.'

Ashleigh hoped she was talking about Ben's parents and the great name debacle, and not her and Archie, who had to make a plan just to sit down together and eat a bloody lasagne.

Remy

Remy did her best at these events to look like a young and hip mum who took life in her stride. It certainly felt like the kind of place where that was required. She'd carefully selected her fitted Fair Isle tank top that she wore over a white shirt, her Uggs, obviously, and her good jeans. An outfit that she hoped said *cool mum who can sing along to The Streets, a mum who is up on the latest trends, a mum old enough to have wisdom and yet young enough to rock these boots.*

The arts college where so many clever kids went to study painting, textiles, fashion, sculpture, and ceramics, was another world. Sophie's world. Just to be among it gave her a thrill! As ever, to be in a place of higher learning, any college, made her think about the prospectuses she had hoarded under her mattress, quietly plotting and imagining a different kind of life, before the universe had kicked her in the face and busted her shoulder and she had understood the value of staying close to home, of keeping the world at bay.

Oi! There it was, the gunshot.

She reached for Midge's hand.

As she made her way into the foyer with her mum also by her side, she remembered the open day, nearly three years ago, when she had been in awe of the displays right here, the paintings on the wall, the sculptures in the studios.

'I can't believe someone *made* this! A youngster – it's incredible! Wow, Soph! Have you seen this?' She had pointed to a stunning frock on a mannequin. 'A student designed and created this dress – I can't believe it! Look at it. So beautiful!'

Her daughter had pulled her to one side in the corridor and flicked her blunt, long, pink fringe from her face. 'Mum, I love that you're enthusiastic for me to take up a place here' – there had been much discussion about how some of her friends' parents were against their children following a less than academic path – 'but for God's sake, stop being so . . . impressed!'

Remy had nodded, hadn't realised she was being overly keen, but crucially aware that she was embarrassing Sophie in the process. All she wanted was for her daughter to grab every opportunity and to know that they supported her, no matter what. It was a freedom she and Ashleigh could only have dreamed of, a life without academic pressure, hence why they had kept this secret for so long, understanding that for her mum and dad it was St. Jude's or bust.

Sardinia or Southend . . .

'Sorry!' she'd mouthed, and mimed zipping up her lips and throwing away the key.

The truth being she *was* impressed, massively so! It was awe-inspiring to see the creations and artistic outputs of these young creatives, who were still mere babies in her book. She couldn't wait to see what the future held for them all. None more so than her very own baby Sophie, who at nineteen was the confident, non-conformist, kind, strong, brilliant woman she had always known she would be. Remy knew she had been similar, until that damn night that had changed everything.

With Sophie's ever-changing look, subtle wit and her incredible style, Remy knew her first-born little dove would set the world on fire! Harper was different, more considered, more concerned with what others thought and without the defiant spark that made Sophie question everything. Remy hoped Harper had had a better day at school. With Sophie, it was as if she understood, even as a baby, that she couldn't rely on Jamie, and therefore she *had* to rely on herself. Neither of them could have guessed that eventually

Midge would come into their lives and help build a solid dock on which they could all rest, come rain or shine.

'I'm a bit nervous!'

Remy smiled at Ruthie.

'Don't be. She's been working on the show for months, and you know what a perfectionist she is.'

'I've never been to a fashion show before.' Her mum beamed and adjusted the navy silk scarf at her neck. 'Hope we get good seats. I promised your dad I'd try and take a photo. I've got a disposable camera.' She rummaged in her bag for the thing and held it up. 'You'll have to show me how it works, Midge. Last time I used one was when we went to that open garden in Bath. It was only when we got the film developed that I realised I'd had the camera the wrong way round. We got twenty-four pictures of my left eye!'

'Don't think you're allowed to take photos, Ruthie,' Midge laughed, 'but you can see the pieces up close afterwards and you can photograph them then, just not during the show.'

Remy stared at her man, who had shaved and put on his cologne. It seemed he too was overly aware of making the right impression. Her dad had very kindly agreed to babysit for Harper and Bertie, who would no doubt have him playing a board game at which they could cheat while they all ate more Maltesers than was good for them.

'What do I do if they won't go to sleep?' he'd asked as she left.

'Tell them all about concrete, Dad. That can send anyone to sleep.'

'Cheeky mare!' He'd winked.

'Let's sit down, shall we?' She knew her pulse would only settle when they were in situ. Her heart sank a little, as they entered the large hall, to see that most of the seats seemed to be taken, and the excited burble of conversation that hung in a pungent cloud over the crowd suggested they'd been here for some time. The invite had said seven o'clock, and here they were at seven o'clock. These keeners must have been queuing around the block! Not that there was a darn thing she could do about it now. Getting everyone in from school, home from work, fed and watered and dropped and collected, had been a chore in itself. She heard Graham's nasal tone in her mind: *By the skin of your teeth, Remy Hughes . . .*

'Are we going to be able to get three seats together?' her mother asked with a nervousness she could relate to.

'Four, Mum. Jamie's coming,' she reminded her, and saw Midge stiffen.

'Oh, gawd, I forgot!' Ruthie's eye-roll and tight-lipped response kind of summed it up for them all.

'There's two.' Midge pointed. 'You and Ruthie take them, and I'll go and stand behind. I don't mind.'

'Are you sure, love?' She didn't want to be separated, but equally wanted to get her mother seated.

'Of course. I'll be right behind you.' He pointed to a gap between the rows of chairs and the wall where a couple of people were already standing. Touch was their love language, and she brushed his arm as she walked past, sidling into the row.

'Excuse me.' She smiled, pointing to the two spare chairs in the middle of the line. 'Thanks. Thank you. Sorry.' She guided her mum, as those already seated moved bags from the floor and twisted their legs to the side to allow them access.

'We can move down, make space.' One lovely lady spoke out as she did just that, and hey presto! There were three seats.

'Midge!' she called, pointing and beckoning. He nodded and made his way over. 'Thank you. That's so kind!'

The woman smiled her acknowledgement and Remy felt all her worry over the logistics of the night fade away, as the three took their seats and opened their programmes. Jamie would just have to find a spot when he arrived. There wasn't a whole lot she could do about it. She scanned the pages, and there it was, Sophie's name and the name of her show, the third in the programme.

Sophie Aller-Hughes BA Hons Fashion Design presents 'All or Nothing!'

'There she is, look!' Ruthie held up the pamphlet and pointed to Sophie's entry.

'Yep, I've got it right here, Mum.' She raised her own copy, but did so without irritation, knowing her mum felt exactly as she did in that moment: so very, very proud.

'Here we are then!' She heard him before she saw him, wincing as she turned her head to face her ex, who spoke at his usual volume, as if she were on one side of an empty field and he were on the other. 'All right, Rem?' He clasped his hands and sucked air through his teeth. 'Any seats?'

'Erm . . .' She looked up and down the row and pointed to one in front.

'I need two!' He stood to one side and pointed at a woman, his guest, his date, his latest, who raised her hand in a wave. 'This is Lauren!'

'It's Laurel,' Laurel corrected him.

'We can all shove up, again.' Lovely woman did the honours and, just like that, two free seats appeared next to Midge.

'Cheers, darlin'!' Jamie yelled to the woman who had been so kind, and gave her a double thumbs-up. His leather jacket squeaked as he raised his arms.

'All right, Midge, me old mucker!' Jamie punched him lightly on the arm as he liked to do and Midge nodded, quietly, slowly.

'Yep, all good, Jamie. Nice to meet you, Laurel.' He twisted to greet her.

'Hi!' Remy, too, waved at Jamie's very attractive date, who wore a tight-fitting leopard-print dress.

'This is something, isn't it?' Jamie bounced in his seat like a child at the cinema. 'A bloody fashion show! She'll be in Paris next, or Milan, you mark my words!'

She felt her face colour, as it did whenever Jamie spoke loudly in public, paying no heed to the room, none at all, as if he were unaware that everyone there was supporting their own Sophie and all of them harboured the same kind of dream.

'Yep.' Midge, it seemed, was in the firing line to deal with the man and had no choice but to converse. She felt her insides flip and knew she owed her husband big time.

'You all right then, Ruthie?' Jamie leaned across and raised his voice as if her mother were deaf or deficient in her understanding.

'Yes, thanks.' Her mother smiled briefly at him and his date before burying her head back in the programme.

Ruthie had always been cool yet civil to the man, and Remy silently thanked her for it, knowing that if Sophie or Harper turned up on her own doorstep in a similar predicament, she couldn't guarantee the same treatment. Not that it was entirely Jamie's fault. It wasn't.

Without further ado, the doors at the back of the hall closed and the lights dimmed.

'Here we go then!' Jamie shouted.

She reached for Midge's hand and took comfort from the way he squeezed her fingers. It spoke volumes, it said *I love you, Ren. It's okay. He's loud, but harmless. We're good. This is exciting. Let's do this for Soph!* So in tune were they, she got all of that from one tiny squeeze.

There were, throughout her day, markers that reminded her that she was no longer in the first flush of youth. The ache to her shoulder in the cold morning, the way it took her eyes a while to properly focus at the start of the day, her need to devour the news on the radio while the kettle boiled, her colleagues' lengthy discussions about *Grand Theft Auto*, in which she had absolutely zero interest, their in-jokes, laughing heartily as they quoted from *The Osbournes*, all of it left her feeling, if not old, then certainly much, much older than them. And in those moments she wondered how her life had sped by so quickly, remembering being of a similar age. Her life had been different, tethered as she was to her mum and dad, trying to make amends for the keeping of secrets from them. And then the accident, confirming the thought that it was better, safer, to stay close to all that was familiar, to hold tightly on to the foundations of her life and close her eyes.

Deafening music filled the room, so loud she couldn't hear herself think. Her mother put her fingers in her ears. Remy wished she could do similar but was aware that she was trying to be a young hip mum who took life in her stride. A young hip mum who *loved* this kind of techno blasted into her eardrums! She found a smile that she hoped wasn't a grimace and stared at the stage.

The light show was spectacular. The white flashes and pulsing neon did much to distract from the music and as soon as the first models appeared she almost forgot the infernal noise. The clothes were breathtaking! Sharply cut suits with oversized structured jackets and loose pants with hanging straps, all worn by androgynous students with deadpan expressions that absolutely would not have been out of place on the catwalks of Milan or Paris. The crowd clapped with heartfelt enthusiasm, and when the boy who had designed the pieces came on to the stage in his own fabulous suit, it felt entirely right to rise and give him a standing ovation! She had no need to ask who his parents were as she spied the couple sobbing into their hands as their son did his thing. And she understood. That feeling when your kids did good . . .

'What were you thinking? Why would you do this to me? All you had to do was one thing, one thing! Go and sit the exam, a couple of hours of your time, that was all . . .'

She blinked away the memory.

The next show was similarly high octane, the music more of the pop variety and the light show in shades of crimson and fuchsia. This collection was of evening gowns – beautiful, beautiful dresses with gathered waists, boned bodices, and acres of tulle that floated down the runway and lifted the skirts to make them full and vast. Again, the crowd went wild! The designer of the stunning frocks crept out to take her bow with obvious reluctance, pushing her glasses up on to her nose and fiddling with the tape measure around her neck that hung down over the shoulders of her ratty T-shirt. Impressive didn't come close! Remy was in awe!

'This is it!' Jamie shouted, leaving no one in any doubt who he had come to see. Remy smiled at him. It was impossible not to be wrapped up in the electric atmosphere, and she was glad he had made the effort, knowing it would mean a lot to Sophie.

Midge's leg jumped with nerves and her mum sat up straight in preparation to take it all in. Remy held her breath, excited, nervous, and desperate to see her clever girl's designs.

The room plunged into darkness, which was as surprising as it was intense, and everyone gasped, before the room slowly filled with a quivering blue light as if they were underwater. The music was soft, the gentle roll of waves crashing, whale song, and in the background, the melodic hum of a folk-inspired tale about the sea, sung by a voice of such clarity and beauty it made the hairs on the back of her neck stand up.

The music went on and still no model appeared. Remy turned to Midge and pulled a wide-mouth smile, a smile that said, *Hope it's all going to plan. Shouldn't someone be on the stage by now?*

He bit his lip, eyes wide in anticipation.

Even leopard-print Laurel sat forward in her seat, her look one of excitement.

A girl did eventually appear, wearing jeans with a plastic shopping bag fashioned into a halter-neck top. With a sparkling microphone held close to her lips, she began to half talk, half sing, her words a rolling montage of facts mixed with words that everyone concentrated to hear.

'Hundreds of thousands of tons, hundreds of thousands of tons! That's how much clothing we throw away each year! Clothes we won't wear because we don't like the colour, the style, outdated-after-one-wear clothes, cheap, cheap clothes for which the earth pays a high, high price! You should weep! You should weep for our planet, but weep too for our seas! Hundreds of thousands of tons of microplastic, that's what the fashion industry puts into the ocean each year – fish and chips and plastic, you want salt and vinegar with that?'

Remy looked at her mum, whose face was contorted as if she was confused. Granted, it wasn't what they had been expecting, but it was brave and fearless and memorable!

The girl on the stage continued.

'Water polluted for dyeing, for finishing, for fashion, for what? All or nothing! That's it, all or nothing, so we say choose nothing! Re-wear, re-use, recycle! Stop the waste! Choose nothing! Choose the planet!'

And then came the models.

All barefoot, wearing plastic bags, crudely stapled together to cover their modesty. All with eyes rimmed with dark kohl and hair wild and tied with the plastic that cans usually sat clustered in. The girl's voice got louder, the models grouped on the edge of the stage in a crowded, haphazard jumble, crammed together, and then came Sophie, her beautiful girl, herself in a bin liner.

'Enough!' the girl shouted, and the music stopped, and the lights held still, and Remy fully understood the expression 'to hear a pin drop', as a collective silence held them in thrall. 'All or nothing, and we choose nothing! We choose change!'

It was perfectly choreographed; as she shouted the last word, everyone on the stage pulled the plastic bags from their bodies and stood in their underwear, the terrible statistics that still rang in her ears scrawled on their arms and legs in black paint. And then darkness, total darkness, before the first clap and then a whoop of approval, and then Sophie got *her* standing ovation and Remy thought her heart might burst from her chest, as she clapped and stood and did her best to swallow the tears that snaked into her mouth.

'Brava!' was the chorus, and she could only nod and clap as emotion rendered her mute.

Midge grabbed her and held her tight, and as she looked over his shoulder, she saw Jamie, crying and clapping. 'That's my daughter!' he repeated to anyone who caught his eye. 'That's my daughter!'

And she was glad he had come.

Ashleigh

Ashleigh read the message and put her phone face down on the counter before digging the big spoon into the bubbling lasagne and dolloping a portion into the white ceramic bowl. It was lovely to be home with Archie. The mellow sound of Norah Jones floated from the surround sound, she'd even lit a candle on the island, and now she sipped from her glass of red. Doing her best to calm her pulse, putting her worry over Guy, over the business, over her trip home this coming weekend and a thousand other mental paper cuts out of her mind, on this rare early evening when they were all together.

This was how she made things better: a family dinner, being present, this was how she brought them closer together, how she gave her daughter the kind of memories that sustained her. When life threatened to overwhelm Ashleigh and her feelings of low self-worth almost drowned her, this was how she felt like she belonged, had a right to be here.

Just breathe . . .

Evie lay on the rug with a book in her hands, and just the prospect of the three of them sitting down to supper was enough to lift Ashleigh's spirits. The fact they had Marguerite's fabulous food to tuck into, a bonus. She was hungry.

'Was that a text from Guy? How're they doing?'

She hadn't spoken to Guy and felt decidedly awkward at the mention of him. 'No, it was my mum, saying she has the spare room all set up if we want to stay with them after Dad's birthday lunch tomorrow.'

'It'll be fun.' He sipped his wine.

'Yep.' She handed him the bowl.

'Smells delicious!' Archie grabbed his fork, sleeves rolled up, ready for his supper.

'There's plenty more.' She smiled with a pride she had no right to. This was, after all, not her handiwork. 'Have some salad too.' She pushed the wooden bowl full of fresh green leaves towards him. Trying not to be bossy but wanting him to eat something balanced.

'Is there any garlic bread?' Evie asked, as she took a seat and looked hopefully towards the oven.

'Garlic bread? No! This is filling enough. Have you been listening to your dad, who likes to double down on carbs?'

Evie looked at Archie, who winked at her. It felt exclusionary, and Ashleigh's cheeks flamed accordingly.

'Marguerite always gives me garlic bread with lasagne.'

'Well, Marguerite isn't here.' She placed the bowl in front of her daughter and served herself a small portion, knowing she would have to hit the pavement early in the morning to work it off.

Evie picked up her fork and sniffed it, before taking a minute bite of pasta. Ashleigh found it a little infuriating. This was not the action of someone who was happy to be eating as a family. It wasn't what she had envisaged.

'So is there any news on Ben Baby?' Archie asked with gusto, designed, she knew, to create a tributary, diverting them from the slightly tense flow that they were in danger of getting carried away on.

'Is that how we're going to differentiate, Ben Baby and Ben Dog?' She pulled a face at the absurdity of it.

'I think so. It will be easier when we're with them physically and we can point and say, *this little chap!*'

She shook her head, not knowing how it would be, to see their friends, to make small talk, still trying to come to terms with the sneakiness of Guy and Ada's behaviour, and the disloyalty that had whacked her around the chops so hard she could almost feel the sting.

Adding to her discomfort was the fact it was now a secret she kept from Archie, feeling humiliated, embarrassed that Guy had done this, had kept her in the dark. Proof that their relationship had broken down.

She was also mindful that the men had been friends since their days at Clifton, and the thought of her putting a splinter in that was almost too much to contemplate. She knew the pain of realising an old, reliable friend was slipping out of reach . . . picturing Remy exchanging a wide-eyed look of irritation with Tony when Ashleigh had told them with much excitement about the boy she had met at uni whose name was Archie. It had hurt. It hurt still.

It was as unfathomable as it was upsetting, how quickly things had turned a little sour with Guy, and how she felt unable to even call the man who had been her great friend for the longest time. One of her pillars.

The sheaf of paperwork sat in her bag, unread, humming like a toxic thing that drew her thoughts in the early hours and at any other gap in her busy day.

Did he want her out completely? Was this what it was about? A stepping stone to replacing her with Ada? Ada, who had never worked in their industry. Ada, who had not worked much full stop. Remy had told her not to overthink it. If only it were that simple.

'Ash!' Archie shouted as he banged the flat of his palm on the counter. It was jarring.

'What?' She looked up.

'Evie was telling you about her project. You were miles away!'

'Evie!' She wiped her fingers over her face. 'I'm sorry my love. Daddy's right, I was miles away! Please tell me about your project. Is it still the Romans?'

She smiled and took a mouthful of lasagne. Archie was right, it was delicious, but when your stomach had shrunk with anxiety and sat somewhere beneath your throat, and your thoughts whirred and you felt sadness at a visceral level, making your bones feel brittle, as your friend's betrayal was lodged like a stick in your heart, it was hard to enjoy anything. Even Marguerite's fabulous lasagne turned to ash on her tongue and threatened to choke her.

'Romans was last term. We're doing World War Two now.' Her daughter spoke with reservation, clearly disappointed her mum did not know this.

'World War Two! Wowsers! Well, you should speak to Grandad Dennis. His daddy, my grandad, fought in that war. His name was Charlie, and he was a porter in a field hospital in France, and he got a medal. I think he had great adventures, even though it was terrible.'

'Yes,' Archie boomed, 'and *my* grandfather was in the cabinet office. He worked for Winston Churchill himself and was knighted to the Most Nobel Order of the Garter for his services to King and country.' Her husband sat tall in his seat.

Ashleigh held her fork and stared at him, quite unable to voice how dismissed she felt, how he had nullified her grandad's efforts. She didn't want to bicker, not tonight, when she had been so looking forward to this supper.

'A knight! Wow! Did he have a suit of armour and a horse?' Evie was clearly quite taken with the idea.

Archie laughed loudly, so loudly.

'Plenty of horses, yes. I remember their stables very well, but no suit of armour that I can recall.'

'I expect he also knew to make garlic bread when serving lasagne, did he?' Ashleigh fired the sarcasm across the table.

'I doubt it. He had a cook.' They locked eyes and the tension flared. 'But he did know the value of a decent family dinner where kindness and conversation were allowed to flow. He knew it was the glue that bound.'

Kapow! His words landed like a punch.

'Wow! He sounds marvellous!' She gave a fake smile.

Evie stared at her.

'Are you okay, Mummy?' Her little girl's voice was small and croaky.

Ashleigh put the fork down, knowing she couldn't stomach even the smallest mouthful.

'I'm sorry, Evie.'

'That's okay. I don't really need garlic bread.' Her child stared at her with big eyes that carried worry beyond her years.

Evie swallowed, and Ashleigh studied her. Her little one looked as if her heart was beating very quickly and like she might feel a little sick. Ashleigh understood how it could happen like this sometimes, when the world felt very big, and you felt very small and entirely uncertain of your place in it. She pictured sitting at the kitchen table on exam day and wishing she could disappear. The thought that she might have made Evie feel similar was gut-wrenching. The very opposite of what she wanted to achieve with this dinner.

'Can I . . . Can I take my supper and go and watch a cartoon?' Evie almost whispered.

'Course you can.' Archie reached out and ruffled her hair. 'Tell you what. I'll pop our grub on trays and come and join you. We can watch and eat from our laps. How does that sound?'

Ashleigh watched as her daughter nodded and climbed down from the high stool. Her podgy bare feet made a sticking sound as they padded across the wooden floor as she made her way towards the refuge of the den and those infernal cartoons.

'Sort it out, Ashleigh!' Archie spoke firmly, as he reached for Evie's bowl. 'Whatever it is, please just get a handle on it!'

She sat at the table long after the two had left, could hear their laughter and the ping and boing of the cartoon soundtrack filtering back into the vast, handcrafted kitchen. Making her way to the den, she put her hand on the door that was ajar, wanting so badly to jump in and sit with her husband and child, wanting them to invite her in, to budge up and make space on the sofa. They were laughing, the two of them, laughing at those infernal cartoons, a team of two. She stood for a few minutes, willing them to notice her, to smile at her, let her know all was forgiven, but they didn't. It reminded her of being at school, that feeling in her gut that she didn't quite belong, that this was not her place. At home too, as a teenager, while Remy and Tony danced in that tiny bedroom and she lay on her bed, listening to them, waiting for an invite that never came.

It felt easier to walk away, to go back to the solitude of the kitchen.

Lonely and alone, she wondered what Remy was doing, and was looking forward to seeing her tomorrow in a way she hadn't for a while. It would be good to get out of London, away from the house, where she felt the walls were closing in, away from the business that felt like it was slipping through her fingers, away from Archie, Guy, and the Bens. Good to spend time with Evie in the car, and good to catch up with the other little dove.

So good.

Remy

Remy sat at the kitchen table, sipped her morning coffee, and mentally replayed images from Sophie's fashion show. She was barely able to contain her tears as pride rose up in her throat and spilled over. It was amazing to her, the confidence of her daughter, who had set her own course and was running towards her future. It was something Remy was unable to imagine, having never fully cut the ties of duty and penance that kept her close to her mum and dad.

Midge walked in with a fistful of dirty mugs, no doubt gathered from the far corners of the house, and usually only retrieved when the mug tree was bare.

'All set?'

'Yeah. I can't stop thinking about Soph last night.'

Midge rested his hands on his hips. 'Me too. I didn't fancy going, not really. I mean, I want to support Sophie, always, but a fashion show? I didn't really think it was my thing, but honestly, Ren. It was breathtaking.'

'It was.' She bit her lip, wondering how long the warm, fuzzy glow of joy that she felt inside might last.

'You look nice.' He studied her and she liked the way his eyes sparkled.

'I washed my hair and ironed my knickers.'

'Impressive.'

It wasn't far from the truth. The days of her going full glam were behind her.

'So, is Ashleigh picking your mum and dad up on the way? She'll practically be driving past.'

'No.' She faced him, waiting for his commentary. 'The plan is I'm taking Soph and picking them up in the car, which means you and the little ones are in the van.'

'That makes no sense! None at all.' He dumped the china into the sink, if not aggressively then certainly with a clatter. 'Three cars, instead of . . .'

'I know! Midge. I know! I tried!' She sighed, without the energy or inclination to have this conversation again and feeling that warm, fuzzy glow of joy dim a little.

'Bert, Harper, get your trainers on, loves. We're heading off in a minute,' he called to the kids, who sat side by side at the dining table, eyes glued to the wall-mounted TV.

'Can we watch the end of our programme? It's nearly finished,' Bert asked, his tone urgent, as if his life depended on it.

'Yep.'

Midge sighed and reached for the van keys. 'There's always these ridiculous shenanigans. Can't believe we're not just all jumping into one car, like a normal family on a day out. I don't know why you let them tie us up in knots like this.'

'Midge,' she implored, wanting him not to dwell on it, 'we are not a normal family.'

'That much I do know.' He smiled. There it was, the slight thawing, the love, the understanding.

'It's just how it is! They drive me mad too!' She wanted him to know she got it, was on his side.

'I just wish you'd put your foot down, just once.' He spoke calmly.

'I know it doesn't make sense, love. Mum insisted, and you know what she and Dad are like when they get a plan into their heads.'

'You could always say no.'

She laughed out loud before his expression told her he wasn't joking. And had it not sounded like pure sarcasm, she would have told him that, truthfully, she'd not thought of that. Aware that she never challenged the ridiculous, overcomplicated plans, never; aware that at a subconscious level she was always trying to please her parents, to make amends for letting them down. Every day, since she was ten years of age, trying to make them forgive her for not taking the exam and changing her life when she'd had the chance. Even though she had of course taken the bloody exam but had changed Ashleigh's life instead.

Not that she could tell him this. Not now, with so much time having passed. It was a horrible, spiky betrayal that sat between them that she didn't know how to fix.

She called up the stairs to their daughter. 'Ready when you are, Soph! Don't forget Grandad's present, your protest placard, that kind of thing!'

'Very funny.' Sophie slunk down the stairs, fully dressed and looking gorgeous in mustard knitted tights, a green faux-suede miniskirt and a striped hand-knitted jumper that fell off her shoulder. Her wide, blunt fringe framed her face, and her only make-up was a dark lipstick.

'I can joke, but honestly, little dove, Dad and I were just saying how incredible you were. We're so proud. And you look great, by the way!'

'Thank you. All thrifted.' She lifted the fluted edge of her skirt and curtseyed.

'You're so clever, Soph. You really are.' She loved these moments when pure pride coursed through her veins at this wondrous woman she had grown. A young woman who ran her own race.

'Take after my mumma.'

'Or your Auntie Ashleigh, if you listen to your nan.' She kissed her eldest child on the cheek.

'Haven't seen Evie for ages,' Sophie pointed out.

'Me either. I'm excited!' She hunched her shoulders, knowing that her relationship with her niece was a casualty of Ashleigh living so far away and their less than regular communication. She thought about the phone call yesterday; it had been nice, her sister reaching out to her in that way. 'Right, gang, Sophie and I are leaving the building. We'll see you there.'

Midge walked over and kissed her on the face. 'See you in a bit.' It felt a lot like forgiveness.

'Yep, see you in a bit, my love.'

Remy pulled the car up in front of her parents' house and Sophie ran in to knock on the door. They were of course loitering in the hallway, ready to go.

'Happy birthday, Dad!' she called as he climbed into the back of her Corsa, Sophie next to him. Her mother, as befitting the matriarch, took the front seat.

'Thank you, Remy.' He crinkled his eyes shut in love for her.

'You don't want to sit in the front? A birthday treat?' she teased, nodding at her mother, who was busy adjusting her skirt.

'No, it's easier for her to co-pilot from there.' He winked at Remy in the rear-view mirror. 'I see number twenty-two have left their wheelie bin out again!' He shook his head as they drove past. 'How hard can it be to pop it inside the gate? It clearly states on the council leaflet that bins are not to be left out on the pavement after collection day. It's these small details that can wreck a neighbourhood!'

Remy stared at her daughter in the mirror, and they exchanged a knowing look. Sophie, no doubt, like her, thinking that if the worst thing a neighbourhood had to contend with was a misplaced wheelie bin, then it was hardly wrecked.

'Will there be something you can eat at the pub, Sophie?' Her mum spoke through the gap between the seats. 'I know you don't eat meat or chicken or anything like that.'

Remy decided not to point out that chicken was meat. *Potato potarto . . .*

'There will be, Nan. Last time I went they had a chickpea curry and a couple of starters to choose from. I'll be fine.'

'Don't you ever want to try a nice steak or a bit of crispy bacon?'

'I don't, Grandad, no.'

'Well I never.' Her dad shook his head as if he just didn't get it. 'Do you think they'd be offended if I reminded them at number twenty-two of the rules about bin stowage? Don't want to fall out with anyone, but it is a bit much.'

And just like that they were back to the bins.

'Slow down, Remy. We want to arrive in one piece.' Her mum tutted and gripped her seat belt as if this might, in the event of an accident, make all the difference.

Remy felt it churlish to point out that A) instead of tutting, her mother might acknowledge that she'd come out of her way to collect them and that it had caused ripples of unease between her and Midge, and B) she was doing thirty-three miles per hour on a stretch of road where the speed limit was forty. It wasn't lost on her that whether fourteen or forty, she still didn't feel able to answer back.

'Although we don't want Ashleigh to be kept waiting,' her dad pointed out. And for a split second, Remy genuinely didn't know whether to pump the brakes or hit the accelerator. This was what they did, confused her, turned her into her seven-year-old self without confidence in her own decision-making or her ability to get a task done. It was bloody infuriating!

'Shame Archie had a work thing.' Her mum changed the topic. 'He's a very busy man, has a very important job.'

'Apparently so.'

Remy stared straight ahead. It bothered her, how *busy* they thought Archie was, whereas Midge, who ran himself ragged trying to keep all the plates spinning and everyone happy, doing everything and anything for his family and anyone else who cared to ask, well, to hear her mother talk, you'd think Midge spent his days sitting on his arse.

'How's the outside tap working out, Dad?' She slowed and indicated at the junction.

'Oh, it's grand! Everything's so much easier. I can water all the tubs, clean the car.'

The car you never use . . .

'Good,' she breathed. 'I'll let Midge know.' She subtly made the point.

The car park at The Plough was rammed.

'Goodness only knows where Ashleigh's going to park. She's got that big old car!' Again, her mother came in with that tut.

'Or Midge in that big old van!' Remy clicked her tongue against the roof of her mouth.

'You might have to drop us off and go and find somewhere to park, love,' her dad suggested.

'Yes. Why don't I do that?' She bit her tongue. Literally and figuratively.

With her parents decanted, shepherded by Sophie, she reversed out of the awkward, narrow car park and drove back out to the main road, abandoning her car a little way along, with two wheels up on the grass, where a couple of others had done the same thing. She took a minute, gathering herself, calming her pulse and reminding herself that it was her dad's special day, and everyone was very excited. Emotions were bound to run a little high, and it would be over soon enough.

Midge pulled up behind her and jumped out.

'I've just dropped the kids with your mum and dad. Didn't want them tackling the verge.'

'Good idea. Sorry about all this.'

'It's fine, love. Sorry I moaned. We'll have a lovely time. Not often we all go out together, and it is Den's birthday!'

'I bloody love you.' She stared at the man who was good, kind, and had the power to make everything feel just a little bit better. He always had.

You're in shock. But don't worry, these guys will get to you in a mo . . .

'I know.' He winked at her and gripped her hand. 'Posh not here yet?'

'Obviously not, or you'd have heard the fanfare and seen the red carpet.'

'Good point.' He squeezed her fingers.

They walked back to the pub hand in hand and found her parents and the children cluttering up the foyer. A woman with a clipboard stood at the entrance door like a gatekeeper.

'There you are!' Her mum looked less than happy.

It occurred to her then that she'd not called to request the big table under the window, figuring they'd give them the best table they had available and that, for a large party, it would likely be the one they wanted. Harper held her grandad's hand. Bertie was selecting leaflets from a rack of information on the wall and studying them like an old man on a walking holiday. It made her laugh.

'Right. Let's go in, shall we?' Midge rubbed his palms together. He loved a good roast.

'We would' – her dad spoke slowly, his eyes darting towards his wife who looked a little pale – 'but they can't find our booking.'

She felt all eyes on her as a warm blush of discomfort rose on her chest and neck.

'It's under my name.' She smiled, knowing there would be a simple solution.

'We tried that.' Her dad widened his eyes at her.

'Well, I definitely made the booking.' She felt the first flash of fluster. 'Have you tried under the name Hughes, our surname?' She smiled at the woman with the clipboard.

'Hughes . . .' The woman ran her pen down a list. 'Nope. Nothing.'

'Okay.' Remy moved closer to her, hoping she might be able to have this conversation without the scrutiny of her entire family breathing down her neck. 'I definitely made the booking. I emailed you.'

'This is a printout of all the emails for today.' The woman was unflinching as she raised her clipboard. Remy remembered that dealing with issues and making people feel better when things went wrong was her actual job. She took a breath and painted on her smile.

'I am sorry about this mix-up. It's my dad's birthday. There are nine of us. My name is Remy. R.E.M.Y.,' she spelled, 'or maybe I put it under my parents' name, Brett? Ruthie Brett? Or my dad's? Den, or Dennis?'

'I'm sorry.' The woman looked up at her with an expression that spoke more of irritation than remorse. 'I have no booking for nine people under any name.'

'Did I get the time wrong? Are we early?' she pressed, desperate to find the booking.

'No. Nothing at all. I've checked.' The woman looked over her shoulder, as a couple entered the already overcrowded foyer space.

'Right, well, in that case, can we please have a table for nine. For lunch. For . . . for my dad's birthday!' She smiled widely, showing they were friendly forces, friendly forces who needed to catch a break, and who deserved a bloody table.

'I'm sorry. We're fully booked. No tables free at all. You could try again for next week?'

'Well, it won't be his birthday next week, will it? And we are all here now!' Remy felt her blush intensify.

'And Ashleigh, our daughter, is coming all the way from *London,* just for this. She has her own business.'

Remy turned to look at her mother but chose not to speak, knowing this was not the time or place to inflame the situation.

'I don't know what to do.' She stared at the woman as the words left her mouth. 'I honestly don't know what to do. I'm sure I emailed. I composed the email. Did I send it? I thought I'd sent it. But did I?'

The woman sighed. 'Look, I just can't help you.'

Remy turned to look at her husband.

'Right.' Midge spoke to the crowd. 'First let's move so these people can get in.' The family parted, and the couple walked through the gap between them like sheepish participants in a country reel. The man lifted his hand in a reticent wave, as if it were his fault they would not be getting their gnashers into roast beef and Yorkshire pud. 'What's plan B? We could try and find somewhere else? We could go into the centre of Salisbury and try our luck?'

'It'll be heaving.' Dennis put the kibosh on that idea.

'What about if I go and buy some hot chickens and fresh bread from Sainsbury's and we can do hot chicken sandwiches at your house, Mum?' Remy took her lead from Midge and went into solution mode.

'We could go to the cathedral and see the Magna Carta!' Bertie held up a leaflet.

Sophie laughed.

'Hot chickens? She's coming all the way from bloody London!'

Remy knew it was bad when her mum said 'bloody', but at least she hadn't pointed her finger. Yet.

'Could I ask you to move outside, do you think?' the woman asked. 'It's just that we are expecting guests. Guests with bookings.'

The downcast troupe made their way into the car park, while Remy continued to fret. She had been wondering earlier how long the warm, fuzzy glow of joy she'd felt at Sophie's marvellous triumph might last. It was apparent that this was the moment it faded, if not disappeared entirely.

Shit. She had messed up.

Catching Midge's eye, she felt the bloom of tears. It was all her fault, all of it. This realisation turned her once more into her seven-year-old self, without confidence in her own decision-making or her ability to get a task done, knowing it was the small details that could wreck not only a neighbourhood, but a birthday too.

It was as they clustered like a bunch of hungry nomads in the car park that her sister's shiny Range Rover pulled into the tight space.

'It's Ashleigh! Ashleigh's here!'

Her mother squealed with more emotion in her voice than those women who saw tears coming from the eyes of the Holy Mother's statue at Lourdes.

'Hello, family!' Her sister waved as her window wound down. 'Where am I supposed to park?'

'You look like my mum!' Bert shouted. It always blew his mind. 'But shinier!'

'None taken,' Remy quipped.

'It has been said before.' Ashleigh shot her a look, and Remy smiled, because it was true. Ashleigh, her identical twin, was now a younger-looking, shinier version of her. Remy also smiled because her twin was home.

Her twin was *home*, and theirs was a connection that was beyond the material, and it ran deep.

Ashleigh

'Don't be long!' Her mum waved from the front door. 'We'll do pressies and cake after we've eaten!'

'We'll be as quick as we can!' Remy replied from the passenger window. She smacked the dashboard and shouted, 'Drive! Drive! Drive!' as soon as they left the road.

Ashleigh laughed. 'That bad?'

'Mum is driving me frickin' crazy!'

'Well, in fairness, you did mess up the booking and therefore spoil everyone's weekend, not to mention ruining Dad's birthday.' She made a clicking noise with her tongue.

'Do you think she'll let that rest any time soon?'

'Nope.' This was nice, easy, just chatting to her sister. A lovely reminder of how good it felt to be together, reunited.

'I'm dreading it already. She'll probably cut me out of the will, and I was really looking forward to getting my hands on Great-aunt Bet's trifle bowl.'

'God, that trifle bowl! Do you remember when it sat on its own special doily on the table, like an Oscar! To be admired by all!'

'I do. Bless her.' Remy sighed. 'I mean, don't get me wrong, Ash, I'm pleased to see you, you know I am, but my God, she goes like a loon before you get here. I heard her asking Dad if he thought they should get the front path jet-washed. I had to explain that even you probably had moss between your paving stones in that fancy house of yours in London.'

'I don't, actually. I have a man that takes care of things like that. And I am now definitely going to ask if they've seen the state of their front path when we get back.'

'Please don't. She'll make Midge get out there with a scrubbing brush and bowl.'

'Good old Midge.' Ashleigh liked her brother-in-law enormously, knew how much he did for her parents and how happy he made her sister. He had brought back her spark after those awful, awful years when Remy seemed to have faded, closed down. The terrible attack and then her short marriage to Jamie Aller. *Jamie Aller!* Ashleigh would never forget the moment she'd met him, barely able to disguise her look of horror, knowing he wasn't smart enough, committed enough, not in *any way* enough for someone like Remy.

Her sister's words had resonated, yet Ashleigh knew she'd never say how alienating and upsetting it was to be so considered a guest, a rarity, highlighting how much their lives had drifted apart and how much of a novelty her return.

Whose fault is that? The question rattled in her thoughts.

'Shame Archie had a work thing, although with hindsight, having to abandon him at Mum's or let him come with us in search of food . . .'

'He'd be fine! He does muck in, Remy. He's great with Evie.'

'I didn't say he wasn't!' Her sister's voice had gone up a little.

'We both know it's what you *don't* say that is always the most telling.'

'That might be true,' Remy conceded. 'I guess it's just a bit odd for me, odd for us that we don't really know Archie that well.'

'Of course you *know* him!' There it was again, that alienation thing.

'Yeah, but do we? We see him at Christmas and maybe on the odd visit once a year, but we never really spend any time with him. I couldn't pick up the phone to him, wouldn't call him for a chat or to check in. It's always via you.'

'I wouldn't call Midge,' she fired in her husband's defence.

'No, but you *could*, and you'd chat, and it would be fine.'

'So you're saying you wouldn't want to chat to Archie?' Ashleigh felt the flare of self-consciousness. The trouble was, it was true: Archie was a little aloof with her family and it bothered her more than she could say. Just another aspect of her marriage that didn't compare well to Remy's. Her isolation last night during dinner, that feeling of impotence and not knowing how to make it better, how to get closer to Evie and to communicate with Archie without rowing had all rippled through her.

'It's more that I don't know him, and he doesn't know me, and he doesn't know my kids or Midge. And I don't think he's a bad person. I like him! But I don't think he minds that he doesn't know us all. I always get the impression that he has enough people and doesn't need any of us.'

'That's . . .' She tried and failed to find the words to knock this theory on the head. Her sister wasn't done.

'He's my brother-in-law, but I have no idea if he prefers tea or coffee, whether he has any allergies, his favourite board game, has he ever broken a bone, all the things that would come up in conversation if we spent time together.' Remy shrugged. 'Just normal stuff.'

'I see, normal stuff,' she echoed.

'It's a bit like . . .' Remy hesitated.

'Go on, spit it out.' Ashleigh braced herself.

'It's a bit like it's the first time I've ever met him, whenever I see him. We're ill at ease. He seems awkward, like he doesn't know whether to kiss me or shake my hand and doesn't look me in the eye, like he's nervous.'

'Maybe you make him nervous! Maybe he can sense you are about to bombard him with questions about board games and broken bones!' she deflected, because this felt easier than to admit there was truth in her sister's words.

'Maybe.' Remy pointed ahead. 'You need to get into the lane on the left, and then it loops back around to the drive-thru.'

Ashleigh indicated and followed her sister's outstretched hand. 'Can't believe we're getting KFC for lunch on Dad's birthday.'

'Don't worry. None of your friends in *London* will ever know!'

'Don't be mean!'

'I wasn't. I was trying to be funny! It was a joke!' Remy laughed.

She shook her head. It was hard enough coming here and trying to pick up where they'd left off, to find the path that would take them back to different times, when they were as one, without feeling the wrap of guilt around her shoulders.

'Besides, we do have KFC in London.'

'Do we?' Remy asked in an affected voice that made Ashleigh laugh.

Ashleigh pulled the car into the drive-thru lane and sat behind a white van.

'Come on, Ash, when was the last time you shoved a bit of greasy chicken in your gob?'

'A while,' she admitted, 'but that's got nothing to do with where I live, but more that I want to look after myself.'

'How long is a while?' Remy turned in her seat to face her.

'I've not had a KFC for years! Like, literally, years!' She felt excitement fizz in her veins at the prospect.

'Do you remember when they opened the kebab wagon in town, and we were so excited!'

'Tony came with us!'

'Of course he did. I love him so much.' Remy sighed. 'I still miss him, I know it's daft. Nearly two decades since he left, but I still miss him. Even now, I prefer not to go past his mum's house if I can help it, because I don't want to see his old bedroom window and know he's not there.'

'He loves you too. I know.'

'What we went through, Ash.' Her sister took her time, looking out into the middle distance. 'I still think about it, not all the time, but often.'

'Of course you do. It was terrible.' Ashleigh hated to think of the moment she had walked in the front door the morning after the ball. Her parents grey-faced, exhausted and whimpering. Remy on the sofa, a blanket over her legs, her arm and shoulder in a cast. Her face stitched, her lip a swollen strawberry of mess. Eye blackened and closed. The house had been so quiet, eerily so, as if no one dared make a sound.

'Sometimes I think it was a dream, like I still can't believe something that bad could actually happen, happen to us! And I hear the, the . . .' Remy paused, hesitated.

'You hear the what?'

Remy bit her lip. 'I hear them shouting at us, the word *Oi!* That's what they said before it all kicked off, and I still hear it, like a . . . like a gunshot in my head and just as loud.'

Ashleigh reached out and squeezed her sister's leg. 'Do you think you should talk to someone about it?'

'Who?' Remy faced her.

'I don't know – a doctor, a therapist?'

Her sister shook her head. 'It was so long ago they'd probably just tell me to get on with it.'

'I don't think it works like that. It might help?' She hated the thought of Remy living with flashbacks like that.

'Not sure,' Remy whispered. They were silent for a second.

'Tony seems happy, though. I speak to him very occasionally, but it seems he and Raul are living their best lives.'

'They are. I worry about him though. I've been worrying about him since we were little!'

She smiled in acknowledgement of Remy's words.

'It bothers me, the fact that only he and I know what it was like that night, and yet we don't talk about it, not really. It's too hard to bring up. And I guess that's why I don't want to talk to anyone else about it, a doctor or whatever.'

'I can't imagine.' She thought of Guy, and how hard it was to bring up the fact he wanted to make Ada a partner, not that it was comparable. 'You can always talk to me.'

'I know you say that, and I appreciate it, but it's different when you don't see someone every day.' Remy spoke the truth, and Ashleigh felt the weight of it; they had shifted on their axis a long time ago now, no longer sharing that closeness that some might assume was standard when it came to twins. 'I can't imagine calling you up for a goss and launching straight into my latest nightmare.'

'You have nightmares?' It was another revelation that Remy suffered in this way, after all this time.

Her sister nodded. 'Don't tell Midge. He worries enough as it is.'

'Welcome to KFC. May I take your order?' The man's voice cut through the moment.

'Thank you, yes. We'd like some chicken.' The moment she said it, she knew it was going to make Remy laugh. And not just a little laugh, but that nose-snorting kind of hysteria when something was so ridiculous. It set her off too, and she did her best to take a deep breath and remain composed. 'I'm sorry!' she managed, wheezing with her hand on her chest. 'I just need a minute!' Ashleigh howled her laughter and couldn't look at her sister directly, knowing it would only make her laugh harder. Remy leaned forward in the front seat, her mop of curls spilling over her legs. Hair that looked quite beautiful, she thought. On Remy.

'Thank you, yes. We'd like some chicken!' Remy repeated, the funniest thing, it seemed, she'd ever heard!

'Well, you're in the right place!' The man, thankfully, had a sense of humour.

'Oh, my goodness. I am so sorry. My sister is from London, and she doesn't get out much,' Remy yelled, doing her best to compose herself, before leaning further across her lap, and shouting their order into the speaker, speaking with such fluency it was like she'd learned another language. Ashleigh thought of Elaine and Dickie, who liked to impress with their command of French and Italian. She doubted they'd be impressed with her sister's impressive chicken-speak.

'Is that everything?' the man asked, after Remy had recounted the long and convoluted order.

'Hang on a sec!' Remy sat back and counted on her fingers, as she named members of the family, 'Mum, Dad, Midge, Soph, Bertie, Harper, Evie . . .' Checking she hadn't forgotten anyone.

'Sides?' came the voice from the wonky pole.

'I'm sorry?' Ashleigh pushed her straight blonde hair behind her ears as though this might help her understanding.

'Sides?' the man repeated.

'I'm not sure!'

'You're such a dipstick!' Remy laughed, which set her off again, that word . . . it had been an age since she'd heard it. Remy leaned forward with her arms over her head now, laughing and hiding.

'Remy! Don't leave me hanging. Help me out here!' she giggled.

'Corn? Beans?' the man asked.

'Yes, corn beans would be lovely,' she replied as politely as she could.

Remy bashed the dashboard with her flattened palm, wheezing her laughter.

'What?' Ashleigh managed.

'It's corn *or* beans!' she practically shouted.

'Oh, right! Corn.'

'No! Beans!' Remy shouted again.

'Oh God! I am so sorry! Just beans.' Ashleigh was laughing so hard, her tears sprang.

'And to drink?' The man, sounded, understandably, like he was beginning to lose his patience.

'I don't know!' Ashleigh was struggling through her hysterics. She turned to her sister. 'What drink?'

'Lemonade? Fanta? Coke?' the man prompted.

'Oh, okay . . . Fanta, please.' She knew the answer to this one, having heard the kids ask for it.

'Sorry,' the man boomed. 'We are out of Fanta.'

This was the final straw. Remy shrieked, 'Ash! I'm going to wet myself!'

With her head on the steering wheel, she fought for breath. It happened like this sometimes, rarely, but it happened, these moments when she let a little laughter out and a whole rush of happy came tumbling after, as if it had been lurking there in the crevices of her mind, just waiting. And only in acknowledging the release did she understand how tightly she was wound, and how much she kept in. It was like being a teenager again, and with it came a freedom, a lightness of being that was rare and precious, reminding her how she used to be, before she felt the weight of the St. Jude's blazer on her shoulders. It was as if her worries took flight, spiralling high into the sky overhead, and she gladly watched them go. In the immediate aftermath of such release she felt enthused, optimistic even, that everything would work out. She and Guy would talk, regroup. She and Archie would iron out the kinks, and things with Evie would get easier, she was sure. It used to feel this way when her mum tucked her in before sleep, as she lay in the little bed opposite her sister.

'Night night, little doves, sweet dreams . . .'

And they were – her dreams sweet, her sleep deep, as she sank down into the sheets feeling warm and happy. Until that word 'exam' was first mooted and she felt the threads of her joy slowly unravelling.

By the time they collected their food from the second window, they had mascara-smudged eyes, blotchy skin, and had released enough tension that their muscles were soft, their spines relaxed, and they breathed easily.

Sitting now in the parking area at the drive-thru, their laughter subsided.

'Honestly, what a carry-on.' Ashleigh smiled.

'That was so funny.' Remy beamed. 'I haven't laughed like that in ages.' *Thank you, yes. We'd like some chicken!* 'Why did you say that? It sounded like a royal decree!'

'I don't know! I panicked, thought it was better to say *something*!'

'You maniac. Right, we better get this grub back to the masses. Hope it doesn't make your car smell. Don't want Archie having to whip out the Febreze the moment you get back, and I know you'd blame me.'

It made her think, how Remy assumed that Archie would do this, something Midge would probably do. Archie wasn't quite so hands on, wasn't like Midge at all, in fact. She hoped he was not still mad at her in the way he had been last night, and was looking forward to getting home and making up, hoping this new frivolous mood would last until then. They might not be perfect, but he was her man, her love, and always had been.

'In answer to your earlier questions about Archie: coffee. Latex. Uno. Wrist.'

'Ah.' Remy popped a chip into her mouth, stolen from the bag, and smiled. 'Well, there we go. Now I have the basis of a great conversation with him.'

Ashleigh smiled, but knew there was truth in her sister's assessment of Archie's aloofness, disinterest almost. She was right: it was as if he had enough people. Ashleigh wished it were different, wished *he* were different, knowing how much easier her life would be in some ways if she could better integrate her married life and her family, if only he had that everyman approachability that was such an attractive trait in Midge. But it was undeniably her fault too. Even only at a subconscious level, there was an element of keeping her two worlds separate, so that neither discovered she was a fraud.

'I know what you mean about Archie, but it's not personal, Rem. It's just how he is. His upbringing, his family, all quite odd compared to us.'

'Christ, they must be really *odd*!' Remy swallowed her chip and stared at her.

'It's not like it is here, at Mum's.' It was scary opening up in this way, rare for her, but the atmosphere of fun, the connection, certainly made it easier.

'Well, no. Mum doesn't have a pool in the back garden or staff!'

Ashleigh ignored her; this wasn't what she was driving at. 'I sometimes' – what did she want to say? – 'sometimes when I'm in the house, Archie might be reading the paper, and Evie will be in the den watching her bloody cartoons.' Remy made a tsk noise, as if recognising the behaviour in Bertie. 'And I get this feeling like I want to go home. I close my eyes, and I think, I want to go *home*, but I am home. Do you ever do that?'

'No.' Remy's tone was quiet now, her expression pained. 'No, I don't.'

She turned to face her sister, her own face, the other half of her. 'I'm happy most of the time.' She felt the need to add the caveat.

'I don't think anyone is happy all of the time, little dove.' Remy reached out and held her hand. A hand the same size and shape as her own.

'I'm tired,' Ashleigh confessed, knowing if she could close her eyes, right there and then in the KFC car park, she'd sleep soundly. 'Probably because I've got the worst period!'

'Ah, I thought you were looking particularly cool and interesting.'

'What?'

'Nothing.' Remy smiled.

'Do you ever think we should tell Mum and Dad?' The words flew from her lips without too much forethought, wondering if this might be the first step to making everything better, easing her guilt, removing a layer of deceit, coming clean.

'Tell Mum and Dad what?' Her sister threw another chip into her mouth and crunched loudly.

'About, about the exam, about St. Jude's, about all of it.'

Remy stopped crunching and seemed to have difficulty swallowing the mulched-up chip as if it were a boulder.

'I guess I might have considered it once or twice, especially since you mentioned it last, but then I ask myself why. Why would we?'

'Because, because it feels important. It weighs me down, Rem. The thought that it's waiting in the wings. I sometimes feel sick just thinking about it. I thought it would get easier as I got older, but if anything, it grows in my worry, like we can't keep getting away with it, surely we must be getting close to discovery.' Ashleigh placed her hand on her forehead as if just the suggestion of discovery gave her a headache, noticing how that carefree happiness was already on the wane.

'I get it. I haven't liked lying to Mum and Dad, or Midge. It's the worst. And I know what you mean, the feeling that it's lurking somewhere with leaves over it in a shallow grave, waiting for discovery. Midge is proud of how close we are, he loves that we have no secrets, that we really *know* each other, and I have to smile and look him in the eye.' Remy paused, and Ashleigh could see the anxiety in her anguished expression. 'How the hell would I tell him that we do actually have secrets, that I'm not the open book he thinks I am?' She shook her head as if it were non-negotiable. 'I worry he might stop loving me if I told him, and it wouldn't be about the exam – who gives a shit? It was such a long time ago – we were kids! It would be about the lying to him, and I get it. I'd be gutted if it was the other way around.'

She understood, trying and failing to imagine how it might feel to tell Archie the truth, worried too that he would see her as the fraud she felt herself to be.

'I'm not sure what coming clean now would serve?' Remy pulled her from the thought.

'Peace? It sometimes wakes me up in the early hours – often, in fact. It's the thing I'm most ashamed of, the thing I've *always* been most ashamed of, because I didn't deserve the place and I've always had this feeling, ever since, that I don't deserve my life!'

'Wow! Ash! That's – that's huge!' Remy stared at her, open-mouthed.

'Tell me about it.'

'You deserve *all* of your life! You've worked so hard, and we both know you would have passed, passed easily. Of course you would!' Remy spoke emphatically. 'I think that's another way I justify it, don't let it eat me up, because, without doubt, you would have passed it anyway.'

'But I didn't, did I?' The shame of her ten-year-old self wrapped her every word. 'It looms larger when I've got other stuff going on. You know how that works.' Remy nodded. 'This thing at work, it's really thrown me, and Evie and I' – Ashleigh didn't want to go into detail; it was too painful, too exposing to admit she feared her child didn't like her that much – 'and I kind of wonder if maybe by righting this big wrong, things will start getting on track for me!'

'I'm sorry things are a bit rough for you. I hate that. But I don't know how I feel about telling everyone. Mum and Dad . . .' Her twin looked out of the window and spoke slowly, as if considering the outcomes. 'I think they'd be angry, yes, but gutted too. And actually, I can cope with them being angry, but the thought of them feeling hurt . . .' Remy turned to face her. 'You're golden, Ashleigh. I think they'd be *really* upset, but, like Midge, not so much about the exam, but how long we've kept it from them, and I don't want that for them. And selfishly, I don't want to deal with the fallout of it all. Midge and I *don't* have secrets!'

'Apart from this one,' she reminded her.

'Yep, apart from this one. Oh God!' Remy rubbed her eyes.

Ashleigh felt bad for bringing it to her sister's door, for wiping away her smile, for replacing the lovely atmosphere with growing tension. 'Look, just forget I mentioned it.' It was too much, the thought of distressing her parents, creating a bow wave and leaving Remy to face it, even causing trouble between her and Midge. 'Just forget it. I was having a moment.' Ashleigh figured it was probably better to let sleeping dogs lie, understanding she really was probably just reacting to the whole Guy thing.

'Well, now *I* feel really bad! Like I'm saying you *can't* tell them, and I'm not saying that, not at all. I just—'

'It's okay, Rem. Honestly, please just forget it. Come on, let's get this feast back to the birthday boy.'

'Yep.' Remy lifted one of the heavy bags.

'Do you think Mum might have calmed down a bit?'

'No chance.'

They both laughed loudly in response, laughter that wasn't entirely natural but felt necessary to cover the conversation they had just had, *exactly* like putting leaves over a body in the forest, knowing it would do the job for a bit, but ultimately they'd blow away, exposing the crime.

And all Ashleigh could do was wait.

Remy

Remy unclipped her seat belt as Ashleigh pulled up outside their parents' house. She was almost reluctant to get out of the snazzy Land Rover, where the seats were about as comfortable as her sofa. This was also the perfect place to talk, just the two of them. Even though it now felt very much like they had unfinished business. It had never occurred to her that her sister might want to come clean about the exam. The thought of it put the fear of God into her, and she was genuinely worried about her parents' reaction, and knew Midge would, understandably, see it as a betrayal. Her whole failure to get to St. Jude's had been one of their running jokes for as long as she could remember. The idea that he might not be able to get past it, that she might lose her love, her protector . . . she felt her heart beat a little too fast, and there it was, that gunshot in her mind: *Oi!*

Her head spun.

Ashleigh was clearly going through something, and she wished they had more time. As was always the case, Remy felt guilty for having dreaded her visit when it was clear to her that despite this very fancy car and the mansion awaiting her in London, there was an underlying sadness to her sister's words. She couldn't imagine not feeling at home in her own house, or not wanting to be wherever Midge was.

'You know it goes both ways: you can talk to me whenever you need to. Any time. It was nice when you called me, crying, this week.'

'Oh, cheers!'

'No – you know what I mean; not nice you were crying, but it was nice for me to know you'd call me when you needed me.'

Ashleigh nodded. 'As I mentioned, I've got a lot going on.'

'Yep, I got about half of it. You weren't making much sense, and it was hard to make out your words through all the sniffing and sobbing, but something about a dog called Ben, and Guy pissing you off at work.'

'Succinctly put.' Her sister thumbed the diamond eternity that was wedged on her finger under her wedding ring and the diamond engagement ring that was so big, Sophie, as a little one, had asked if it was a lump of ice. 'So you know who Guy is?'

'Yes, bit posh, has a wife you don't like?' Remy remembered he had been good to chat to on the occasions when their paths had crossed at Evie's christening, and the housewarming.

'I wouldn't say I don't like her.'

'So you do like her?' Remy pushed.

'I wouldn't say I *like* her!'

And again the two spurted their laughter.

'He's gone behind my back and is trying to make Ada, his wife—'

'The one you may or may not like,' she interrupted.

'Yes, that one.' Her sister blinked slowly. 'He's trying to make her a partner in the business. And he hasn't told me about it. The first I heard was when the paperwork turned up.'

'Oh, so that's what you didn't tell me! Can he do that?' It sounded horrible, especially coming from someone her sister trusted. Again, with a bloom of unease, she thought about having to tell Midge about St. Jude's.

'Apparently so. Truth is, I think he wants me out of the business.'

'But it's *your* business!' Remy pointed out the obvious, knowing how much of her life Ashleigh had poured into Gallow and Fitch and how very proud she was of it.

'Yep, but he's the bigger shareholder.'

'Does that make a difference? Sorry to sound stupid. I don't know how it all works. I spend my days with a headset on taking calls about broken washing machines and trying to ascertain what has gone wrong with a fridge as a customer on the end of the line imitates its whir.'

Ashleigh stared at her as if unable to imagine this life.

'I don't know if it makes a difference, but more upsetting than the legality of it is the thought that he feels that way at all. The fact he's trying to get Ada involved, it's like they're ganging up to kick me out. Otherwise, why not mention it?'

'I thought she was against working, devoting herself to bread-making and spending Guy's salary.' This much she remembered about the woman.

'She was, she does, I don't know what's changed.' Ashleigh swallowed. 'Actually, that's not wholly true. It's me that's changed, I think. I've made a few mistakes, messed up, said the wrong thing, lost an instruction on a big house when we need the money, that kind of thing.'

'Christ, we're all allowed to make a few mistakes, Ash. Some of us can't even manage to book a table for lunch at the pub.' She gave a wry smile. 'But you work so hard, it doesn't seem fair. What did Guy say when you confronted him?'

'I haven't spoken to him about it yet.'

'You have to!'

Her sister let out a sharp breath. 'I know! I want to see him, but I don't want to call him in. They've just had their baby.'

'Oh, yes, of course.' Remy remembered her sister saying something about this on the phone.

'The baby they've called Ben, same name as their dog.'

'Ben's a funny name for a dog.'

'That's not really the point!' Ashleigh yelled.

'Suppose not.'

'I feel a bit like' – Ashleigh took her time, giving Remy the impression this might be the first time she had said any of this out loud – 'you know like before you have kids, if things aren't going great, at the back of your mind is the thought that you can always jump on a plane or a train and go and work in a bar or go to Ibiza, or backpack somewhere hot and dusty, change course, whatever! It's a mental escape hatch, that feeling that the whole wide world is out there waiting for you. But once you have a kid and you're a mum, you can't, can you? You're stuck! I mean, in a good way, but you're stuck. Even if you feel like it's not a life for you, there's no going back. You can divorce a husband, leave a partner, but you can't stop being a mum, and so it means you plod on, and you put up with things you might not have before your choices were limited. Because there's that . . . that expectation.'

'I've never . . .' Remy spoke with caution, shocked by her sister's words, yet careful not to undermine her view or make her regret her candour.

'Never what?'

'I've never felt the whole wide world was out there waiting for me, but I've also never felt stuck, not really. Never wanted to be anywhere other than where my kids are.'

'Well, lucky you.' Ashleigh folded her arms across her chest. Remy didn't take offence at her sharp tone, knowing Ashleigh got this way sometimes, a little snappy, a little mean. She was, after all, tired.

'Do you *want* a divorce?' she asked quietly, tentatively, as if unsure if she should be asking at all.

'No!' Her sister shook her head, vehemently. 'God, no! I love Archie, I love our life, and we work, we have everything we ever wanted.'

'So . . .' She paused, beyond fearful of asking if Ashleigh wanted a divorce from Evie. She wouldn't know what to say or do if her sister admitted this, a thought too terrible to contemplate. 'When you say you feel stuck . . .'

'Just forget I said anything.'

'So, you want me to forget about coming clean to Mum and Dad about the exam, which, I confess, I'm relieved about, forget you might just have told me that you are not happy. What else do you want me to forget, and what if that's not an option?' She felt advice cueing up on her tongue but knew her sister had to be in the right frame of mind to receive it.

Ashleigh turned to face her, her expression almost pained. 'If it's not an option, then add everything I've said to our one secret, just make it a bit bigger, and hide it away. You know we're good at doing that.'

'For God's sake, Ash!'

There was a sudden loud tap on the windscreen, and Remy felt her heart jump in her chest.

Oi!

'What do you two think you're doing? I've got hungry kids and a hungry husband in here!' Ruthie pointed at the house and shouted through the glass, and there it was, the pointed finger. 'Of course, we wouldn't have to be doing any of this if someone had remembered to book the table!'

'Yep, she's definitely calmed down.' Ashleigh sighed.

'I'd say so.' Grabbing the big bags of stinky food from the footwell, Remy got out of the car.

◆ ◆ ◆

Her dad settled back into his chair and placed his hands on his rounded tum.

'Well, that was lovely. All that chicken, and those little pots of beans, just smashing!'

'Once again, Ashleigh, I'm so sorry about the whole . . .' Her mum flapped her hands as if unwilling to voice for the thirtieth time just *how* sorry she was that Remy had not booked a table.

'Stop apologising! It's been great. Not a scrap of chicken left. Everyone's enjoyed it.'

Remy was thankful for the support. 'Although how hard can it be to book a table?' Ashleigh tutted.

Remy raised her middle finger and made out to scratch her cheek. Juvenile, yet still funny.

'Well, you know what your sister's like.' Her mum pursed her lips.

'I am right here! And honest to God, it's not like I've been getting my nails done or sitting on a yacht! I messed up because I'm busy, so busy!'

'A poor workman always blames his tools.' This her mum's parting shot, called over her shoulder as she left the lounge.

'What the fluff has that got to do with anything?' Remy asked, her arms outstretched, palms upturned, her tone as jovial as the sinking feeling in her gut would allow. Her mother's nagging and the thought of having to come clean to Midge was enough to throw her completely. And why, again, was it all her fault? Why was everything? Why was she still feeling the negative effects of a kind and loving thing she did aged ten? Why didn't everyone just sod off? This was, she reminded herself, what happened when Ashleigh arrived like a well-groomed hurricane and upset the balance of everything.

'Do you want a cup of tea?' Midge asked from the sofa, where he was sandwiched between the kids.

'I'd like some wine. Maybe a bottle with a straw in the top.' Remy answered in the voice of a needy teen, and Midge jumped up.

'Tea it is.'

She loved the way he looked out for her, knew what she needed. It was built on understanding and trust, and this was her fear when it came to Ashleigh's request. What would she do in a world without Midge to love her? Swallowing the threat of tears, she dug deep to find a neutral expression, not wanting to spoil anyone's day any more than she already had.

'Ready for your pressies?' Her mum came back into the room, arms bulging with gifts wrapped in *Star Wars* paper, no doubt left over from Bertie's birthday. Ruthie spoke to her husband with her head tilted to one side, voice high, as if he were a child.

'I've been ready since first thing this morning!' he chuckled. The sparkle in his eye made a mockery of his reputation as a man who didn't like a fuss.

'Come on, Midge, we're opening pressies!' Ruthie called to the kitchen, as usual wanting everyone there to witness the event.

He appeared at the door; tea would clearly have to wait. Her dad ripped the paper from his first gift as the kids clustered on the carpet in front of him.

'Oh, Maltesers! My favourite. Thank you, Soph!'

Sophie, her fabulous girl, beamed in the glow of his praise. 'Happy birthday, Grandad.'

'Can I have one?' Bertie shouted.

'In a minute.' Her dad winked at him.

'What's this then?' He took a stiff yellow gift bag into his hands and struggled with the silky black ribbon that formed a generous bow. Ashleigh's gift, obviously. She felt Midge staring at her and knew ordinarily she'd turn to face him, and he'd widen his eyes as if to say, 'wonder how much that cost . . .' and she'd smile at him. But with Ashleigh's words still ringing in her thoughts, her apparent unhappiness, and all they'd discussed, she didn't want to do that. Not at all.

'Fancy shower gel? Well I never!'

'It's Acqua di Parma,' Ashleigh enunciated. Remy looked straight at Midge and pulled a face, *I mean, come on!*

'Is that right?' Her dad nodded, clearly no clue as to the value or brand. 'Your mum gets me the stuff I like from Aldi. What's the flavour I have, Ruthie?'

'Oh, it's like a spicy smell, very nice.'

'And about fifty pence a bottle,' her dad added.

'*Fifty pence?*' Ashleigh's voice was shrill. 'How can shower gel that costs fifty pence be any good for your skin?' She was clearly rankled. Remy could only assume that the gift wrap alone on his present had set her back nearly a tenner.

'What do you think shower gel is, love?' He looked at Ashleigh in earnest. 'It's only water with a splash of chemicals and some smelly stuff shoved in! All of it. You should look at the ingredients, and I guarantee they are all mostly water! I mean, they might tart it up by saying H2o or aqua or some other such rubbish, but it's all water at the end of the day.'

'Did they not teach you that at St. Jude's?' Midge piped up, and Ashleigh scratched *her* cheek with her middle finger, giving her brother-in-law the subtle, childish and funny sign. Remy felt her stomach roll with anxiety at the topic, which seemed to be all around her today, or maybe that was just her sensitivity to it.

Midge laughed and retreated to the kitchen to make tea.

'Well, now I know!' Ashleigh folded her arms across her chest.

'That's from us, Dad.' Remy spoke as he lifted a white envelope and rattled it next to his ear.

'Gift voucher?' he asked.

'Yep.' She wished she weren't so predictable.

'Garden centre or B&Q?'

'Garden centre.'

'Smashing. I need a bag of compost.'

Marvellous . . .

'Do you still get that staff discount?'

'No, Dad, I worked there nearly twenty years ago! And yet you still ask me!'

'Twenty years, a blink . . .' Ashleigh spoke directly to her, her words spiked with lament.

'Yep, a blink . . .'

'Say thank you, Dennis!' her mum prompted.

'Thank you, Dennis.' Her dad spoke on cue and winked at Remy.

'Honestly! You get dafter with age!' Ruthie tutted, but her expression was one of love.

'What are we having for supper?' Her dad looked at his watch.

'Supper?' Ashleigh shot a look at her sister and they both gave the small smile that meant they knew exactly what the other was thinking.

'You've only just had your lunch!' Her mum trumpeted their thoughts. 'You can't be hungry, Den!'

'What's hungry got to do with it? We have supper at five! It's not about being hungry, it's about being supper time, about routine and sticking to it!'

Remy suppressed a laugh.

'Right.' Ashleigh clapped and looked at her mother, as if expecting the predictable sigh of disappointment, the look of irritation and the general air of a balloon deflating fast as she took a pin to the celebrations. Remy knew this couldn't be easy, as if Ashleigh's presence, however long she was here for, was never enough. She understood it was probably the last thing her sister needed, on top of having a lot to deal with at work and, she suspected, at home. 'I think we should hit the road. The M3 and M25 will probably be nightmares, and Evie has school tomorrow.'

'Oh, that's such a shame.' Her mum, right on cue, hung her head, mouth turned down a little, shoulders slumped.

Remy offered her sister a wink of understanding; she knew more than most what it felt like to be a source of disappointment.

'Come and give your nan a hug.' Ruthie opened her arms.

Evie leapt from the rug and embraced Ruthie with a fierceness that was as tender as it was telling. Remy watched Ashleigh look away, aware of her words earlier and how she sometimes felt a little stuck.

'I'll see you very soon, littlest dove,' her mum whispered to Evie with obvious emotion.

Remy smiled to hear the words of affection; it spoke volumes, letting her niece know that they might not see her all the time, but she was very much part of the fold.

It was a reminder to Remy that no matter what happened, or how much they might irritate each other or upset the balance of a gathering, they were still family, forever connected.

Ashleigh

Ashleigh smiled as she navigated the roads of West London, where the traffic, at this time of night, was manageable. It made her laugh to think of her dad, opening his birthday gift, and extolling the merits of his fifty-pence shower gel. She did the maths in her head and made a mental note to next year go to Aldi and get him almost a hundred bottles for about the same money. It was always hard leaving, her mum's expression one of disappointment, whether she was there for an hour, a week, a month. It was never enough, leaving her with a new branch growing from the cold kernel of failure in the pit of her stomach.

This, she knew, came from a place of love. They *loved* her, and they loved her being near them. *Golden*, that was what Remy had said, not that this made dealing with the aftermath any easier. She was looking forward to getting home, to smoothing things over with Archie after last night's supper-time debacle. Sex, she decided, would be nice, sex and wine, after she'd made him chuckle with an embellished account of their day: *Everyone was up in arms! We had to go forage for KFC! And then Dad was enquiring after his supper when he'd not long had lunch . . .* She felt a frisson of excitement at the prospect of the evening ahead, thankful that her husband still had that effect on her after all this time.

It had been a long day, but a lovely one. Those hilarious moments ordering chicken in the car with Remy. To see her after any time apart meant they built a bridge, and topped up their love, which would see them through to the next visit. The very best part of her trip, however, was spending time with Evie. There had been moments throughout the day, getting lost in the pantomime of life with her family, when it had felt like a breakthrough. Watching her daughter interact so easily with her cousins, and not a cartoon in sight. She smiled now to think of it.

'I liked today, Mummy.'

Her daughter interrupted her thoughts. Ashleigh adjusted the rear-view mirror and framed her daughter, wanting to capture this second like a photograph. It was easy, relaxed, because Ashleigh let herself *behave* differently and *feel* differently. Distracted by the mayhem, the noise, she didn't carry the weight of the world on her shoulders, wasn't, in those moments, worrying about Guy or the business or Ada or supper or winning her place at a table she felt she had no right to be at, or any of the other paper cuts of concern that occupied large chunks of her brain. It was that feeling of freedom and lightness that had settled over her after laughing so hard.

Yes, it had on balance been wonderful, but she'd missed Archie too, missed him driving and allowing her to doze as she liked to on a long journey, missed his quips about Midge, who he privately referred to as Arnie on account of his very macho career and his good-looking, bare-chested, slight Terminator vibes. Missed the post-visit dissection, where they would laugh over her mother's slightly manic air, her burbled clichés, as she spoke in riddles and platitudes and threw salt over her shoulder and knocked on wood and crossed her heart and pressed her hands together in prayer to keep her family safe. And Ashleigh didn't doubt Archie would have loved her dad's dire summary of her gift. She hated having to admit to her folks that, yet again, Archie wasn't in attendance because of a work thing. She was determined to find a way back to him, to find a way back to being 'them', remembering when they had laughed as long and loudly as she and Remy had earlier, before life had placed her on a busy path that meant they conversed in short snaps as one ate breakfast and the other rushed out of the door. It wasn't good enough.

Yes, she missed him and would tell him so. He always found her parents' ways amusing and it left her feeling a little torn, as she did too, but her judgement came from a place of affection, and she wasn't sure he had the same right to comment as she and Remy. Her sister's words about his aloofness she'd analyse over the next few days. To have her husband and twin closer would be nice, no doubt. Trouble was, they were all a little late out of the gate to make the necessary changes, should have worked harder when they'd first met. And maybe it was impossible to have that shared, easy closeness, and still keep her life compartmentalised. One thing was for sure, she was too tired to think it through tonight.

'I liked today too, very much.'

'Grandad Den gave me this!' Evie peeled the five-pound note from her pocket and waved it in the air, her face split with delight.

'Lucky girl.' It made her smile too. Her parents never really gave her money, didn't need to. She remembered her grandad giving her a fifty-pence piece and the joy of holding it in her palm. This clearly felt the same, albeit with a note. That was inflation for you.

'What are you going to buy with it?'

'Sweets!' Evie answered without hesitation.

'And toothpaste, to brush off all that sugar when you've eaten them!' she joked.

'Can you read to me tonight, Mum?'

This in itself was an honour. It was always Archie's job or Marguerite's if Ashleigh was late home. It had become a habit, part of Evie's routine. Grabbing a book and calling for her dad to read her to sleep. It filled Ashleigh with a potent mixture of joy and sadness, delighted to have been asked, and yet distraught at the novelty of it.

'I'd really, really love to.' She swallowed the lump in her throat, as the car pulled into the gates of their palatial home in Clarendon Road. 'Come on, let's get you inside.'

Ashleigh put the key in the door and tutted to see Archie's brogues in the middle of the hall where anyone could trip over them. So this was what he got up to when he had the house to himself for a few hours, flagrant shoe flinging! There were worse things. She smiled, knowing he'd probably eaten croissants for breakfast, lunch, and dinner.

'Can I get a drink?' Evie followed her into the kitchen.

'Course you can.' She switched on the lamp that filled the room with just the right level of glow for this time of night, as her daughter ran the cold tap and filled her beaker. Ashleigh walked towards the den, where the flicker of the TV screen sent turquoise and white lights to dance on the ceiling of the hallway.

The movie was turned up loud and she felt a little mean, knowing she was about to disturb his solitude, the joy of watching a movie, sprawled on the sofa in the den, probably with a very large bag of crisps and a couple of cold bottles of beer. This was quickly diluted by the fact she was going to make him a promise of sex, kiss him hard and tell him how much she loved him. She pushed the door open slowly, quietly, not wanting to startle him, figuring she'd coo her hello and slip down beside him for a hug of reconciliation before going upstairs to read to Evie.

Ashleigh did not slip down beside him for a hug.

She couldn't.

Because the spot on the sofa that might have been hers was already occupied. She felt a cold creep of ice through her veins and was rooted to the spot.

'Fuck!' the woman yelled, and let go of Archie's hand, as Ashleigh, jolted into action, raised her palms, about to take a step backwards, on the verge of apologising for making the woman jump and for disturbing their movie.

'Jesus!' Archie shouted and leapt up, staggering and part falling to avoid the open bottle of wine on the floor by his feet. Although it wasn't the sight of Jesus in the doorway that caused him to jump up and slip, slopping his overfilled glass of red all over the deep, pale rug, and splashing his chinos, the ones with the belt and fly undone. Nor was it Jesus who stared, mouth falling open, as Archie did his best to button up his shirt, his complexion wan, his lips dry, his expression one of anguish, as he rushed at the door and pushed her into the hallway, doing his best to keep her away from his guest. No, it wasn't Jesus. It was her, Ashleigh, his wife.

'Ash! I can . . . I can explain,' he stammered.

It was the line she'd heard in movies, the mealy-mouthed catch-all that somehow made the situation more sickening with the predictability of it.

'What the fuck is going on?' The woman appeared in the hallway, as if it were her who had been inconvenienced, unnecessarily alarmed. Ashleigh took a second to make mental notes about her: nice jeans, good hair, bare feet, a decent pedi with hot-pink toenails, soft sweater, a little too much foundation and a lower lid sweep of heavy kohl that made her eyes look small. Her accent was strong, distorting W to sound more like V, the T to D, and the S more Z. Germanic. German. *The German.*

Ah . . . Suddenly it all made sense. And she felt like a dumdum, having assumed the partner was a man, a beer-loving, hairy-handed colleague, and trusting her husband, the father of their child, her friend and lover since university, who had not corrected her.

'Go on then.' Ashleigh folded her shaking arms across her chest as if this might help contain the pain, the raw sorrow that threatened to spill from her. She couldn't take a full breath, felt a little high, a little wired, as if the discovery had sent her brain into overload. She held his eyeline and he looked at the floor. The coward.

'Go on . . .' He shook his head. It was then she noticed the slight unsteadiness to his legs, the slur to his words, suggesting much booze had been taken.

'Yes, you said you could explain.' Her smile was brief, as this clipped, controlled version of herself that contained so much rage, so much hurt, stood her ground and spoke with clarity, knowing that in the remembering she would be proud of her stance, her demeanour, all the while battling the desire to throw up.

'You said you were staying at your mum's!'

Laughter burbled from her that she quickly suppressed.

'Oh dear.' She sucked air through her teeth. 'I didn't. I said she'd asked if we wanted to. More to the point, that's not really an explanation, but a very big reveal.'

'What's going on here?' the German repeated, as she placed her hands on her slender hips. *Actually* put her hands on her hips, as if fed up at having to miss a chunk of her film, to have had her cosy evening in another woman's home disrupted.

Ashleigh turned to face her, her heart now threatening to jump right out of her chest. Archie, she noticed, had slunk back against the wall, his face strangely porcine in the dimmed light. The bloat of good living she hadn't properly noticed before.

Probably all them croissants.

'What's going on is that you have mere minutes to get out of my house. Because one of two things is going to happen. Either my daughter is going to come and see you here with her dad, which I will not allow, or I will lose my shit, like *really* lose my shit, and trust me, you don't want to see that or be on the receiving end of it. So I suggest you fuck off, right now!'

'Archie?' The woman turned to address Archie, who looked as if he might actually topple over or had received a punch to the paunch.

'Did you not hear me? I said fuck off, right now!' Still Ashleigh kept her voice level, watching as the woman grabbed her knee-high boots from the floor of the den before running upstairs, no doubt to retrieve toiletries or whatever else she had been relying on to make her sordid sleepover more comfortable. Ashleigh felt unable to move her legs, her breathing loud in her ears like she was underwater. She wanted to call Guy, wanted to tell him what Archie had done! Before remembering she wasn't talking to Guy. *No Guy, no Archie . . .* this time she was actually a little sick in her mouth, and swallowed it, as she trembled.

'Ash.' Archie reached out as if to touch her and she almost jumped back. The thought of any physical contact repulsed her, especially from those fingers that had been holding the woman's hand.

'Who's that lady?' Evie asked, staring after the skinny arse that was hightailing it up the stairs.

'Daddy's work colleague, but she's leaving now. Their meeting is over.' She smiled.

'We had a lovely day, Dad.' Evie twirled.

'That's' – he swallowed – 'that's good.'

'Auntie Remy forgot to book the table, so we had KFC and cake at Nanny's house. And Grandad got Maltesers. Bertie and I played football in the garden. Harper taught me how to do cheerleading, and Sophie was there too. She's got a tattoo of a sewing machine on her wrist.'

To hear their child so sweetly and enthusiastically recounting the details made her stomach fold. How *dare* he do this to them, to her?

'That's – that's . . .' He licked his dry lips, and she despised his drunkenness, his lack of control, his deceit, his weakness.

At the sound of feet running down the stairs, Ashleigh instinctively placed her hands on Evie's shoulders and held her close.

The woman said nothing, declining to look in their direction as she headed across the hallway, and her boots, now on her feet, trotted out of the vestibule, disappearing into the night.

'Bye!' Evie called sweetly. 'Shall I go and get my PJs on, Mum, and then you can read to me?'

'That's a great idea.' She smiled, doing her best to control the shiver to her limbs, which now shook violently. Her fingers twitching, her head jerking, her voice a warble. The moment they were alone, Archie again reached out as if to hold her.

'Don't you dare touch me!'

She made her way to the kitchen, hoping a glass of water might help calm her down and wanting to put some distance between them.

Staring out into the garden, she found it hard to hold a thought, overloaded by all she was trying to process. Her heart beat very quickly and the room spun. It happened like this sometimes when the world felt very big and she felt very small and entirely uncertain of her place in it. Her limbs tingled. *Freefall* . . .

'Ashleigh,' he began, speaking as he took a stool at the island, slumping down as if weighted by the pain of discovery. 'Ash,' he began again, suggesting any more coherent thoughts or speech might be tough.

'What, Archie?' She put the glass down hard and stared at him. 'What are you going to say? That nothing happened? That it didn't mean anything? That you'll work hard for forgiveness? That you love me, love Evie, love our life, our home, our little family?' she spat.

He sat straight up then and wiped his hand across his mouth. He shook his head slightly and in that moment she was glad he wasn't going to patronise her with his bullshit.

'No.' He swallowed. 'No. I wasn't going to say any of that.'

'Good!' she fired. 'Because that kind of cliché would do both of us a disservice.'

'I was going to say' – he took a deep, slow breath – 'I was going to say that I want a divorce.'

Ashleigh knew he was speaking, knew what he had said, but it was as if his words were edged with an echo that made it hard to comprehend.

'What?' She needed the repetition to allow her a moment to think, to understand not only what he was saying, but also how best to respond. There was a shift in their dynamic. Ashleigh had thought she was holding all the cards, having discovered his infidelity, was mentally figuring out how he could make amends, wondering if he *could* make amends, but with these words she understood that it was Archie who was in control. He was upending their life; he wanted out.

'I . . . I want a divorce,' he repeated.

She stared at her legs, just to make sure they were still attached to her body, as she had the most curious sensation that they were not, that she was somehow detached from her lower limbs, cut, halved.

'Mu-um!' Evie called down the stairs, impatient, it seemed, to get story time underway.

'Coming!' she replied in the brightest voice she could find. 'Are you in love with her, the . . . the German?' Her distress came then, as she sobbed, and to her horror, as it confirmed the very worst thing, Archie cried too, matching her tear for tear.

'No. I'm not in love with anyone,' he managed.

'Not even me?' Her mouth curved and twisted, as sorrow shaped her lips, which tasted of sadness and regret.

'Not even you,' he admitted, his eyes bloodshot as he used the flapping sleeve of his shirt to wipe his face.

And there it was, the words she knew would linger in her thoughts long after the image of her husband and the German holding hands on the sofa in the den of their home, drinking red wine, clothes suitably disturbed, suggesting they had been shagging in her beautiful house, had ebbed away.

'You don't love me, anymore?' Her words were the faintest whisper, wary as she was of putting them out into the world, and of hearing confirmation, making it real.

'I don't.' He coughed, as if understanding that this honesty, this openness, was best in the long run.

'When did you' – she sniffed through her tears – 'when did you stop loving me?' She was curious, wanting to know, despite his every word landing like a sharp thing in her heart.

He doesn't love me . . .

Archie doesn't love me . . .

My husband doesn't love me . . .

You are under my skin and inside my bones . . .

'I'm not sure, but a while ago.'

'How long, Archie? A month, three months, a year?'

It felt important, to know at what point he had emotionally pulled the plug on them and for how long he had been pretending. The thought was enough to make her quietly retch again, as she swallowed the bile that rose in her throat.

'I guess, since not long after Evie was born.'

'Hooooooh.' Gripping the edge of the granite countertop, she let out a strange sound, as if the air had been squeezed from her lungs. This was not what she had expected, wondering when in recent times he had fallen out of love with her, but Evie was now six years old, which meant he had been pretending for a very long time. Going through the motions as they finished renovating the house, chose paint colours, while she built the business with Guy, and they picked a nursery and then a school, while they took holidays, did laundry, ate supper, drank coffee, saw friends, made love, all of it a lie. *All of it* . . . She gave a small nod of understanding, having waited for this moment, this revelation, this dismantling of all she had held dear since . . . since they had first met, when she feared she would be discovered, outed as a fraud, rejected as just not good enough.

Now she stared at her feet, because everything she had thought was solid, everything she had taken for granted, now needed to be questioned, even the ground beneath her. She fully expected a large hole to appear and swallow her life whole.

'That's – that's a long time.' She met his gaze.

'I thought it might get better, thought I might fall in love with you again.'

'I don't think it works like that.'

'No. I don't think it does. I just didn't want to upset you, didn't want to . . .' He ran out of words.

'Didn't want to *upset* me?'

The irony wasn't lost on her, as tears sheeted her face.

Her next thought was to call Guy, to go to Guy's flat, to nab his spare room and howl into his shoulder after tucking Evie up on the back seat and telling her it was an adventure, before she remembered that Guy was busy with his wife and the Bens, preoccupied in his baby bubble. And of course there was no spare room, now that Ben baby had arrived and it was his nursery. She pictured the file with the paperwork in it, knowing Guy too had kept secrets, wanted to make Ada a partner, all discussed and set in motion behind her back. She wondered then if Guy and Archie chatted openly; were they aware that the other was lying to her, *pretending?*

'Shit!' She felt the cloak of loneliness and desolation wrap tightly about her shoulders.

'I am sorry, Ash.' Archie spoke as on unsteady legs she made her way across the large kitchen.

'For what?' she asked over her shoulder as she paused at the door, leaning on the frame for support.

'All of it.' He placed his splayed palm over his mouth and spoke through his fat fingers. 'All of it.'

Walking up the stairs to go and read to Evie, it took all of her strength to put one foot in front of the other. One thing was certain: Ashleigh knew she had never felt less golden in her whole life. She pictured her family, crammed into her parents' sitting room earlier, watching her dad open his gifts, teasing each other, the kids huddled together, arms and legs overlapping, and the air weighted with love. It made her cry all over again, wishing she had stayed right there in that place that had once been her home, before she'd started at the school that had set her apart and made her chase a life that was not really hers. How could it be? A life that was now being taken away from her, just as she had always expected. And wishing she could go back to exam day and be stronger, speak louder, let Remy wear the crown, while she slunk off to Milton Road with Tony Newman, because then it might be her at home with Midge and her sister standing at the foot of this grand staircase, trying to figure out how to keep climbing.

Not that she'd wish this feeling on Remy; not that she'd wish it on anyone.

Remy

'Hey, Mum.' Remy called before climbing the stairs to bed. 'Just wanted to thank you for a lovely day, and I'm sorry about the whole table mix-up thing. Obviously my fault, and I feel dreadful about it, but I think everyone had a lovely day.'

'I don't think Ashleigh minded. In fact, she seemed to like tucking into her chicken!'

'And Dad, whose birthday it was, did *he* mind?' She did her best to find the humour in it, how quickly her mum had zeroed in on Queen Ashleigh. Not that it was her sister's fault, and it had truly been so good to spend some time together, just the two of them. The echo of their conversation about coming clean was still in her mind. She hoped they'd put the subject to bed, unable to imagine the damage a revelation like that might cause and feeling shame at this truth.

'Oh, you know your dad. Doesn't mind much, doesn't like a fuss.'

She pictured the look of delight on his face when the prospect of a KFC in the lounge had first been suggested and smiled.

'Yep, anyway, bedtime for me, but thank you for a great day, Mum. It was nice.'

'I told Ashleigh that next time she should bring Archie if he's not working, and they can stay. We got rid of the bed to make space for storage, but I've got the blow-up mattress that we got for Auntie Joan's back when she had to sleep on the floor at Jane and Angelo's wedding, do you remember?'

Remy didn't remember, could scarcely place Auntie Joan, one of her mother's cousins who apparently had a dicky back, but was too tired to listen to what she suspected might be a convoluted explanation in which she had only the tiniest bit of interest.

'Oh yes, yes I do.' The lie was swift, tasted of guilt, and yet was preferable to having to hear Auntie Joan's life story.

'I told her we could put that on the floor of her old room, and she and Archie can sleep there, and Evie can go on the single in your room. It'd be cosy for one night.'

'I think they'd love it.'

The excitement in her mother's tone for an event that was no more than a vague idea was as sobering as it was sad. A reminder of how little her mother needed and how she so loved her family. It also reinforced Ashleigh's words, how uncomfortable it made her to be the star attraction, and in part the reason she deliberately wanted to sabotage the view their parents had long held about their two daughters.

'I think so too, and don't worry about the pub. You have a lot on your plate, Remy, you work so hard.'

It was recognition that warmed her from the inside out, as any compliment from her mum always did; forgiveness, almost, for not taking the raffle ticket that had been handed to her, for not, in their eyes, grabbing it with both hands.

'Thank you. Love you, Mum.'

'And I love you, little dove.'

Remy checked the doors and windows were locked and climbed the stairs. Midge was already in bed, reading the sports results on Ceefax.

'Three–nil, Remy! Three flippin' nil!'

'Oh, I'm sorry to hear that.' She had no idea of the team or even the sport, but by the look on her husband's face it was not the result he desired.

'Can you believe it!'

'No. No, I really can't.' She feigned interest.

'I sometimes think I'd be better off as their manager. Do you know what I mean?'

'I do, love.' She gathered her hair into its curly pineapple and popped it inside the silky scrunchy. 'Like my mum, but shinier! Did you hear what Bert said?' She laughed at the audacity of the boy she loved.

'Did he have his glasses on?' Midge looked away from his phone.

'He doesn't wear glasses!' She hopped into bed and pulled the duvet over her shoulders; the heating went off at 8 p.m. and she was beginning to feel the chill.

'Well, maybe he should start.'

'Very funny.' She snuggled against his warm body, putting her cold feet on his calves.

'There is nothing dull about you, my love. You shine brighter than anyone.'

'You say the nicest things to me.' She felt the glow of love spreading over her, doing her best in that moment to dilute her fear over having to come clean about taking the exam for Ashleigh, or more specifically for keeping it a secret from him.

'It's true, plus, I'm kind of hoping to get lucky and thought that by saying that you might be more receptive.'

Propping her head on her wrist, she studied his handsome face.

'You know it's not flattery that puts me in the mood.'

'Isn't it?' He looked a little surprised. 'It's just that I've read articles in those women's magazines in the doctors' surgery, and it seems that a box of chocolates and flattery is a time-old tradition, it's how to woo a woman.'

'Hmm, maybe in 1953. For me, it's unstacking the dishwasher, folding laundry, helping the kids with their homework, things like that. It's doing chores that I find most alluring.'

'In that case, I should probably remind you that this week, unasked, I have babysat, cooked supper, cleaned out Morty's cage, and provided a very reliable taxi service. And so if we're keeping score—'

'We're not,' she interjected. He ignored her.

'Then I'm actually down on the deal.' He sighed.

'Can I just say' – she spoke as he abandoned his phone and shifted to face her – 'that you haven't babysat.'

'I have! Nearly every day!'

'No, Midge, it's not babysitting when they're your children. It's just parenthood. It's what we do. Keeping an eye on the kids that live in our house, the kids we had, *our* kids, feeding them, keeping them from harm. It's almost a prerequisite.'

'But . . .' She could see the crease of confusion at the top of his nose. It made her laugh. He was right: he did a lot and was loved a lot, and without doubt his honesty was the one thing she loved about him most. This itself a small needle, reminding her of her own duplicity. 'It's okay. I love you. You're going to get lucky anyway.'

The landline rang, and they looked at each other, he, like her, wondering who would phone the house when it was dark, and they were off to bed.

'I'll go.' Grabbing her dressing gown from the end of the bed, she hared down the stairs, trying to get to the phone before it woke the kids, if it hadn't already.

The sound of crying came down the line and her stomach dropped, before she realised that Sophie was asleep upstairs, Bertie and Harper too. She'd only just spoken to her mum, and so that left . . .

'Ash?'

'Just . . . just give me a minute.'

'Okay, my love, take your time.' She sat on the bottom stair and let her sister sob, as she fought for breath.

'I need you, dove. I need you right now.'

'It's okay, my love, don't cry. Ash, take deep breaths, I'm right here.'

Ashleigh Brett and Remy Hughes

2012

Aged 50

Ashleigh

It was rare, almost unheard of, for Ashleigh to have enjoyed an afternoon nap, yet here she was in her sister's cottage, waking to the sound of the door creaking. It took her a second to remember where she was. Remy jokingly called this *Ashleigh's bedroom*, as it was where she slept at Christmas, and on the three or four times a year she made the trip. The light in the room was certainly not that of the bedroom of her ground-floor flat in a red-brick villa in Queen's Park, North-west London. The place she called home, bought with the proceeds of her divorce.

This room was bathed in sunshine, unfiltered by the roman blinds that kept her privacy, and it was quiet, eerily so. Missing was the honk of horns, wheeze of brakes, whir of skateboard wheels, shouts of kids, music from passing vans, all of it providing a background noise that meant even though she predominantly lived alone, she hardly ever felt lonely. How could she when she was surrounded by so much life?

What she didn't want to admit to herself, today of all days, was that on the rare occasion when loneliness *did* strike, it did so with a vengeance. Usually in the early hours when the streets quietened, her bed felt too big, and the sheets too cold. Reaching across to touch the neighbouring pillow, remembering what it had felt like to find the warm skin of her husband beneath her touch, believing it would ever be so. She would then howl her tears and desolation until dawn broke, mourning a life that was so nearly hers. Her heartache all the worse for having glimpsed it.

But never in public, never. The fact that divorce had been foisted upon her was her own private sadness. Something that had shaped her, scarred her, and meant she would never marry again, unwilling to take the risk and unsure she could survive that level of rejection again.

Besides, who would she marry? Despite his dire treatment of her, his lack of love, his infidelity, she still couldn't see how anyone was going to measure up to Archie Oxton Fitch, the boy who had held her hand as they'd walked into the wine bar in their finery, and she had felt like . . . like someone.

In the immediate aftermath of their separation, and after much deliberation back and forth, it was agreed that Evie would spend her weekdays at Archie's but come to the flat at weekends. Evie herself had been involved in the conversations, and Ashleigh knew she'd never forget the crumple of her daughter's face and the flow of tears at the mere suggestion of a life away from her school, away from Marguerite, and the house on Clarendon Road. It had been a hard pill for Ashleigh to swallow, the hardest, just as it felt she and Evie were making headway and she was doing her darndest to be a better mum. She was, however, far more concerned with what was best for her daughter than her own feelings.

'I do love you, you know that, right?' she'd whispered on the night she left with her car packed and her heart feeling like it might fall out of her ribcage. She had knelt down on the driveway to say goodbye, able in the dying light of dusk to hold her baby without reservation, inhaling the scent of her and wondering why she hadn't done so more often, feeling the pull of something in her gut. Desperately afraid that she might just lose her baby, as well as her house and husband.

'I know that, Mummy.' Her little girl's words were the sweetest balm in her ear.

'We'll have quite the adventure, you and me. I'll make sure of it!' Finding a voice of optimism had taken all of her strength.

On a Friday night she could barely contain her excitement, quite transformed from the harried woman who had been so busy keeping all the plates spinning. As if, away from that pressure, and not so concerned with her role as Archie's wife and all that came with it, she was free to concentrate on Evie. Free to make mistakes, to figure out motherhood away from the glare of the Fitch family. In the little flat, alone with her daughter, she finally felt worthy of being this little girl's mother and understood the attraction of it. It was just her and Evie, the two of them against the world! Watching TV under a blanket, eating snacks on the sofa, and living in such close proximity it fostered a new kind of closeness. It reminded her very much of what it had felt like when she and Remy had formed a similar duo. Before she'd gone to St. Jude's. That warmth in her stomach and the feeling that she was safe, that she was home.

How she longed for the sound of her ex's car pulling up and the ring on the doorbell! Having waved her little girl off on a Sunday evening, her sense of loss was acute. After sitting on the sofa, the warmth her child had created lessening with every minute, Ashleigh would then almost crawl to bed, feeling the loss of her family and her old life acutely. Torturing herself with images of Evie's return to the fold, the celebration, the party-like atmosphere in the palatial kitchen. Did they maybe laugh at her efforts? Did the German sip wine and ask, '*She made what? Macaroni cheese? Urgh!*'

Ashleigh was not proud that these imaginings had the power to haunt her for days after, almost until the next Friday, when she would again clean the flat, find a smile and wait patiently for the sound of the idling engine and the doorbell ringing.

Now aged sixteen, there was often a reason Evie couldn't make it to the flat for the weekend: a party, a meet-up, a coffee date, a school assignment, a library trip, even having to babysit for her two younger brothers, Jakob, aged seven and Otto, nine. And while she tried to understand, make light of it, these absences punched a hole in her routine that left Ashleigh feeling flat, bereft, and strangely exhausted.

Ashleigh's contact with Archie was minimal, busy as he was with two kids and life married to Leni, the German, who *still*, in her humble opinion, wore too much foundation and eyeliner. But when for the third weekend running she received a text from Evie explaining that she'd been asked to babysit *again*, and would therefore be staying in Clarendon Road, Ashleigh called him.

'Ash, hi.' He sounded irritated, hurried, as he always did when she rang. It upset and irritated her in equal measure.

'Yep, erm, just a quick call.' She didn't want to waste a second of time on pleasantries, didn't want to chit-chat to the man who had stopped loving her and who had married another woman who now lived in the house Ashleigh had spent years renovating. Another woman who had popped out two handsome boys who no doubt rough-housed in the den while Leni cooked at the hob that Ashleigh had deliberated over choosing. *A proper family.* She had coughed to clear the thought and the bitter taste of envy. 'I really don't think it's fair, Archie, asking Evie to babysit! Not when it's a weekend—'

'I would agree!'

His almost jovial interruption only served to irritate her even more.

'One weekend, I understand, but three in a row, it's not on. The weekends are all the time I get with her, I like to cook, we like to—'

'Sorry, Ash, are you suggesting that Evie has babysat for the *last* two weekends?'

'Yes! And as I say, once is fair enough if you were stuck, but this weekend too, it's not—'

'I have to stop you there.' He drew breath, and when he spoke his tone was quiet, as if trying to keep it between the two of them, to spare whose feelings she wasn't quite sure. 'Evie is a wonderful girl—'

'She is.' It was her turn to interject.

'But she has never, to my knowledge, babysat for the boys on a weekend, not ever. She's kept an eye on them maybe when one of us was late home or sat with them when we've been out to supper once or twice, or if Marguerite was running behind schedule, but, *babysit*?' He laughed. 'It's not something that Leni . . . I mean, she doesn't really.' He swallowed as if suddenly aware that she was holding the phone tightly to her face, with her heart beating too quickly for comfort and her tears gathering.

'My – my mistake.' She sniffed. 'My mistake, Archie. Forget I called. I must have got the wrong end of the stick.'

'Do you want me to get Evie? She's just painting Leni's nails. I can take her the phone if you like?'

'No, no, that's . . .' She'd ended the call.

Painting Leni's nails . . .

It conjured a picture that was so intimate, suggesting a strength of connection between the two that was something she could only dream of. In her imaginings, Evie kept the woman at arm's length, this interloper who had stolen Ashleigh's life; she figured Evie would side with her, not that they were taking sides, of course, but still. Harder still was the fact that Evie had lied to her – *lied* to her! How many other times had she been lying too? And there was only one reason for doing so; because it was easier for her daughter to lie than admit she preferred to stay home, would rather spend time in Archie and Leni's house, *choosing* Archie. This despite how very hard Ashleigh had worked to build a bridge. She felt the flare of distress in her chest and rubbed the heel of her hand over the space where it hurt most.

When Evie had pitched up the following weekend as if nothing was amiss, she chose not to mention it, doing her best not to pressurise her child, understanding that life picked up a gear at this age. It was when she had learned so much about herself, spending time with boys in the sixth form at St. Jude's, practising for grown-up-hood that had felt just around the corner, and watching with envy as Remy and Tony danced to their favourite music and shared in-jokes that left her feeling a little excluded.

Conjoined!

This one word alone used to send them into hysterics, making her feel like an outsider. She had no idea why it was funny but was damned if she was going to ask.

Each weekend without Evie's company was a jab to the ribs and a small erosion of her confidence when it came to her mothering skills. She had done her best to get to know her daughter, cooked for her every Saturday night and even attempted a roast dinner on the odd Sunday. They shopped together, if not harmoniously, an almost impossible task when their tastes were so different, then certainly with a sense of commitment. There were moments of laughter too that she carried in a small pocket under her heart, like the time Ashleigh had parked up so that Evie could run into the store one rainy night to get milk, chocolate and crisps, watching as her daughter left the shop and attempted to jump in a random car parked in front, getting a little confused in the dark and drizzle. It was made all the funnier as the car for which she tried the handle, and banged on the passenger window, belonged to two police officers on patrol who had not quite seen the funny side, as her teenage daughter tried to force entry with an armful of snacks.

She smiled at the sight of her sister, who now stood by the bedroom door, grinning. It was lovely to be here, like this, knowing Evie was having a good time and was just along the hallway with Bertie. At sixteen, the cousins shared a love of *Call of Duty*, whatever that was, a game, apparently, that they played on Bertie's computer.

Her sister's village home was cutesy, with a quaint porch and roses around the door. It made her laugh, it was so twee, so perfect and just the right place for her and Midge to be, living in their blissful bubble. She didn't envy her twin, exactly, but was certainly made aware of what she might be missing. Especially when Remy squeezed into any gap next to her husband and he, without hesitation, placed his arm about her shoulders, on her thigh, her neck, anywhere contact was possible. It was no more than Remy deserved, and was, she observed, a nice way to live. Not that it was a life for her. No matter how lovely it was to be here for a long weekend, she knew she'd be glad to get back to the hustle and bustle of London life, her regular haunts, the coffee shop and bakery where she was guaranteed a warm welcome, and the market where she took her time picking fruit and vegetables. She also missed the pristine desk, her workspace in the hallway from where she ran her bespoke agency, finding homes for wealthy foreigners who were househunting in London. It was hard work, but lucrative and, crucially, it was all hers.

'It's about time we started to get dolled up, and you need to put these on!' Remy reminded her as she walked towards the bed.

'No! Don't even think about it!' Ashleigh slunk down under the duvet and tried to hide from her twin, who was wearing a pair of oversized sparkly sunglasses and brandishing an identical pair in her hand. They were made up of the numbers five and zero!

'You're in my house, and you *will* wear my celebration glasses!'

'I've told you already, I'm not being fifty! I'm staying at forty-nine. In fact, I might go back to forty-eight.' Ashleigh giggled like a teen and knew there was no better place or way to spend this day, which she had been slightly dreading. It was hard to explain why, but fifty felt like the beginning of getting old. Not that she was old – no way! In great shape, a keen walker and tennis player, her tweakments kept any threatened wrinkles at bay and her hair was still, with the help of regular visits to JoJo, her beloved hairdresser of many years, blonde and straight. But fifty – *fifty!* It felt a bit like turning a corner and finding herself on a one-way street. Not that she'd be sharing this with Remy, who by the look of things was intent on embracing their half century.

'We have to wear these all night!'

'We should be somewhere fancy! Are we sad, having a joint fiftieth with the family?' she half joked, thinking of the kind of birthday Archie might have prepared for such a milestone.

'Yes! We are sad, but my house is fancy, thank you very much.' Remy flopped down on the end of the bed. 'I'm here for it. Besides, there's no backing out now. We have the CDs loaded, Mum's made enough sausage rolls to build a replica of the Great Wall of China, and Sophie has made bunting, which Harper is putting up as we speak! Our guests will be arriving in approximately' – she looked at her watch – 'an hour, and Midge has enough prosecco chilled to ensure the evening goes with a pop!'

'How's Harper doing?' It was a tentative enquiry, aware as she was that her sister worried so about her middle child, who found life trickier than most. She was a wonderful girl who was dogged by anxiety and moved as if she had the weight of the world on her shoulders, and Ashleigh was wary of stirring up concern when Remy's mood was so buoyant.

'She's having a good day, and so let's focus on that!' She clapped.

'Yep.' Ashleigh nodded. 'And Sophie's so clever!' She was, as ever, in awe of her niece's skill with a needle and thread. 'Can't believe she's found time to make bunting.'

'I know – superwoman!' Remy spoke with obvious pride.

It was hard to fathom how quickly Sophie had grown into a woman and was now a mum herself to one-year-old Elio, and married to the wonderful Riccardo, who was a gem.

'Mum called. Her and Dad are going to come over early, so they get a seat, apparently.' Remy rolled her eyes.

'What do they think? That it's like musical chairs, last one here has to stand?' She laughed, kind of loving their eccentricity and their funny little ways.

'God only knows what they think, but I do know Mum has been fretting over her hair and which handbag to bring. She's spent an age pressing Dad's good shirt and has bombarded me with messages, asking *exactly* what time they will be eating the buffet, as Dad likes to know!'

Buffet . . . The word reminded her of her wedding, a long time ago now and a most stressful couple of days at Mulverton as she had run around trying to get everything ready. This, of course, made her think of Guy, her lovely friend, who she still missed and whose awkward confession she had never told to a soul.

If the hurt she had felt at Archie's betrayal was a splinter, then the same from Guy, in her weakened state, had been a whole log that flattened her. After she had confronted him about the partnership, he had gone quiet. This man who had been her great mate, her confidant, her rock, had simply gone quiet, the coward.

He too had, quite obviously, chosen Archie. Her hurt, even after all this time, still had the power to bring her to tears.

After Guy's silence, letters began to arrive from solicitors, all communiqués signed with a friendly flourish, *very best wishes* . . . but not even the pleasant sentiment or the handwritten signature could disguise the proposals of a gut-wrenching nature, all suggesting how they might proceed.

The options were numerous. A few stuck in her mind still:

To redefine the partnership, three ways, with Ashleigh as a minor partner . . .

To rename the company Gallow and Gallow, cutting out the Fitch bit altogether . . .

To close the company down, both walk away, start over, and Guy would take over the rental agreement and retain the premises . . .

To buy Guy out, with money that she didn't have . . .

To let Guy buy her out with money that he did have . . .

The latter had felt like the least unpalatable option. Ashleigh had reluctantly agreed, upon the completion of which Guy had installed Ada, who no doubt sat at Ashleigh's desk and maybe made her jam from there, with Ben and Ben running around her ankles as Clara poured coffee for their wealthy clients. It was as hard for her to imagine as it was gut-wrenching.

The people she would have discussed such options with were Archie and Guy. And with her phone in her hand, sitting in her car, unable to go home, unable to go to the office, unable to phone either of these men, she knew she had never felt so desperately alone. Remy, true to her word, had been on the end of the phone, but knowing how full her sister's life was, Ashleigh never wanted to overburden her. It was some weeks before she found the courage, dried her tears, and called Gigi, telling him to buy her out and that he could shove their friendship up his arse.

He had, without hesitation, done both.

Many nights had been spent analysing when the cracks had appeared in their friendship. Cracks she hadn't seen opening up beneath her, unaware she should have been clinging on for dear life or finding safer ground. At first she put the blame squarely on Ada's shoulders. Jealous Ada, who had requested his oldest friends did not call her husband Gigi. Jealous Ada, who despite her smiling mouth and Mother Earth vibe, apparently wanted to be a partner in their business! Jealous Ada, who had hooked Guy with home-made suppers, cosy interiors and enough preserves to sink a bloody ship. But deep down, Ashleigh knew it wasn't Ada. Having painfully peeled back the layers of their friendship, she could see that, actually, things had shifted after his admission in the library:

'You do love me, don't you?'

'Since the moment I met you.'

She might have smothered the exchange with arm punches, bluster and the belief that never mentioning it made it go away, but it had not. He had looked at her a little differently, and there was, on reflection, an increased formality in his manner, only by the smallest degree, something undetectable to anyone who didn't know him as well as she did, who didn't share their closeness, but it was, she realised, there. Not that this insight helped or changed a thing. It was all too late for that.

As her luck would have it, with debt hanging over the business and a rather insipid sales pipeline, he had not had to pay her very much at all.

She hadn't spoken to Guy since, learning only a year or so later that Archie had invested in the business and had become a silent partner, ensuring the name Fitch stayed firmly above the door, as the business and the brand grew and grew.

'Promise me you'll wear them!' Remy thrust the revolting sunglasses towards her.

'Do I have to?'

'Yes!' Remy bounced like a child who'd been on the sugar.

'Ren? Ash?' Midge called from the bottom of the stairs.

They both responded:

'What?'

'Yes?'

'Can you come down here a sec?'

Remy pulled a face. 'It'll be that he can't find the scissors or figure out how to put crisps in a bowl or some other life-altering dilemma that requires my input! Good job he's handsome.' She spoke with a love that even her sarcasm couldn't disguise. Ashleigh felt a flash of envy, wondering what it might be like to share her life in this way. She dated, sporadically, but the disappointment of men who were never quite what she was looking for, never quite Archie, made her rather not bother. She was fifty, more than set in her ways, and with an understanding that it was to be the single life for her. The odd dinner, the company of men a nice diversion, but never more than that. Just as she now, with the glorious benefit of hindsight, understood how things with Guy might have started to shift after her wedding weekend, she also understood how the same was true of her life with Archie. She had found motherhood difficult; dogged by self-doubt, she had retreated, distracted herself with being busy and never looking up. It meant not having to deal with the disintegration of her marriage, which was staring her in the face. Instead she simply painted on a smile and waited for the axe to fall, as if believing it was almost inevitable, the punishment she deserved. Another consequence of that damned stunt that Remy had pulled, leaving her feeling like a passenger rather than the captain of her ship. Steered this way and that since her sister had leaned in and told her, *'Don't say anything! It's done! I did it for you. I love you, Ash . . . No one will ever know, and that's all that matters!'*

But she knew.

She had always known.

'Don't know why *I* have to come!' She had planned to take a shower and then spend time putting her make-up on.

'Ren! Ash!' he called a little more forcefully now.

'For the love of God, we're coming!' Remy adjusted her glasses and Ashleigh reluctantly put hers on.

'How do I look?' Ashleigh posed in the shades and sucked her cheeks in.

'Marvellous, little dove, absolutely marvellous!'

Remy

Remy loved having her sister under her roof. Things between them had been so much nicer since Archie had upended their lives, and Ashleigh had, in the immediate aftermath, spent a week living in Sophie's room at their old house, while Sophie bunked on the floor with Harper, and Evie slept on the floor in Bertie's room. All those years ago now, it had been quite glorious, one big, happy family! Eating together, as they shared tales of their childhood, growing closer in a way that was just wonderful. And occasional weekends thereafter spent in each other's company, laughing over the silliest things, and never able to order KFC without announcing, *'Thank you, yes. I'd like some chicken, please!'* before falling apart. There had been a family holiday to Cornwall, birthdays, Christmases, graduations, Mother's Days and Easter weekends too numerous to mention, but which were the building blocks for a lovely future. The dream. It gave her an enormous sense of peace, to have some of their closeness restored, part of her joy rooted in how happy her parents were whenever their *girls* were together.

'Midge, where are you?' Remy now shouted as she made her way down the stairs with Ashleigh close behind. She was excited about the gathering. Nothing formal, just family, a decent chocolate cake and a bit of a boogie in the kitchen. Perfect. Her husband stood by the sink in the square kitchen of their lovely little cottage, their haven, the house of their dreams on the outskirts of Amesbury. They had lived here for nearly six years now, and she couldn't imagine being anywhere else. Not that it had been easy to walk away from their old house, which held so many memories, but it had been time. The cottage had felt like home the moment they walked in. The garden was private, the light on the blond wood floors warmed her soul, and the pretty front door with the half-timbered porch a design she had always dreamed of.

'What's up?' she asked her handsome husband, who stood with his arms folded across his chest, his expression hard to read.

'I'm afraid you've got some early guests.' He nodded towards the sitting room.

She turned to her sister. 'Bloody Mum and Dad! I *told* you!' Her complaint was wrapped in affection, aware that it was their special day too: fifty years since she and Ashleigh had been plonked in their arms.

Walking ahead, she set foot in the sitting room and couldn't help the scream that left her throat! She jumped up and down on the spot and felt quite light-headed, to the point where she thought she might fall over.

'No! No way! Oh my God!' Her tears were automatic. A visceral reaction of love, loss and relief all rolled into one.

Ashleigh too started to cry, as one of the early guests ran forward and caught Remy in his arms, lifting her clean off the ground.

'Tony!' She held him tightly, eyes shut, letting the realisation sink in. Her very best friend was here, all the way from Sydney. He was *here! In her house!* 'Tony!' She hardly dared let go and look at him in case he disappeared. 'I can't believe it!'

'Hello, darling.' His emotion matched her own.

Finally he put her on the ground, and she stared at the face she had known so well. He had aged, a little, of course, but was still the same twinkly-eyed, kind man she had always loved. His tan was enviable, his hair styled, although with a lot less hairspray than he had once favoured. The years melted away: *he was here, her marvellous friend . . .* the touch, scent and sight of him enough to take her back to a time when they had been inseparable and the thought of not seeing him would make her so miserable!

'I can't believe it!' was all she could repeat. 'I just can't believe it!'

'Hey, Ash!' Remy watched as he hugged her sister too, still quite unable to accept that he was actually *here!* She turned to smile at Midge, who looked just as swept up in the high energy of the minute. 'This is Raul!' Tony pulled away and pointed to his handsome other half, who held out his hand, which she rejected, pulling him in too for a hug.

'Raul!' They had of course only previously met via Skype.

'Love the glasses!' Raul pointed at her face.

'She's making us wear them.' Ashleigh laughed, quickly removing hers. Remy followed suit, having quite forgotten they were there.

'When was the last time you were all together?' Midge asked, his face split with the satisfied smile of one who had pulled off a master surprise!

'Too long,' she managed. 'Tony, I can't believe it!'

'Okay, you have to stop saying that!' He tutted. '*Believe* it – I'm here! Midge and I have been plotting and planning for months!'

'Midge! I never suspected a thing.' She beamed, full of love for her man, who would know how much this meant to her.

'It's not been easy keeping it a secret, you have no idea how many times I nearly let the cat out of the bag! We were even on a call once and you walked in. I had to say, "Okay, mate, speak soon!" And end the call!'

'I didn't know what the hell was going on.' Tony laughed, 'I said to Raul, I hope I haven't offended him. I mean, the last person you want to offend is a bloody Royal Marine! Especially not Batman!'

They all laughed at that, but she heard the emotion in his words, saw the twitch to his eye. It seemed he too could still only recall that night with the same level of emotion as her.

'It hasn't felt good keeping it from you.' Midge swallowed.

She caught the look Ashleigh cast in her direction and got the message loud and clear; it hit her in the gut, the subject that kept rearing its bloody head. The deceit that sat between them like a spiky thing. It caused a flicker of anxiety that she would not let spoil the moment.

'You did good, Royal!' She blew him a kiss.

'You haven't changed a bit! My beautiful Remy.' She saw his eyes settle on her facial scars, and this time his tears gathered.

'I still miss you, Tony. Even after all this time, I miss not having you close by.'

'Same.' He wiped his eyes.

'Hi!' Bertie waved from the doorway, shoulders hunched, hands shoved into his jeans pockets. He was of that age when a cloak of self-consciousness engulfed him, almost as potent as the cloud of Lynx Africa that hovered over him.

'Hi!' Evie stood by his side, the two cousins of similar height and build, both now wearing dark-framed glasses. They too could have been twins.

'Look at you two!' Tony put his hand to his mouth. 'You've got so big.'

'Yep.' Bertie looked more than a little embarrassed, whereas Evie looked only delighted.

'Where's Harps?' Remy looked beyond them, hoping her daughter had come to say hello.

'She's just nipped to her room.' Midge winked at her, his smile fixed, but his eyes with the desperate haunt of worry that he, like her, was consumed by, whenever life felt a little too much for Harper.

'How long are you staying, Tony?' She felt the dread in her stomach that he would be leaving, knowing that whenever it was, it would be too soon.

'We're here for a couple of weeks. Going to spend time with Mum, obviously, and we want to go to London and a few other things.'

'I'm going to drive you crazy and want to see you all the time.'

'Nothing new there then.' He smiled at her. 'God, I've missed you!'

'Same.' She smiled.

'We were just about to get ready.' Ashleigh pointed upstairs.

'Oh, I'll come with.'

'Do you fancy a beer, Raul?' Midge, darling Midge, knew his job was to entertain Raul and allow the three some catch-up time. Her heart swelled with love for her husband.

'Always!' Raul who seemed just as lovely, placid, and calm as he'd been on the phone, followed him into the kitchen.

It was surreal and wonderful, as she, Ash and Tony sat on the bed in the guest room, where Ashleigh had made herself at home.

'I love your cottage!' He took in the chintzy drapes and soft-yellow painted walls.

'Me too.' His approval meant the world, their little home a symbol of how hard they had always worked.

'And you've finally figured out how to hang clothes in a wardrobe and not chuck them on the floor!'

'Don't look in my bathroom!' She pictured her pyjamas and dressing gown, lobbed into a heap by the sink.

'Well, this takes me back, the three of us sharing a bed!' Tony laughed. 'I must have been the envy of every boy in the postcode. If only they'd known!'

Remy laughed too, having never really given it much thought.

'You guys helped me not only understand I was gay but accept it too.'

'Ah, that's so sweet. Because you found us so physically repellent the only explanation could possibly be that you weren't into girls?' Remy laughed, putting her hand on his arm as if only physical contact would do.

'Kind of.' He stuck out his tongue. 'No, I remember sharing a bed with you two hot chicks and all three of us lying there staring at the poster of John Taylor you had taped to the ceiling.'

'I remember the one.' Indeed she did.

'And it was like . . . ah, I see what's going on here.'

'I still love him,' she declared.

'Do you?' Ashleigh sounded surprised.

'God yes, I've already told Midge that if John happened to be passing through Amesbury with his entourage and his car broke down and he needed the loo and a cup of tea, and he knocked on my door and came in and used the bathroom and had a cuppa and then, as he was leaving, said to me, "I've fallen madly in love with you, Remy Hughes. Come with me and live in my mansion in America, and let me peel you grapes all day and we can swim naked in my pool and play *Rio*, the album, on repeat, while we lay in the sun," I'd go. Just so he's prepared and knows what to tell the kids.'

'That, my love, is a weirdly specific and detailed scenario, if you don't mind me saying so. It suggests you've given it quite a lot of thought.' Tony stared at her.

'Not really.' She smiled, knowing she had maybe envisaged this very thing at least a dozen times.

'Hang on a minute!' Tony reached for his phone and the sound of 'Hungry Like the Wolf' filled the room. 'Oh my God!' She jumped off the bed and danced with her hands above her head, watched by Ashleigh and her beloved bestie. 'I'm sixteen again!' she yelled, as the music filled her up and she did her best to blink back the tears that threatened at just how quickly it had all passed, all of it, and for what she and Tony had endured, unaware of what lay in wait for them, just around the corner in a dark car park one Saturday night.

The bedroom door opened and in walked her mother.

'For of the love of God, Tony Newman, please turn that down. I can barely hear myself think!' Her mum shielded her eyes with her hand as if this might quieten the music.

'Sorry, Mrs Brett.' He hit the volume button.

'Keener!' She pointed at him.

Ruthie Brett rushed over and held the man in her arms. 'Welcome home, love.'

Remy knew she'd never forget this wonderful, wonderful moment on this brilliant day. Her fiftieth birthday was shaping up to be the best one ever!

Ashleigh

With the party in full swing, Ashleigh helped herself to a glass of wine.

'You all right, little one?' her dad asked, as he ate a sausage roll and wiped crumbs from his V-necked sweater with the back of his hand.

'I am, Dad. So lovely to have everyone here under one roof.'

'Makes me prouder than I can say!' His voice carried the quaver of emotion as Sophie and Riccardo danced, and her mother sat in the corner, no doubt grateful for the seat, with little Elio on her lap. Bertie and Evie giggled in the doorway, partners in crime. It made her happy to see the cousins getting on so well. Ridiculously, it felt like a win for her side. Given the lure of Archie, his little boys, and all that his family and their wealth could offer, at least she had Bertie and his deftness at computer games in her corner. Midge and Raul chatted and reminisced like old friends, as Remy and Tony leaned on the windowsill and occasionally bent double over something that was so funny they couldn't possibly remain upright!

She took a sip of wine, unwilling to admit that having Tony here had rather robbed her of something. She was fond of Tony, most definitely, but they were never a comfortable trio, not once she'd left primary school, as if Remy only knew how to operate as a twosome. It hadn't bothered her much when she'd had Guy to hook arms with, but it had of course been a while since that was the case. It *was* lovely to see their old friend – of course it was, they shared history – but she knew that if Tony was on the scene, then she faded into the background. It had always been that way, and wasn't going to change, even on her special birthday. It was uncomfortable to recognise this as jealousy, plain and simple.

'Can't believe my kids are fifty!' Dennis tutted.

'That makes you very old, Dad.' She laughed.

'It does that!' He reached for her hand. 'I don't know if I tell you enough, Ashleigh, but I am so very proud of you.'

'Don't know why.' She looked at the floor, unable to accept his simple compliment for what it was.

'Oh, so many reasons.' He took a deep breath. 'Getting into St. Jude's. I'll never forget it, all those kids vying for that scholarship, and they gave it to you! Them teachers knew, like I did, that you were always going to make something of yourself. I've never been so proud. I used to tell all the blokes at work, *my daughter goes to St. Jude's Academy*. You should have seen the look on their faces! I might not have made it to the boardroom, never got the big promotion, but I had that.' His words were like tiny spikes that peppered her skin and stung just as much. Her sweet, sweet dad. 'How you've handled splitting up with his lordship.' He never said Archie's name, not anymore. 'I'll never understand the fella, never! The way you've looked after Evie, setting up your own business *again*, as if it was easy, not letting life knock you down – you've done it all, Ashleigh, and you should never forget it.'

She took another sip.

'Den!' her mum called. 'Come and hold your great-grandson!'

'Duty calls.' He leaned in and kissed her gently on the cheek, let go of her hand and went to take Elio into his arms.

It was an odd moment.

Here she was, on her birthday, surrounded by her family, yet feeling, in so many ways, like an outsider, as if she had been put on a path when she'd taken up the scholarship that had made her travel in the opposite direction to her family. Remy had remained at the heart of it, walking to Milton Road Comprehensive every day and singing her way through her teens with Tony by her side, but that hadn't been possible for Ashleigh. She'd had no choice but to try every day to prove she was entitled to wear the blazer for the place she had taken by deceit. The ripples were still felt far and wide, even here, today, on her fiftieth birthday, when her dad was so very proud.

'Are you having a nice time?' She hadn't heard Riccardo approach, and started.

'Yes! Lovely, thank you! Elio is wonderful.'

'He really is. Hard work, but wonderful! He's a clever little thing.'

'Takes after his mumma!' she joked.

'Oh, no doubt! She wants a drink.' He reached for a Diet Coke.

She smiled at the young man who had slotted in so well with the family, as if he had been there forever. An architect, who was smart, patient, and adored Sophie in a way that, Ashleigh knew, had made putting her daughter's hand in his on their wedding day far easier for Remy than it might have been. Midge had remained stoic and calm as Riccardo had given his speech, pledging to always love and respect his new wife, and there'd not been a dry eye in the house. Including Jamie and his girlfriend Daina, who had been part of the proceedings. True to Riccardo's word, he had encouraged Sophie to follow her fashion dreams and was keen to tell anyone who would listen about his wife's incredible couture business, with a keen eye on sustainability, that she operated out of her flagship store and workspace in Spitalfields.

It had made her wonder about Evie's wedding day, if and when it came, trying to imagine how it would be with her, Archie, and Leni all in attendance. That was the thing. Unlike her dad, who could simply not say his name to make Archie disappear, she was stuck with him, replacement wife and all.

Remy shimmied her way across the kitchen. 'Happy birthday!' she called, clearly high on life.

'Yep, happy birthday!' Ashleigh raised her glass.

'Isn't it great to see Tony? Can you believe he's here?' Her sister's tone was one of pure delight.

'It's really great.'

'What did you say it like that for?' Remy's face fell.

'Like what?' She was unaware of anything other than trying to sound joyful.

'So flat! Like you're fed up, or . . . or angry!'

'Not everything has to be fun and roses, Rem! People are allowed to be a bit pissed off or a bit thoughtful!' she snapped.

'Yes, but not on their birthday, *at* their birthday party, on a lovely, special day!'

'Jeez, that's exactly what I'm talking about! It doesn't have to be *lovely* and special!' She decided to get some fresh air and made her way out into the back garden. Remy followed her.

'What's wrong, Ash? Where has this come from? You were fine earlier. Tell me.' Her concern was touching.

'Nothing. Ignore me. I'm just . . .' She didn't want to have to explain it all to Remy, who was clearly having a ball.

'Just what?'

'I don't know.' Ashleigh felt the full effect of her sipped wine on her fuzzled thoughts. 'I'm just not in the mood for making out everything is great!' There, she'd said it.

'Do I do that, Ash? Try and make out everything is okay when it's not, is that what you're saying?' Remy sounded hurt, and this in turn hurt Ashleigh; she could hear the slight slur of prosecco on her words.

'Don't overthink it. We all do it, don't we? The small lies of communication that paint a picture. I mean, you and Midge are always, just . . . perfect!'

'We are, yes! We are perfect! It's not a front we put on. We are *that* happy, because we work at it, and I'm sorry if it bothers you! Jesus!' Her sister shook her head.

'Well, good for you. I *want* you to be happy! I want things to be wonderful. All I'm saying is that I can't tell you how many times *I* say I'm okay when I'm not,' she admitted.

'You think that's what I do?' Remy stared at her. 'You have no idea! I am happy! I am!'

'All right! No need to shout at me!'

'I'm not shouting!' Remy shouted. 'But you think it's *easy* for me, trying every day to make it up to Mum and Dad? Not being able to tell them that, actually' – her voice wobbled – 'I didn't let them down, I didn't rip up the raffle ticket to win at life that had been offered me! I bloody won! I won the bloody raffle! I just gave you the prize. And I don't want your life, none of it! I want *my* life, my cosy life in my pretty cottage with my Midge. That's all I want. And I know you want me to come clean, which, ironically, might just cause the one thing that scares me, the one thing I want to avoid – putting a dent in my lovely, lovely life!'

'This is what I'm talking about!' Ashleigh laughed. 'Small lies and big lies, we all do it every day in so many ways. "How are you?"

"*Oh, I'm fine!*" We smile, fix our hair and say, *I'm fine!* Even when our hearts are broken, or we're keeping shit to ourselves, even when we're lonely.'

'Do you get lonely? Is this what this is about?' Remy held her gaze.

'A bit, but again, doesn't everyone?' She shrugged. 'And it doesn't feel like a lie though, does it, when we say those things? It feels like self-preservation and a lot like consideration as you say it, to spare the feelings of the person who's asking, knowing they can do very little to mend the situation anyway, and so why offload? I've done it for years! Presented myself as this capable, smart, go-getting businesswoman, when the whole time I feel like it could be snatched from me at any moment because I don't bloody deserve it!' She clicked her fingers.

'You do deserve it. You deserve all good things, Ash!'

'So you say.' She took a beat, and they were quiet for a moment, both calming, as the night air cooled them.

'I guess I don't always tell Midge how I'm feeling, don't want to worry him. Particularly if I'm concerned about Harps. I don't see the point in both of us lying awake until the early hours. I prefer that he, at least, gets some sleep.'

It was heartrending to hear of her niece's struggles and how it affected her twin.

'I understand. I keep things in. There's lots I don't talk about.' Aware now that she was really delving into the honesty pot, she was more than a little nervous about how to proceed.

'Like what?' Remy sat down hard on the step that ran along the back of the patio, and Ashleigh joined her.

'Like . . .' She slumped, aware her posture was slovenly. 'I yell at random strangers in the car. I do it a lot. I've sworn at someone on the crossing who didn't say thank you. I called them a fucking twat, just shouted it, randomly, at this bloke who ignored me when I stopped to let him cross.'

'That's not nice, but there are worse crimes. I think if you were sent to hell it'd be an interesting conversation, you standing there with warmongers and murderers, having to explain that you once swore at a man who didn't thank you at a crossing.'

'I've done it more than once. I can't help it. I don't plan it, it just comes burbling out . . . and then I cringe at myself, I feel so bad,' she admitted.

'So don't do it. Stop yourself. Think before you speak! Isn't that what they say?' Remy offered the cliché, and Ashleigh smiled.

'Yes, they do, and they make it sound so easy, but it's not. I don't know why I do it.'

'Well, I'm no psychologist, but it sounds like you have latent anger that is waiting for an opportunity to show its face.'

'Latent anger?' Ashleigh laughed, partly at her sister's earlier outburst. 'There's nothing latent about it – I'm *angry*!'

'What are you angry about?' Remy asked with barely disguised incredulity, as if trying to figure out what her sister, who had been given the prize, had to be angry about.

Was she not listening?

'Where to start . . . The way Archie's parents treated me, viewed me, as if I just wasn't good enough. They never wanted to spend time with me.'

'That was a long time ago, and actually, having met them, I think that's a blessing.'

Ashleigh ignored her, not in the mood for her humour right now.

'I'm angry with Archie too, angry that we built a life, and I imagined a future that was never going to be mine. And Guy, our business – *my* business – all that work, all those dreams.' She clicked her tongue on the roof of her mouth. 'I still feel very angry about how it was all taken away from me, even after all this time.'

'That's sad.'

'I know!' she fired, not wanting anyone to find her sad, especially not Remy. 'And I'm angry at Evie for not picking me more often, for lying to me rather than just saying, "I don't want to spend time with you, Mum!" And I'm angry at myself for not . . . for not being the best mother on the planet. For not figuring it all out sooner.'

'Well, no, because that award went to me. Have you spoken to Harper? I don't know where I went wrong.' Remy rubbed her face.

'Rem, I see how you are with your kids. They love you, and you love them, you all get on so well, and it's something I just can't emulate, although God knows I've tried.' Her voice, she knew, carried the falter of imminent tears. It was as her sister opened her mouth to comment that Ashleigh felt a surge of wine-fuelled confidence and the contents of that pot of honesty came pouring out, quicker than she could consider the consequences. 'And I'm angry with you. I've always been angry with you, I think.'

'With *me*?' Remy half laughed, as if trying to mask her surprise and embarrassment. 'Really?'

'Yes, really.' Ashleigh paused and drew her verbal dagger from its sheath. 'I'm angry because I'm a fraud. You made me a fraud. Complicit in a crime I knew nothing about but a crime with my dabs all over it!'

'For the love of God, Ash!' Remy laughed – actually laughed!

'What? You can't deny it!'

'I don't deny it! But we were ten – *ten*! Babies! And as I always say to my kids, you can't regret a decision you made if you made it in good faith at the time, and I did, I really did! I made the decision I thought was in your best interests, and that set wheels in motion and here we are!'

'Yes, here we are, Remy. But you could have told the truth. Could have got me out of this.'

'Got you out of it? What does *that* mean? My God, you look like you're so mad at me right now!' Her sister raised her voice.

'I am! I told you I am. You made me the golden girl, and I've had to live up to that. What you did, it's dictated so much of my life, trying to prove that I was worth that place, trying to live up to the person Mum and Dad thought I'd be once I'd been through the system at St. Jude's, trying to please *everyone*, trying to be tough, trying to make money, trying to win!'

'Win what?' Remy's expression told her that she just didn't get it.

'Approval! Affection! First place! A successful husband! A big house! A fast car! You fucking name it!'

'I thought I did a good thing, I thought you wanted that place – *needed* it – and I didn't give a shit where I went to school, not really. I was happy to stay with Tony, so it made sense to do it and hand it to you.'

'*Hand it to me!* You just don't get it, do you?' It was in the moment impossible to pack the words away, to stop spewing truth at her sister. 'I'm a fucking fraud, and I've been a fucking fraud since I was ten years old. Bogged down by the secrets I carry, and it's been hard lugging that much weight. It meant I never felt like I'd earned my place at the table, like I'd got there through duplicitous means, not just at St. Jude's, but everything that came after – university, landing a man like Archie, all of it! I had to try really hard, every single day, to be good enough. But I never was. I never could be! No wonder Archie chose Leni. Because I don't deserve any of it, do I, Remy? Not the house, the job, my marriage, my kid, none of it!'

Remy stood now and stared at her, her face ashen, eyes close to tears, nose running, mouth twisted, voice hoarse with all it tried to contain. 'Are you saying you blame me for every single thing that you have fucked up in your life because I did something with love that I thought was a good thing?'

'I don't know what I'm saying.' Ashleigh thought she might throw up, as drinking wine on an empty stomach caught up with her.

There was a beat of silence as they mentally regrouped.

'I thought – I thought I was doing a wonderful thing, a kind thing.' Remy now sobbed, her voice quieter now. 'We were just the littlest doves.'

'We were, the tiniest doves, but it messed me up, Rem. I've spent my whole life trying to be as good as you, as brave as you, to be more like you in every way.' She took a deep breath.

'That's . . . that's insane!' Remy cried and wiped her face on her sleeve.

'It's not though. It's the truth, and the worst thing, the very worst thing, is that for years, for nearly all of my life, I've been lying to Mum and Dad, so scared they might find out.' Her tears came hard then, as she remembered what her dad had said to her earlier. 'And when I told you, all those years ago, that it might be a good idea to tell them, you said I couldn't!'

'I did not!' Her voice squeaked with indignation.

'You *did*, Remy! You told me not to say anything.'

'I don't . . . remember saying that. I remember saying we should be cautious, and I told you what that might mean for me, but I never said you *cannot*!'

'But it's true, whatever way you split hairs, you *did*! And I felt I couldn't say a word, aware of what it would cost you, cost me, but it's changed my whole life. What you did changed my whole life, gave me a different life to the one I maybe should have had. I lost my foundation, my honesty, my authenticity. You took it from me.' She had thought often about how it might feel to say it all, to get it all out into the open. It had, in her mind, felt a lot better than this.

'Well, Ashleigh, the good news is I can fix it right now. I can fix it all! Because I can't have this conversation with you again. I can't live with it hanging over me, not anymore!'

She watched as her sister stood, raced across the patio, and threw open the back door. Ashleigh followed her, watching as Remy walked into the lounge, and began clapping loudly. 'Everyone!' her sister called. 'Everybody, listen up!'

'Remy!' she shouted, wanting to stop this any way she could. 'Remy, no!'

'Shut up, Ashleigh!'

All present stared at them both. Ashleigh felt her face flush red.

'I have an announcement.'

'Remy!' she shouted again, as Midge, Sophie, Bertie, Tony, her mum and all the assembled looked from Remy to her and back again; it was excruciating to be under the microscope. It was, however, too late for Ashleigh to stop her, as her sister did something that was crazy, stupid and risky, speaking quickly and loudly. *Very* loudly, as her hideous, sparkly sunglasses rested on her head.

'I would like to tell you all something that I probably should have said a long time ago. I owe it to my sister, to my parents, my husband, all of you, and it's this.' She paused, swaying slightly. 'It was me that took the exam for St. Jude's Academy. Me pretending to be Ashleigh, me that passed with flying colours, me that actually won the place and the full scholarship, and it was Ashleigh who hid in the mower shed, wetting her pants about it! And she's *still* wetting her pants about it, and so that's why I need to tell you all, to make it stop. To make it all just . . . fucking stop.'

Remy

As her arms fell to her sides, Remy was aware of the room spinning and that her speech had been hastily and carelessly delivered. She'd thought about this moment, of course she had, imagined the after-effects of words that slid over her tongue and out into the world in an impetuous moment! Would she feel relief, freedom from the burden, finally erasing her sister's icy glares, subtle gestures, and suggested negative outcomes, forever? It was nothing like she had imagined. Instead it was like standing in a blast zone, feeling the full force of detonation, and about as scary. She waited for the relief to kick in. It didn't.

The moment Remy stopped speaking, she placed her hand over her mouth, instantly regretting every single word, as her tears sprang and ran over her clenched knuckles. The room seemed to grow smaller as there was a collective gasp. Her mother stared at them, her face pale. Midge seemed to study her, looking more than a little perplexed, and Sophie grabbed Elio, who leaned back against his mother's legs.

She had half suspected that Ashleigh might come and stand by her side, take her hand, and explain how that long-ago day had unfurled, how Remy had found her in the cubicle, crying . . . but that was not what happened. Instead, Ashleigh raced out of the house, leaving her quite alone to deal with the fallout. Her heart sank. Where was she going? It was dark outside, and it was their birthday!

One thing was, however, crystal clear and would be preserved in her memory for always: the way Midge now looked at her. It was a look she'd hoped never to receive from him, something close to disappointment, and a knife to her heart. It weakened her, made her feel vulnerable, and for a split second she remembered what it had felt like to sit on the damp cobbled floor wrapped in his coat, with blood in her mouth, one eye closed, as the blue light coloured the air and they wheeled her broken friend into the back of the ambulance. Or to sit in Jamie Aller's shitty flat and wait for him to come home, while baby Sophie slept and she tried to stop trembling, feeling as if she could quite easily fall right through the floor.

'Is this some kind of joke?' Her mother was the first to speak.

'No, Mum. *I* took the exam.' Calmer now, having hurled the verbal boulder, she saw how her parents stared at each other.

'But . . .' Her dad's eyes narrowed, head shaking, as if he couldn't find the words.

Tony walked to Raul and leaned on him, as if he were his safe place, and she more than understood.

'Are you kidding me?' Midge muttered as he made his way past her, up the stairs and away from the party.

'Wait, Midge . . .' She called after him, wanting him to hold her tight and tell her it was all going to be okay, because she had been ten, a baby, and it was a long, long time ago.

'We'd, erm, we'd better be getting back to Mum's.' Tony looked a little flustered. 'It's been a long day, long journey and . . .' Even he ran out of words as he wrapped her in a hug and kissed the top of her head. 'See you tomorrow, darling.'

Raul squeezed her hand as the two made their way out of the front door. It wasn't quite the end to the party she had envisaged.

Sophie picked up Elio as Riccardo packed away the baby things.

'We'd better make a move too, Mum. You've got a lot going on.' Her oldest daughter seemed keen to get away. 'Thank you for a lovely party, and happy birthday.' Sophie kissed her cheek, and she held her hand briefly as they left.

Harper was nowhere to be seen, which wasn't a surprise.

Bertie and Evie disappeared upstairs, and she was left with her parents, who sat clearly stunned by her revelation.

'All that time.' Her mum shook her head, as if the fact just wouldn't land.

'Why didn't you say anything?' her dad asked, softly.

'I honestly didn't think it was important, Dad. Didn't think it mattered, not for the longest time, and by the time I understood that it *might* matter, years had passed, and I didn't know how to tell you. I was worried about what it might mean for Ashleigh, worried about what you'd think of me, and I didn't *want* to tell you! Didn't want it mentioned, not ever. I thought it was between us and that we'd got away with it and that we'd never talk about it and that would be that.' She decided it was the time for complete honesty.

'You've made us look so stupid.' Her mum sniffed.

'I haven't! I didn't mean . . .'

'Well, whether or not you meant it is another thing entirely, Remy, but nevertheless you have.' Her mum stood and reached for her handbag. 'What are we, monsters? So terrible that you couldn't tell us?'

'No! Not that, it was just this pressure . . .' she started, unsure how to finish.

'Come on, Den.' Her mum made the call to leave.

She watched her parents, shoulders sloping downward, trundle out into the darkness.

Remy looked around the room, the beautiful bunting Sophie had gone to so much trouble to make, the cake still on its stand, yet to have the candles lit or be cut. Her tears were drawn from deep inside, as she flopped down on to the sofa, riddled with regret, and wishing she had kept her big gob shut.

'Where is everyone?' Harper asked as she came down the stairs, reading book in her hand.

'They've gone, darling. Evie and Bertie are in his room, Ashleigh's gone out, your dad's upstairs and everyone else is travelling home.'

'What happened? Why are you crying?' Harper tucked her hair behind her ears nervously and put her fingernail between her teeth to rip it. A habit Remy deplored.

'I think I messed up, Harps.' She nodded through her tears.

'Wanna talk about it?' Her daughter sat next to her, and Remy laid her head on her child's narrow shoulder.

'I love you, Harper Hughes.'

'Love you, Mumma.'

These were the sweet words she needed to hear right now as this changed world settled around her.

It was nearly midnight and Midge was yet to appear. Remy had sobered as she scrubbed, having spent the latter part of the evening clearing up the kitchen, pulling down the bunting, sweeping the wooden floor, stacking the dishwasher, and washing glasses in the sink. All while Harper read her book on the sofa. The cake she left on the countertop with a knife next to it, should anyone fancy a slice. Cowardly as it was, she was still plucking up the courage to go and face her husband, having fully expected him to appear at some point. Whether they would row, chat or cry, she had no idea, possibly all three, but either way, she was dreading the interaction, unable to get the way he had looked at her out of her mind.

With tiredness now pawing at her muscles and her thoughts a little less than crisp, she knew she couldn't delay it any longer; it was time for bed and to go and face the man who was everything to her.

'I'm going up, Harps. Will you be okay?'

'Yep. I'm not sleepy, just going to sit here and read.'

'Okay, my darling.' She peeled the soft blanket from the arm of the sofa and placed it over her daughter's legs. 'I love you. I'm so proud of you.'

'See you in the morning, Mum.'

'See you in the morning, and don't bolt the door, Ashleigh has a key.' She wondered where her sister had got to and checked her phone again. Still no reply to the two texts she'd sent asking where she was and if she was okay.

It was as she held the banister and put her foot on the first stair that she heard the clatter and bang, as Ashleigh more or less fell through the front door. Her dress had ridden up and her eye make-up was smudged; she was certainly making a good go of ridding herself of that golden girl image.

'What the hell!' Harper's anxious tone was one of concern, as she jumped up, alerted by the crash.

'She's fine!' Remy smiled, to show there was nothing to worry about, knowing her girl was sensitive to any extreme situation, easily overwhelmed. Rushing towards the front door, her sister lay laughing on the mat, hair falling over her face and with too many buttons of her frock undone, revealing her lacy cupped bra. She was giving off more booze fumes than The Dog and Duck at chucking out time on market day. 'You're fine, aren't you, Ash?' she asked through gritted teeth, smile fixed.

'Fine is debatatatable!' Ashleigh snorted. Harper smiled awkwardly, concerned, on high alert, yet it was undeniably funny to see a sloshed adult on the hall floor.

'Harps' – she clapped – 'why don't you go and read upstairs? I'll be up in a bit.'

'Sure.'

Her daughter had given her a sideways glance, indicating she understood it was not actually a suggestion, but more of an instruction.

'For God's sake, get up!' Remy hissed, watching as her sister managed to haul herself into a crawling position and, on all fours, slowly made her way into the kitchen. She came to rest by the table, slumped against the wall with her legs straight out in front of her. It was then Remy noticed she had one shoe missing.

'What on earth? Look at you!' Remy ran her a glass of water, knowing there was little point in getting angry or even expressing an opinion; her sister was too drunk to take anything in.

'I've hadalovelytime.' She beamed.

'So I see.' She handed her the water and decided to make coffee.

'I've got something to . . . t' tell you.' Ashleigh hiccupped.

'Is it that you've consumed your body weight in wine? Because I hate to be the spoiler, but I already know this.'

'Funny!' Her sister pointed at her, before trying to stand on her booze-addled pins, and swaying, resting her hand on the wall to steady herself. 'It's a secret that I think might make you mad.'

'Oh, you know me and secrets.' Remy felt a headache pulse; this was the worst possible end to the worst evening.

'You can't keep them, can you! You told *everyone!*' Her twin laughed as if this were the funniest thing she'd ever heard.

'You wanted me to, and I did! So don't throw it back at me, Ashleigh. You've wanted me to come clean for years, and now I have. And thanks for sticking around to help me deal with the aftermath!'

'Ssssh! You're very shouty.' Ashleigh put her finger over her lips and slid back down the wall, landing with a thump in a sitting position.

'So what's your secret? Spit it out,' she snapped, wanting to get the interaction over so she could go upstairs, wanting her sister to sober up enough so she could send her to bed, out of the way.

'I have been to the pub!'

'No shit.'

'Come here! Come here!' Ashleigh beckoned her over, as if about to reveal big news. Remy bent down.

'I have had sex,' her sister whispered, and Remy caught the full whiff of sour wine notes on her breath. It was far from pleasant.

'Two things: you're a mother and therefore I guessed this might be the case.'

Again Ashleigh roared her laughter. 'Wha's the second thing?'

'You need to use mouthwash, that's the second thing. You smell like an old brewery mop.'

'I want to tell you more about my secret, Remy.' Her sister pulled her arm, until she was sitting next to Ashleigh on the floor, suddenly a little tired, her body flagging.

'Go on then. Just tell me.' She was running out of patience.

'I had it just now! *Tonight!* When I went out, I ended up in the pub and had sex! The best kind of sex, unexpextedsex!'

'You met someone in the pub and had sex?' Remy didn't know how to process this. Her sister was a grown woman, and yet she felt horrified. Had someone taken advantage of her? Her gut churned with all the terrible possibilities.

Ashleigh howled her laughter. 'No! Well, yes, but I knew him already.'

'You don't know anyone here.' She was confused, Ashleigh was a London girl. Who did she know who might be drinking in a pub in Amesbury?

'I had sex with Jamie!'

The words were easy enough to understand, yet made little sense.

'*Jamie?*' She felt her mouth go a little dry, and was confused, because the only Jamie she knew was Jamie Aller and . . . surely not! 'My Jamie?'

'He's not your Jamie anymore, but *that* Jamie, yes. Sophie's dad, Jamie the bozo!'

Remy stood and held the edge of the countertop. 'That's . . . are you actually kidding me?' It was a thought as yucky as it was surprising. Not only was Jamie a dipstick, but Ashleigh knew exactly how he had treated her when they were married.

She shuddered; the connection was revolting for her. *She had been married to Jamie, had a baby with Jamie, it was . . .*

'Are you angry?' Now her sister looked close to tears.

'Go to bed, Ash. Go to bed and sleep it off and we can talk about it in the morning.'

'You *are* angry with me.' Her sister stifled a sob.

'No, no. I'm not angry.' Remy turned away, unable to look at her, and pausing by the door, she spoke plainly and loudly. 'I'm grossed out, just completely grossed out!'

Halfway up the stairs, she could hear Ashleigh bashing pots and clattering pans in the kitchen. God only knew what mess she was making physically to match the one her behaviour would undoubtedly create.

The bedroom was in darkness. It was hard to tell if Midge was sleeping. She could just about identify his shape under the duvet. Her body was stiff as she lay on the bed next to him, arms by her side, breathing heavily, staring wide-eyed at the ceiling as her thoughts spun and her upset brewed, and all thoughts of a restful sleep this evening were relegated in the face of this . . . this . . . turmoil!

Midge turned on to his side and she heard him sigh.

'Well, that was quite the night.' He spoke clearly, far from sleep.

'Yep.' She wasn't sure how to be, what to say, feelings alien when it came to her marriage.

'She's right though, Remy, he's not *your* Jamie. He can't be, because you've got me, you've got a Midge, and Jamie is old news, the past.'

So he had heard; at least it spared her having to say the words out loud.

'You know what I meant. He's still Sophie's dad. Are you telling me it's not weird?'

'Oh, it's weird all right, but that doesn't change the fact he's not yours.'

His tone was loaded, hurt, and she knew it was about so much more than this one incident.

'I don't *want* him to be mine. I don't want him at all!' She balled her fingers into fists, distressed at all that was unfolding. 'I also don't want my daughter to have to deal with the fallout of her aunty shagging her dad! I mean, what next? A relationship? More sex between them? We are twins! *Identical* twins! It's . . .' Words other than 'weird' and 'gross' failed her, and she'd already used them.

'Well, there's lots of things that I don't want.' Here it was; she braced herself as he sat upright against the headboard. 'We've laughed and joked for decades about your snooty sister, your smart-arse sister, the way Ruthie and Den coveted that bloody school, and you never thought to tell me?'

'I didn't know what to say or when to say it.'

'Are you trying to tell me that in all the years we've been married, you haven't been able to find a single suitable moment?' He gave a wry laugh. 'We talk about *everything*, we always have, only it turns out we haven't, and I'm still trying to get my head around that.'

'I'm sorry,' she whispered, aware of the inadequacy of the words.

'I'm sorry too. I don't give a shit about what you did when you were a little girl, but I do care about what you've done every day since we've been together. I feel left out, like a bit of an idiot. What else don't I know?' He clicked on the bedside lamp; the light, usually soft and welcoming, was tonight stark, brutal. It was the worst feeling to know she had made him feel like this.

'There's nothing you don't know.' She hung on to his arm, imploring him to keep loving her, to forgive her.

He stared at her, the atmosphere in the room now quite charged.

'What?' she asked, his silent scrutiny uncomfortable.

'You never say "our daughter", you always say "my".'

'I meant *ours* – of course I do!' His expression was one of hurt, and to see it wounded her also, knowing she had inadvertently armed her words.

'I've been her dad since she was little. Jamie's never been there for her, not really, he just pops up at events, shouting! He's not been there for her like I have!'

'I know, I *know*.' She too sat up straight and folded her arms across her chest, trying to contain the shame that she thought might spill from her. She felt physically sick. She had caused this, all of it.

'I'm her dad. I am. I'm her dad.' It was hard to hear the croak of emotion in his voice.

'You are. You know you are.'

She moved across the divide, coming to rest against him, feeling his usually yielding body a little cool, a little strange to lean on, like they were strangers.

'What the hell just happened, Ren? It was supposed to be a celebration. I've worked so hard to get Tony over here. We were so excited, and then, bam! Out of nowhere a fucking tornado struck!'

'I'm . . . I'm sorry.' Those words, again. 'I just, I don't know, I wanted to tell everyone, wanted to get it out there!'

'Well, you certainly did that.' Midge put his arm around her and held her close. But there was something fundamentally different in the way it felt, a hesitation, the slightest formality in his manner, a subtle brittleness to his grip. She had caused this, aware that she had only spoken the truth earlier: *We are, yes! We are perfect!*

But what if we're not? This thought left her reeling, her heart cleaved open at no more than the possibility.

And then she heard it, loud and clear in her mind – *Oi!* – and she jumped.

Midge held her tighter.

'I guess there – there is something else.' She closed her eyes. 'Something I haven't really . . .' It was easy to start, but a lot harder to finish.

'Tell me.' His tone was worried, as if wary of what revelation she might be about to make.

'I am still a bit . . . no' – she shook her head – 'still *very* scared of those men.'

'What men?' His voice was quiet now; she could feel his heart racing against her skin.

'The men that attacked Tony and me. I still hear them shout at me, just before it all started, and it happens quite a lot, whenever I'm feeling vulnerable or stressed, or a million other times, I hear that shout and it's like I'm still there in the car park, in the minutes before you came along.'

'Why haven't you said anything?'

'Because it was bloody decades ago. I should be over it by now! It feels ridiculous to still be this afraid!'

'Oh, my love.' He kissed her scalp. 'I think you need to talk to someone.'

'I can talk to you.' She lay her cheek on his chest.

'Someone better equipped to deal with this kind of thing. Someone cleverer than me.'

'Is there anyone cleverer than you?' She kissed him, willing to talk to someone, to do anything to get rid of the fear, yet equally fearful of opening that particular box.

'You, apparently. Winning that full scholarship. That was really something.'

His recognition of her achievement, the acknowledgement of her smarts for the first time since she was a child, had a profound effect on her, and as her tears flowed, he held her close, and she was thankful.

Ashleigh

Ashleigh woke with the headache she deserved.

'Oh, God!' She remembered instantly that she'd slept with Jamie Aller! It had been sordid, quick, and thrilling, but right now the thought was enough to make her feel sick. And then came the recollection that she had told Remy.

'Shit!' Sitting up in the bed, she brought her knees up to her chest and sat with her face in her hands, the door of this pretty bedroom the only thing between her and the sister she would have to face eventually. She looked at the window and half wondered how sturdy the drainpipe might be. Not that there was humour to be found in any of it.

'Shit!' was the only word that would suffice.

Jamie. The man had always set her teeth on edge, irritated her beyond belief, barely tolerating him when he was with her sister. Her emotional disgust only matched by the physical, she needed a shower, desperate to wash the whole experience and the dire ending of the party from her skin.

. . . it was me that took the exam for St. Jude's Academy. Me pretending to be Ashleigh . . . me that actually won the place and the full scholarship.

She had heard every word and her legs had turned to jelly; she had wobbled and felt like she might fall. Unsure what to do, where to go, what to say, it had been a feeling not dissimilar to that night sitting in her car all those years ago, knowing she had lost Archie and Guy and was without a home, without a haven. But this felt worse, much worse. Yet what she would always remember from that moment was her dad's face. He had looked . . . bereft. And she had felt the disappointment in it. It wasn't only that they'd lied – that *she'd* lied – but also that he now saw her as she saw herself, a fraud. This, she knew, was the hardest thing to deal with. It was a strange feeling to be divested of the guilt, the dishonesty; it was certainly freeing. Yet she had lost something too, lost her podium place, her status diminished, her stature reduced. The world now knew that it was her who, as her sister had so succinctly put it, had been wetting her pants in the mower shed. Hiding in the pub had felt like a good plan, and who should have been propping up the bar, but Jamie.

There was a knock at the door, and she caught her breath.

'Yep?'

Remy walked in with a mug of coffee.

'Thought you might like this.'

'Thank you.' She took the mug into her hands and did her best to avoid eye contact, relieved her sister seemed calm, at least.

'How are you feeling?' Remy sat on the end of the bed, this debrief happening whether she wanted it or not.

'As you'd expect. Rough.'

'I don't know what to say, Ash, not really.' Remy stared out of the window, looking towards the green rolling fields in this, her little slice of heaven.

Ashleigh sipped the coffee, feeling it instantly doing much to lift the fug of her hangover.

'What happened after I'd left?'

'Oh, we cut the cake and carried on dancing like nothing had happened!'

'Really?' For a second her heart lifted at the prospect.

'No, Ashleigh, of course not! What do you *think* happened? Mum and Dad barely kept it together and left looking like I'd socked them in the face. Midge went off to bed, Tony and Raul left a bit sharpish, and I don't think I even properly said goodbye to Sophie, Riccardo, and the baby.'

Her coffee was becoming less appealing with every sip, as guilt sat on her tongue and distorted the flavour.

'You just left me! Literally raced out of the back door and left me to face everyone!' Remy looked right at her now; she looked tired, distressed. It struck her how markedly different things had been yesterday when they'd sat on this very bed and laughed, putting on those hideous glasses.

'What was I supposed to do?'

'Erm, I don't know, stay by my side, support me, help explain?'

'Explain what?' Ashleigh wasn't sure what she might have been able to add that would have made the situation any less awful.

'Are you kidding me right now?' Remy's mouth fell open.

'I'm not. I *told* you not to say anything, I was calling out to you, but you just ignored me.'

Remy laughed then, and it took a while for her to regain her composure. 'I don't believe this, Ashleigh! Are you are saying now you *didn't* want me to tell them, that maybe *I* was right all along, and that we might just have been better off not saying a word?'

'No, I'm not saying that. Christ, I'm scared to say anything in case you jump up and go and make a public declaration.'

'You've been pressuring me for ages! And last night you backed me into it and then left me to take the hit.' Her sister's words were as relatable as they were upsetting.

'We're not to mention it, not ever again. Just make out it hasn't happened, let everyone believe what they know to be true, that you took the exam, Ash. That's the end of it. Promise me!'

'You just don't get it, do you, that's exactly what you did to me!' It was crazy that Remy just couldn't see it. 'You landed me in it, *told* me what you'd done, never asked! Never gave me a chance to back out! You made the plan, the announcement, set up the scene and then left *me* to take the hit!'

'I was ten!'

'And *I* was ten! It was a lot! And besides, you were ten for *one* year, and then you've been eleven, twelve, sixteen, twenty-six, thirty, forty-four and every other age up until this point, but still not acknowledged that what you did might not have been in my best interests, and you weren't even willing to talk to anyone about it!'

'Well, I've certainly told people about it now! And it feels like you might be a little bit delighted by the fallout, as if it's my turn, and that's really shitty!'

'What a bloody awful thing to say to me!' She was hurt; her throat tightened with the pull of sadness.

'And you slept with Jamie – *Jamie!*' Remy stood up. 'What were you thinking?'

'I wasn't.'

Remy ignored her. 'It meant Midge and I had an even bigger row.'

'Well, that's not my fault.' Ashleigh chose not to make a quip about the fact they were supposed to be perfect.

'Oh, nothing is ever your fault, Ashleigh! Last night was horrible.'

'It was, but I didn't do anything – *you* did!'

'But you pushed me to do it, you've always been pushing me to do it. Is that why you slept with him? To punish me more, create a ripple?'

Ashleigh put the coffee cup down, fearing her trembling hand might shake the contents all over the pale bedlinen. Her words, when they came, required no forethought but were a confession of sorts.

'I suppose, in my pissed state, I wanted Jamie to want me because I thought it might prove, in some way, if he wanted me too, that I was as good as you.'

'As good as me? That's nuts! You were always the bright one, the one who was going places, according to Mum and Dad.'

'Yes, I *was,* but not now, not now they know the truth.'

'But you *wanted* them to know the truth!' Remy raised her voice.

'My God! My head is spinning! And if it's any consolation, Remy, we were drunk, as you saw when I came home, and I'd actually sobered up a bit by then. We were very drunk.' She rubbed her forehead, as more of that shame seeped from her pores.

'It's no consolation. I don't know why people think that makes a difference.' Remy wasn't giving her an inch.

'Because it does make a difference. When you're incapacitated like that, you make crazy decisions. Do stupid things. Take risks that you wouldn't dream of taking when sober. Like standing up and blurting out a lifelong secret!'

'I wasn't *that* drunk, not at all. And you and Jamie aren't fourteen-year-olds, sharing a bottle of scrumpy at the bus stop. You're fully grown adults!'

'You sound like Mum.'

'I'll take that as a compliment in this instance,' Remy retorted. 'You slept with Jamie, Ash. It's . . . I just still don't know why.' Remy looked as stunned as she had last night, that much she did remember. 'He was awful to me, bloody awful, and you know this, and he's Sophie's dad, and . . .'

'I don't know what you want me to say!' She felt everything had already been said.

'I don't either, but I can't imagine a scenario where I would sleep with Evie's dad.' Remy visibly shuddered, as if horrified by the thought. 'I mean, how *would* you feel if I shagged Archie? Not that I ever would.'

'It's not the same. It's just not the same!' Ashleigh did her best to defend the one stupid mistake.

'Isn't it?'

'No! And no matter how much you want to verbally batter me, I can't change what happened, Remy! And besides, if you wanted to shag Archie, you'd have to fight off the German, and she's pretty strong. Not sure I'd fancy your chances.'

'I can't laugh about it, Ash. It turns my stomach when I think about it. It's icky.'

'So don't think about it.'

'Now why didn't I think of that?' Remy smacked her forehead.

They were quiet for a second, until Ashleigh broke the impasse.

'I think Evie and me will head home today.' She spoke as the thought formed, picturing the packing of her case, and wondering how quickly she could get into the car, just wanting to be gone from here, away from her sister.

'I think that's probably best.'

It was telling that Remy didn't try to dissuade her, not at all. If anything, she looked a little relieved. Ashleigh couldn't believe that the birthday weekend that had started with so much promise, so much fun, could have ended this way. She felt a little bit heartbroken and a whole lot like running away.

◆ ◆ ◆

Having loaded up the car and buckled up, just before they pulled away she spied Remy through the kitchen window, standing as

Midge pulled her close to his chest, enveloping her in his big arms and leaning his chin on the top of her head, about as close as two people could get, as if she was under his skin and inside his bones – yes, exactly like that.

'Is it true you slept with Sophie's dad?'

Her young daughter's words were like punches, and she felt the bruises form in a place deep inside.

'Yes.' There was, she figured, no point in denying it when Evie had been present, had probably heard enough to already know it was true.

'Is that why we're leaving early?'

'Yes,' she whispered, unable to control the emotion and absolute desolation she felt at how it had all turned out, knowing Evie had been having the very best time with her cousin, building bridges.

'Don't cry, Mum.' Her girl reached out and wiped a tear from her cheek.

'I'm sorry.'

'I don't want you to be sad. It doesn't matter, not really. I was getting bored of playing computer games.' Evie's tone, trying so hard to convince her that this might be true, suggested it might actually matter a lot.

'I am sorry, darling.' She sniffed, found a smile, and shoved the car into gear. 'I really am. Let's go back to the flat and' – she wiped her eyes – 'and I'll cook something.'

'Oh, I'd love to, Mum, but Leni called and, err, she needs me to babysit. If that's okay?'

'Sure.' Ashleigh indicated and pulled out on to the road with a heart that felt heavy with sadness at the prospect of a lonely night ahead. 'Of course it's okay.'

Ashleigh Brett and Remy Hughes

2022

Aged 60

Remy

On top of all the other thoughts and emotions fighting for top spot today, and in spite of the exhausting list of chores and the many moving parts, concern at having to face Ashleigh was right up there. It wasn't too extreme to say that she was dreading her sister coming home. This immediately filled her veins with guilt, knowing Ashleigh had just as much right to be there as she did. Their relationship was fractured. They saw each other only sporadically. This was just the way it was now, as if it were too hard to hurdle over the wall of hurt, mistrust and awkwardness that sat between them. A wall Remy could see over and yet found almost impossible to climb. It bothered her how her relationship with her sister hijacked her thoughts when today it needed to be all about her lovely dad, the loss of him and coming together to support their mum.

The last couple of times she had seen Ashleigh, at Evie's wedding to Katrina, and then Sophie's party for London Fashion Week, she had smiled and nodded politely, and they had managed the briefest of exchanges, both with rictus grins that reflected their discomfort.

'Evie looks so happy.'

'Yes.'

'You must be so proud of Soph.'

'Always . . .'

She was aware that her parents had kept them in their sights, which only added to the pressure, as they waited for the thaw, the reconciliation, the open-armed hugs that meant all was forgiven, so that they could breathe a little easier, knowing their girls were reunited and all was well.

'I just don't understand it . . .' her mum was fond of repeating, and Remy would try to explain.

'Not all siblings get on, Mum! Not all twins! We're very different people.'

'I know that, I'm your mother, but you never used to be very different people. You used to be the same!'

And Remy would nod and make a cup of tea or nip to the loo, anything other than try to explain that they had not been the same for a very, very long time and that spending time in each other's company only seemed to goad the other, like putting a flame to touchpaper. Being on edge when the other was present was now a default, and it didn't really matter how it had started or how they had got there, it was just how it was. After their fiftieth birthday, the night that still lived bright in Remy's memory, they hadn't called each other. Sulking, healing, reflecting, it all led to the same thing; days that turned into weeks and then months without contact, and suddenly it felt too awkward to make the call, to reach out. She didn't know how, wasn't sure what to say, and if she were being honest, she quite liked not having to worry about the confrontation, concentrating instead on smoothing things over with her parents, looking after her own family and committing to her therapy. Midge's suggestion had been a good one and she now wished she had sought help earlier, only able to marvel at what a wonderful thing hindsight was.

At Evie's wedding, Remy had been overly aware of her sister's presence, making sure Ashleigh always had someone to chat to, so as not to be left by herself like lone prey. She also deployed avoidance tactics like taking five in a corridor, being preoccupied with a drink or her handbag, clinging to Midge like he was a rock that kept her weighted and she was therefore in no danger of floating into Ashleigh and their worlds colliding. Remy wasn't sure it was going to be quite so easy to avoid her twin today.

Standing in the bathroom in her bra and knickers, she twisted to the side and studied her slender frame in the full-length mirror, running her finger over the bumpy red scar along her abdomen. *Hysterectomy.* The word itself had been scary enough, followed by the very best words that came soon after: *non-malignant, all good, no need to worry . . .*

And something she'd not shared with anyone: the post-operation distress. It felt ridiculous that, aged sixty, she had perched on the side of the bath in paper knickers and with a gauze-covered pad over the incision and sobbed. Mourning the loss of her womb and the fact that she would never again carry a baby. Not that it was possible or had been possible for over a decade. A post-menopausal woman; it wasn't even a consideration. But still. To know that the nest which had nurtured her children, the soft, fecund tissue where memories and cells of conception lurked, was no longer part of her body was a lot. She found herself dreaming of being pregnant, bathed in sunshine and running her hands over the full-bellied satisfaction of taut skin, the distended nub of navel, smug and smiling at the miraculous thing that brewed within. Waking placed her in a reality that was cold, riven with loss, and where it was hard to explain to anyone just how much she missed the years when having a baby was possible, missed them with a strength that was alarming to her. With this came the realisation that those had been her best years, when with the optimism of her youth, the wisdom of her experience and an energy for whatever might come next, she had eaten up life!

Not so much now.

Never one to obsess over her weight, accepting the pockets of plumpness that had graced her hips and bottom in her forties, it was odd to her that now, and from this angle, she looked decidedly flatter, squarer. No bum to speak of, no handfuls of flesh; even her boobs had deflated. It was as if the universe had decided that with the decrease of her sexual appetite, and no need to concern herself with reproduction or attracting a mate, they may as well remove the lovely soft bits that she felt made her more desirable. She supposed it helped her to accept the ageing process, the slow fade from siren to sixty, not that she'd ever been a siren. Sixty felt like the gateway to becoming old, and she had to dig a little deeper to find that optimism. She could feel it, the edging towards invisibility, becoming an *older* lady before she became an *old* lady, and they all looked the same, didn't they? Milky eyes, grey hair, comfy shoes, breathable fabrics. It was all a ghastly thought.

Hey ho.

Grabbing her fleece dressing gown, she welcomed the softness, the warmth against her skin, and headed downstairs.

'Penny for them?'

Midge stood by the sink. They had lived here in their cottage for sixteen years now, and she still couldn't imagine being anywhere else. She liked that each room held memories of get-togethers, the comings and goings of her family and grandchildren. It only made her love the place more.

'I'm not looking forward to seeing Ashleigh.'

'I know.' As usual, Midge offered his unconditional support by not saying too much, but rather giving her a look that told her he was right there and he understood. It was inevitable that with her sister's imminent return, she would think about the fallout from their fiftieth, a long time ago now, but it had been a marker, and had certainly changed things for a while between her and Midge.

The fact that she'd lied to him had placed a tiny fissure in their blemish-free marriage, one she had had to work hard to polish out. He had been adamant that it was nothing to do with the actions of her ten-year-old self, but rather her actions as a grown-up, when honesty and transparency had been their bywords and she had let him down. This, coupled with the fact she had never truly told him of her lingering trauma, not given him a chance to help fix or even understand it. All of it they had had to slowly unpick, spending quiet nights, side by side, talking as the fire flickered, she cried, and they held hands, drawing strength from the other as they shed skin. Time and patience had played their part. Stripped bare, talking openly and honestly was often far from comfortable, had made her feel vulnerable, scared even. But waking now each morning with a lightness to her conscience gave her new-found freedom, specifically the ability to exist without the worry of discovery lurking. The worry of Ashleigh exposing the secret. The worry of those men hurting her again.

'I knew I'd have to face her today, but . . .' She clicked her tongue against the side of her mouth.

'I guess if it's any consolation, she'll be worried too, I'm sure. She looked really nervous at Soph's party. I think we all need to remember there's other things to think about today. It's all about your mum.'

'I know that.' A steady stream of tears now striped her face. Her sadness was in plentiful supply. In the face of fatigue, Remy's sorrow found the cracks and wheedled its way into her thoughts. 'Am I selfish?'

'Ren, you are the least selfish woman I know.'

'I told you she sent me an email, saying she wanted to give the eulogy!' she snorted, and wiped her eyes. 'Can you believe that?'

'He was her dad too.'

'Whose side are you on?' she fired.

'Yours, always yours, but he was, and if she wants to say a few words . . .'

'Yeah, well, I left it to her and Mum to sort out, and they've made a plan. I'll say my bit and she'll say hers. It's a bit cringe though, isn't it, like how many speeches does there need to be?'

'Well, you don't need to do one. You could leave it to her.'

'Are you joking?'

He exhaled and held his hands out, as if aware that there was no right thing to say and that he was damned if he did and damned if he didn't.

'I spoke to Soph earlier. She said Mum was quiet, but seemed okay.' She gathered herself.

Her mother's stoicism in the wake of losing Dennis, a couple of weeks ago now, was admirable. Ruthie, who made a meal out of everything, who greeted the most minor crisis with much ado, had been calm. It seemed the magnitude of such a loss, the shock and life-altering ripples that came from it, were enough to cow even the strongest of personalities. It was another element to her grief, to see her mother so altered, so quiet, and knowing there wasn't a thing she could do to put it right.

It had made sense for Sophie, Riccardo, and Elio, now eleven, to stay at Ruthie's; she did after all have the two spare rooms. Not three, like Mrs Jenkins who used to live over the road, but still. This nostalgic thought pulled on those darn tears again. Remy had figured it would be a lovely distraction for her mum, having her granddaughter and great-grandson to fuss over.

'Is Elio going to the funeral?' her husband asked.

Remy nodded. 'Soph thinks he should be exposed to all aspects of life, thinks it would do him more harm to be left at home with a babysitter, wondering what was going on while we all traipsed out to be together. I'm not sure I would have taken my kids aged eleven, but what do I know?'

'Soph's a great mum.'

'Oh, she is a great mum, no doubt. I'm not saying that, and I suppose it's different, isn't it, nowadays? Kids are exposed to more things than we can imagine, thanks to the internet. I guess I'm more worried about Elio seeing us upset, seeing me cry.'

'I think that's exactly Sophie's point about us being open, showing how we're feeling, saying that it's fine to have a whole range of emotions and not shielding him.'

'I guess so.'

'Did you not cover that in therapy? I'm not prying, it's a genuine question. I'm not being . . .'

'It's fine, my love.' She found a smile. There was still hesitancy in his tone whenever they discussed her sessions, still a smidge of awkwardness at the whole topic, as if he was unsure what was up for discussion and what was off-limits, respecting her privacy and her journey. Therapy had been a murky and vague word, something she felt was for other people. Turns out she was other people.

They rarely spoke about the detail of her one-to-ones, more how the last few years had helped her put into perspective so many of the things that had hampered or preoccupied her. Things she only thought about occasionally when reminded, like the guilt at hearing that Tyler, her loud colleague, had jumped from a bridge and taken his young life. Always positive Tyler, who it turned out might have very much needed *someone* to talk to who was not a customer on the end of a line. To the bigger things that impacted her daily; being one of two twins who were almost estranged, and the complicated range of familial difficulties that brought with it. Her short-lived, failed first marriage that she had rushed headlong into without a thought for the consequences. The fact that Ashleigh had more or less disappeared when Remy had made her confession, and how shitty that still felt. The unappealing thought of her sister sleeping with her ex, and of course, the trauma of her attack, quietly and painfully reliving it in so many variants, without the courage or confidence to talk openly about what she had been through, about what *they* had been through. As if believing that if she were strong enough, laughed enough, kept busy enough, she could simply brush it under the carpet. It had helped massively, talking to a dispassionate stranger. She would always be thankful for being given that perspective, now able to look back on it as a terrible random thing, a chilling chapter in her life but just that – a chapter, and not her whole story, and certainly not the thing that she should allow to dominate and shape her life.

'I don't think so, nothing that specific, but maybe Sophie's right. Yeah, why not let him see us, warts and all!'

'He's a good kid.' Midge smiled, his role as grandad one that he cherished, in the way she could have predicted.

'They're all good kids, they really are. We're so lucky.'

She smiled, picturing Bertie's twin girls, Clementine and Topsy, now eighteen months old. Bertie and his wife Ulla Lumi lived a fantastic life on the coast, where he worked as a ranger for the South Downs National Park, and she taught at the local primary school. It was idyllic, but how she missed them all! Wanting them to live their best lives, to be happy, she understood how important it was for Ulla Lumi to be near her family, and not that she'd ever mention it, but it came at a cost to theirs. She was very much looking forward to seeing them both later. Ulla's mother was looking after the girls.

Harper would not be coming.

It was more than she could cope with. Her darling middle child, who lived in a flat in Salisbury and whose life was not without its struggles. Harper, who, in her early twenties, had been diagnosed with severe depression, anxiety and a whole host of complex labels that formed a knotty ball which her girl did her best to navigate each and every day. Remy knew if she could have one wish, *just one*, it would be to make Harper's life easier, to give her clarity of thought, a good night's sleep and for there to be one day, *just one*, when her daughter didn't feel the need to phone her several times to unload all the things that jostled in her mind for position. Remy loved her girl, loved her with her whole heart, as she did all of them, but she'd be lying if she didn't admit that those interactions left her feeling exhausted. The call late last night had been no exception.

'Mum, I . . . I was going to wash my hair so I could come to Grandad's funeral, but I've run out of shampoo—'

'Do you want me to get you some shampoo?' she interrupted, looking at the clock, even at this hour wondering how long it would take her to drive in, make the drop, drive home. She'd do it, no matter how long, how tired, she'd do it . . . do anything.

'No, no, no, please don't.' Harper sounded almost panicked by the prospect. It was like this sometimes when she was hiding. *'Anyway, I went on Amazon to see if I could get a hat delivered, like a . . . a . . . beret-type thing, but they can't guarantee it will be here in time, and I can't find my dark shoes. I spoke to Sophie, and she said she'd pick me up, tomorrow, but I know that it's hard to pull up right outside sometimes and I got really panicked about where they'd park and being able to find the car. I thought they had a white car, but Sophie said they'd changed it last year. I'd hate to get in the wrong car. And I don't think I want to go to the party after the funeral, don't really want to see everyone, and just thinking about that, having to chat to people who are all going to ask me how I am, it made me feel awful.*

I had a nap, but, honestly, Mum? I loved Grandad, but I think he'd understand that it's just too much for me . . .'

'He would, my love, he would.'

Midge, in his calm way, would remind her that if it was that exhausting for her, just imagine what it must be like for Harper. Part of the reason for giving up her job at the insurance company, almost eight years ago now, was so she could be there for her daughter. To field her calls, help her out in a crisis and give her the time and attention she needed to get through the day, being that *someone* to talk to.

The timing had all worked out, as it was around the same time that Midge had expanded the garage and hired her to take care of him and his staff of four. She made bookings, took payment from customers, ordered parts, stashed car keys, brewed coffee, you name it . . . three days a week. Just enough.

This latest call had left her feeling a complex range of emotions; as ever worried for her daughter's mental state, a little relieved that she wasn't going to have to watch over her tomorrow – one less thing to stress about – and guilt, as she accepted the latter.

She wondered for the first time if Ashleigh would be coming alone, or whether she'd bring her new partner. She wasn't sure of his name but knew there was a new partner. There was always a new partner. Her sister's life had always been somewhat unstable in the romance department.

'I love you, Midge.'

Her voice a squeak, as she remembered why they were all gathering and that her daddy had died. This in turn encouraged more tears, as she sniffed.

'I love you too. Come here.' He reached out and pulled her towards him, holding her close; one hand on the side of her head, the other across her back, making her feel safe and warm in this space that was hers alone. He whispered now into her scalp.

'You'll blink, and before you know it the day will be over, and we'll be back here sitting at the kitchen table with a cup of tea talking about how it went. You know that's how it goes.'

'Yes, you're right.'

She didn't share that this was how her life went; one minute she was ten, then twenty, thirty, forty, fifty, and now sixty – *sixty*!

Her mother was right: it had gone in a blink.

Ashleigh

Victor Perera indicated and smoothly changed lanes on the motorway. Ashleigh sat back in the passenger seat of his Aston Martin Vantage with its buttery-soft leather interior, a lovely car in which to make this, the most dreaded journey.

'It's funny, isn't it, you think about your parents dying from when you're a child, fret over it, and yet you still don't really believe it's ever going to happen, can't properly imagine it. Then it does happen, and no matter you might have considered it in any number of scenarios, it's still a tremendous shock.'

'You were lucky to have had them both until you were fifty-five.' He spoke with clarity and there was a brief moment of confusion, before she remembered she'd shaved five years off her age when they met, just because.

'Yes.' Glancing at her reflection in the tinted window, she liked what she saw. Her blonde, straight bob was timeless, her wrinkles kept at bay by regular appointments with her aesthetician. Her lips ever so slightly plumped to replace the pout that would by now have undoubtedly thinned. A routine of facials, collagen supplements, turmeric shots, vitamin drips, skinny jabs, yoga and clean eating ensured she could get away with fifty-five for a while yet. 'Are both of your parents alive?'

'Yes.' He nodded, eyes on the road.

They were at this stage, her and Victor, where they were sleeping together rather successfully. She knew he had grown up in Sri Lanka, was divorced, had a penchant for Jo Malone candles in his fabulous Mayfair penthouse, as one sat next to a framed photo of him with Charles and Camilla, all mid-laugh. She was aware he didn't approve of public displays of affection, knew he wore handmade shoes and shirts, that his favoured food was a hearty full English served in a good old-fashioned café, and he liked to listen to Coldplay on repeat. But the more detailed stuff, how he had made his money, did he play an instrument, had he ever been to jail, been very sick, made terrible mistakes, his plans for the future . . . it was all out there to be learned.

This thought reminded her of a conversation a long time ago with Remy, who had wanted to know all about Archie, and she had answered in the misguided belief that she knew him. That was a time when she and her sister were still close, still speaking. When Remy was one of her pillars, someone she could call in an emergency or because the world felt too big. It hadn't been that way for a while. They had drifted, were estranged almost. A situation that had arrived on the coattails of that disastrous weekend. She thought about Remy, of course she did, not least when she was having to verbally dance around conversations with her parents, who had constantly pushed for some kind of reconciliation. If only it were that straightforward.

Her sister's upset at the fallout, once she'd come clean about the exam, proved to Ashleigh that they'd been right to tell the world. If it had been the small thing Remy had always professed, no big deal, then there wouldn't have been any fallout in the first place; people would have laughed it off, had another drink, scarcely given it a second thought! But it was not like that. The irony wasn't lost on her that her sister was now, when it came to their parents, having to deal with the weight of the deceit, that feeling of being a fraud, of disappointing the people close to her, exposing her lie . . . all the things Ashleigh had had to live with since she was a little girl. That and the fact she had drunkenly slept with Jamie, which in all honesty she couldn't believe Remy was so freaked out about, given that she'd been drunk! Very drunk. It wasn't as if she'd planned on making a habit out of it. She could, in fact, almost guarantee that recalling it was far worse for her than it was for her sister. *Jamie Aller – urgh!*

She clenched her jaw, wondering how their reunion was going to go down and hoping that the solemnity of the occasion might be enough to keep high emotions at bay.

Victor was handsome, accomplished, funny, and she felt quite optimistic for what might come next. She had given up entirely on finding love, but whatever *this* was, with this successful man, was nice. The last few years of solitude and reflection had helped her understand that post her divorce from Archie, she had entered a period of mourning, that, with hindsight, had taken her decades to recover from. Although that wasn't strictly true: she wasn't fully recovered. It had damaged her, changed her, and she knew without doubt that she'd never again experience a love like theirs. Never again be so willing to commit, to dive in filled to the brim with enthusiasm for whatever might come. It had been special, easy, comforting, passionate and true, rooted in the heavy excitement of their youth. The only shame being it wasn't reciprocated. And her biggest regret, a nagging thought that maybe if she'd tried harder, worked less, cooked more, been more involved with Evie, he might not have stopped loving her.

'When did you stop loving me?'

'I'm not sure, but a while ago.'

His words, there for perfect recall whenever she needed them, venom that she rolled along her tongue, feeling its sting, and knowing that to swallow it would only cause her infinite harm.

She had trusted him, adored him, Archie, that fabulous boy who had chosen her and made her feel like she had won the world! And no matter how much time passed, it still irked her that he now lived with Leni in the house Ashleigh had designed; every room they had christened with sex and champagne. She wondered if Leni knew that? Not that it was her fault; it wasn't. It was his. Leni had merely entered the play when they were halfway through the first act, unaware of the promises Archie had made and how she had believed them entirely. Besides, Leni and Archie had now been married for far longer than she and Archie had. It was an achievement that rankled, along with the fact that in every snap she saw of them with their two teenage boys, they all looked so goddamn happy! Evie included.

Evie, who lived in Canada with her wife, Kat. Far away from her. They liked the outdoors, hockey, skiing and watching cartoons. Ashleigh did her best to keep in contact, they swapped texts, birthday cards and met for lunch whenever Evie and Kat were in London, which they were at least twice a year, trips paid for by Archie, when they slept in Evie's old room in Clarendon Road. Ashleigh did her best not to picture the family dinners around the table of the fancy house, the one with the Crittall windows and the turnaround gravel driveway and the grandest of hallways.

It was odd and bothered her enormously that Evie was yet to bring Kat to Ashleigh's flat. It was her greatest sadness; the lack of closeness between her and her only child. She had tried, tried hard, but it was as if that lack of closeness in those early foundation years was not something she could catch up, not ever, and no matter the emotional pain this caused her, she understood. Evie, as a little girl, had sought out the arms of Archie and Marguerite, safe harbour in that busy, slightly fraught world she had inadvertently helped to create.

'Would you like a mint?' Victor reached into a cubby and shook a little green tin of Marks and Sparks mints at her.

'Why not?' She helped herself.

She tried not to imagine Evie and Kat in that spacious kitchen, sharing food, laughing as they caught up with Leni hosting and Archie drinking, music playing, her own private torture.

'How often do you come back to visit?' His enquiry casual, she tried to answer in kind and not give a hint of the boulder of destruction that had been lobbed into her life here, her childhood home.

'I had sex with Jamie!'

'My Jamie?'

'He's not your Jamie anymore, but that Jamie, yes. Sophie's dad, Jamie!'

The memory made her cringe.

Home . . . it hadn't felt like home for quite a while.

'Not too often. We're all – all busy. You know how it is.'

'I do indeed.' He spoke with the suggestion of laughter, indicating he got it; a busy man, no doubt. 'So you used to work for *Gallow and Fitch*?' he asked with an impressed tone.

There were very few who lived in the capital who were unaware of the successful chain of luxury estate agents. She'd spy their classy logo everywhere and did so with a gripping feeling of hurt in her gut. She had, over the last couple of years, slowed down, working a bit less and socialising a bit more. It was all about that work–life balance.

'I . . . I used to be a partner, actually. One of the founding partners. The Fitch bit, my . . . my married name.'

Damn! There it was again, that desire to cry, the shame, the loss, the grief, the rejection, just as acute at times when the topic caught her unawares, as if it had happened yesterday.

'Oh? What happened?'

'It's rather complicated.' She swallowed her distress, and smiled, doing her best to change the course of the conversation. 'It's very good of you to drive me all this way, Victor. Thank you.'

'My pleasure. This beast likes nothing more than a good run.' He patted the steering wheel. 'And I shall visit the cathedral, have a gander at the Magna Carta and find a café that knows how to fry an egg and make a decent mug of tea.'

'Sounds like bliss.'

'They're weird things, aren't they, funerals?' he mused.

'Uh-huh.' And just the mention of it, the imagining of her dad in a coffin and recalling his final words, spoken down the phone when she had called without any idea that this chat would be their very last: *'Night night, darling. Sweet dreams . . .'*

Enough for her to feel a pull of tears far stronger than her ability to keep them at bay.

It would forever be a great sadness to her that in his final years, he hadn't looked at her with the same beam of delight, the instant bright-eyed wonder whenever he saw her, his golden girl. It had dulled, as if she had let him down, badly. This coupled with the fact that as she did her best to avoid running into her sister, went home less, engaged less; she had missed so many opportunities to see him, to be with him, believing she had more time. And all because she wanted to avoid seeing Remy. Remy, who lived close by and got to pop in whenever she liked.

She hadn't been lying. It *was* rather complicated.

Reaching into her bag for a tissue, she did her best to blot under her mascara, not wanting it to smudge. A little embarrassed, a little awkward, as Victor was not yet someone she knew well enough to sob in front of.

Not at all.

Sensing her discomfort, he pressed a button on the steering wheel and the sound of Chris Martin singing '*Fix You*' filled the car.

It was kind of him, but only made her cry harder.

Remy

Remy took a seat on the sofa, finding it very odd, being in her mum and dad's house, without her dad in it. Sorrow hovered in the air like a fine mist. Two weeks after his passing, there was no wailing, no tears, no chest beating in a rage of grief, nothing like that. It was more a sneaky, silent anguish that left a cold residue on every surface, inhaled with every breath. The lamps were on, yet each room was in shadow.

When she was in the cottage or helping Midge at work, she could kid herself that her dad was pottering in the garden, rattling tins, looking in jars, as he hunted for something in his shed, or oiling wheels and widgets, as he was wont to do, but there somewhere, mumbling about the recycling or the weather, in the place he had been since she was born.

To be here, to see his shoes paired up by the radiator, his favourite mug in the cupboard, his pyjamas in the laundry hamper in the bathroom, his wristwatch on the nest of tables by his chair, the chair with the slight dent in the cushion, where he rested his head every day at approximately 3 p.m. for his afternoon nap, all of it left her feeling empty, bereft, and unbelievably sad. The sight of these redundant items helped her understand the finality of his passing, knowing he would never have need of them again. To throw them away felt rude – *his* things! She wondered how long it was prudent to hold on to them, knowing it could do her mother no good to stare at them day after day, yet the thought of seeing them discarded was just as hard.

'Are you okay, Mum?'

'I'm about as okay as I was when you asked me less than five minutes ago.' Ruthie took a slow breath, her gnarled fingers running back and forth over the lace edge of the handkerchief that was scrunched in her palm.

Remy felt flustered, aware of the repetition, the banal question that felt like a safe and necessary thing to ask. Constantly checking, still looking for the opportunity to fix something, to make it better. How she wished for a different answer from her mum.

How am I?

. . . Well, I'd like a cup of tea.

. . . I could really do with a hug.

. . . I'm a bit chilly. Is there a blanket?

Practical requests to which she could provide a practical solution. Something, anything, to make it all a little bit better. *If only.*

'Your hair looks nice.' She tried again.

This one of many small phrases designed to break the silence, lobbing a verbal pebble, hoping to provide a moment of distraction, of joy. Joy maybe too much of an ask. But wanting more than anything for the time to pass, so she could do as Midge had said, gather around the kitchen table with a cup of tea and talk about how it had all gone.

'Janet did it.' Ruthie didn't look up from her handkerchief.

The hairdresser had indeed done a good enough job in styling her mum's sparse grey locks. Old-lady hair. Remy patted her own mop, almost entirely grey and still as wiry and unruly. Her curls, her trademark. She had in recent years chopped it, so it sat below her chin, far easier to manage now that practicality took precedence over trend and beauty.

'Sophie and the boys have gone for a walk. God only knows why, it's bloody freezing.' Ruthie tutted.

Remy's shoulder ached on cold days such as this. She now rolled it, making a face as the muscles pulled and twinged in a way that was so familiar she could almost count, *one . . . two . . . three . . .* knowing that until it had popped and caused a needle of sharp pain to fire right through it would remain a dull, pulsing throb of discomfort. Far better the ritual and routine of the predictable hurt that eased after she encouraged it with this movement.

Having spoken to Tony last week, he had commented something similar about the cold exacerbating his old bones, now held together with pins and wire. Not that he had much cold to contend with, living just outside of Sydney. The lucky thing. He and Raul were still toned and handsome and looked a good ten years younger than their ages. He'd explained how tweakments were the key, not that she liked the sound of it. Needles, urgh!

'We must suffer for beauty. You know this!' Still his go-to phrase, that had made her laugh out loud.

Remy envied their sunshine life, not that she'd willingly swap her cottage for the surf at Bondi; she'd never been too good in the water. It thrilled her that her darling friend had found such love, such happiness. It was no less than he deserved.

FaceTime was a godsend, to see his lovely face at the press of a button. He had called last week to say how sorry he was about her dad, how Dennis had never judged, and only ever shown him kindness, and how much it had meant to a teenage boy doing his best to navigate a less than conventional life in a small suburban place.

'He loved you,' she had told him in earnest.

'Not all dads would have been so good to me. Your whole family . . .' He paused, and they shared a knowing smile. 'Particularly you and Ash.' As was his habit, he took the opportunity to try and bring her and her sister closer, to restore harmony.

'Your sister's not here yet then?' Ruthie called across the lounge and pulled her from her thoughts.

Yes, she is, but I've gaffer-taped her mouth, shoved her in a cupboard and not told you.

Actually that didn't sound like a bad idea.

'No, not yet, Mum. Shouldn't be too long.' Her pulse jumped at the thought.

'You did tell her two, didn't you? She knows to be here by two?'

'I did, and she does.'

'Maybe someone should give her a shout and make sure she's on her way. No hold-ups.'

'She'll be fine, Mum.'

It wasn't easy, the awkwardness between them. Not easy on her, not easy on her mum, and she knew it hadn't been easy on her dad, a fact that filled her with regret. Her lovely dad.

'You spoken to your sister?' he'd ask softly with a crinkled smile of hope around his eyes. She couldn't stand to think of it now.

Midge walked in, her handsome marine. There was a split second when, admiring him, she forgot why he was wearing his dark suit, white shirt, black tie, and the moment she remembered, a rush of sorrow caused her throat to almost close. She had to gasp to take a breath.

'You okay, Ruthie?' He walked over and quietly yet confidently placed his palm briefly on his mother-in-law's shoulder.

'For the love of God! Don't you start!' Her mum closed her eyes, as if exasperated, as she folded her hands into her lap. Her thin legs clad in black tights dangling in her wheelchair. It had felt practical to get her into it to save having to shift her from the sofa into her chair, then from her chair into the car. This, she figured, was one less move, like a game of chess for their queen.

'And how's my girl?' Midge sat on the arm of the chair and ran his hand over her back.

'Don't know really. Bit wobbly.' She smoothed invisible creases from her black shift dress.

'It's ridiculous.' Ruthie shook her head, as she unfurled her handkerchief and wiped her eyes. 'Do you know what he said to me?'

'What, Mum?' She had no need to ask to whom her mother referred.

'He said he hoped that, this year, we could all spend Christmas together as a family; none of this you here Christmas Day, your sister coming the day after and you staying away. Years of it! That's what we've had – how ridiculous! And what a waste! Selfish!' Ruthie breathed in juddery bursts. 'That was all he wanted, to have his girls here together, for Christmas. It wasn't much to ask, was it?'

Remy wanted to respond, but hearing that this was her dad's wish and that he had not lived to see it was a knife to her breast, the blade tipped with guilt.

'There's a bit more to it, Ruthie.' Midge did his best to pour oil on to the troubled waters.

'There's always more to it, Midge! Always.' Her mum raised her voice. 'But life is too short. That much I do know!'

Ruthie sat forward in her chair, her voice as strong as she could make it, but with the wobble of age and distress.

'Today should be about Dennis, my husband, who is not yet cold in his grave, but all people will want to talk about is the girls! Why are they not speaking? Why don't they get along? Right here in the house he worked so hard to make nice for them, to give them everything they ever needed, so they could lead good lives! Selfish is what they are!'

'All right, Ruthie.' Midge stepped up. 'I don't think this is the time or the place. And all families have hiccups, all siblings spar with each other – it's the nature of it! Doesn't mean they don't love each other.'

'Well, they've got a very funny way of showing it!'

Remy was as hurt by her mother's words as she was warmed by Midge's. Before she could mount a word of defence, there was a knock at the front door.

'I'll go.'

She decided it was better to get it over with, to face her sister and be done with it. Having mustered her courage, she walked slowly along the hallway, recognising the shape of the head through the glass, a head the exact same size and profile as her own. Having taken a deep, slow breath through her nose, and waiting for a second to compose herself, she turned the latch.

She might have practised in her head what she wanted to say, thought about how she would act, but such rehearsals paid no heed to the rare, deep connection between the two women. It was a visceral reaction, the need to hold her, be close to her, to cry with her. There was no forgiveness, nothing that instant or idealistic, but it felt entirely necessary to sweep away her suspicion, her defence, to pause their estrangement in recognition of their unifying loss.

You need to look after each other, always. You are, after all, miracles, two babies from one egg, rare and special!

The moment their eyes locked, all reserve and pre-planning fell away, as they stumbled into each other and held each other tight. Toe to toe, cheek to cheek.

'I can't believe he's gone!' Remy cried into her sister's hair, taking comfort from the closeness of her twin. Remembering their childhood, the way her dad had made them laugh at the breakfast table and had gone on about concrete. His red company tie with the little gold logo on it, resting against his pressed shirt, as he ate his toast and marmalade, smiling, kind, working hard to give them the very best kind of life.

'I miss him, I never got the chance to . . . to say goodbye!' Ashleigh stuttered.

'Our dad!' Remy sobbed.

'Our daddy.' Her sister matched her tear for tear.

'He built our . . . our Cindy shelf!' She could barely get the words out.

'He did, he built our brilliant Cindy shelf . . .' Ashleigh echoed.

Ashleigh

Ashleigh sat on the bench at the back of her parents' garden, part shielded from view by the enormous shrub that grew by the side of the shed. An ugly thing, really, that flowered only briefly at the start of the summer. Two or three weeks of flame-red blooms that for her did not justify its ugly, woody green presence for the rest of the year. She lit the cigarette and exhaled the smoke in a thin, satisfying line out into the early evening air.

In no mood to chit-chat to the assembled crowd inside her mum's house, not wanting another warm, crustless egg mayonnaise sandwich, and knowing to have the exact same conversation with any number of family members might drive her over the edge, she took refuge here, hiding.

'Yes, still in Queen's Park.'

'Not for me, I don't really like quiche, but thank you.'

'Oh, you went to London? How lovely. No, I'm not near Buckingham Palace.'

'She's doing great, her and Kat are happy, loving life in Canada!'

'No, my friend brought me down. He's picking me up later.'

'Yes, yes, he will be missed. He really will . . .'

'Look at you with a cigarette – when did this start? I can't believe you smoke!' Remy wafted her hand in front of her face as she took a seat next to her. It was easier, somehow, to talk while sitting side by side. It was with nothing but relief that she stared at her sister, grateful at how they had found common ground today, letting their love, their history, blunt the sharp edge of mistrust that seemed to have flared over the years.

'And I can't believe you mentioned concrete in your eulogy!'

'He loved concrete,' her sister justified.

Ashleigh thought *her* words had been more fitting, her tone more reverential, better. Not that she'd be sharing this.

'It was a lovely service though.'

'It was.' Remy nodded.

'And to kind of answer your question, if I smoke, I don't want to eat,' she admitted.

'Why don't you want to eat?'

Was it a trick question?

'So I don't put on weight.'

'But you've never put on weight. We're built like Mum, luckily.'

'Dad loved anything sweet, didn't he, especially Maltesers!' It felt good to talk about him and laugh, to remember his funny little ways, to remember him positively, rather than give heed to the gut ache that had dogged her since his death, knowing she had disappointed him, let him down.

'I don't know if I tell you enough, Ashleigh, but I am so very proud of you.'

'For your information, I smoked occasionally at university, then Archie and I smoked when we were drunk. Then I stopped when we went our separate ways but had a cigarette at a party about three years ago, and I just started doing it, but only when I have a drink.'

'How often do you have a drink?'

'What are you, my doctor?' She pulled a face. 'Don't you worry, it's all about balance. I eat well, drink rarely, and take a whole handful of supplements and potions, so I figure the odd cigarette won't kill me.'

'Unless it does.' Remy spoke plainly.

'Give me a break. Today is an exceptional one. I've just buried my dad.'

'What a coincidence!' Remy gasped.

'Talking of doctors, are you well now? Feeling better? Mum said you'd got the all-clear.'

'Yes. Thank you for your card and the flowers. Are you getting checked?' Remy's expression was one of concern.

'Yes. I did, nothing found, so . . .'

'I wasn't surprised. I mean, to get to sixty without being sick felt like an achievement. I know so many people who are either battling something or waiting for results or getting over an illness.'

'I guess we're at that age when the wheels are starting to fall off,' Ashleigh admitted reluctantly. 'Sniper's alley, isn't that what they call it?'

'Yep.'

There was a moment of silence.

'How did you get down here, anyway?'

'My . . . friend brought me, Victor. He has an Aston Martin.'

'I didn't ask.'

In no mood to row with her sister, Ashleigh bit her lip, before taking another drag. It was always this way when they hadn't seen each other for a while, the verbal jousting, the tension, like shouting at yourself in the mirror; exhausting, confusing, and just as fruitless when it came to resolution.

'So, is he your boyfriend?'

'What are you, six?' She shook her head.

'No, Ashleigh, I am not your doctor, and I am not six. I was just trying to make conversation. Forget it.' Remy stood, as if to make her way back inside.

'I'm sorry. Please stay here. I'd like the company. Mum is still telling everyone about my D.I.V.O.R.C.E., like *that's* the worst thing I've ever done, and as if it wasn't a million years ago now! Then she mentions that Evie is married to a woman – a *woman*! Big deal! I left before she got to the part where I stole your place at St. Jude's. She tries to do it all in hushed tones that are anything but.' She pulled her sister's arm until Remy plopped back down next to her.

'They never said you stole my place, I think they always went down the line that it was more that I *forced* you into taking it, that kind of thing.'

'God!' she sighed. 'How's it still such a fucking mess?'

'I don't know, but it is.' Remy gave a snort of laughter, suggesting she found the whole subject as taxing and ridiculous as her sister did. 'I can't very well hide from you today.'

Ashleigh smiled at her. 'No, you can't. You look good, Remy.' She really did, her curly hair, now greying, suited her, and she was ageing well, owning those wrinkles and still beautiful.

'I do not! I am now officially about a hundred years older than you! You look like my little sister! With the . . .' Remy pointed at her own mouth and forehead. 'I mean, you look amazing, but I don't know how you do it! I couldn't be arsed. Does it hurt?'

'Yes.'

It was easier, Ashleigh figured, for her to spend money on her aesthetics. It wasn't as if she had a mortgage, grandchildren, a husband to consider financially, and her time was her own, no cooking of supper, no Sunday roasts, no babysitting, no having to be there for Harper, day and night, no . . . nothing. She was free, as a bird, almost. No matter that it was a freedom that came with its own kind of cost and its own kind of loneliness.

'Plus, I have to be arsed. It's cut-throat out there in the dating pool, especially at our time of life. Fifty-five is no age to be on the hunt.'

'Fifty-five?'

'Yes, if Victor, my lift, asks you, we're fifty-five.'

Her sister laughed out loud. 'You're terrible!' The energy shift eased the atmosphere and they sat quietly, for a minute, until Remy turned to face her. 'Should I be worried about you, Ash?' Ashleigh watched as her sister studied her face for clues. She knew how this worked, recognising the small tells of her own expressions that were the same, and therefore revealed much.

Shaking her head, Ashleigh looked towards the house, where Bertie and Ulla Lumi were taking a moment, holding each other tightly in the kitchen, unaware they were being watched. It felt invasive to stare but it was beautiful too. She was happy for Bertie, a quirky kid who had turned out great, the father of twins, no less. What a gift.

'I know what you're asking, and the answer is no. I'm not depressed, not struggling, just thoughtful, reflective. Which I think I'm allowed to be today.'

'Yes, you are.' Remy nodded. 'But I just wanted to say that losing Dad has made me think about everything, Ash.'

'Me too.' She could only agree.

'I was dreading seeing you, and that's not right.'

'It's not, Rem.'

'I might not always like you, but you *can* always talk to me if you need to. Always. Just call.'

'Can I just call you?' Her question was genuine, her confusion real. Her sister's words had hurt more than she could express. She *wanted* Remy not only to like her, but to *love* her, to forgive her too, for how far she had slipped out of reach, how far they both had. It was a two-way street. But right now all she wanted was for them both to find a way forward.

'You can, Ash, of course you can. And maybe you should. We're not getting any younger. Well, one of us isn't.' She smiled.

'I'd never take my life, Remy, if *that's* what you were driving at. I love my life, love my friends, my people.'

'That wasn't what I was—'

'Wasn't it? You think I'm unstable.'

'I don't!' There was a beat of silence, and an overenthusiasm in her sister's tone that suggested she had lied. 'I think you're a train wreck sometimes, but generally not unstable.'

For some reason she found this funny. 'Don't hold back, Rem!'

'I'm in that frame of mind where I think maybe we'd benefit from some open and honest communication, don't you?'

'Oh God, did you learn that in therapy? This was always my fear that with your new-found understanding you would try and fix me!'

'Not that you need fixing.'

'No, not that I need fixing.' Ashleigh took a drag on her cigarette. 'I'm worried too that the last time wine levered open the honesty portal, it didn't exactly end too well.'

'There's the understatement of the day.' Remy bit her lip.

'Perhaps you're right. Talking openly *would* be good for us. God only knows there's a lot to say. We've drifted apart, and I find it hard to explain, to justify.'

'Me too. I hate saying that it just happened!' Remy faced her.

'I guess it felt easier not to call you than risk arguing with you, going over the details of what happened with St. Jude's, the Jamie thing.'

'Yep, all of it.'

Spurred on by her burst of confidence, Ashleigh decided to test the water. 'I'm okay. I really am. Most of the time. I think we all crave the same things, don't we? A haven, love, and hope. Life is busy and hard sometimes, but it's never too hard if you've got those three things.'

'Yep.' Remy swallowed. 'And do you have those three things?'

'In the words of Meatloaf, two out of three ain't bad . . .'

'Huh!' Again, that beat of silence while they mentally regrouped. 'When I told everyone, I thought you'd be delighted. It's what you'd always wanted, and it came at a huge cost to me, to me and Midge—'

'It came at a huge cost to me too,' she interrupted, thinking again of her lovely dad and how things had never felt quite the same after.

'I know.' Remy gave a stiff nod of acknowledgement. 'But you weren't delighted. If anything, it only seemed to make you angrier! I couldn't believe I'd got it that wrong *again*, when I only thought I was doing a good thing, getting it right.'

'Not angrier' – she took her time – 'but I hated how you did it and when you did it. I guess I'd envisaged sitting down quietly with Mum and Dad and explaining what happened, but you just pulled the pin and lobbed it into the middle of a family celebration. Our kids were there, Tony . . .'

'I know, and I'm sorry about that. I really am. In the moment, I just felt I couldn't stand the thought of that conversation again, you making hints and suggestions. It felt like it was dangling over me, always dangling over me.'

'Well, ditto that!'

'And then you slept with Jamie!' Remy's face creased, as if to even say the words was enough to make her cringe. 'I found it gross. Too close a connection. You knew what he'd done to me, how toxic we'd been, how hard I've worked for all these years to find balance, to let him in without letting him in, all for Sophie, and you did that.'

Ashleigh felt her body stiffen. She had prayed that today she could parachute in and out without this analysis, but deep down she had known it was inevitable and this was why she had dreaded coming face to face with her twin. 'I' – she felt her jaw tense – 'I was definitely going through stuff. Evie was pulling away from me, and it was a real slap in the face, my love life was in the gutter, the business was thriving without me in it, Archie was living his best life with his hot wife and fabulous kids all living in *my* house, and it all felt a bit unfair. I'd spent the weekend with you and Midge, the love birds in your cosy cottage. Jesus, there were literal roses around the front door, and then the cherry on the cake – Tony appeared to whisk you away into a corner to gossip!'

'So you were jealous?' Remy's eyes misted.

'No, not jealous, not really, more reflective, sad, looking for a quick hit of dopamine that fast, thrilling sex might provide, and it did. I was so sloshed I didn't stop for a minute and think about the fact that it was with Jamie.' She took a final drag and trod the cigarette butt under foot. 'If I'd been sober . . .' She let this trail.

'For the record, *I* wasn't jealous, couldn't give a shit. It wasn't the physical thing, it was just yuck!'

'We kind of unravelled after that, didn't we?'

'We did,' Remy whispered. 'I remember saying it was probably better to get all the shite over at once, and just let the avalanche knock me off my feet.'

'And I remember thinking it would be better *not* being knocked off my feet at all!'

Remy licked her lips. 'I guess I meant better than life-altering things happening by paper cuts. Better, I thought, to take the mighty thump that would see us land on our arses. The pain and humiliation would be the same, but I figured, at least it was going to be over, and we could dust ourselves off, and get up, stronger, nothing waiting in the wings for us.'

'But we never really got up, did we? I still feel like I'm sat on my arse some days. I am happy, I am, but I don't know what happens next, and that's unsettling at my age.' It was her truth, and it felt like the right time to say it. Ashleigh reached out and took her sister's hand, and there they sat for a while.

'I hope it's true, Ash, that we can get up stronger, closer.'

'I hope so too.' She held her sister's stare. 'I've hated not being in contact with you. It's been lonely.'

'For me too. I just couldn't figure out how to mend things. Was it better to keep a distance and try and let things blow over, or face it head on, or make out it had never happened, or ignore you? I just . . .' Remy looked a little overwhelmed, and she understood. This felt a lot like progress.

'Listening to you now, it sounds like you're posing one of those conundrums that Guy and the knobhead used to debate when drunk: would you rather get attacked by one horse-sized duck or twenty duck-sized horses . . .'

'Gee, that sounds like fun!' Remy gushed with fake enthusiasm, her smile turned to a sneer. She clearly wasn't a fan of either man. This smacked of loyalty that was very nice to see. It made her laugh.

'Oh, it was. *So* much fun!'

'I'd rather neither, Ash. If I had the choice.'

'You were always the wise one.'

'In some ways.' Remy huffed. 'Thought I had all the answers, even when I was ten.'

'Well, my problem, sis, or one of them' – she puffed on her cigarette, deciding to wade even further into the honesty pool – 'is that I've never been as confident as I present. And it's hard to breathe sometimes when you feel a little less than.'

'You've never been less than, Ash. You have so much going for you. I mean, you can be an arsehole, but you have that lovely life in London. And if you ever worried about not measuring up to that prick you married and the people you hung out with . . .' She gave a wry laugh. 'None of them deserved you.'

Ashleigh shook her head. 'Not just them, although yes. I wanted so badly to be liked by his parents.'

'Oh God! I remember them – what were their names?' She clicked her fingers, the well-known aide memoire. 'Margot and Freddie?'

'Close. Elaine and Dickie.'

'Elaine and Dickie! That was it!' Remy chuckled. 'Now they *were* arseholes!'

'She liked me far more after we divorced. Don't think the German tolerates her arseholeness.'

'Well, there's a lesson.'

'Yep.'

Remy stood. 'Shall I go and get us a cup of tea?'

She nodded. She liked the sound of it; her and her sister having a cuppa at the back of the garden, just the two of them. 'That sounds like a plan.'

Remy wiped the seat of her dress with her palms.

'People always ask me when they find out I'm an identical twin if I can feel your pain; they want to know if we have a psychic link. The look on their faces, Rem, when I tell them no is always one of disappointment.'

'Yep. I've had similar conversations.'

'I did once though, that night, when you and Tony . . .' It was almost instinctive, the way her sister rubbed her shoulder as Ashleigh spoke. 'I got this sharp pain in my shoulder and felt winded.'

'Weird!' Remy acknowledged, this the first time Ashleigh had mentioned it.

'Yes, weird. But over the last few years, I've known you were mad at me.'

'Don't think you need a psychic link to figure that one out, Ash.'

'I guess not, but more than that, I could feel it, like *really* feel it, if that makes any sense, and it hasn't felt good.'

'I could feel it too,' Remy whispered.

'I guess what I want to say, is that I'm, erm' – she felt the flare of emotion and exhaled through bloated cheeks – 'I am sorry, Remy. I am. I'm sorry.'

'I'm sorry too.' Remy looked directly at her, and it was a moment of connection, of understanding in the way twins did, that this was the start of healing. 'I'll go and get the tea.' She offered a small smile.

Ashleigh watched as her sister made her way along the path towards the back door.

Remy

Remy walked towards the house with a lightness to her being, this despite it being the saddest of days. It was what her dad would have wanted, reconciliation between his girls. The most fitting way to honour him. She filled the kettle, set it to boil, and put teabags in the old earthenware teapot, before sloshing milk into two mugs.

'All right, Rem.' His voice came from the kitchen door. She grimaced at no more than the sound of him.

Oh Christ!

Jamie walked into the kitchen. He was the very last person she wanted to see. She stared at him, her mouth pursed. Having barely spoken to him in recent years, other than the most perfunctory 'hello' and 'goodbye' when their paths had crossed and only when it was absolutely unavoidable. A thought persisted, that if she was talking to Ashleigh, then maybe it was time she spoke to him too, no matter how uncomfortable. She'd keep it as civil as she could, just like she always had, including him, inviting him, for Sophie's sake.

'It was a lovely service, I thought.'

'It really was,' Remy replied curtly, reminding herself that it was good of him to have come and paid his respects to her dad. She poured the boiling water into the teapot and replaced the lid.

'Elio did us proud, didn't he?'

Us . . . She shuddered.

'He really did.'

'You still not talking to me then?' He waggled his eyebrows.

'You still think it's funny?' She turned to face him, his apparent amusement enough for her to momentarily forget her pledge of civility.

'I don't know what you want me to say.' He looked a little sheepish, but with a smirk around his mouth, his lips parted over his sparkling veneers, stark against his perma-tan.

'I don't want you to say anything, Jamie, but we're Sophie's parents, Elio's grandparents, and therefore I think it's wise if we find a way to be around each other without awkwardness.' She knew her therapist would be proud.

'I don't feel awkward when I see you.'

'Just me then,' she confessed.

'Seems like it!' He laughed. She didn't. 'You are so serious, Rem, you need to lighten up!'

'Jamie, I have to be serious because it seems you think everything is a joke. You create mayhem and then scarper.'

'I don't!' He laughed again, and it was akin to jabbing her in the ribs, provoking a reaction.

'You do. You make every situation a little trickier. If I told you I was searching for an escaped mouse in a room, you'd throw a hundred snakes in and stand back. It doesn't help! It makes everything much worse!'

'Actually, one of those snakes would definitely get the mouse, job done.'

'And how would you suggest we get rid of the snakes, a thousand wildebeest?'

'You see, this is your problem, Rem, you're never happy! You'd ask me to get rid of the mouse, I'd do it, and you'd still be moaning.'

His words, his suggestion and his dismissive manner caused fireworks of frustration to go off in her gut. Gaslighting at its finest. But that was nothing new.

'Because your methods, your behaviour – it causes trouble and, actually, I'm not a moaner. I'm happy. I'm nearly always happy! And I have been since—' She stopped talking, aware of going too far.

'Since you chucked me over.' He jutted his chin and folded his arms.

'I chucked you over, as you put it, because you were a shit. A shit to me. The life and soul of the party to everyone else.' She remembered so clearly what it had felt like to be so young, expecting Sophie and waiting for him to come in after a night out, stumbling through the door of their grotty flat in the early hours, reeking of booze and with a grin that told her a good night had been had by all. All apart from her. It felt good to finally have the confidence to say it to him out loud, cathartic.

'I didn't mean to be, I was just a kid, and I didn't – didn't think it through, didn't understand the consequences. It all felt like a bit of a game. I was just too young, too dumb to get it.'

'And here you are in your sixties, Jamie, and you still think it's all a bit of a game. All the years I've spent being nice to you, making allowances, including you, because it felt like the right thing to do, and you slept with my *sister*!' She kept her voice down. 'Sophie's auntie! You did that, Jamie! We are a *family*, and I know it takes two, I'm well aware, but . . . what a rotten thing to do to us, to me.'

'We were drunk.' His voice quieter now, he looked at the pointed tip of his boots.

'Why do you think that makes it okay? Why does anyone? It's not the law, that anything goes if you've had a couple of pints or a glass of plonk. It doesn't work like that.'

He nodded.

'All those years ago, but still it makes me feel – eeuw.' She pulled a face. 'You're my ex; we were married, and you slept with Ashleigh.' She shook her head to help remove the unpalatable images that popped up.

'I don't want Ashleigh, I never have, she just . . .' He paused and exhaled from air-filled cheeks.

'She just what, Jamie?'

'She just reminded me of you.' He spoke slowly and she felt a potent mixture of irritation and sadness. She didn't want him to have any feelings for her other than those of a platonic nature; it made her feel uncomfortable, disloyal to even be hearing it; and sad because he was an idiot and he was Sophie's dad and she should have chosen better, should have waited for Midge.

'I really don't want Soph to hear us arguing. She is so busy with work and the baby, and is obviously upset over my dad,' she pressed.

'Yep, I don't want her to worry about us, either.'

'Well, look at that, we're in agreement!' She reached for the teapot, poured the tea, grabbed mugs, and walked back out to the garden, glad to be gone from him and to feel the fresh air on her face.

Ashleigh took one of the mugs from her.

'Did I just see you talking to Jamie?' her sister asked, taking a sip of tea.

'Yep.'

'How did it go?'

'Same as ever. He's a div.' Remy rolled her eyes.

'He is a div.' Her sister smiled, as if thinking, like her, how lovely it was to be on the same page. 'I've hated not being able to see you, not being able to chat to you, absolutely hated it.'

'Me too.' Remy sat back on the bench. Confession felt easy in the moment; besides, it was the truth. 'At first I was so riled I didn't want to speak to you or look at you. By the time I'd calmed, months had passed, and then it was a new year, and I didn't give it as much thought – it was no longer an obsession like it had been – but it also meant I gave you less thought, and then more months passed.' She took a deep breath. 'I didn't know how to undo it, how to start over, go back to the beginning.'

'I understand. But honestly? It's been the opposite for me. Each month that passed without contact, I've thought about you more and more. *Missed* you more and more.' Ashleigh took a swig of her tea. 'I wanted to call you.' She rested her mug on her thigh. 'But didn't know what to say. And I didn't want to be picking over the conversation for weeks after, reading between the lines of all the things you had chosen not to share or didn't say.'

'What a bloody mess.' The day's events suddenly threatened to catch up with her; she felt tired.

'You could say that. It's not too late though, Rem?'

The two shared a quiet moment of connection and Remy knew she'd hold it close to her heart for the longest time.

'No, not too late, Ash.'

'Are you two hiding?' Midge called from the back door. 'Come and help me out. I can't have the same conversation with your Auntie Jan about her high cholesterol again. I just can't!'

'Okay. We'll come in if we have to.' Remy smiled at the man, and he let his gaze linger on her. It was everything, that look, that love, still there.

She was reluctant to go back inside, feeling a lump in her throat as she was reminded of the neighbours and relatives, all clad in black, the realisation of why they were all there. It had been possible to dilute this sadness out here in the back garden, building a bridge to her twin.

'Is this a bad time?'

A voice came from the side patio. A nice voice. Remy turned to see a man in a camel coat standing awkwardly, a fixed smile on his handsome face.

'No, it's perfect timing.' Ashleigh smiled at the man who had an Aston Martin. 'Midge, Remy, this is Victor.'

'Two of you!' He pointed at them with his index fingers, his expression one of perplexation.

'Yup!' Ashleigh's grin was wide, and she understood it had always been a novelty, the thrill of someone spotting the fact there were two of them.

'Ah, monozygotic, I'm deducing . . .'

'Exactly that.' Ashleigh sat up straight, as if paying this man full attention for the first time, with an expression that suggested she might be ready to dive in, filled to the brim with enthusiasm for whatever might come.

'Yes, a little over fifty-five years ago now!' Remy added, for no reason other than to make her sister laugh.

And she did.

Ashleigh Perera and Remy Hughes

2028

Aged 66

Remy

Remy put the phone down.

'What did he have to say, love?' Midge ran his hand up and down her back. She took comfort from both the contact and the warmth.

'He said they're going to keep going with the chemo, but that he's very weak. Didn't sound good.'

'Poor Raul.' He and Midge had formed a close friendship over the years, a remote friendship, of course, but one that was important to her and Tony, in the way that it was when your other halves were mates. It made everything a little easier.

'Poor Tony.' Her heart ached for him. She was beyond worried.

'Yes, my love, I know.'

'I wish I could see him, Midge, wish I could just sit by his bed and talk rubbish, make him laugh, get him some soup. I don't know, something!' It was a dire feeling, to know her best friend was ill, ailing, and that she was unable to help. Very much as it had been post their attack all those years ago, when he had taken to his room and she had been kept at arm's length.

'He's a private man in that respect. Don't think he wants people seeing him so unwell.'

'I know. And I'm glad Mrs Newman lives out there now, and his brother Greg, of course, I just' – she hardly dared say it – 'I just want to see him again, one more time.' It was the first time she had acknowledged just how poorly her friend was.

'You can go – of course you can! I can book you a ticket, come with you if you like?'

She squeezed his hand, her sweet man, always trying to make things better, to find a way.

'It's expensive. Not like nipping up the motorway, is it? And it's too far, my love. Plus, you're right. I don't think he'd like me turning up to gawp at him.'

'He knows you love him.'

These were the words that caused her distress to flare.

'Maybe if the timing was different, but I don't want to be far away when Ulla has the baby. She's due in a couple of weeks. And we've already said we'll go and stay to take the twins to school and pick them up. Don't forget, when she had Clemmie and Topsy, her mum was close by to help out. Ulla will feel the loss of her even more.'

'Flippin' 'eck, Ren! Feels like they're dropping like flies!' His face crumpled as if instantly aware of the insensitivity of his remark. 'I didn't mean—'

'I know, love. It's fine. It was a shock when Ulla's mum died so suddenly.' Unpalatable as it was, she couldn't decide if it was better or worse for Tony having had months to get used to the idea. Midge was right: poor Raul . . .

'Are they still going to call the new baby Nettle?' Midge pulled a face, deftly changing the subject.

'Yes.' She smiled at her beloved. 'And it's not our place to say what we think!'

'What happened to all the old-fashioned names like Sarah, Olivia and Charlotte!'

'Time, my love. That's what happened, time passed, and they became just that, old-fashioned, but no doubt they'll come back around. Names seem to go in phases, don't they?'

'I guess.' He stretched his arms over his head. She knew that since he'd retired he felt the pull in his muscles, punishment for all those years spent running with a heavy backpack and latterly the hours spent hunched over an engine. 'But I don't remember Nettle ever being in fashion.'

'We will love little Nettle! And once we see her face, won't be able to imagine her being called anything else.' This she knew to be true, exactly as it had been with Bertie's twins, who were nearly eight and doing so well at school. *Well enough to pass the scholarship for one of the fancy schools in the area . . .* This she kept to herself.

'What time are we off to your mum's?' He glanced at the kitchen clock.

'Ashleigh said they were arriving about midday, so we'll give them some time to get settled and head over.'

'Can't imagine Evie with a little one. I still think she's a baby herself.'

'Same age as Bertie,' she reminded him.

'Yep. And remind me' – his memory, especially where names were concerned, was a little hazy – 'what's their baby called?'

'Levi.'

'As in the jeans?'

'Yes, but please don't say that to Kat and Evie!' She smiled for the first time that day at her super-klutz darling.

'And Elio is bringing his girlfriend. Must be serious; don't remember him introducing us to anyone before, much less bringing them to Ruthie's with some of the family present.'

'Her name is Pia, and Sophie said he's keen as mustard. They study together and apparently it's love. But they're only seventeen. The heart is fickle at that age. I expect they'll go off to uni and meet other people.'

'Well, I won't bother learning the name Pia then!' he teased her. It was a nice distraction from the sadness that underlined her every thought, worrying about Tony.

Ashleigh

'Oh! Will you look at him.' Ruthie placed her hand on her chest and shook her head. 'He's the image of your dad, don't you think?'

'Erm . . .' Ashleigh gazed at the face of her grandson in her arms and felt the quickening of her pulse and the melting of her heart, the falling away of all negativity and worry at the sight and scent of this beautiful baby. Surely the most beautiful baby ever to have existed! He was perfect, absolutely perfect. 'I guess he does a bit.' She winked at Kat and Evie, who sat side by side on the sofa. No one had the heart to explain that it was Kat's egg, fertilised by their trusted friend, that had made Levi, and therefore Dennis Brett's DNA was not directly involved.

'Is he good, a little sleeper?' her mum asked, the visit already putting a sparkle in her eyes and her posture the best Ashleigh had seen in a long while.

'Well, he's yet to figure out which is day and night, but luckily Evie is great at night feeds, so . . .' Kat beamed at her wife.

'Well, he's a lucky little boy to be so loved.' Ruthie spoke in earnest and it warmed Ashleigh to hear such approval from his great-grandma.

Levi made the smallest sound and emitted a light snuffle.

She raised him to her shoulder and stood, holding him against her with his head resting in her palm, safe against her chest.

'No need to worry, my boy. Your nana's got you. I'm right here. Go back to sleep, little Levi. Your great-granny is right, you are so very loved.'

She looked over his head to Evie, who stared at her with an expression of love. It would have been hard for her to explain just how connected she felt to the little one, understanding the first time she saw him the swell of unconditional love that so many people had spoken of. It was also the most terrible confirmation that she had not felt this before, not with such immersion. Something she would never, ever admit or discuss. How could she? It wasn't that she didn't adore her daughter, she did, but rather it was a love that had grown over the years, as they survived the ups and downs of divorce, and had got to know each other.

It was easy for her to see now that when she was trying so hard to figure out life, dogged by so much self-doubt, it had felt almost impossible to love herself, let alone love Evie. The only person she had truly thought she loved was Archie. More than loved, *worshipped*, as if he knew the secrets of life and, if she was good enough, he might just reveal them to her one by one.

The love that had come to her in recent years had taught her that true happiness lay in equity and respect. Right on cue, she heard his voice in the hallway.

'Couldn't find Cheddar, so I got Wensleydale instead. Hope that's okay?'

'Lovely, Victor, thank you. How much do I owe you?' Ruthie reached for her handbag, always within reach, where her purse nestled.

'No, no, that's fine, Ruthie. My gift to you.'

Ashleigh shared a lingering look with her husband, the kind of look that spoke of a deep love and affection. The kind of love and affection that meant they were both in it for the long haul, come what may.

'Can I hold him?' Victor walked forward.

'No, Grandpa!' Ashleigh teased him. 'You have to wait your turn.'

'I think I'll have a long wait, eh, Evie?' He smiled.

'We literally haven't had a look in since we got here,' she laughed.

'Don't moan.' Kat jabbed her, playfully. 'I'm enjoying the rest!'

'How's your dad doing?' Victor took the empty chair and asked in earnest.

'Oh.' Evie swallowed. 'Okay, I guess, but it's certainly scared him.'

'Heart attacks will do that,' Ruthie piped up with almost comic precision.

'Leni's running around doing everything, and he's grumpy because she's now in charge of his diet – no wine, no croissants! He eats them every day, always has, loaded up with butter and jam, and does very little exercise. Can't be good.'

All those croissants, no good for him! Who knew? It was a churlish thought. Ashleigh of course took no joy from the fact that Archie had been sick, hated that it had caused Evie an ounce of worry.

'Hello?'

Midge's voice came from the front door. He walked in, followed by Remy, who looked a little older, a little frailer than when she had last seen her. Ashleigh hoped she was okay, making a note to remind her of the importance of her annual check-ups.

'Hello, Nana.' Remy stood close and peered at the face of her sister's beloved grandson.

'Is he the most beautiful baby you have ever seen?' To show him off to her sister was a wonderful, wonderful feeling!

Remy laughed and smiled at Kat and Evie. 'I think he might be. Can I have a hold?'

Her sister rubbed her hands together.

'Nope.' She took a step away, and inhaled the scent of her grandson. 'You'll have to wait your turn.'

'Hi, everyone!' Ashleigh turned to see Elio walking in hand in hand with a pretty girl who looked a little shy. 'This is Pia!'

She smiled at the girl who clung to Elio, leaning on him like he was the anchor in a stormy sea. Remy caught her eye and the two shared a knowing look. There was something about the way the two youngsters held each other that was full of promise, so lovely to see.

Remy

'You've actually let someone else hold him?' Remy smiled at her sister, who sat, baby free at the kitchen table.

'No, he's asleep, so no one's holding him, but I'm keeping an ear out for the monitor, so the moment he wakes . . .'

'You're obsessed, Ashleigh!'

'I actually am.' She beamed. 'Is it like this with all of your grandchildren?'

'No.' Remy shook her head. 'I only really like the first one. The novelty wears off, so I can kind of take or leave Clemmie, Topsy and the new baby. It's all about Elio for me.'

'Really?'

'Of course not, you idiot! I adore them all! Each one a tiny miracle, a magnet that pulls me to them and means I can't get enough of them.'

'You've always been funny.' Her sister laughed.

'Funny weird,' she quipped. 'Pia seems very nice.'

'They are clearly smitten!'

'I said to Midge before we came that they're very young and so . . .' She let this trail.

'Well, in my humble opinion, they might be young, but they're not messing around. Did you see the way they looked at each other?'

'I did.' She beamed, happy that Elio seemed to have found someone as lovely as him. She knew Sophie approved, and she'd always been a great judge of character.

'I notice we never sit in Dad's chair,' Ashleigh pointed out, as they both looked at the seat at the table that would forever be where Dennis had tucked into his toast in the morning, his sandwich for lunch and his shepherd's pie for supper.

'It doesn't matter how many times I walk through that door, I still expect to hear him call hello to me.' She wondered if this would ever cease to be, kind of hoping not, as she could hear him loud and clear whenever she arrived.

'Me too. Mum seems to be doing okay; older, yes, but managing. I know how much you do for her.' Her words seemed tinged with guilt that she wasn't close enough to help more, to relieve her burden of care. Not that it was a burden to Remy, not at all.

'She is, she's great. And it's just part of my routine, always has been, really. I don't mind.'

Ashleigh drew breath, took her time; Remy got the feeling that what came next had been long cued up on her tongue. 'Do you think – do you think he forgave me, Rem?'

'Dad?'

'Yes.'

'Forgave you for what?'

'For letting him down, lying to him. Mum said I'd made her look stupid.'

'She said *we'd* made her look stupid,' Remy clarified.

'You're right, but that doesn't make me feel much better. I hate the thought that he never quite got over it, that it sat like a thing between us.' Ashleigh's words seemed to almost choke her as she spoke. She coughed to clear her throat.

'He wasn't like that. Not that kind of man. You know that,' Remy reasoned.

'I do. I just wish – wish that I'd apologised again, helped him understand our reasoning. I wish that I'd met Victor sooner so that he could have known Dad, and vice versa. I wish I'd given more time to Evie when she was little. So many things.'

'We all do that, Ash. I wish I'd run a mile from Jamie Aller, but still got Soph, I wish I'd met Midge sooner, wish I'd not gone out that night with Tony, wish we'd stayed in and danced in my bedroom.' She looked up to the room that was overhead as her shoulder twinged on cue. 'I wish he wasn't sick now, wish Dad was still here. But it's pointless, isn't it? It's just another way of regretting things, trying to rewrite our lives, and that's futile. What's done is done and we are where we are. We're far better off looking forward and accepting what we can change, what we can do.'

'Yep.'

'And you know Dad would have loved Victor – we all love Victor! Married life suits you.' It did. Ashleigh was calmer, smilier, since she had become Mrs Perera almost two years ago now. A quiet ceremony without guests in Sardinia, it sounded blissful. And it had made Remy laugh; her parents had, after all, predicted the destination.

'You're right, of course you are, but I can't help it. And I do love being married to Victor. He's so nice to me!'

'As he should be! It makes me mad that might not have always been your experience.'

'I know that feeling. I remember being so angry that you'd settled for Jamie.'

'Yet it didn't put you off him entirely . . .' she teased. It was harsh but funny.

'Please let's not go there!' Her sister blushed and changed the subject. 'I know you'll be upset about Tony. How's he doing?'

'Midge spoke to Raul earlier. Not so good.' A tear bloomed and trickled down her cheek.

'That's rotten, Rem.' Her sister ran her fingers over the tabletop. 'Do you remember the morning of the exam? Sitting here with Mum asking us questions, testing us.'

'God, I'd forgotten that! She used to do it all the time!' Remy laughed to be reminded of the memory; it was nice to have the mood lightened.

'Random questions about geographical locations or our times tables!' Ashleigh shook her head. 'My God, the pressure!'

'I didn't feel it, not really,' she admitted.

'Well, that much I do know.'

Remy pictured the morning, eating breakfast, then their mum driving them to school so they didn't have to get the bus because it was a special, special day.

'Some of the happiest times in my life were when we were little and shared that tiny bedroom, I loved going to sleep and waking up knowing you were right there.' It was true; being in close proximity to her twin had made her feel safe in a way that had been lacking until she'd met Midge.

Ashleigh took her time responding. 'Those years when we didn't chat much, when we were sulking' – Remy smiled at this description of the great chasm into which they'd fallen – 'it was awful. I never felt whole. I hated it.'

'I hated it too,' she admitted. 'I'm still ashamed to think of how it had spiralled until contact was minimal and forced. But that's behind us, Ash. I meant what I said: we're far better off looking forward.'

'I feel like I have a lot to look forward to, possibly for the first time ever! Victor and I are just starting out, really, and little Levi! He's stolen my heart!'

'You're a good mum, Ash, and a brilliant nana.'

'Well, coming from you, that's the best compliment.'

Remy felt a rush of affection for her sister. 'I'm going to stay with Bertie and Ulla when the new baby comes. Midge and I can look after the twins so they can enter their baby bubble.'

'Ah, lovely. Have they got any names yet?' Ashleigh asked casually, and so she tried to answer in kind, knowing her response would cause a ripple.

'Yes, they're going to call her Nettle.'

'Nettle? As in stinging or tea?' Her sister wrinkled her nose as best she was able with all that Botox.

Remy felt the smallest flare of defence at the name, which was, after all, going to be how she referred to her baby granddaughter.

'That's the one.' She held her sister's gaze. 'And it's not the weirdest thing. Do you remember your friend who named his baby after his dog! What was it? Ben and Ben?'

'Yep, the Bens!' Ashleigh laughed. 'Ridiculous. Can I ask you a question, Rem?'

'Course, fire away!' She braced herself for some more name-related teasing.

'Would you do it again? Would you make out you were me? Sit the exam?'

'Oh.' This was not what she had expected. 'I've thought about that in the past, and the answer is yes, yes I would.'

'Even though it caused us problems further down the line, put a rift between us, almost, made us fight?'

Remy reached out and took her sister's hand inside her own, the same hand, one egg, split in half, *miracles* . . .

'Yes, Ash, because I would only do what I thought was right at the time and I *thought* that was the right thing to do, because I *thought* it was what you wanted. Because I love you that much.' It was her truth, would always be her truth. She would do it all again.

'I know. I loved you that much too.' Ashleigh's words were hoarse, her vocal cords pulled thin with emotion.

'Loved?' Remy pulled a disapproving face.

'Love. I *love* you that much, little dove,' Ashleigh whispered.

'I love you that much too, little dove . . . always have, always will.'

'What are you two conniving about?' Ruthie asked, pushed into the room in her wheelchair by Pia.

'Nothing.'

'Nothing.'

They replied in unison. It was that way with twins. In sync, in tune and always having each other's back.

Remy Hughes

2042

Aged 80

Elio shut the passenger door. He was a wonderful young man, popping in often to her little flat overlooking the river in Salisbury, not far from where Harper lived with her boyfriend, Frank, and their three dogs. Harper, who had, in recent years, found a certain peace, and thankfully now had more good days than bad. Elio was a wonder, her rock, who didn't talk to Remy like she was deaf or daft. His partner, Pia, also a doctor, was about to give birth to Remy's first great-grandchild. She couldn't wait.

She wished Bertie and Sophie would take a leaf out of Elio's book, her wonderful son and daughter, who she had to remind, 'I'm eighty, kids, not deaf or stupid. My body might be a little slow, but my mind isn't.'

She wished this were true, but actually, she had got a little slower, as well as forgetful. It was allowed. A brain that had done its best for eight decades to juggle the never-ending stream of information that bombarded it twenty-four hours a day. A brain that had known love, laughter, loss – a brain that had *lived!*

'How are you doing, Nan?'

'I'm fine, darling.' She smiled at her handsome grandson, who drove slowly, no doubt because she was in the car.

'Feels weird, knowing this time next month, Pia will have had the baby. I'll be a dad!'

She watched his slow exhale, the only suggestion of nerves.

'You'll be a great dad, Elio.'

'I hope so. So, come on, what advice would you give me?' He turned briefly to smile at her.

'Advice?' She took her time. 'Treasure every second. No one really tells you just how quickly it goes by. But it does! We all need to appreciate the now and waste less time!'

'Waste less time on what?'

'On everything!' she replied quickly, her eyes, for a second, bright again. 'Less time worrying about all the rubbish that doesn't matter. All the small stuff that occupies your mind – and don't get me started on slowly squashing your joy with the twin knives of comparison and regret. If a thought starts with "*if only*" or "*I wish*" then strike it through and don't dwell on it. Enjoy the moment, the air in your lungs, pain-free movement, movement at all! The changing seasons, a belly laugh, the sound of your children's voices, birdsong, sunshine on your face, the shade of a tree! And books – read all the books. *ALL* the books! And above all, be thankful for every day that you see a rising sun, for one day it *will* be your last, and in that moment you'll understand one thing – how very quickly it has all passed.' She paused then. 'Listen to me going on. Bet you wish you hadn't asked.'

'No, I'm glad I did, but it certainly took a turn. I was hoping for something a bit more upbeat!' He made her laugh, not an easy task on a day like this, and she was thankful for it.

'My old mum, your great-gran, Ruthie, always used to say, "time flies, no more than a blink!" They were just words to me really. But not now. I'm better at it, I think, better at appreciating it all, now I'm waiting for my timer to ping!'

'Oh, don't say that.' Elio shook his head.

'We should talk about it more, love. At least I think so. I do hate the frailty of this chapter in my life. I prefer to think about the younger, stronger me. When I could race around in trainers and rely on my body in a way that I thought would last forever. Now, I walk like a newborn lamb for fear of falling. And even the slightest knock will see me landed with an almighty bruise, as if I've gone ten rounds with Tyson Fury! I don't expect you know who that is. He was a boxer, a heavyweight boxer, back in the day.'

'I've heard of him.'

'It's true though. One minute you're a child at the start of the summer holidays, playing with your Cindys and eating Arctic Roll, freewheeling through sun-filled days, sharing a bedroom with your sister and thinking it will be that way for always, and the next minute you're a teenager, being moulded and influenced in ways you can't even begin to imagine by all that comes your way. Then suddenly you're in love and you build a life, share a home, kids. And you think of all the chances you had not to meet that person and how odd it is that of all the people on this planet, you chose each other. Then you grow older together if you're very lucky, and POW! Just like that you are not just older, but old! And that's that. Off you pop.'

'Who knows what comes next?' Her grandson spoke with something close to encouragement.

'I suspect nothing at all, my love. My guess is that it really will be just a big old sleep, like before I was born.'

Born special, one egg, split in two . . .

'But, I have to admit, Elio, that just the smallest possibility that there *might* be more, now wouldn't that be something.' Something Remy daren't hope for.

'I see a lot of death, Nan.'

'Of course you do, darling.' It was still a wonder to her, how this little boy was a doctor! Helping to save lives.

'It doesn't scare me, not at all. But what does amaze me, every time, is how small the margins are between life and death, paper thin. The difference between that last but one breath and the very last, no more than a second.' He snapped his fingers. It made her jump.

'I look back on my life and see it like a giant lake. Even the most spontaneous of decisions, the simplest and seemingly most matter-of-fact choices, all caused ripples that had the power to change the course and rhythm of my life in ways I could never have imagined. Ripples that got bigger and bigger as they travelled. And so, actually, that would probably be my advice: make good choices if you can, darling.'

'I'll try, Nan, I promise. Here we are.' He parked the car.

She felt the usual tremor of trepidation as she climbed from his very low vehicle, taking an age to hook first one leg over the lip of the passenger door and then the other.

'I fear one day I'm going to get in and am never going to be able to get back out!' She smiled at the handsome boy. 'You'll have to let me sleep in it!'

Elio offered her his arm, which she grabbed, as he comically hoicked her upwards. It might be a devil to get in and out of, but she had to admit, it was as comfortable as it was quiet, almost gliding over the roads. She didn't drive anymore. She *could*, was perfectly capable in her opinion, but the new road rules, the complexity of junctions, slip roads and intersections where traffic control systems were paired with the dashboard, made her feel less than in control. Yet more technology that had very much left her behind.

It was to be expected, and she accepted it with a certain fatality, knowing for a fact that she had enjoyed the very best era, a time when everything had felt a little calmer, a little easier to grasp. Her heart lurched in pity for the youngsters, Topsy, Clementine, Netty, and all like them who it seemed worked so hard just to stand still. Hers had felt like a world of opportunity that seemed to be lacking nowadays.

She liked to tell her grandchildren about the stick shift in cars that had meant you had to clunk, clunk up and down the gears while depressing the clutch with your foot, as the car sped up and slowed, at every corner, every bend, every junction. On her old . . . *What was the make of that car . . . Corona, no . . . Corn . . . Corp . . . Corsa! That was it, a Vauxhall Corsa!* It was with the usual flare of delight that she remembered something that had not yet fallen through the ever-widening fissures in her memory.

They would laugh, quite unable to imagine it.

'You had to do it with one hand, and what, the other hand on the wheel?'

'Yes, pretty much . . . and there was nothing to help you park – no camera, no sensor, no beeps . . .'

'How did you manage?'

'We just did!'

'Vauxhall Corsa!' she said out loud, before realising she had done so.

'You all right?'

Elio gave her a tight-mouthed smile that smacked of concern.

'Yes.'

'We'll take it easy. No rush.'

He linked arms with her, and they set off from the car park at a slow pace. It suited her, and she was grateful for it. He was smart enough to know not to rush her, with her milky eyes, and not to steer her, as that could lead to unsteadiness. She thanked goodness for her comfy shoes. He seemed happy to meander with her, seeking out the flatter surfaces of the path, avoiding the little tufts of grass and weeds that had sprung in the gaps between the stones.

It was a winter-blue-sky day, and the air was crisp, the kind of weather that was invigorating, restorative and happy-making, if she ignored the chill that tore through her shoulder like a knife, slicing through her very flesh, cutting her to the bone. That darned shoulder that had insisted, year on year, on reminding her of that terrible night a long, long time ago.

It was funny the way time worked.

How she would have loved to hold so many other thoughts with the same clarity. Like the first time Midge had kissed her or one of the nights they had laughed until they cried. The births of her three beautiful babies – so many things. They were still all there, of course, in the crevices of her memory, but were now a little worn, a little fuzzy, a little faded. Precious things, pasted into the honeycomb of her mind which she liked, on occasion, to dust off and recollect.

'You okay, Nan?' Elio pulled her arm tightly, checking on her again, as was his habit.

She nodded. Not trusting herself to speak, as her emotions hovered very near the surface. Cemeteries did that to her. Wandering as they did in this expansive wood, a garden of remembrance where all her loved ones had plaques, all reunited beneath a tree. Their ashes interned under the spreading protection of the beautiful flowering red dogwood.

It was an odd thing that she'd not fully understood when she was younger, how the first death takes all of your thoughts, engrossing you with the novelty of loss, and the first painful realisation of infinite separation that is very hard to fathom.

Her lovely dad had been the first, of course.

I don't like a fuss . . . this the phrase she still heard from his mouth as he smiled at her in her mind, and *More money than sense . . .* whenever she splashed out or left the lights on.

Her mum, the most marvellous, meddling matriarch, Ruthie Brett, had lasted another nine years without her beloved Dennis. She'd become quieter, as if without him to corral, the family no longer at home to fuss over, she had lost a lot of her purpose. This, too, Remy now better understood.

Hello, love, it's me, it's Mum . . . This her phrase, uttered every single time she called, no matter that Remy explained, each and every time, *Yes, I know, Mum, your name comes up on the . . .* It used to irritate her, but my goodness how she would love to receive a call from her now. The death of her mum had somehow diluted the grief of losing her dad, and so it went on, as if experience taught her how to cope, how to better handle the devastation. How to carry on.

Tony's was a grave she had never and would never visit. Too far away. *His* words in her head: *Turn this one up!* Before they would sing along or dance or nod their heads to the glorious sounds of their youth. And just to think of it meant she smelled the White Musk that had been their signature scent and heard '*Geno*' chanted in the background. Still she loved him, her wonderful, life-long friend who had succumbed to cancer aged sixty-eight. Too young.

Yet now, at this juncture in her life, when her bones creaked, her joints were inflamed, her skin too loose for her bones, her teeth weak, eyes myopic, feet sore, blood pressure high and her bladder no more than a slack and useless thing that contained nothing with great effect, it was somehow strangely fitting, for him, the beautiful boy, to be so preserved in his prime, in her thoughts, anyway. She knew he would have liked that.

Raul had remarried quickly, couldn't bear to be alone, he said, and this too she understood. He and Scott still sent her a beautiful Christmas card. One of only a handful she received now, knowing it was very out of fashion, the waste of paper and the cost of postage, when a personalised digital card could be sent so easily.

Still she remembered the Christmases of the 1970s, when her mum would fasten sharp, garish tinsel in loops along the tops of the walls and hang card after card on them to create their festive bunting. Remy could see her now, reaching up, as she stood on the sofa in her tights, with a paisley orange-and-yellow apron tied around her waist, *The Harry Secombe Show* on the telly. They had looked wonderful, all those cards, and the walls seemed quite dull when she took them all down before Twelfth Night.

It was, however, Midge she missed the most.

Midge, her darling, her marine . . .

Just the thought of him was enough for her to feel the sharp needle of loss pierce her heart and for her tears to start falling. The loss of him, her greatest love, her very best thing, the hardest thing she had ever faced. Now living half a life without him, the man who had made her whole. He who had given her absolutely everything. Midge's death, eight years ago, meant her parents, Tony, all of them, were relegated in the grief scale.

Eight years . . . it was a wonder to her that she had survived at all.

The ache to feel his presence, to stand inside the arc of his arms, to see his face smiling at her in the way that he used to, to hear his voice, *my beautiful girl,* to sit next to him on the sofa, to know the comfort of his warm skin in a cold bed, all of it.

Yes, she missed him the most.

See you in a bit . . .

His voice now clear and distinct in her mind, and her reply, encouraging the corners of her mouth to lift in a small smile.

Yep, see you in a bit . . .

A sharp wind flared, blowing on the embers of her aged bones. The thief of time no doubt watching, hovering in this place where death lurked, before the cold air retreated leaving the fabric of her ashy, brittle, and frail.

There was also something strangely comforting about being here among the trees and grass, where all life was represented, all ages, all fates, all people, knowing she would soon enough be among them. Her very own little plaque, nestling among those of her family.

Not that she minded, not at all. To have lived this long, to have known such love, was, she knew, the greatest privilege.

'Here we are, Nan.' Elio spoke softly, she suspected both in reverence and to give her a heads up, as if aware it was no small thing.

And there it was.

The new plaque.

Designed to match the others, yet standing out by the fact it wasn't weathered. No moss gathered on the stand that drove it into the ground; rain and snow were yet to give it the patina of age. There was no trail from inquisitive creatures who had slithered or hovered on the words that meant little to them.

'There she is.'

Remy felt the lump rise in her throat that duly pushed tears up and out of her eyes, which now trickled down her ruddy cheeks. The leaves rustled, trees danced, and the breeze, softer now, lifted her grey curls.

'Could you give me a minute, darling.'

'Sure.'

Shrugging free of Elio's arm, she walked forward and bent low, slowly dropping to her knees in front of the plaque, as he walked on, giving her the privacy he understood she needed.

'Well, my love, my sister, my Ashleigh. I shall come here and visit you. I'll come and tell you what Evie and Kat are up to, and that darling grandson of yours. I'll tell you all about everything.' She felt the breath catch in her throat as her sorrow made it tricky to get the words out. They had seen each other with regularity over the last few years, although living in different cities made it difficult, but they had managed a reunion at least once a month. Victor was always happy to drive her in his fancy car. 'I've been thinking a lot, Ash, about when we fell out. It bothers me still. I'm sorry for being stubborn, for not seeing more of you when I could, for not fully understanding that we were wasting precious time. I'm sorry for telling Mum and Dad in the way I did. You told me a while ago about what you wished to happen. Well, I wish I'd done as you suggested and sat them down quietly, and explained what happened, instead of pulling the pin and lobbing my truth bomb.'

With her hand at her throat, she took a moment to compose herself. 'I hope you forgive me. I never stopped loving you, never, even when we were miles apart and not talking. How could I? We are one egg, split in two. One person, really, always connected, always.' She took a breath and wiped her face. 'You were the best – *we* were the best! And I shall miss you. Every day I shall miss you, more than my old tongue can say.'

It was as she spoke that sun broke through the clouds and she felt the warmth on her silvered scars, barely visible now among the lines and blemishes that covered her face. A mask, behind which the girl she still sometimes felt herself to be hid. A mask by which others judged her, quite unable to see themselves as an old lady like her.

This too she understood, because life happened in a blink.

It was just as Ruthie had always told her:

'One minute you're twenty, then forty, then sixty, then . . . and it goes fast, so fast.'

'Doesn't it just,' she whispered, feeling a roar of regret and love surge in her chest.

A sound overhead caused her to shield her eyes and look skyward, and there it was, a single white bird, spiralling up and up into the bright blue winter sky.

'Fly high, little dove.' Remy smiled, closing her eyes as the sun kissed her skin. 'Fly high!'

If you enjoyed *Life As Planned,* why not read *Ever After,* available now.

Chapter One

Enya Brown's phone buzzed in the middle of the night.

Throwing back the duvet, she sat up straight, skinny legs dangling from the side of the bed, widening her eyes to help clear the foggy edges of sleep. She took a moment to centre herself with a long, deep breath through her nose and out of her mouth, just like the lady she had found on YouTube had suggested.

It helped, a little, in that her flustered pulse calmed and she was able to quietly locate her glasses, which were on top of the book on her nightstand. There was something about a text or call arriving in the dark when the world was sleeping that had the power to put the fear of God into her. Her first thought was for her son, was he okay, had something happened? Her second, a prayer that he was safe and sound. Then came the devastating prediction of utter desolation, knowing that if anything should ever happen to him, her life would lose all of its meaning.

It was daft really, the idea that bad news could only be delivered after office hours, or that the Grim Reaper preferred to work the night shift, understanding that the very worst news had far more impact when delivered to someone in their pyjamas. They might have a point.

She wondered what percentage of people died at night, not underestimating the powerful addition of booze, drugs, poorly lit roads, inclement weather: *were* we more likely to die in the dark?

She wasn't sure who she could ask.

Feeling far more alert, she reached for her phone. The house was quiet. She detested the silence of the empty hours. Similarly, small noises of irritation like the creak of a door, the whistle of the wind and the chirp of birds, as they only served to remind her that she had once lived in a home with so much noise, so much life, that she would never have noticed such an inconsequential thing! What *had* she become? *Who* had she become?

'Sometimes, Jonathan, I feel that I'm no more than a trick of the light,' she whispered. 'Almost invisible.'

This she spoke as she opened the text, incredibly relieved to see it was a message from Jenny. Any contact with her friend triggered a thunderclap of joy that pulled her out of any potential panic.

GOT ANY KITKATS?

These three words from her best friend, akin to opening a window in a stifling room to welcome a breeze, or a warm hug on a cold day, were crucial reassurance when she needed it the most. Invisible people did not receive messages like this.

The text had been sent some five minutes previously, at precisely 3 a.m. She smiled.

NO, BUT IVE GOT A TWIRL, HALF A TOBLERONE AND THOSE CHOCOLATE DIPPED SHORTCAKE BISCUITS FROM MARKS THAT YOU LIKE. OH AND HALF AN EASTER EGG

ON MY WAY – the instant reply.

Throwing her kimono over her cotton PJs, she made her way down the stairs and opened her front door, taking a moment to look along the street, very much liking the pink-edged, lilac-tinged light that hovered over the terraced chimney pots, giving the place an ethereal quality. It promised warmth tomorrow and she felt it a privilege to see this little corner of suburbia in its idling time, where only the scamper of tiny creature feet foraging, the flutter of leaves disturbed by breeze, and the thump-thump of her friend's slippers as they made their way down the path of the house next door but one, cut through the quiet.

Enya smiled and waved. Jenny smiled and waved back. Their faces, devoid of make-up, crinkled in delight, shoulders raised, fingers on lips. The two more like excited kids who were sneaking out, breaking curfew, than grown women, who could, if they so desired, venture out and about whenever the fancy took them. Even at this hour.

Enya made her way into the kitchen and filled the kettle. What was a 3 a.m. snack without tea to accompany it? She heard the front door close, and the sound of her friend, babbling, as soon as she walked in, as if it were mid-afternoon, normal.

'Who in the world has *half* an Easter egg hanging around? It's nearly July!'

'I am aware.' Enya gave a slow blink as she plopped the teabags into the mugs, comforted by her friend's presence, aware of how having someone else near her halted all feelings of despair.

'I hate people who save their Easter eggs, it's not natural! They're designed to be shoved in your mouth, eaten in one go and then you have to dispose of the foil and cardboard as soon as possible, hide the evidence.' Jenny took a seat at the kitchen table.

'This actually speaks volumes about your secret chocolate habit, the fact you feel the need to hide the evidence! It must be hard being married to a police officer, does he check the recycling for dabs? And also, hate is a strong word. I don't *hate* anyone, but if I did, it wouldn't be because I disagreed with how they did or didn't eat their chocolate!'

She pulled the pretty tin with the chocolate stash in it from the shelf inside the larder and grabbed the biscuits, placing both on the table in front of Jenny.

'That's the difference between you and me.' Her friend levered the lid from the tin with her thumbs and, with something close to urgency, ripped the wrapper from the Twirl, before stuffing a whole stick of the stuff into her mouth. She continued to speak with her gob full of chocolate. 'I hate lots of people, and for the most ridiculous reasons, not that they're ridiculous to me. I have a list.'

'You have a list?' Enya was shocked.

'Yes! And don't look at me like that, Angela gets it, she has a list too.'

She poured water into the mugs, fascinated, unaware that her sister also had a list. 'Who does Angela hate?'

'Well, I wouldn't want to break any confidences,' Jenny pulled a face and carried on, 'but I know for a fact that woman who does the weather – too smiley, too keen, with undertones of smug.'

'I can't believe I'm last to know about this! So who do you hate and why?'

'I hate Poirot,' Jenny over-enunciated.

Enya whipped around to face her friend; this was a revelation that she couldn't allow to pass without comment. 'Oh you can't! I love him!' She fished out the teabags and lobbed them into the sink. 'Why do you hate him?'

'It's the moustache, it looks like liquorice, and it makes me feel sick.' Jenny shuddered. 'I imagine it going soft and then having to eat it.' The thought clearly didn't repulse her that much, as she reached for the second stick of chocolate.

Enya laughed loudly. 'You can't hate Poirot because you fear having to eat his moustache!'

'I told you it was ridiculous, and I think you'll find that, actually, I can hate whoever I want. It's my list.'

'So, who else?' It was always a delight when after two decades of friendship, they revealed new facets of each other; she loved how her friend checked in like this regularly, chocolate craving or not. Although unspoken, it was obvious that Jenny understood how much Enya needed this companionship. She sloshed milk into the tea and took the mugs to the table, where she sat opposite her friend.

'Erm, Blake Dunlop.'

'Blake Dunlop?' She repeated the name of a gangly boy who had been in their kids' class at primary school. A name she hadn't heard for a while.

'Yes.' Jenny, straight-faced, sipped her tea. 'If he walked in right now, I'd punch him in the face!'

'You would not!' She did her best to contain her laughter.

'I bloody would!'

'You know he runs the reclamation yard up by the quarry?'

'Does he now? Hmmm . . .' Jenny stroked her chin as if making a plan.

It made her chuckle. 'Why do you hate him?'

'He made Holly cry.'

'What, recently?' Enya felt the flicker of concern. She loved Holly Hudson.

'No!' Jenny tutted. 'Of course not recently. If it was recently, Phil would have punched him in the mouth.'

'Or Aiden would,' Enya pointed out. She had known Holly since she was in nappies on account of the fact that she had grown up next door but one. Holly had been (almost) surgically attached to her son, Aiden, by the hip, for the last decade. 'Not that I can imagine Aiden, or you, punching anyone, for that matter.'

'There's always a first time.'

'Mmm.' Enya sipped her tea. 'What did he do to make her cry?'

'Karate-kicked her art project, broke it clean in two. I'm sure I told you about it at the time.'

'Probably. But a lot's happened since then.'

Enya swallowed, thinking of that time when Aiden was little, and she'd been so busy. Busy with mum jobs, her actual job, looking after the house, running around with a timer in her head that meant she leapt from chore to chore like a bee harvesting pollen. *Busy* . . . Unlike now, when lonely hours stretched ahead of her each evening and the night often felt endless.

'Ain't that the truth.' Jenny nodded. 'Holly spent hours making it, don't you remember? They were about seven and had to build a puppet theatre in a shoebox?'

'Vaguely.' She couldn't remember what she'd had for supper last night, let alone an event decades before that hadn't concerned her.

'Well, Holly walked into the playground with hers in her hands, she'd gone for a *Wind in the Willows* vibe, river background with weeping willow, Toad, Ratty and Mole stuck on to lolly sticks, it was lovely. Then Blake bloody Dunlop comes along, high kicks it right out of her hands and runs off. The little turd.'

'That was over twenty years ago!' She pointed out the obvious.

'Your point being?' Jenny sipped her tea.

'Holding a grudge for that long only damages you. I bet Blake won't even remember it!'

'I'd still like to punch him.'

Enya laughed at her diminutive best friend, a talented florist whose hands were more used to arranging stunning floral bouquets than brawling. 'I take it you couldn't sleep?'

'Nope. The usual.'

Enya understood only too well the debilitating pattern of insomnia that meant she often went to bed dreading a disturbed night ahead.

'I slept soundly from ten until three, then my cogs started turning. I'm thinking about the shop, excited for our plans!' Jenny danced her slippered feet on the wooden floor.

'Me too.' She beamed.

'Shall we redo the sign, put your name next to mine?'

It was a lovely, generous suggestion that thrilled her. 'Oh, Jen, as wonderful as that sounds, let's give it six months before we do that, just in case I'm pants and you have to fire me!' There was a subtle truth to her words, a lack of confidence that meant she tended to err towards the negative.

'You won't be pants, you'll be ace, and I can't fire you if you're my partner, can I?'

'I'm not sure, actually.' Enya sipped her tea. She was indeed excited for the venture that would see her become part of Jenny's business. An excitement tinged with the inevitable nerves; she didn't do too well with change, who did? But losing her job of over two decades was a big deal.

She loved her job at the solicitors', working for the genteel Messrs Greengate and Greengate. Mr Richard Greengate and Mr Robert Greengate whom callers, on occasion, referred to as 'Mr *R* Greengate', with great emphasis, as if this might be defining enough. To say it made for much confusion was an understatement.

The building on the pretty, curved High Street, where she spent four days a week between the hours of nine and five, was from a bygone era, and one where sunlight highlighted the rich soup of historical dust. Six decades of particles swirling right there in the room that made her wonder if she ever breathed in the tears her mother had shed when listening to the will of her father being read, or inhaled the fear and shame of her great-uncle Maurice as he dealt with the paperwork pertaining to his bankruptcy. Or maybe she had sniffed Jonathan's laughter, as she'd cradled their newborn and he'd jovially taken care of business.

'So, Mr Greengate, this is our son, Aiden Jonathan, who needs to be added as sole beneficiary and also we think it worth making a note about his guardianship, should the worst ever happen.' Jonathan had shot her a look then, with a wink. It was what he had done, protected her, soothed her worries, smoothed her path, letting her know it was just a precaution. Nothing to worry about. *'He would be placed into the care of Mrs Angela Rudd . . .'*

It felt like weeks ago, minutes, this another reminder that the whirlpool of life seemed to spin quickly, and it was all she could do on some days to keep her head above water.

It was a jolt to think this would be her last few months in their employ, as they had decided to retire, shut up shop and spend time with their respective Mrs Greengates. The ending of her job of over twenty-five years, another change of routine that would require adjustment, another severing of rope that kept her pleasantly anchored to all that was familiar.

Her old life.

A life she missed. Not that she wasn't looking forward to joining Jenny at the florist's and being surrounded by that glorious scent each and every day, learning all about the business and honing her creative skills. Her best friend had thrown her a lifeline, and she had grabbed it with both hands. It occupied a lot of her thoughts as she chased ideas, imagining how glorious it would be at Easter, Christmas, Valentine's and all the days in between.

Jenny swallowed her biscuit and continued. 'Then I started worrying about how Holly will cope over the next three weeks, you know how she frets when Aiden is away for work.'

'It ain't easy!' Enya sighed, glancing up at the ceiling towards her bedroom, trying to remember what it had been like when she and Jonathan were of a similar age.

They'd been desperately in love, that much she knew, but the feeling like she might crumble if he were not within reach? She couldn't quite remember, preferring to think of herself as capable and grounded.

'Well?' Jenny raised her voice.

'Well, what?' Enya stared at her.

'You were miles away! I just asked you if you think I can fit this half an Easter egg in my mouth and eat it in one.'

Laughing now at her friend, Enya shook her head. 'Without a doubt. For someone so tiny, you have a very big mouth.'

'None taken.' Jenny took a deep breath, like an athlete preparing to perform, before cramming in the half an Easter egg.

She stifled a yawn as she watched Jenny's antics.

'Ta da!' Jenny opened her mouth to show that the egg had indeed disappeared.

'Magic!' Enya smiled, wishing she believed in such a thing, knowing that if it were possible, she'd wish to turn the clock back to a time when her life had felt full, and she had thought loneliness and anxiety were what happened to other people . . .

Chapter Two

Enya felt a little out of sorts, a residue no doubt of the disturbed night just spent. Not that she hadn't enjoyed Jenny's company and the unexpected laughter that had filled the kitchen. It was her best friend's superpower, the ability to make everything feel just a little bit better.

'Where *are* you?'

She now leaned against the kitchen sink and spoke firmly down the phone while rubbing her temples, feeling the beginnings of a headache. It was too hot and too early on this sweaty June day to feel this harried. Only thirty minutes out of the shower and already she wished she could pop back upstairs for another one. She pushed out her bottom lip and blew upwards, an act that was habit, and yet curiously did very little to cool her down, bar maybe lower the temperature of her rather downy top lip, another gift bestowed upon her by the menopause gods.

'Yeah, I'm just . . .'

She could hear her son on the other end of the phone, fannying around.

'Aiden, it's so unfair! I'm feeling all the anxiety of wanting to get to the airport on time. I'm worried about a queue at check-in, the hassle of having to cram my decanted liquids into one of those slightly too narrow plastic bags, which I can never quite close properly. I'm watching the minutes tick; my pulse is through the roof and it's not even me who's flying! I'm happy to drop you off, love, of course I am, but you said you'd be here by ten past and it's nearly half past and I already thought you were cutting it fine, supposing we hit traffic!'

Aware she sounded a little manic, it was, she thought, preferable than admitting to her only child that Holly wasn't the only one who was anxious about him being out of reach for three whole weeks. When had she become this needy?

'Mum, just take a minute, chill, please! Jim has only just left and I'm getting my stuff together.'

Suddenly, it all made sense! Jim, her son's rugby friend, was always big on drinking and seemed not to pay any heed to timekeeping. She liked Jim, liked him very much, but he was that friend whom, at the risk of sounding like one of *those* mothers, she'd describe as a bad influence.

Memories of her boy as a teenager calling from a field in the middle of Wiltshire filled her mind. There had apparently been a mix-up and two cars had driven off leaving Aiden in the wilderness, each car believing he was a passenger in the other. The whole jaunt planned and poorly executed by Jim. Jonathan had sleepily grabbed the car keys, ready to retrieve their boy from wherever he'd been abandoned. She had watched him shuffle out of the door with a sweatshirt over his PJs and his hair sticking up at all angles. A good dad. The kind of parent who, like her, didn't think twice, but was simply always on the end of a phone, for whatever their son might need, whenever he might need it.

'Getting your stuff together, you mean you haven't packed yet?' She felt the flare of anxiety at the thought. 'And you want me to *chill*?'

This word enough to see her teeth clamp down hard and her jaw flex. What was it about being told to calm down or chill that was almost incendiary!

'What would happen if you missed your flight?' This was how she parented, getting him to think things through, figure out the consequences that she hoped might inform his future decision-making. It mattered little that he was now twenty-seven. Old habits and all that.

'Erm, I'd probably get the next one?'

His sarcasm wasn't lost on her. She glanced across the room at Jonathan, who sat at the dining table with a smile that suggested that, like their son, he found the whole thing highly amusing. It didn't help. She gave him a slow blink of dismissal.

'Get the next one? It's not like buses! You're going on an aeroplane!'

His laughter was loud and instant, and she could hear Holly joining in. She felt outnumbered, ganged up on, and a little dismissed, *silly old Mum, getting her knickers in a twist*, and this too did not feel good.

'Actually, Mum, it's exactly like buses! In fact, I had to go up to Manchester three weeks ago and my train ticket from Bristol cost three times more than my flight to Rome today. In fact, my plane ticket cost the same as when you, me and Holly went to the cinema! So, I can just get another one.'

Really? This was certainly food for thought, even if he had missed the point.

It was another salient reminder of how the world had moved on. A fact trotted out that made her feel older than her mid-fifties, a scythe to her belief that she was smart. Was she getting dumber? Did that happen? It was as if by staying in more, avoiding all sources of news and current affairs, sometimes finding the world a little too hostile and unkind, she was getting softer, losing her sharp edge of reason. It worried her. That, and the fact that because she was unaware of trends and technological advances, she lost skills or, rather, was getting left behind. When your life was a little set and unchallenging, it made it hard to keep up. Was that the answer, to challenge herself more? Possibly. She wasn't sure. But as a proficient taker of shorthand, someone who used to be able to remember everyone's telephone number, map reader extraordinaire, the best dahlia grower this side of

Cheltenham, a dab hand at photocopying and a whizz on the Rubik's cube, this downward slide was also a scythe to her confidence.

She hoped that going into business with Jenny would be the mental shot in the arm she needed. And even if it wasn't, just being in her friend's company made her happy, like she was part of a team, protected, loved. Especially now she knew that should the need ever arise, Jenny was not averse to slugging her way out of trouble. The thought made her smile.

'I just don't want . . .' she began.

What didn't she want? To have her day disrupted, not that she was busy, and in fact had nothing else in her calendar, but she liked to know what she was doing and when. Any last-minute change of plan had the potential to throw her completely. What *did* she want? To spend as much time with her son as possible, even the thirty-minute drive to the airport was something she looked forward to. It wasn't that she missed him, not exactly, but she missed seeing him alone, and not that she didn't like Holly, she did, in fact she *loved* Holly. Her headache pulsed, maybe she was overthinking it. Maybe Aiden was right, she needed to take a minute.

'I'll see you when you get here.' She ended the call. 'What's wrong with me, Jonathan? Have I always been like this?'

Her phone buzzed. A text from Jenny.

LET ME GUESS, THEY'RE LATE AND YOU'RE PACING!

She laughed out loud and replied immediately.

AM I THAT PREDICTABLE?

Jenny fired back with:

NO BUT THEY ARE!! WHERE DID WE GO WRONG??

It was true, but my goodness how the two women adored this young pair, loving nothing more than to chat about the time when they would both be grannies to the same baby! Something on the horizon that filled them both with excitement at the mere prospect. She pictured her days full of trips to the park, reading stories and the feel of a little hand in hers once again, the thought alone enough to move her to tears. She couldn't wait, knowing the arrival of a little one would be the most glorious gift, a focus for her life that in recent times had felt lacking.

Pickle meowed at the back door. Enya let her out to go wandering, no doubt to catch up with other cats, chew the fat, swap stories, sit in the sunshine, a bit of mutual grooming. It was a sobering thought that the cat had a better social life than she did.

Taking her son's advice, she tried to *chill*, did her very best not to let the tick of the clock on the kitchen wall grow louder in her thoughts. She filled the time by watering the plants in the hallway, even the one that was hard to reach, meaning she had to teeter dangerously on the spindly chair that lived in the corner and on to which they piled anything that needed lugging up the stairs. A holding bay for items heading to the bedrooms, clean laundry, letters, replacement tissues, parcels. There was always something in need of ferrying up. She stood on tiptoes and eased the jug of water into the planter of the devil's ivy that she didn't particularly like. More than that, actually, she hated it, but the fact that it thrived made it hard to get rid of, as if it were daily trying to earn a place in her affections by growing well and never moaning when she neglected it.

As she stepped down from the chair she spied Holly's car pulling up, dropping Aiden off.

Finally!

Her son jumped out and retrieved his carry-on bag from the boot. Enya ditched the watering can and grabbed her handbag, car keys and water bottle. She waved, awkwardly, watching the young love birds out of the window, wondering when it might be opportune to interrupt them. Entwined was the best way to describe them, thoroughly entwined. She pulled a face. She wasn't a prude, not at all, but found watching people smash noses together and stick their tongues into each other's mouths quite revolting. Especially when one of those tongues and mouths belonged to her only child. This too, she was aware, was probably a view that was out of step with more progressive parents, quite unable to imagine carrying on in this way in front of her own mother! It occurred to her then that maybe she was *actually* invisible . . .

She stared at the back of her hands where the skin was a little crepey, the small bulge of prominent veins, a scar around the tip of her finger from a winter's night eight years ago when she'd slipped while peeling potatoes with a short, sharp knife. Hands that no one held anymore.

With one eye on the clock, she made her way outside and banged the front door shut, loudly. Giving the snogging duo the opportunity to part, should they so desire. They did not desire and so she mumbled a vague commentary on how lovely it was to see them, which was ignored, and jumped into her little Audi, taking her time, setting the sat nav to the airport.

Aiden opened the rear door and shoved his bag inside.

'Don't leave me! Don't go!' Holly spoke in a mock whine with distinct undertones of moron.

'Come with me!' Aiden laughed. 'Hop in my pocket!'

Enya resisted the temptation to mock-*gag*, knowing it was both unkind and ungracious. Why did she feel this way? What more could a mother ask for than a partner who looked at her child and saw only starlight?

And that partner was Holly, who right now had her head in the small of Aiden's back and her arms clamped tightly around his waist, pulling hard as if this might prevent him leaving.

Enya beeped the horn; it was all she could think of and took no pleasure in from the way they both jumped.

'You're going to be late!' she hollered, wanting to get going, wanting to get back, wanting something other than to sit here witnessing their shenanigans.

'Sure you don't want me to drive?' her son asked, yawning.

'No, I'm good.'

Enya and Aiden shared the car. It made sense.

Finally, they were underway. Holly had waved until she was no more than a dot in the rear-view mirror, and Aiden had nearly cricked his neck making sure he didn't miss a glimpse.

'Do you mind if I nap, Mum?' Without waiting for an answer, he settled back in the seat and folded his arms across his chest as he closed his eyes.

'Course not. You nap.'

She swallowed her disappointment, having planned the conversation she wanted to have, wanting his advice on so many things, her new business venture with Jenny, the damp patch on the kitchen wall, did he know where she kept the will in case of emergencies? Things like that. Nothing, she realised, that wouldn't keep.

The sound of her son's gentle snoring wasn't nearly as rewarding as the chatter she had envisaged. Their animated discussions in her head were always far more engaging than the reality. In them they reminisced, and he laughed, as they turned the clock back and she felt the warm glow of a memory that could sustain her in the early hours, when she might sit on the edge of her bed and breathe slowly in through her nose and out through her mouth. Woken and alarmed by no more than a text, a noise, a dream, a paper cut of worry . . .

He woke as she pulled into the car park.

'Shit! I'm cutting it fine!' He pulled a face, and she mentally pulled her hair out. 'See you in three weeks, thanks for dropping me off.' He leaned over and kissed her roughly on the cheek. 'Love you!' She could feel the imprint of it on her face and would treasure the contact long after he had gone.

'Love you, too. So very much,' she whispered into the ether as, with his bag slung over his shoulder, her boy ran along the covered walkway and into the terminal without looking back. With the confidence of youth, his stride that of someone who was sure of where he was heading and how he was going to get there. In that second, she envied him. Her life, her place in this world, felt watered down, diluted to the point where she sometimes gasped when she caught her reflection in the mirror.

A trick of the light . . .

She didn't leave immediately, but sat in the car, staring ahead. For someone who felt as if her life was stagnating, it was nice to see people travelling.

It was interesting, watching the bronzed and bedraggled returnees pulling cases on wheels, wearing jumpers loosely draped about their shoulders, shivering to confirm they had come from somewhere much, much hotter, as they clutched souvenirs and duty-free booze in sturdy plastic bags. If these travellers had arrived at the airport hand in hand on an excited high, this felt like the other end of the budget flight conveyor belt.

It was more than a little depressing. She had seen many couples over the years bickering on this very spot, no doubt travel-weary and miffed at the prospect of tackling the sunscreen- and sweat-soaked laundry that hummed in their cases. Plus, the thought of going back to work tomorrow without the joy of a holiday looming was probably enough to knock the gilded edge off their tan.

She was lucky on two counts: her mother's Irish heritage meant never having a tan to preoccupy her, and she and Jonathan had never stopped laughing, chatting, always looking forward, planning. It wasn't always roses and wine, of course not, there were days when she could happily have throttled him, and there were a thousand small things he did that drove her to distraction, but in the main, they were good.

More than good.

And then, as she did sometimes, her mind wound back to trips she'd taken years ago. The three of them, arriving at the airport, Aiden jumping up and down, so excited to be going on a plane, his little backpack bulging with comics, Top Trumps, sweets and puzzles to keep him occupied, and keen to hold her hand, always so keen to hold her hand.

'I do, I miss it. I miss it all. I miss being that important in his life.'

She felt the ache of longing for those times, wondering, as she often did, how time had passed so very quickly. Jonathan loved to travel, to sit in the sun, excited to swim, try new food, drink cold beer, and let the giddiness of a holiday change his whole personality, as he shook off the responsibility of the day to day and danced in the street, twirling her around and around.

'Shit!' Enya simultaneously swore and jolted in her seat, as her car suddenly rocked.

Almost instinctively, her hands grabbed the steering wheel. She looked up to see the front of the silver Mercedes crashing into the passenger door of her Audi. It made the loudest bang, so much so that several of the weary travellers stared and winced. Her face coloured under their scrutiny.

She wasn't a habitual swearer, but the shock fired the word from her mouth. 'For the love of God!'

Lost in daydreaming, the loud noise probably had more impact on her than if she'd been more focused on the world around her.

From her vantage point, she could now see the long legs of a man standing between the cars. This was the last thing she needed. Was her car invisible too or just her inside it, she wondered? Unbuckling her seat belt, she prepared for a confrontation with the navy-jean-wearing, car-crashing klutz.

ABOUT THE AUTHOR

Photo © 2023 Paul Smith @paulsmithpics

Amanda Prowse is a multimillion-copy bestselling author who has published more than thirty novels and is one of the most prolific writers of contemporary fiction in the UK today.

Crowned 'the queen of family drama' by the *Daily Mail*, she writes about life's challenges – from heartbreak and loss to dysfunctional family dynamics – but also about the pockets of delight that can be found in our relationships with others, often when we need them most.

Amanda is known for her relatable characters, emotionally compelling plots, and the sense of connection that readers feel with her stories.

She is an ambassador for The Reading Agency and feels passionately about supporting other women, spending as much time as possible outdoors (preferably by the sea!), and her family.

Follow the Author on Amazon

If you enjoyed this book, follow Amanda Prowse on Amazon to be notified when the author releases a new book!

To do this, please follow these instructions:

Desktop:

1) Search for the author's name on Amazon or in the Amazon App.
2) Click on the author's name to arrive on their Amazon page.
3) Click the 'Follow' button.

Mobile and Tablet:

1) Search for the author's name on Amazon or in the Amazon App.
2) Click on one of the author's books.
3) Click on the author's name to arrive on their Amazon page.
4) Click the 'Follow' button.

Kindle eReader and Kindle App:

If you enjoyed this book on a Kindle eReader or in the Kindle App, you will find the author 'Follow' button after the last page.